STREET RATS OF ARAMOOR

BOOK 3

written by

MICHAEL
WISEHART

Copyright

ROCKSLIDE is a work of fiction. Names, characters, places, and incidents are products of the author's imagination or are used fictitiously. Any resemblance to actual locales or persons, living or dead, business establishments, or events, is entirely coincidental.

1st Edition

Cover Design by Janelle Wisehart
Cover Art by Dongjun Lu "Russell"
Map by Maria Gandolfo | RenflowerGrapx
Interior Illustrations by Elwira Pawlikowska

ISBN-13: 978-0-9981505-6-7

Street Rats Of Aramoor: Book 3

Rockslide

Books

<u>STREET RATS OF ARAMOOR</u>

(*First book takes place 20 years prior to The Aldoran Chronicles*)

Book 1 | Banished

Book 2 | Hurricane

Book 3 | Rockslide

<u>THE ALDORAN CHRONICLES</u>

Prequel | Shackled

Book 1 | The White Tower

Book 2 | Plague of Shadows

Map of Aldor - West

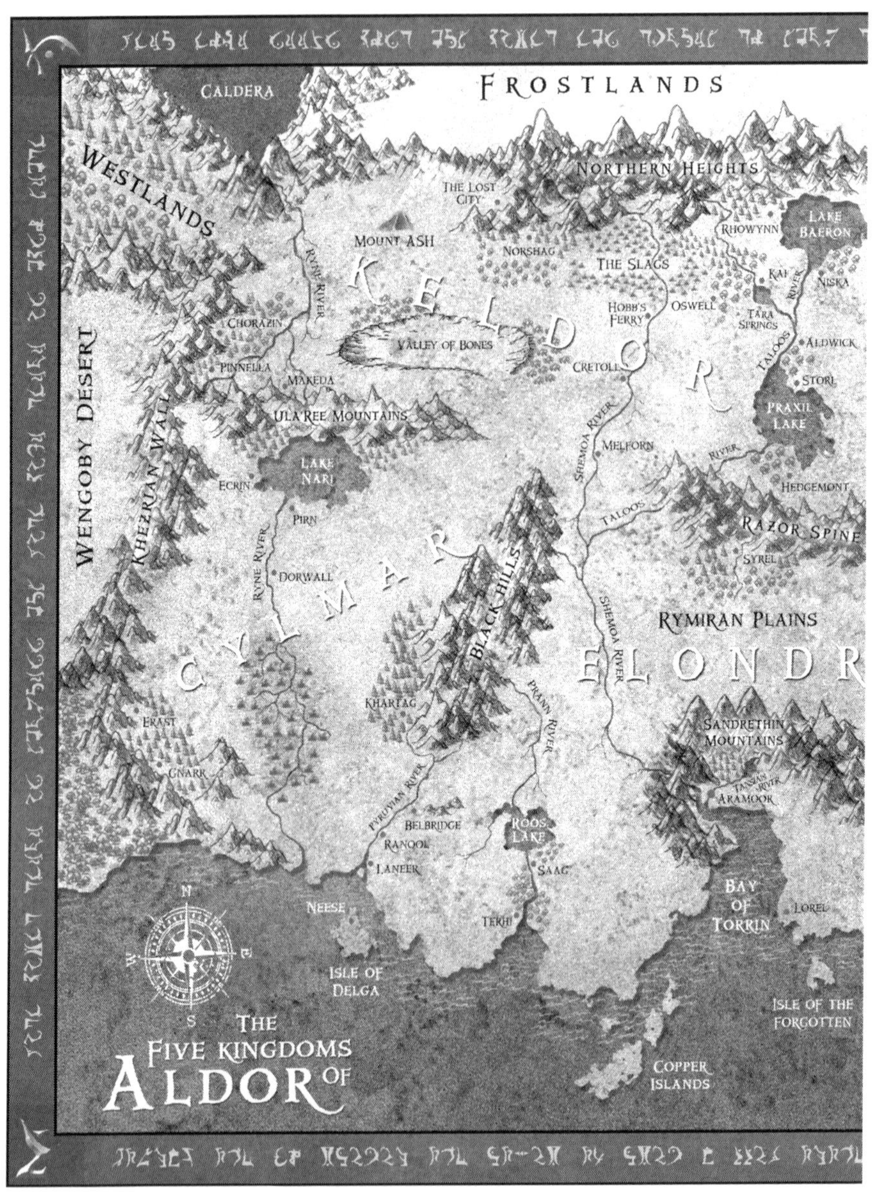

Hi-Resolution maps in the Shop:

« *www.michaelwisehart.com/aramoormarket* »

Map of Aldor - East

Hi-Resolution maps in the Shop:

« *www.michaelwisehart.com/aramoormarket* »

Map of Aramoor

Hi-Resolution maps in the Shop:

« *www.michaelwisehart.com/aramoormarket* »

Foreword

ROCKSLIDE is the third book in the Street Rats of Aramoor series, a prequel to the Aldoran Chronicles saga. If you haven't yet read the first two books, *Banished* and *Hurricane*, I recommend doing so.

This series ties directly into the Aldoran Chronicles saga, twenty years prior to the first book: *The White Tower*.

As with my other books, there is a Character Glossary at the back if you need it.

Street Tribes of Aramoor Logos

Chapter 1

VENGEANCE FILLED MY HEART, a burning sensation that threatened to overwhelm all reason. I barely noticed the night wind off the bay as it lashed at my face, doing little to dampen the rage desperately trying to claw its way out.

Spats had this coming.

Thoughts of what I would do when I reached the Temple had me running all the faster. My feet pounded the worn cobbles, their echoes announcing my coming and the swift hand of justice that would soon follow.

The city seemed eerily silent tonight, which was a reprieve from the growing clamor at the Granary. As the number of rejects continued to rise, so did the chaos. It had been a week since our battle at the Pit, and new arrivals were continuing to show up at our doors, looking for refuge. The noise from all those kids—many of whom had been members of enemy tribes not so long before—had worn a hole through my patience, almost to the point of snapping. That anger needed to be directed somewhere.

Where better than on the coward who had sold me out?

As I made my way through the old city, memories of Oswell and my time spent infiltrating Magistrate Sirias's estates with my father flooded back. Once again, I was on a mission, but unlike my father's contracts, this one was personal. The sooner I dealt with Spats, the safer we all would be.

I stopped at the head of the brick drive leading back to the Temple's gates. Torchlight dotted the walls through the trees. Spats would have doubled the guard, depending, of course, on how many watchers had survived the battle. Hurricane had been one of the first tribes out of the Pit grounds, so hopefully they hadn't taken too many casualties. Even though I was no longer a part of Hurricane, I held most of its members no ill will. It wasn't their fault they were led by the biggest buffoon ever to command a tribe.

Before crossing the street, I took a moment to scan the surrounding buildings, checking to make sure Spats hadn't decided to post a sentry or two outside the Temple walls. He hadn't. I knew the gates would be closed to me, which meant I needed to find another way inside, so I headed into the trees.

The small grove surrounding the Temple was densely populated with brush and briars, leaving small cuts across my arms and face as I pushed my way through. I stopped at the edge of the tree line and studied the opening between me and the twelve-foot wall ahead. Nothing but loose roots and piled rocks. The spot I'd chosen was directly between two of the guard stations, giving me a better chance than not at making it across unseen, since the light from the watchers' torches barely reached halfway.

I unhooked one of my swords, the one with the least amount of wear, and stashed it behind a nearby tree. Trying to climb the wall with a sword strapped to either side of my waist was a greater risk at the moment than the possibility of needing them both inside. It would be too easy to knock one against the stone wall and alert the watch. The last thing I could afford was being spotted and losing my one advantage. I was only going to get one shot at this. I had to make it count.

I tightened the wrap over my injured ribs, took one last look at the wall, and sprinted from my hiding spot. Barely five steps out, my foot caught a root, and I almost went down, just managing to right myself before hitting the dirt. *Stupid!* My focus had been on the guard stations and not where I was placing my feet. With my eyes on the ground, I scurried the rest of the way across.

I stopped at the base of the wall and took a moment to test my ankle. It was a little sore, but it didn't feel like there was any real damage. Thankfully, I'd made it across without sounding any alarms. The short run was enough to set my chest on fire, a solemn reminder of what I had to look forward to over the next month or two as my ribs healed.

Careful not to let my sword clang against the stone, I started up the wall. The decorative etching in the blocks gave my fingers a better grip, and before I knew it, I was at the top. I waited to slip over until I'd made sure no one was walking by on the other side. Not that I'd expected there to be. Spats had never established a perimeter watch before, relying solely on the makeshift guard stations to warn if anyone was coming. And those were only good if there happened to be a full-scale attack. A lone assailant would be the last thing they would expect.

A quick push and I landed inside, behind a short row of evergreen shrubs that were in some serious need of pruning. Some of the branches looked like emaciated fingers reaching out to grab anyone wandering too close.

I took a moment to open Reevie's bag. Each bottle was wrapped in wadding to keep from clanging, or in the case of the glass vials, to keep from breaking. I pulled the corks on a few before finding the right one. My eyes watered, and I quickly thumbed the cork back into place. *Yep, that's it.*

Placing the bottle in my trouser pocket, I hooked the satchel back over my shoulder and headed across the yard, following the garden path toward the back of the compound. The Temple was quiet, most of the kids in bed. Still, I kept my eyes open for any stragglers who might be making a late-night privy run.

Once inside, I followed the corridors toward Spats's chambers, stopping only long enough at the infirmary to refill Reevie's bag with whatever supplies I could find. I'd spent most of my brief time at Hurricane right in this room. A lot of memories there. Good and bad.

But I wasn't there to reminisce. I had a job to do.

Quickly, I walked the shelves, snatching anything I thought

might come in handy. Unfortunately, it appeared the only ether left was the little I had tucked away in my pocket.

It didn't take long before the satchel was brimming, and I was forced to leave the rest on the shelves. I even found an old cloak of Reevie's while digging through one of the trunks. It barely reached my knees, but it had a hood I could use to hide my face, so I slipped it on.

At the door, I stopped and listened, taking a moment to grab the bottle of ether from my pocket and the rag sheathing it. I didn't like the idea of dosing any of my former compatriots, but if it meant getting rid of Spats once and for all, it would be worth it. Besides, if I did feel guilty, all I needed to do was remind myself that there were more than a few from Hurricane who had been cheering for my defeat at the Pit.

Not hearing any footsteps in the hall, I turned the knob and opened the door.

"Healer?"

I froze. Thankfully, my head was down, so the girl couldn't see my face. Why was she up at this time of night? Without saying anything, I popped the cork on the bottle and doused the rag. The girl stood there watching, seemingly too confused to know what to do. I didn't like doing this, but I was already committed.

As soon as I finished, I stoppered the bottle, placed it back in my robe, and leaped into the hall. The girl didn't even have time to open her mouth to scream before I had the cloth over her face. She jerked for a moment, words muffled by the wrapping, but soon went still. I dragged her into Reevie's chambers and stuffed her behind the door, leaving the cloth over her face just in case. She must have been standing just outside when I first listened, which was why I hadn't heard her.

I took a moment to catch my breath. The unexpected leap into the hall had left my chest thrumming. I didn't think my body could have handled an actual battle. Stealth was my greatest asset at this point.

I looked down at the girl and shook my head. She'd left me in somewhat of a bind. There was only enough ether left for a single dose, and there were always two guards watching Spats's chambers. But with little other choice, I swung the bag over my shoulder and started for the door, racking my brain as to what I was going to do to get past them.

This time, before opening the door, I got down on my hands and knees and looked under. There was no one there. Sparing one last look around the infirmary, I slipped into the hall beyond and made my way to the end of the corridor. Two guards stood in front of Spats's office about halfway down the next hall.

The problem wasn't just overpowering them, which was going to be difficult enough with my injuries. The challenge was not waking half the Temple when I did.

Lifting my hood, I stepped out from the hall and started forward, carefully pouring what was left of the bottle on the rag. Its sweet scent tickled my nose. I kept my head down, not wanting my Upakan eyes to reflect the light coming from the hall torches and give me away.

I counted down the steps. How much closer? With my head down and hood lowered, I could only see a foot or two in front of my own feet. I had to be close, though. I strained to listen, hoping to hear the tap of a boot, the release of a breath, the grumble of a hungry stomach, anything that gave away where they were. Then I saw them—the guards' boots.

I stopped. "Keep moving," one of them said. It sounded like Forehead's rough voice.

My hand tightened around the cloth. Forehead was the bigger of the two and would be the hardest to take down, so the ether had to be for him. I was about to make my move when it hit me. Why was I hiding my face?

I was the champion of the Pit. I'd defeated Flesh Eater, something no one had ever come close to doing. Having them see me might actually be to my advantage. With that in mind, I lowered my hood and turned to face them.

Both guards drew their blades when they saw me.

"You know who I'm here for," I said, standing as tall as I could with broken ribs.

Forehead raised his sword, eyes full of rage. "I had friends who didn't make it back from the Pit." His words practically lunged out of his mouth, like asps looking to sink their teeth into my flesh.

My heart dropped. This wasn't going to work. I needed to come at this from a different angle. "Yes," I agreed, "but that wouldn't have happened if Spats hadn't run off and left them there."

Forehead stared at me for a moment, seemingly mulling over what I'd said.

"If you want to blame someone for their loss," I said, pointing at the door behind them, "it's that pathetic excuse for a leader you have hiding in his bedchamber. Did you see him raise a finger to help save his tribe?" I didn't give them a chance to answer. "No. He was too busy fleeing like a coward."

Forehead's grip on his sword tightened.

"Is that the sort of person you want leading this tribe?"

The tall guard didn't respond, other than to grind his teeth.

I was growing desperate at this point, but I held my ground, staring the boy down, willing him to listen to reason.

Finally, he turned and looked at the other guard.

I held my breath.

Forehead nodded, and both stepped aside.

I released a small sigh of relief and cautiously stepped between them and put my ear to the door.

"He's been snoring for the last hour," the second boy said.

"Here." Forehead pulled a dagger from his belt. "Use this."

I stared at the weapon briefly, not sure how I felt about the guards' desire to kill Spats in cold blood. I guess I couldn't blame them.

With Forehead's knife in hand, I lifted the latch and slipped inside. The door clicked shut, and the light from the hallway vanished. They weren't kidding. Spats's snores could have woken the dead.

I had no problem using the ambient light shining through the windows to see where I was going. The clouds parted momentarily, sending a pale glow across the lower half of Spats's bed, which was pressed against the left wall between an upright chest of drawers and a rack of swords.

Thick quilts hid his shape, leaving only a thin lump in the middle and a tuft of red hair poking out the top. I moved across the room, not too worried about being quiet with all the noise Spats was making.

He had his blankets tucked up under his chin, his head the only thing visible, like a big red cabbage sitting on the back of a farmer's cart, just waiting to get plucked. It would have been so easy to reach out and slide the blade across his throat, like slicing a moist plum, one that had already fallen from the tree and started to rot. That was Spats—a rotten plum. No one would have faulted me, not even his own guard, apparently. Besides, wasn't this what I had been trained to do?

My hand lifted slowly as I recalled Spats's high-pitched voice shouting above the crowd for Flesh Eater to finish me. But above the noise of the chants, I heard my father's voice whispering in my ear: *Just because something is easy, it doesn't make it right.*

As much as I wanted to peel this nasty plum, I knew I'd have to live with myself afterward, so I lowered the dagger, walked around to the foot of the bed, and climbed up.

Spats continued snoring as I slowly worked my way across the bed and up to his waist. As badly as I wanted to beat him senseless, scaring the snot out of him would have to suffice. I raised my hood once more and drew my sword, poking him in the stomach with it. The only reaction I got was a flinch before he was snoring again. I poked him again, this time not so nicely, and he startled awake with a snort.

He blinked, then jerked upright and screamed at the top of his lungs, scaring me half to death in the process. I dove on top of him, and the force of my weight hitting his chest stifled his shrill cry as the air was driven from his lungs. He gasped for breath as the back of his head sank into his pillow.

I couldn't help but take a little pleasure—or perhaps a lot—in Spats's terror. With one hand over his mouth, I pressed my sword to his neck, and the redheaded boy stiffened like a sweat-dried collar. In fact, he was so paralyzed with fear that I was able to release his mouth long enough to lower my hood without him screaming again.

One look at me and he started crying. "Please don't kill me. Please . . ."

I sneered. "Have some dignity, won't you?"

He continued to beg for his life, tears streaming down his cheeks.

"You tried to kill me," I said.

Spats sobbed so hard, he choked.

"Stop your crying, or I'll stop it for you." I pressed the blade even harder.

His mouth snapped shut.

"Now answer my question! Why did you try to have me killed?"

"Because," Spats said with a frightened whimper, "I placed a wager with Noph that you'd lose." He started sobbing again. "That way, when you did, I'd be able to cover my debt with Cutter." He cried some more. "It wasn't personal. I was just trying to save Hurricane."

"The Defiler you were!" I said, losing my temper as I leaned in closer, the tips of our noses practically touching. "It was flaming personal for me."

He gulped and went back to whimpering.

"Justice needs to be served," I said firmly. "You tried to take my life. Now it's my turn."

"No. Please. I'll do anything. Anything." He closed his eyes, snot running down his upper lip. It was a sad, pathetic sight.

"Anything?" I asked.

Spats lay as still as he could while I hefted him over my shoulder. I whimpered as the added weight sent lances of pain shooting through my chest, practically stealing my breath. Once at the door, I kicked twice with my boot and waited. A moment later, it cracked, and Forehead peeked in.

"You done?" he asked.

I nodded.

"I heard him screaming," he said with a smile. "I hope you made him suffer."

Spats squirmed, and I quickly shifted him higher on my shoulder to hide the movement. *Idiot!*

"Your friends have been avenged," I said, trying to hurry the conversation along as I pretended to wipe Forehead's dagger on my pants as though cleaning off the blood.

"You want us to dump the body?" he asked.

"No," I said, handing him his belt knife back. "I have something special in mind. What I want you to do is continue guarding this door."

The two guards looked at each other.

"Why?" the second guard asked. "He ain't in it. And I want to get some sleep."

Spats was starting to get heavy, and standing there answering questions wasn't something I had planned on. "Because," I said, letting them hear the frustration in my voice, "we don't want people knowing what happened. What do you think the members of Hurricane would say, let alone the Guild, if they were to find out that a chief's own guard had a hand in murdering the head of their tribe?"

Their eyes widened. "Didn't think of that," the second guard stated.

"We'll stand watch," Forehead said, saluting with his hand over his chest as though a member of the Elondrian Lancers.

"If you haven't heard back from me in the next couple of days," I added, "then go in and act surprised when you can't find him. Tell everyone that he must have snuck off in the night."

The guards nodded and turned back to their posts.

I quickly hobbled down the hall toward the back exit. Once outside, I lowered Spats to the ground and stretched my back. My shoulder was aching. Surprisingly, the former chief didn't say a word. Probably one of the first times that had ever happened. "This way," I said, taking the south path. Spats followed me around to the side wall without argument. Having witnessed his own guard willing to murder him in his sleep was enough to encourage a speedy retreat.

It took us three attempts to make it up the wall. Spats fell twice, and by the third time, I was practically carrying him on my back.

It was a miracle we made it to the other side unseen. We stopped only long enough for me to collect my second sword before heading through the trees.

We left the Temple grounds the same way I'd entered, then made our way west through the Maze and out to the lower docks. Spats carried a small travel bag he'd stuffed with a few of his belongings, mostly a change of clothes, a few coins, and one knife.

"Where am I going?" he asked nervously as he followed me down the boardwalk toward the ships.

"I don't care, just so long as it's far away from here. You show your face in Aramoor again and I'll come for you. And next time," I said, slapping the hilts of my swords, "I won't give you a choice."

He gulped and took a step back.

I slowed when we reached one of the watchmen on rounds in front of a tall three-mast ship. "How much to stow him on board?" I asked, pointing over my shoulder at Spats, hoping the watchman could be bought off.

The stout man crossed his arms, revealing a sleeve of tattoos, one of which ran from his wrist all the way up to the base of his neck. I recognized it immediately, having seen several similar markings during my time spent on the *Wind Binder*. It was the geographic representation of the Shemoa River. This man had clearly been a river boatman at some point in his past. His shaved head and thick mustache reminded me of Kettle. "We got us a frigate heading for the Blue Isles at dawn," the sailor said. "Can't say it will be a pleasant trip below deck, but it'll get the young master there in good order." He took another look at Spats, then at me. "It'll cost ya, though. Two silver, and none of that soft stuff."

"Two silver? For him?" I was dumbfounded. "You can stuff him in a barrel of onions for all I care."

"And if the captain finds the boy, he'll toss him overboard, and me along with him."

"Fine," I said, pulling a small purse from my trousers that I'd pilfered from one of Spats's chests, along with a fresh pair of socks and two apples. I laid the two pieces in the man's palm.

The watchman stuck the coins in his mouth, one at a time, and bit down. "Is that the extent of your belongings, lad?" he asked Spats.

Spats nodded, or he was quivering so badly it looked like a nod.

"Then get a move on. Need to get you below before the crew wakes." He spared a quick look at the sky. The stars were still there but faint. With a brisk grunt, the sailor turned and started for the loading ramp.

Spats lifted his bag and ran to catch up with the watchman. He didn't look back, and I didn't bother waving goodbye, or good riddance. As much as I had wanted to drown him myself, this seemed a far better punishment. For someone like Spats who enjoyed being at the top, with others bending to his every wish, to be sent away in shame, completely destitute, forced to survive on nothing but the handouts of others . . .

I smiled. He was getting exactly what he deserved.

Chapter 2

INSTEAD OF GOING STRAIGHT back to the Granary, I decided to clear my head by taking a stroll around the city. The sun had risen high enough to force the stars back into hiding, which meant I would reach the east markets just as Master Endle opened his bakery. He had the best tarts in Aramoor, with honey thick enough to stick to your ribs on the way down. I winced as I patted the injured area around my chest. A little thickening around the ribs might do me some good.

By the time I arrived at the bakery, the sun was just peeking over the top of the east wall, and Mistress Storella, Master Endle's wife, was stacking the tarts on the cart out front. It looked like the usual lineup today: blueberry and raspberry, followed by pear, apple, strawberry, fig, two types of melon, a couple of sweet cheese, and my personal favorite—honey, filled with sweet cheese and cinnamon.

My mouth watered as I stood in an alleyway on the other side of the street and waited for her to finish. The tart I was after was on the top shelf of the cart, all the way to the left, making it easier to get to. Sure, I had a bag of gold in my pocket, but for a street kid like me to pull coin like that out in the middle of town would have led to harsh scrutiny and possibly the calling of a patroller. Easier to just grab a tart while no one was looking.

The longer I stayed in Aramoor, the more my scruples seemed to disappear. At one time, the thought of stealing a tart would have repulsed me, but now I could almost justify the necessity. I assuaged my conscience by determining I would only pick in small quantities and only things that were required to survive, and while one of Master Endle's tarts might not have been the difference between life or death, the thought of sinking my teeth into it had me convinced it would be. It wouldn't hurt, just this once. I could leave some money the next time I passed this way.

I waited until a gaggle of women swarmed this side of the street before making my move. It was always best to blend in with other shoppers. Children who stood apart tended to draw more eyes than those accompanied by a parent.

Leaving the shadows of the alley, I followed the trail of dresses, poking my head out every so often to see around them. I made sure to stay close, but not so close that they paid me any notice. Besides, they were too busy gossiping about the week's events to notice me tagging along in their wake.

Finally, we were only a few steps away from the cart. Mistress Storella stepped back inside the shop to grab another basket of fresh baked goods, and Master Endle had stopped what he was doing to talk with a couple of the ladies in front.

Carefully, I slid up alongside one of the women who was standing next to the cart. Her back was turned to me. This was perfect. I spared one last quick look up toward the front. Hopefully, Master Endle was too focused on his sales pitch to notice my hand slipping out from the back of the group. As soon as my fingers wrapped around the tart's flaky crust, I yanked it back.

Yes! I almost shouted, staring fondly at the warm pastry in my hands, grateful for—

"Stop!"

I looked up.

Mistress Storella was standing in the doorway with a basket of fresh bread. "Stop him, Hubert! He just stole a tart." She tried pointing in my direction but almost lost her basket instead.

I took off running, straight through the women, hoping their skirts would hide me, but the cluster quickly scattered, apparently not wanting the shopkeeper to think I belonged to any of them.

Behind me, I could hear Master Endle shouting as his heavy boots stomped the cobbles, no doubt hoping to stomp me as well.

I ran as hard as my injuries would allow, whimpering at each jarring step, desperation the only thing keeping me going—that and knowing the angry man with the long-handled bread peel was catching up. One look at Master Endle's oven paddle and I picked up speed. It was as big as a boat oar.

Shockingly foul language sprung from Master Endle's mouth like crossbow bolts aimed at the back of my head, letting me know that if he caught me, my life was going to be short lived. I was almost impressed with the eloquent way he strung them together. He would have put a riverboat captain to shame.

By the time I reached the fourth or fifth shop up, I had to stop just to catch my breath. I glanced behind me to see if he was still giving chase.

He was.

I hadn't expected Master Endle to continue the chase past Rossen's quilt stand, let alone halfway down King's Way West. I clutched the tart to my aching ribs and started running again.

"I'll get you, you . . ."

I didn't hear the rest. I didn't want to.

The street opened into a park just ahead. If I hadn't found a way to give him the slip by then, it would leave me with nothing but wide-open spaces for him to pounce. The only thing that had kept me out front so far was the fact that Master Endle's stout bearing was making it difficult for him to scramble around shoppers.

I could almost feel him raising his peel to strike as the hairs on the back of my neck stiffened. I ducked to the right around a cart, then quickly switched back left into another small crowd, weaving in and out of the stream of people as they meandered up the side of the street. Their pace was as sluggish as the Tansian River on its way through Aramoor, and I was forced to slow.

I dodged to keep from hitting one woman, only to run headlong into a skinny man with sharp elbows. One of them struck my chest. My eyes watered from the pain, but I kept going.

A quick glance over my shoulder let me know that my pursuers had tripled. Two patrollers with their noticeable blue capes and thick batons had decided to join the chase. "Just my luck. All of this for a stupid tart." The pastry was still warm, so I stuffed the entire thing in my mouth. If I was to get caught, I should at least enjoy my last meal as a free man.

The flaky crust melted in my mouth and honey oozed between my lips. It was the best thing I'd eaten since the last time I'd nabbed one.

I turned to see how close my pursuers were and caught the edge of Master Endle's peel right across the face. Sparks filled my vision, and I screamed. The blow knocked me to the side, where I bowled over two kids before hitting the ground.

Suddenly, I was back on the sidewalk running. *Another vision.*

This time, I ducked. I could feel the wind from the peel as it passed over my head.

"Get back here, you flaming sack of . . ." Master Endle's breathing was so labored, he could hardly finish. "I'll have your hands for this."

Scary thing was, he meant it. It wasn't uncommon for a thief to lose a hand as punishment. In my case, I might get away with simply losing the bag of gold I carried.

But it was gold I couldn't afford to lose.

"I've got you now," the baker shouted as he grabbed for my tunic. He caught the back of my cloak but slipped when I dove into the middle of a group of bystanders, who were in the throes of admiring some newfangled gadget on display in one of the shops' windows. They barely registered my presence. I didn't have time to see what they were gawking at or even glimpse the shop's name, but by the awestruck expression on some of their faces, it was probably Trelinder's Emporium.

There was always a steady stream of window shoppers around Trelinder's. His strange and unique inventions were quite the talk. I could have sworn I'd seen one of his dolls turn and look right at me once.

I pushed on. I couldn't afford to lose my hands over a tart or, worse, get sent to the dungeons or the salt mines. I had people depending on me. I wiggled through the crowd's feet on my hands and knees, staying as low to the ground as possible.

For the most part, the onlookers never even knew I was there. It wasn't until Master Endle decided to crawl in after me that the commotion began. Women, startled at the sight of a grown man wriggling up under their dresses, screamed, rousing the men to action. Poor Master Endle found himself accosted on all sides by an angry mob as they thrashed him for being some kind of pervert. It raised such a spectacle that the two patrollers had to forcibly fight back the throng in order to save the man from his own stupidity.

I couldn't help but laugh. I crawled underneath two nearby carts and out the other side. Back on my feet, I looked for a safe place to run.

That's when the patrollers spotted me.

"You there! Stop!" one shouted. "Someone grab him!"

I ducked behind a tall gentleman carrying an age-worn saddle over his left shoulder and peeked between the man's arms.

The patrollers had managed to clear Master Endle's attackers away and were now moving to get around the carts blocking that section of the street.

Behind me, the closest alleyway was at least three shops up. If I could cut across to Tilferd and keep ahead of the patrollers long enough, I could probably lose them near the riverfront. With no better options, I turned and ran—straight into the arms of a third patroller.

"Watch it!" he said, grabbing my arm defensively.

I tried pulling away, but not before he had my arm pinned behind my back. Where had he come from? One of the shops?

For most, this would have been the end. But not me. I was Upakan, after all. Every part of my body was a weapon.

Of course, in that moment, all my training flew out the window, and as desperation took over, I opened my honey-caked mouth and bit down.

The patroller roared as my teeth sank into his forearm. "You filthy street rat!" He swung for my head.

I ducked, and he backhanded a lady on my right, who was trying to pull her daughter away from the scene.

The impact knocked the woman off her feet and into her husband's arms. Her husband might not have been the most intimidating of men, but that didn't stop him from leaping on the officer. The skinny man looked like a woodpecker as he headbutted the patroller, bloodying the man's nose and blackening his face.

It's amazing how quickly people can turn on you. One minute, they're waving at the patroller as they walk down the street, and the next, they're out for blood, like a pack of hungry wolves closing in on a wounded sheep. The arrival of the other two patrollers sent people scurrying.

Quickly, I spat the patroller's blood from my mouth—it didn't mix well at all with the honey—and used the distraction to blend back into the crowd and disappear up the street.

Stopping at the corner of the alley, I turned to see if anyone was still following. The patrollers were too busy pulling the woodpecker man off their comrade and dispersing the crowd to care, and poor Master Endle looked more than a little worse for wear with his ripped shirt and two black eyes. None of them appeared to have any desire to continue the chase. And all this for a tart. I shook my head and made my way up the alley to Tilferd, and from there south through Cheapside.

Once through the Maze, it was only a short jaunt to the old warehouse district. The buildings had all been abandoned years before and left to rot, as a newer establishment had been built just over the Tansian. Apparently, the old shipping district had been too close to the Warrens and had come under frequent raids. Unable to oust the Warren's inhabitants from their network of tunnels, city officials decided instead to distance themselves and relocate north of the river inlet. What they left behind was the perfect hiding place for those looking to remain off the beaten path.

The Granary was one such place. It had been my home since arriving in Aramoor, a place to escape to when things got tough.

But after the Pit, it had turned into a full-fledged encampment.

And word was spreading.

Chapter 3

"WHERE HAVE YOU BEEN?" Reevie asked, barely pausing his cataloging of herbs for Bull to find on the shelves in the corner.

Bull stopped rummaging long enough to turn and smile. "Protector." He wiped his dirty-blonde hair from his eyes. Ever since I'd found the big Avalanche reject and brought him home, there was hardly a time he wasn't at my side, except when I ordered him to stay behind and look after the others.

"I was out," I said, stepping off the landing and unhooking my swords, still debating on whether to mention my excursion into the Temple or my dust-up with the patrollers.

"I didn't hear you leave this morning," Reevie said, smoothing a piece of parchment on our one rickety table. He turned and gave me a scolding look. “Or were you out all night again? What do you do out there every night, anyway?”

“Oh, you know . . . the usual, scouting out new picking grounds.”

Reevie cocked an eyebrow, letting me know he didn’t believe a word of it.

I had considered telling him what I was planning, but Reevie would have demanded I didn’t go. Not that he cared one whit about Spats’s well-being; he simply didn’t like me taking so many risks. Regardless, Reevie would find out soon enough. News of a tribal chief’s disappearance would spread like a Maze fire.

Truth was, I’d been going out every night scouting the other tribes’ compounds to get some idea of what we were up against. Instead of falling to Flesh Eater like a good little pawn, I had instigated a battle that had dealt heavy losses to all the tribes. It would be foolish to think there wouldn’t be some form of retaliation directed my way once it was known I had survived. It was a safe bet that all the tribes, save maybe Wildfire, would be thrilled to see me wiped from the face of Aldor.

One positive note was that Red, and those beaters still left standing after the skirmish, had not relayed my survival to anyone, at least not that I could tell. But after saving Red’s life outside the Pit, it was the least they could do. There seemed to be a lot of chatter about what had happened to me. Some believed I’d been killed. Others believed I’d left Aramoor altogether, too afraid to show my face.

For now, I was fine letting them believe what they would. The fewer people looking for me, the more opportunity I had to move about the city.

I took a moment to stretch my aching limbs. My chest still throbbed from my flight through the shopping district, but I didn't let it show when I joined Reevie at the table. "What are you working on?"

"Inventory," Reevie said as he strategically placed a couple of jars on the corners of the parchment to keep it from rolling up. "It seems that's all I do around here. Healing and inventory. Other than checking on my patients at the Temple, I haven't left the compound in a week. A week, I tell you!" He threw his arms up in frustration. "You know what I need? I need one of Mistress Orilla's mystery-meat sandwiches."

"I agree," Bull said from the other side of the room.

"What do you mean, you agree?" Reevie shot back. "You've never even had one."

Bull crossed his arms. "Yes, I have. The old bookshop, right? I went with the Protector once to get supplies."

Reevie waved it off. "Oh, I forgot."

The thought of one of Mistress Orilla's sandwiches had my mouth watering, especially since all I'd eaten since yesterday's bowl of watered-down stew was a single honey tart and part of a patroller's forearm. I cringed at the thought and looked for something to rinse away the taste. I walked over to the shelf that held our meager food stores, grabbed the jug of watered-down ale from the middle, pulled the cork, and took a swallow. I made sure to swish the contents around for a good while before swallowing and repeating.

"So, how are we looking?" I asked, recorking the jug and returning it to the shelf. I walked over to the table and glanced at Reevie's scribblings. "What are we low on?"

Reevie snorted. "Everything. We can't keep up with the growth. Half of those arriving aren't in good enough shape to even lift a broom, let alone earn their keep. This row here," he said, pointing with the tip of his quill to the right column, "are the numbers we need to reach in order to survive. And this here," he said, pointing at the left, "is where we are right now."

I glanced at the figures on the right, then those on the left, then back again. "That bad, huh?"

"That bad? Blood poisoning! It's terrible! We're going to be out of food in a matter of days, and we're already out of most of the medicinal herbs I need for the injured. Something needs to change." Reevie shook his head and spared a quick glance in Bull's direction before leaning in to whisper something to me. "We've got to stop letting people in. In fact, we need to start weeding out those we already have."

A loud grunt from the corner let us know that Bull had not only heard Reevie's suggestion but didn't much care for it.

Reevie waited to see how I would respond. As a healer, Reevie had a heart for helping those in need, so for him to suggest that we turn people away, things must be really bad.

I sat down on one of our stacked-crate chairs and studied the figures, which had been depressing enough to look at the first time. "There's got to be a way. We can't just turn these kids out. They wouldn't last the week without our help."

"*We* won't last the week," Reevie said. "They're going to die if they stay here, anyway."

"Maybe if I found a better place to pick."

"It won't matter, Protector," Bull said, crossing the room to join us at the table. "There isn't a safe place in all of Aramoor for us to pick, what with every tribe ordered to chase out all those carrying the mark of the outcast. That's not something you can exactly hide, you know." Bull raised his arm and turned his wrist to show us the melted flesh on the inside of his lower forearm, where Cutter—like some of the other chiefs—had branded each of the rejects with an X before kicking them out.

I took a deep breath, almost hoping the additional air would clear my mind and spark an idea. It didn't. "Yes, that does pose a challenge."

"It poses more than a challenge," Reevie fumed. "It's a fungus-festering impossibility."

Disgusting, I thought, shaking my head to remove the latest imagery Reevie had imparted. "It seems, then, that we have one of three choices." I raised a finger. "We can either keep trying to pick and hope the other tribes will be merciful."

Both Reevie and Bull snorted at the same time.

"Or," I said, lifting a second, "we can try to find a new picking ground where the other tribes won't bother us."

"That means picking in the northwest quarter," Reevie said.

Bull shook his head. "No one picks there, and for good reason. You don't have just the patrollers to worry about. The Elondrian Lancers are there too. It's too close to the palace."

"Then the only other option I see is to—"

The door at the top of the stairs opened, and someone came running down. "Protector! Protector!" There was a loud crash as someone hit Reevie's scored step and went through; the resulting high-pitched squeal let me know who it was.

I ran up the stairway to find Squeaks stuck between the steps. As small as he was, he had fallen through far enough that his chest was level with what remained of the stair. Squeaks was one of the smallest of the rejects. He had shoulder-length brown hair and sad eyes. He was the youngest member of Mouse's pack, which included Mouse, Petal, Squeaks, and Tubby. The others tended to look out for him.

"I forgot again, Protector. Stupid thing!" He tried hitting the step with his fist, but when he raised his hand, he slipped farther in. "Help, I'm stuck."

With Bull's help, I lifted the little boy out of the trap and placed him on the step above.

He brushed the dust from his worn tunic and trousers. "Someone needs to fix that dumb step." He managed a small kick at the wood, but without any shoes, he didn't kick hard. "Protector, you need to come quick. One of the pickers just returned, and he's bleeding. I think there's trouble."

I charged past the little urchin, taking the steps two at a time, not thinking about my broken ribs until I reached the top and nearly lost my breath from the pain. I could hear Bull and Reevie coming up behind me.

A crowd had gathered by the front door, and the kids parted when they saw us coming.

"Protector. Healer." String Bean, a lanky boy about eleven,

stood in the middle of the gathering. His face was bruised. The skin around one eye was already turning dark, and he held a blood-stained cloth up to the side of his head.

"Get out of the way," Reevie said as he pushed through the ring of spectators. "I need to have a look at him."

"What happened?" I asked, already guessing the answer.

"It was an attack!" he said, still trying to catch his breath. "They were waiting for us."

"Who was?"

"Beaters."

Reevie lifted String Bean's shirt, and I grimaced at the bruises already visible across his ribs.

"They're trying to kill us."

"Where?"

"North Avis, above the shopping district, just south of the tannery on Dulmar. It's where we've been picking all week. Please hurry, Protector, before they kill them all."

I turned to Bull, and before I could say anything, he nodded. "I'll round up our Guard."

Chapter 4

BULL HAD THE GRANARY'S Guard assembled within minutes, what few there were. Those minutes, however, felt like hours. I grabbed my swords from below and was back in the main room before our beaters had made it outside. Every moment we wasted was another moment our pickers had to survive without help.

I had stopped wearing my black vest. Since the Pit, it had become too recognizable. Instead, I opted for a black suede jacket that a couple of our pickers had nabbed for me. I normally wouldn't have condoned thieving such a valuable item, but it was a nice jacket, and I didn't want to see it go to waste.

The jacket was warm, far too warm for the late summer month of Èldwin, but it allowed me to carry things I couldn't tote in my trouser pockets. It had three buttons at the front, which I left undone to give my arms more range of motion.

My swords bounced against my legs as I jogged across the main floor, heading for the open door. I stepped outside and inspected the troops.

Bull had all five of the Guard lined up in a row. Weapons were hard to come by, so many made do with bludgeons they had crafted from pieces of furniture scavenged from nearby buildings. A couple had daggers, but they were old and dull. My short swords were the best of the lot, and that wasn't saying much.

All in all, we were a sorry sight to behold. But, as my father used to say, "It's not the weapon but the one wielding it that makes the difference."

The ground shook as a gigantic boy rushed out the door to join us. He had his infamous Flesh Eater mask strapped on, and he carried a club that looked like it might have once been a corner post for a large bed.

"No, Tubby," I said, craning my neck to stare up at him. "Not this time."

His shoulders fell as he stepped out of line. "But Tubby wants to go," he grumbled in his low, raspy voice.

"I know you want to go, but you're just too big."

"Huh?" Tubby scratched the top of his head with his club.

I could see I needed to come at this a different way. Because of his size, the former Pit champion tended to draw too many eyes, especially from the patrollers, which made traversing the back streets that much harder. And right now, we needed speed. I laid my hand on his huge arm. "I need you to stay here and protect the Granary. I'm counting on you to keep everyone here safe."

Tubby straightened, his smile returning.

I turned to the others and motioned them forward. "Let's move."

"Protector, wait!"

I turned to find Petal running out the door with Squeaks a step behind. Her sunflower hair caught the light in a way that made me realize how appropriate her choice of name really was. "What's wrong?"

"It's Mouse, Protector. He was on picking duty today."

I could see the concern on both their faces. Mouse was the leader of their little gang of four. Wherever you saw one, the others weren't far away. No wonder Tubby was so eager to go. Mouse had been one of the first rejects to accept the huge boy.

"I'll find him, Petal." It was all I could say to encourage her, though I worried what condition I would find him in. Mouse got his nickname from being small enough to scurry in and out of tight spaces. I hated to think what would happen to the little boy if the beaters got ahold of him.

I ordered the Guard forward.

We started at a steady jog as we left the Granary and headed north up Mora, keeping to the same pace so as not to have us completely winded by the time we got to where we were going. We eventually cut east along the river until we could find a less-trafficked crossing than the one in front of the shipping yards.

I knew we would never make it all the way across town in time for a rescue. The fight would have been over before String Bean made it halfway back to the Granary. I just hoped we got there in time to find some of them still alive. I wanted to know whose tribe it was that had set the ambush. They'd been picking along the edge of Red's territory, but I couldn't see her going out of her way to attack a group of rejects. Then again, this was Red we were talking about. After the welcome her tribe had given me on my first day, I couldn't put it past her.

The longer we ran, the more images my mind conjured of the broken, bleeding bodies we would find. The outcome was all but assured. Our poor, desperate pickers were in no shape to fight, let alone defend against a planned attack. Their sole purpose was to find enough food or coin to feed our people for another day. Their only defense was the swiftness of their feet.

We kept to the back streets as best we could until crossing King's Way West.

"Keep your eyes open," I told the Guard as we jogged up the street. "Let me know if you see anything." At this point, I wondered if we'd find much more than bodies.

Two streets up, I raised my hand, and the Guard slowed. We were about three streets down from the tannery, where String Bean said they had been attacked. The last thing we needed was to run headlong into some kind of ambush.

Hopefully, the patrollers hadn't been called already. We needed to find our pickers before they got there. I kept my eyes open for movement. I listened for any indication of fighting ahead, but other than the usual sounds of the city, the streets of Aramoor were fairly quiet.

Not a good sign.

The road we were traveling was narrow enough that the buildings did a fair job of blocking the sun from our eyes. I slowed our approach, stopping momentarily at each cross-street we came to. The streets were strangely empty, most of the buildings dark. I wondered if they had shut down when the fighting had started in fear of being involved.

Something ahead caught my eye, and I raised my hand, signaling for those behind me to stop. Broken crates were scattered across the side of the road. A careful look revealed a couple of daggers interspersed with several bludgeons amongst the wreckage. This had to be where they were attacked. But where were—

"Look, there," Bull said, pointing to a small alley on the left.

Two bodies lay under a narrow staircase, neither moving. I ran to see who they belonged to, Bull hot on my heels. It was a boy and a girl, both with a reject brand on their wrist. I recognized their faces from having seen them around the Granary. I didn't know their names, though.

"Are they alive?" Bull asked.

I checked the bodies. The side of the boy's head and face was covered in blood, and his chest wasn't rising. More importantly, I could see the blank stare in his eyes. He was gone. I closed his eyes and moved on to the girl underneath him.

"She's breathing," I said. "Here, help me."

Bull moved the boy's body, allowing me to lift the girl in my arms. I hissed at the sharp pain in my chest, but I didn't let it stop me. She had a large bruise under her eye and a small gash on her forehead, where she'd either been struck by something or had hit the cobbles after a fall. Either way, we weren't going to learn anything until she woke up. If she woke up.

"We need to get her back to the Granary," I said, pausing momentarily to look down at the boy. "We need to get them both back." I carried the girl out of the alley, barely having the chance to lay her down when I spotted movement ahead on the right. "What was that?"

Bull looked around, not having seen what I had. "Where?"

"There," I said, pointing to a cluster of stacked barrels on the other side of the street a few buildings up. I drew one of my swords, and we left the others and made our way across the street. I spotted the tips of a pair of shoes sticking out from between the casks ahead. Whoever it was had tried pulling their legs in when they heard us coming, and that movement was what I'd seen.

We scooted quietly along the brick wall, making sure to keep the barrels between us and whoever was hiding between them. It was probably one of our own, but I wasn't taking any chances. I scanned the surrounding buildings. It could be a trap, another group of beaters waiting for us to show up. I stopped on the other side of the cluster and turned to motion to Bull when Bull snagged a loose plank with his foot and went down with a grunt.

Before I could turn around, the stack of barrels came crashing down on top of me. I dove out of the way as the casks hit the walk, rolling right in front of the boy who'd been hiding behind them. He tried to make a fast break for the alley across the street, but I grabbed his foot, and he went down screaming. He swung and kicked, fighting to get loose, but eventually I managed to flip him over to where I could see his face.

The boy went still. "Protector?"

"Steffin?" He was one of ours. I let go of his arms, and we both stood as I motioned for the rest of the Guard to join us.

"Protector, am I glad to see you." The boy wrapped his arms around me, practically crying for joy.

I still wasn't used to people calling me by a title. "What happened here?" I asked, untangling myself from his grip. "Where's the rest of the pickers?"

"They're gone, Protector."

"Gone? Gone where?" Bull asked, walking over to join us. "Did they get away?"

"No. They were waiting for us . . . beaters everywhere. The only reason I survived was because I stopped to make a pick on the way and fell behind. When I heard the shouts and saw what was happening, I hid." The boy lowered his head, sobbing. "I'm sorry, Protector. I was . . . I was too afraid to do anything."

I looked at Bull. He shrugged. I wasn't sure what to do myself, so I laid my hand on Steffin's shoulder. "There's nothing you could have done."

Bull grunted. I wasn't sure if he was agreeing or disagreeing.

"In fact, I'm glad you hid."

Steffin lifted his head and sniffed. "You are?"

Some of the others looked at me oddly as well.

"Yes. At least now we have someone who can tell us what happened. Did you see which tribe did this?"

"It was Rockslide!"

Rockslide? We weren't anywhere near Rockslide's territory.

Why would they be attacking rejects on another tribe's property? "Are you sure?"

He nodded adamantly while pointing to the side of his arm. "They had green bands."

Kore was hardly known for his mercy. A chief who valued strength above all else. I hated to think what he'd do to a bunch of reject prisoners. "What did they do with our pickers?"

"They took them."

"Did you see which way they went?"

He pointed to the next street up. "That way."

"How long ago was this?"

"A while, I think. I've been sitting behind those barrels long enough for my cheeks to go numb." The boy rubbed his backside.

It sounded like Rockslide had a pretty good head start, and I doubted we could catch them as a group. "Bull, I want you and the Guard to take Steffin and the others back to the Granary."

"Where are you going?"

"I'm going to see if I can track our pickers down."

Bull sheathed his sword and stepped forward. "Not without me, you're not."

As nice as it would be to have someone there to watch my back, it would also be a hindrance. Bull was a big kid with a lot of strength, but he hadn't been trained as I had. Sneaking into Rockslide territory would be much easier with just one of us. "No. I need you to let Reevie know what's happening. Set a watch at the Granary when you get back. If they try using our pickers to find us, I want to make sure we have some kind of way to defend ourselves. Tell him to start planning for an evacuation just in case. He'll know where."

I could tell by the sour expression on Bull's face that he didn't like leaving me there, but he nodded anyway.

I started to turn but caught myself. "Steffin." The frightened picker looked up from where he was bent over the unconscious girl. "Did you happen to see Mouse?"

Steffin thought a moment. "No, I don't remember seeing him. But that doesn't mean much. From where I was hiding, it was hard to tell who was there and who wasn't."

I nodded. Maybe the little street rat had managed to escape. Either way, I needed to find out where the rest of our people were being taken. If they were on their way back to the Rockslide compound, there might still be a chance I could catch up with them.

Chapter 5

I RAN THROUGH THE STREETS of Aramoor, heading east, hoping I was going in the right direction. I was nearing exhaustion. I'd already been up all night dealing with Spats and being chased through the market by patrollers, not to mention my full jog across the city to rescue our pickers, and all with bruised and broken ribs. How much use was I going to be if I did catch up with our people? What could one thirteen-year-old boy manage to do—even if that thirteen-year-old boy felt as though he'd aged about ten years in the last several months?

The route I chose was the most direct to the Rockslide compound—at least from what I could remember of my time spent scouting the city at night. However, things looked different during the day.

The thumping of my swords against the sides of my legs grated on my already-exhausted nerves. I needed to put some thought into a better form of transportation for them. Having two swords bounce all over the place was not conducive to either agility or stealth.

I reached the milling yards and started working my way around the outer fence. If this had been at night, I would have cut through instead of skirting the entire perimeter, but the lumberyards were bustling with activity, and I would have been spotted fairly easily.

The wood had a strong lingering scent, mostly sweet, overpowering some of the more unpleasant smells of city life. Most of it would be shipped downriver to the shipyards in the lower port. I had always wondered how something so enormous as the Elondrian ships didn't sink as soon as they hit the water. Growing up in the ruins of the Lost City, I had never had the privilege of seeing anything as wondrous as the Rhunarin Ocean. I still wasn't sure what kept all that water from washing us away.

On the other side of the milling yard, I slowed. I was now entering Rockslide's territory.

I kept my eyes open, cutting down alleyways and side streets where possible, knowing the Rockslide beaters wouldn't drag a group of rejects down the main thoroughfares. The noonday sun had reached its apex. Light poured through the narrower passageways as I made my way deeper into Kore's domain.

So far, no sign of my pickers.

Once across Rigdin, I could see the city's wall, which meant the compound wasn't too far away. I'd spent more than one night studying it—how many guards they had on watch and how far out they were stationed, how many entrances I could use in order to breach their walls, and what sort of defenses they were capable of mustering. I don't know if it was my Upakan training or my own paranoia, but I had a growing need to learn as much as I could about the other tribes as possible.

What I had learned about Rockslide was that Kore was one paranoid son of a faerie, far more than even Cutter. I slowed the closer I got to my destination. Still, there was no sign of Rockslide's beaters or Hurricane's pickers. Had I managed to somehow get ahead of them?

Three streets down, I spotted the first of Kore's sentries. The girl wasn't heavily armed, but I knew from experience that those posted on the outer fringes weren't there to fight. They were there to give quick warning.

The girl sat quietly on an old barrel at the corner of two adjacent streets, perfectly situated to keep a watch on all four directions. Getting past her was the only way in. Unfortunately, I had no idea how I was going to do that. She was in the perfect position to see everything.

I moved into the shadows and waited. Time ticked by; every minute felt like an hour. Looking for another street would have been a waste of time. Kore would have had sentries on all of them.

I couldn't wait any longer. If I was fast enough, I could probably overpower the girl before she got a warning off. I just didn't like the idea of revealing myself. Best to let the other tribes believe I was dead or gone. However, there were bigger things at stake.

Quietly, I circled around to another alley that opened just two buildings down from where the girl sat. It was now or never. Speed was going to be needed here, so I placed Reevie's satchel on the ground. I took a step closer to the entrance and readied myself.

Here we go. Three. Two—

Voices on my right stopped me in my tracks. I peeked around the corner and spotted a small group heading up the street in my direction. It was a cluster of women and children. Luck was on my side.

The kids were about my age, which helped, but their clothing was far cleaner, not to mention their hands and faces. After retrieving Reevie's satchel, I rubbed my face with my jacket sleeve and waited until the group had moved past my little nook before stepping out to join them. It reminded me of Master Endle's all over again. Hopefully, this didn't end the same.

As we approached the girl sitting on the crates, I carefully moved to the far side of the group and picked up my pace, making sure to keep the small entourage between me and the girl. None of the mothers seemed to notice, too busy boasting about their children's academic achievements to pay any attention to me.

Once we reached the next street up, I cut from the pack and slipped into an alley heading east. I was breathing easier, having made it past the first of the watch, but it didn't stop me from scanning every window and rooftop that came into view. I didn't want to take any chances, not this close to the compound.

Quietly, I moved within the shadows of the tallest buildings, the daylight playing tricks on my memory of the streets. Landmarks I had used while traveling after dark felt out of place. The one thing I could always count on, though, was the city wall. As long as I kept it in sight, I knew I was heading in the right direction.

My breathing increased with anticipation as I made my way down a small sliver of an opening between two buildings. I knew what lay at the other end. I was almost there, and so far, I'd found no sign of my pickers. I didn't want to think what that meant.

The space between the buildings was barely wide enough to allow for the noonday sun, making it a challenge to navigate through loose crates and randomly tossed barrels and boxes. The last time I'd come this way, I'd nearly broken my neck when one of the piles decided my weight was too much for it and had crumbled under me.

Nearing the end of the alley, I worked my way around an old desk that had broken apart from what looked like a great fall. I glanced upward to see if I could determine from which window it had been tossed. Last thing I needed was to have another piece of old furniture discarded on top of my unsuspecting head. The windows were shuttered, so I turned my attention back to what I'd come for—the Rockslide compound.

It looked even bigger in the daylight, more menacing. Maybe that was just my nerves as I tried not to imagine what was going to happen to my pickers if I didn't rescue them. I needed to get a better look at the front gate. Was it open or closed?

I took one step, and something grabbed my leg from under the desk. I jumped, nearly falling as I fought to catch myself. With a quick spin, I drew my sword and swung but stopped halfway when I realized I recognized the dirty face smiling up at me from under the desk.

"Mouse? What in the blazes?" I tried keeping my voice lowered, a difficult thing to do, considering I wanted to thrash the little pickpocket for scaring me half to death. I barely managed to sheathe my sword before he leaped to his feet and threw his arms around me.

"Protector!"

"Shhh!" I cupped his mouth with my hand, and we both ducked behind the upturned desk just as a couple of boys wearing green armbands appeared on the street out front. I kept my hand over his mouth, and we waited, peeking out from under the desk until the two finally moved on.

With a deep sigh of relief, I pulled him farther back into the alley and released his mouth.

"What are you doing here?" we both said at precisely the same time.

"I'm following the pickers," Mouse whispered, pointing back toward the compound. "We didn't stand a chance. They were waiting for us. Stupid!" he said, stomping his foot. "I warned them, I did. I told String Bean and the others they shouldn't be going to the same place every day. That's how you get nabbed. But no, they wouldn't listen to me."

Mouse paused for a moment. I wasn't sure if he was going to continue.

"Then what happened?" I asked.

"The vendors hadn't even opened their carts for the day when those beaters showed up. They were all over the place, like flies on a dung cart. Some of the pickers tried to run." Mouse shook his head. "They didn't get far. I'm small enough that they didn't spot me slipping off to the side. I hopped in the first open keg I could find. I don't know what was in it, but it sure stinks." He raised his arm and took a whiff, then stuck it in my face.

I swatted it away. "I don't want to smell that." It smelled like three-day-old fish offal. "What happened next?"

Mouse gave me a look that he typically reserved for Tubby whenever the giant kid did or said something stupid. "What do you think? I waited until they were gone."

I rolled my eyes. "Obviously, but how close were you following them? Have they already taken them inside?" Once inside those walls, I didn't see much hope.

"No. I got here just before you did and hid under the table when I heard you coming. Thought you was a watcher. Figured I'd been caught for sure." He offered me another one of his relieved smiles. "The beaters have been taking their sweet time getting here, no doubt parading our pickers around for everyone to see."

"If they haven't made it this far," I said, glancing back at the head of the alley, "then there's still a chance to—"

A clamor of shouts erupted from what sounded like the next street over, and we rushed back to the opening and peeked out from behind the desk to see what was going on.

My heart sank.

The Rockslide beaters were just now entering the street between the residential buildings and the walls of their compound. Our pickers were right in the middle. There were a lot more of the beaters than I'd expected, at least two dozen, not including those inside the compound. And unlike the Granary's beaters, these were well armed, daggers at each waist, some carrying swords.

Even with my training, I couldn't see a way to manage a daring rescue that wouldn't end with the death of probably everyone out there, including myself. Even if I managed to break the pickers free, where were we going to go? We were standing in the heart of Rockslide territory, another reason why I was hoping to have found them before now.

One look at the pickers and I could see they were in no shape to fight or run, most barely able to stand. They were covered in cuts and gouges, darkening bruises on their faces, dried blood on their skin and clothing. What was I going to do?

"Move it!" one of the beaters shouted and kicked a small picker in the back, sending him flying forward, where he bounced off several other kids. They all went down together. Cries of fear rang out as they were beaten and dragged back to their feet. The frightened kids huddled together, moving as one.

"Aren't you going to do something, Protector?"

"What do you expect me to do? There's at least twenty beaters out there."

"I don't know. You're Death's Shadow. Go kill them or something."

"Go kill them? What do I look like, a wizard?"

I hadn't realized how much my hands were trembling until Mouse reached out and grabbed them. I took a deep breath to steady my nerves as I watched the beaters force our pickers toward the open gates. The closer they got, the slower our people moved. Pretty soon, they were all but backing up, fighting to keep from being pulled inside.

I watched helplessly as one by one they were dragged behind the Rockslide walls and the gates shut behind them.

Mouse stared up at me, eyes full of disappointment. I felt as though I'd been gut-punched by Tubby, or at the very least kicked by a pregnant mule.

Blazes! I crawled back into the alley, far enough to not be seen by those outside, and punched one of the crates. I barely noticed the pain, hardly caring at that point whether anyone heard me or not. This was why Upakan warriors were trained not to care, to never build connections or relationships. This was why being Upaka meant standing alone.

My instructors had been right. I'd broken a fundamental rule, and look where it had led me. I paced from one side of the alley to the other, my mind racing. There was nothing I could do. I'd failed them. What kind of pitiful excuse for a protector was I? I couldn't even save a bunch of half-starved street kids.

Mouse stood off to the side, staring at me with those beady eyes as though I was supposed to magically have all the answers. I guess that was what leaders were supposed to do, or at least pretend like they did.

Unfortunately, I didn't have an answer. I turned and stared out the narrow alley at the front gates across the street. I couldn't let this stand. There had to be something I could do. Could I bargain with Kore? I dismissed the idea as soon as it reared its ugly head. The thought of Kore negotiating anything was preposterous. Still, I had to do something. I had to find a way to—

"I can get us in."

I turned and looked at the little dirty-faced picker. "What was that?"

Mouse looked at the compound, a smile forming at the corners of his mouth. "I said . . . I can get us in." He turned and looked at me. "But we'll have to wait till dark."

Chapter 6

NIGHTFALL ARRIVED WITH the speed of a mountain duskwing, and it couldn't have come soon enough. Getting inside the compound was going to be difficult. Attempting it in broad daylight would have been suicidal. I could only hope Kore held off doing anything to the pickers until morning.

Fog from the bay lay heavy across the worn cobbles by the time Mouse and I crawled out from our hideaway against one of the buildings in the alley. I could taste the salt in the air. Mouse carefully replaced the loose boards we'd been hiding under. "Never know when that might come in handy," he said with a brisk nod, looking down at his creation.

As one of the Upaka, I'd been trained to move about in such a way that would keep most from seeing, usually by blending in, but Mouse could find a way to keep them from seeing even when they were looking right at you. More than once through the day, watchers had passed through the narrow gap between the buildings, looking for intruders, and each time, they'd walked right by without knowing we were there. It was quite amazing to watch what the little picker could do with nothing more than some old print clippings, a few loose drawers, and the twine he used to hold up his trousers.

I left one of my swords and Reevie's satchel in the cubby. What we were about to do required stealth, which would be much easier to accomplish if I wasn't laden down. We stood in silence at the end of the alley, listening for any movement beyond. I heard nothing, apart from Mouse's nervous fidgeting. The fog was so thick, we couldn't even see the wooden wall on the other side of the street.

"It used to be one of the old Elondrian barracks," Mouse whispered as we waited for the next set of perimeter guards to make their rounds.

"How do you know so much about it?" I asked.

"I used to be a member."

I looked at him, surprised. I'd never thought to ask Mouse which tribe he'd been rejected from. Knowing this, I was certainly glad to have him along. Who better to have with you than someone who knows the layout? Then again, it could also mean he might be recognized.

"Are you sure you want to do this?" Mouse asked, a nervous tremor in his voice.

"We don't have a choice," I said.

"I can think of one. I don't want to get caught."

I crossed my arms. "Are you saying you want to leave our members here to be killed?"

Mouse hesitated.

I rephrased. "Would you want me to leave *you* here if *you* got captured?"

Mouse wrung his hands. "No."

"I didn't think so. Besides, what will happen if we don't return with the pickers?" I didn't wait for a response. "We'd starve."

Mouse didn't say anything, just nodded.

"More importantly," I added, "it's the right thing to do."

Another set of watchers neared, torches in hand, so we ducked behind the broken desk and waited for them to pass. Once they did, we crawled out and made our way to the edge of the alley.

"Lead the way," I whispered, and Mouse scurried out from the narrow passageway and headed down the front of the buildings on the left. I followed closely, wondering the entire way if maybe he had been right. Was this a wasted effort? Something inside me said it was.

Our progress was slow. We kept to the shadows, stopping at the corners of each building to listen. I could hear muffled voices coming from the compound across the street, but nothing beyond that.

"Down," Mouse whispered, and we dropped to the ground and pressed against the face of the building. The fog covered us like a moist blanket—uncomfortable to the touch but too necessary to kick off.

Another pair of sentries neared, but they were hardly worried with checking every nook and cranny, too busy regaling each other with stories so boastfully preposterous that they were almost worth listening to. Once they passed, we kept going.

Mouse stopped at the next building and pointed across the street to the wall. He didn't need to say anything. I knew what was coming.

We waited for the next set of watchers to pass before making our move. The light from their torches had barely faded back into the fog when Mouse bolted out into the street. I ran after him and grabbed the back of his shirt so as not to lose him altogether.

The mist was so thick I couldn't see my own feet. I might have had Upakan sight, but seeing in the dark and seeing through the middle of a heavy cloud were two different things.

The voices from atop the wall were the only indication we were heading in the right direction. We were nearly across when the sound of loose rock being crunched underfoot had us both tripping over each other to stop.

Someone was just ahead of us in the mist. My heart raced as I studied the blanket of nothingness. Where were they?

Then I heard it again.

Someone scuffed a pebble with their shoe. I moved in front of Mouse and pulled my knife. Whoever it was had to be up against the wall.

We waited, but there was no other sound to tell us which direction to go. Time was running out. The next set of watchers would be walking in on us at any moment. I grabbed Mouse's hand, and we started forward slowly, hunching over to make ourselves as small as possible. My eyes searched the fog, hoping to catch a glimpse of whoever it was before they saw us and sounded the alarm. If we were spotted, all hope for our pickers would be lost.

We hadn't taken three steps when something detached itself from the stone wall. All three of us caught sight of each other at the same time. I had no idea where the boy had come from, but before he got a chance to realize he didn't recognize our faces, I jumped forward and kicked him in the gut. He stumbled backward, gasping for breath.

Before he found his first gulp, I had my hand over his mouth and my knife at his throat. I knew from experience that having the air ripped from your lungs in such a way left you with the feeling of drowning. The desperation of trying to catch that next swallow of air was all that mattered. And I wanted him desperate.

Quickly, I pushed him back against the wall and realized there was a recess, a doorway where the boy had clearly been hiding. No wonder we hadn't seen him.

I felt a pinch on the side of my arm and turned to find Mouse pointing out toward the haze. A blur of light floated through the fog, growing steadily brighter. I pressed the blade tighter against the boy's neck and hissed, "Get us inside or you die right here."

One look at my grey eyes and his key was out of his pocket and sliding shakily into the lock.

"Hurry." I pressed even harder, keeping my free hand on his shoulder in case he decided to run for it once the door opened. The voices were nearly on us.

". . . seven or eight at least," one of the watchers said. "Caught them up east of Avis. Ought to make for some good fun tomorrow."

The lock finally snapped, and I shoved the three of us inside.

The door clicked shut just as the sentries passed. I could hear the heels of their boots from the other side.

Mouse wiped his forehead. "That was close."

"Too close."

We waited until the steps could no longer be heard, then I pocketed our prisoner's keys but left the door unlocked in case we needed a quick exit. Hopefully, no one would spot the unattended entrance until we were safely gone.

The inside of the compound was surprisingly quiet. Somewhere above us inside the turret, I could hear faint chatter from the other watchers.

"This way." Mouse spared no time in directing us away from the wall and up under a wooden staircase that ran up the side of a stone-block structure.

Our prisoner remained quiet, his eyes lowered. He looked to be about my age, a little taller perhaps, but thinner. He lacked the muscle I had put on from my training. Dark circles around his eyes said he hadn't gotten much sleep, and the gauntness in his cheeks said that he wasn't getting enough to eat.

"What are we going to do with him?" Mouse whispered, eyeing the boy. "We can't very well take him with us, and we can't trust that he'll keep his mouth shut."

I looked at the watcher. I couldn't tell if he was more afraid of the steel pressed against his neck or my eyes. "Look at me."

The boy didn't budge, so I pulled his chin up with the flat of my blade. "I said look at me."

His eyes rose to meet mine.

"What's wrong with you?"

The boy gulped. "You're . . . you're Death's Shadow. You're the one from the Pit. The one who beat Flesh Eater."

I couldn't tell if he was asking a question or stating a fact, so I nodded.

Mouse brandished a long knife from the back of his pants. "Only one way to make sure he doesn't talk. I say we take care of him right here."

"No," I said.

"No?"

"Please, I won't say anything," the boy pleaded. "I promise."

"Like we're going to believe you," Mouse said, brandishing his knife, tip pointed at the boy's chest, just waiting to stick him with it.

The watcher shivered. "Please, don't kill me. You . . . you could take me with you. I can help you."

"Sure," Mouse said sarcastically, "help us right into the beaters' barracks." Mouse looked at me. He studied my face, then frowned. "You don't actually believe him, do you? He's just trying to trick us. He'd say anything to save his scrawny neck."

Every ounce of my Upakan training wanted to agree with Mouse. Never leave loose ends. The simplest solution is usually the best. I could give Mouse the nod, and we would have one less problem to worry about, but that would make me no better than them. I sighed. "We'll take him with us."

"What?" Mouse blurted out, then covered his mouth with his hand. All three of us ducked down under the stairs and watched the open courtyard, eyes darting from one building to the next as we attempted to pierce the fog. If I were truly following my Upakan instructors' advice, I'd probably have killed them both by now and gone on alone, but my father had raised me differently.

When it appeared no one had heard Mouse's call, or cared enough to come investigate, I turned and gave the little boy a stern look. "No need to worry about him giving us away when I've got you around."

He grimaced. "Sorry."

I looked at the watcher. "He comes with us, but if he tries anything, you have my permission to stick him as many times as you want." I hoped the threat would be enough to deter the boy.

Mouse's eyes brightened.

The boy didn't say anything, just nodded.

"What's your name?" I asked.

"J-Jayden."

"I'm Ayrion, and this is Mouse," I said as a way of introduction. "Now give me your armband."

"What?" Jayden gave me a startled look.

"You heard me. Your armband."

He untied the green piece of cloth and handed it to me. I tied the material to my arm, giving him my blue one instead. His armband was a little snug but nothing I couldn't live with.

“What about this?” Mouse said, grabbing the front of my black overcoat. “No one’s going to believe you’re a simple watcher with something as nice as this.”

“Good point.” I took it off and looked for some way to hide it. “Put it in one of those crates behind you. If we have time, we’ll grab it on the way out.” I hated leaving the coat, but I had more important things to worry about.

After swinging Jayden’s cloak over my shoulders, I took a moment to look us over. I figured I could pass for a Rockslide watcher as long as I didn’t look anyone directly in the eyes. Mouse was easy to spot as a picker, and Jayden was thin enough to look like a picker as well. As long as we didn’t stumble across anyone who recognized our thin watcher, we should be fine.

“Which way?” I asked, looking out at the haze.

Jayden pointed left, to a building at the center of the compound, rising just above the fog. It was the largest of the stone structures directly in line with the main gates. “They took the rejects down to the cells.”

Mouse nodded. “I know where that is.”

I looked at Jayden. “If you try anything . . .” I stuck my dagger in my belt and drew my sword.

“Hey,” Mouse balked. “You said I could be the one to stick him.”

I ignored Mouse, but Jayden got the message, as he quickly nodded, swallowing on reflex.

“How long do we have?” I asked.

Jayden looked at me. “For what?”

"What does Rockslide normally do with captured rejects?"

"Kill them, of course," Mouse said with a sneer.

"Yes, but how, where?"

Mouse didn't respond. Instead, he looked at Jayden.

Jayden pursed his lips. "It's late, so Kore will probably leave them in the cells to squirm 'til morning." He scratched the back of his head. "Or he could just decide to get it over and done with as soon as possible. Just depends on his mood."

Well, that wasn't helpful. I tilted my head to see if the stars could tell me how much time we had, but the fog was too thick. "So, how do we get inside? Walk you two through the front doors?"

"No!" Mouse said. "Through the kitchens."

"The kitchens?" Jayden looked confused.

"That's what I said, wasn't it?"

I studied the two for a moment. Didn't seem like I had much of a choice. I looked at Mouse. "Lead the way."

Chapter 7

WE CREPT FROM OUR NOOK under the stairs and started for the next building over, quiet as a pack of snow cats on the prowl. At least, two of us were.

Jayden seemed to have a knack for stepping in every pothole, kicking up every loose bit of cobble, and occasionally tripping on his own feet. Was he just nervous, or was he purposefully trying to get us caught?

"Sorry, I can't see anything in this fog," he said.

"Hush it or I'm going to cut you," Mouse whispered over his shoulder as he directed us along. So far, the sentries on this side of the wall were few and far between. Evidently, the tribe didn't see much reason to post guards inside the compound. Who'd be stupid enough to want to break in?

The first building we reached had well-lit windows at the front, and the large number of muffled voices inside had us crawling on our hands and knees. We didn't want to take a chance of anyone spotting us through the shutters.

"Beaters' barracks," Jayden whispered as we passed under the last window, its light casting strange shadows in the fog around us. At the corner, we stood, and Mouse took us left, down the walkway between the barracks and whatever building lay beside it.

So far, so good.

A door on the side opened, and two beaters stepped out right in front of us. One of the beaters was holding a torch, the other a small sack.

Everyone froze.

"What's going on here?" the shorter boy with the torch asked. He took a step forward and let the door shut behind them.

I angled my head to keep the light from my eyes.

"Well?"

I cleared my throat and made a show of adjusting the green band on my arm. "I found a couple more rejects and was ordered to take them to the cells." I pointed at Mouse and Jayden with my sword. "I think they might have been part of the group that were brought in earlier." I hocked and spat off to the side to show my disgust.

I hoped that the Rockslide tribal members were similar to Hurricane's in that the inner factions didn't co-mingle all that much. Beaters spent time with other beaters. They didn't generally make friends with the cleaners or pickers, or in my case, a watcher.

"Rejects, huh?" The short beater with the torch took a few steps closer to get a better view of Mouse and Jayden, but the fog was making it difficult. At least we had that going for us.

I kept my eyes on Jayden, watching for the first sign of betrayal. "Yeah, I heard a couple of beaters caught them trying to make a run for it." I tapped Jayden on the side of his arm with the flat of my blade to let him know I was still watching, and to encourage his silence. "But no reject is going to outrun a member of Rockslide."

"You got that right," the taller boy on the left said. He swiped his matted hair from his eyes. He, too, hocked up a wad and spat it against the barracks' wall.

The shorter beater finished his inspection of my prisoners and moved back around to where his friend stood waiting. He turned and looked at me. "What'd you say your name was?"

"I'm . . . Toff."

Toff? It was the first thing that popped into my head. Maybe because the short beater's hair had the distinct coloring of the toffee sticks Reevie and I used to snatch near the fishery. I don't know why I was thinking about sweets at a time like that, but then again, when was there ever a bad time to think about sweets?

"Toff, huh? That's a stupid name. Where'd you get it?"

I kept my head lowered. "From . . . from my parents."

"Your parents? No wonder you're on the streets. With a name like that, I'd disown you too." The short beater laughed, and his comrade joined in. "Well, Toff, if you've been tasked with taking this scum to the cells like you say, then why is it we find you skulking about behind the beater barracks like a right dirty little peeper?"

"I, uh . . ." I fumbled with my words, trying to think of an excuse. The hesitation might have worked in my favor since it gave me the appearance of being afraid, which wasn't too far from the truth. "It's . . . it's this flaming fog," I said, waving my sword clumsily through the air as if trying to cut it. "Can't see a thing. I was just following the light." I glanced at the barracks' windows and nodded with my head. "It was just the wrong light, is all."

The taller boy waved his free hand in front of his face. "Thick as turnip stew, if you ask me."

"No one asked you," the shorter boy said.

"Don't mean it ain't true."

The shorter beater raised the torch and grunted. "I suppose." He glanced over my shoulder and squinted.

"I guess we'll just be moving along," I said, using my sword to angle the prisoners away from the two suspicious beaters and back out into the open yard. "Need to get these rejects in the cells before they decide to throw me in with them." I released a nervous chuckle and made a show of pushing Mouse and Jayden forward. "Move along. We haven't got all—"

"Wait!" Jayden suddenly shouted. "I'm not one of them. I'm not a reject! I'm a watcher. I'm one of you." He pointed back at me. "He . . . he's not even from Rockslide! I caught the two of them sneaking—"

I belted out a heavy laugh. "Listen to the scum," I said, my face reddening. "He'll say anything to save his wretched hide." I glared at Jayden. "You better shut your mouth, or I'll shut it for you."

The two beaters took a step back. They seemed to be enjoying the entertainment. I could almost hear the chants from the Pit echoing in the back of my mind. "*Kill him! Kill him! Kill him!*"

Jayden didn't let the threat deter him. "What's wrong with you?" he shouted, pleading with the two beaters to acknowledge his position. "Can't you see who he is? He's—"

My fist connected with the side of Jayden's jaw, and he spun around, crumpling at my feet.

There was a burst of laughter, and I felt a hard slap on my shoulder. "That's the most action I've seen since the Pit! I didn't think you had it in you, watcher." The shorter beater glanced over his shoulder at his friend. "Our little Toff here's got some fight in him after all. Maybe they've been wasting your talents on the wall."

The taller beater grunted.

"Yeah, I think the beaters could use another scrapper like you." He took a step back and looked me over. "What do you think? Why so quiet? Ain't you got something to say for yourself?"

I looked down at where Jayden lay sprawled. "His voice was getting on my nerves."

The two beaters laughed all over again.

"I best be getting these two down to the cells before they're missed. I wouldn't want Kore coming to look for us."

The beaters stiffened. "Probably right." He looked down at Jayden, who was just starting to move his head. "Need some help?"

"No!" I said, a little too desperately. "I've got them."

The short beater stared at me a moment, then nodded, and they headed out toward the open yard. He glanced back over his shoulder just before disappearing into the mist. "I look forward to seeing you around, Toff."

I waved as the two beaters vanished from view.

There was a loud sigh of relief behind me. "I thought we were goners for sure," Mouse said, staring down at Jayden, whose arms and legs were now moving as well.

"You and me both."

"I was about to stick him if you hadn't clobbered him first."

"Yeah, I figured as much, which is why I did it."

Mouse shrugged. "Well, he had it coming."

"Here, help me get him up." I wrapped one of Jayden's arms around my neck and lifted him to his feet. Jayden's eyes were still rolling in their sockets when I started us forward. "Let's get out of here before we run into any more trouble."

Chapter 8

BY THE TIME MOUSE and I had dragged Jayden around the back of the beaters' barracks, he was beginning to come to.

"What happened?"

"You tried giving us up is what happened," Mouse said, waving his short blade under Jayden's nose.

Jayden's eyes widened, and he reached for his jaw. "You . . . you hit me."

"You're right lucky he did," Mouse said, then looked at me. "Obviously, we can't trust him to keep his big mouth shut. Just give me a minute or two with him in the meat shed over there," he said, nodding toward a small wooden structure just off the building on our right. "I'll keep him from talking."

I glanced at the shed. "Who all goes in there?"

"No one but Cook's allowed in there." Mouse twirled his blade, grinning. "The last kid they caught helping themselves to the meat was branded and thrown out."

It took me a moment to realize what Mouse was saying. "You're a reject for pinching meat?" I tried not to chuckle.

"What're you laughing for?"

"I always thought you were branded because of . . . well . . ."

"What? Because of my size?" He crossed his arms. "I'll have you know, I was Rockslide's best picker. No one can get in and out of places better than me. I can pick anything."

"Apparently not," Jayden said, then cowered when Mouse spun on him.

"How was I to know Cook had decided to sleep in the shed that night? I snuck in through the window and landed right on top of her."

"When does she normally go in?" I asked.

"In the morning when she starts breakfast."

I tilted my head to look at the stars, forgetting I couldn't see them through the fog. "I hope we have enough time."

Mouse looked at me funny and then glanced upward as well. "Enough time for what?"

"To get our pickers out of the compound."

"Why?"

"Because that's where we're going to leave Jayden."

Mouse smiled. "Right. They won't find him until morning."

"But I can still help you," Jayden pleaded. "I know where they're keeping the prisoners."

"We already know where they're keeping the prisoners," I said, grabbing the watcher by his shirt to keep him from making a run for it. "You've already proven yourself untrustworthy, and I'm not going to risk my pickers' lives on you keeping your mouth shut again." I shoved him toward the meat shed.

"'Bout time you came to your senses," Mouse said, waving his dagger. "Now you just leave him to me."

Instead of stabbing Jayden like Mouse wanted, I took the watcher inside the shed and tied him to one of the barrels of salted pork. He never even struggled. No doubt due to Mouse and his threatening. The shirtsleeve gag Mouse tied around Jayden's mouth was enough to ensure no one would find him until Cook arrived in the morning.

"I like it," Mouse said. "Very devious. When Cook finds him here, he'll be branded a reject and tossed out along with what's left of the morning rations."

Jayden started to whimper.

"From what I've seen of how Kore treats his members, we're probably doing him a favor." I turned and started for the door. "Let's get going. We don't have long till sunrise."

"Wait." Mouse stuck his dagger back in his belt and made his way to the far end of the shed, where he grabbed a large coil of rope from behind one of the shelves. "We'll need this," he said, handing me the rope on the way by.

"For what?"

"You'll see."

I secured the shed's door and followed Mouse over to the main building on the right.

"This here's the dining hall." Mouse opened the door, and we stepped inside.

It was about the way I'd expected, a large room with rows of tables and benches. The walls and furnishings were plain, which made sense with this having once been lancer barracks. It was the very opposite of the Temple, where everything, including the design of the walls, was built for beauty and elegance.

I helped myself to a lit lantern that was hanging on the wall beside the door. A quick inspection revealed the oil reservoir was still half-full.

"This way," Mouse said as he directed us past the open kitchen to a door on the left, which turned out to be a storage room filled with cooking utensils and shelves stocked with various fruits and vegetables. I sneezed at the strong odor of spices.

"Give me a hand?"

I turned to find Mouse pushing against a set of shelves on the other side of the room, but with his petite frame, he stood no more chance of moving it than a tree rat trying to move the tree his nest was in.

"What are you doing?"

"We need to get to that," he said, pointing to what looked like a trapdoor beneath the shelving.

"Why? I doubt Kore is holding our pickers in food storage."

"Trust me."

I shut the door leading out to the dining hall and placed the lantern on one of the barrels. "Okay, together." I placed my shoulder against the shelf and shoved. It slowly slid away from the wall, leaving a trail in the dust beneath it. Apart from a few of the stacked onions rolling off and scattering on the floor, the legs made surprisingly little noise on the old wood.

A couple more good shoves and we managed to move the shelf far enough to get at the hatch below. The trapdoor had no lock. It also had no rings or handle to use for opening, so I wedged my blade up under the crack and lifted it high enough to get my fingers underneath. The door gave way with a rusty whine.

There was nothing but darkness below, darkness and the familiar smell of mildew.

"What's down there?"

"Our pickers."

I took another look, but even with *my* eyes, I couldn't see the bottom.

"That's the old barracks cells down there. They used to use this to feed the prisoners. They would lower food down to the jailer through this hole instead of carrying it back around to the main building and down the stairs." He looked at me. "There aren't many that knows it's here."

"How do *you* know about it, then?"

Mouse smiled. "'Cause I'm Mouse."

"Let me guess. This is what the rope's for?" I dropped the coil onto the floor beside the opening. "How far down does it go?"

"A ways. But don't worry. I've done this before."

Somehow, that didn't reassure me. "And how did you manage that? It took two of us just to move the shelf."

Mouse gave me a frustrated look. "Because the shelf wasn't

there before."

Had the shelf been put there because of Mouse? What else had the little troublemaker been caught doing? I anchored the rope around a pair of pickle barrels on the other side of the room. Even without the label on the side, I could have guessed the contents by the strong vinegar smell wafting from the lids. I gave the barrels a shove. Neither budged. The pickles and brine had to weigh at least three or four times more than the both of us put together.

"You ready?" Mouse asked, edging toward the opening. He kept a tight grip on the rope as he waited for me to give the go-ahead.

"Right behind you." I gave the rope a few test jerks, then watched Mouse disappear into the darkness below. After grabbing the lantern off the barrel to keep anyone walking through the dining hall from seeing the light, I gave the rope one final tug for good measure, then stepped off.

The hole wasn't all that large. In all likelihood, it might have been a well back before they had built the barracks, and instead of filling it in, they'd decided to use it. Even without the rope, I could have probably kept from falling by pressing my feet on one side and my back on the other.

I kept my climb slow, not just because of my injuries, but because I didn't want to hurry and land on top of Mouse. The feel of the rope in my hand and the free swing over an unknown drop brought back memories of home and the training I'd undergone on the southern peaks. More than one kid had fallen to their death attempting to scale old Dragon Fang, the tallest and deadliest of the mountain peaks.

The smell was growing stronger the lower we went, building to something far less pleasant. With the lantern shining in my face, I couldn't see much farther down than a few feet beyond my shoes. It's amazing how disorienting it can be when you can't see where you're going. It felt like we'd been climbing for hours, but it had probably only been a few minutes.

I wanted to call down and ask how much farther but worried the surrounding stone would funnel my voice straight into whoever's ears were waiting at the bottom.

Holding the light above my head so it wasn't in my eyes, I caught a faint glimmer below. I found I could see it better if I didn't look directly at it but off to the side, a trick I'd learned while navigating the lower tunnels back home. Sure enough, I could just make out a shape swinging back and forth below me.

Not wanting to give our presence away, I blew out the lantern and hurried my descent to catch up. I had imagined the hole at the bottom of the well lowering straight through the ceiling and into the prison itself, but instead, the shaft ended just outside the prison wall. I felt as though I had just climbed down someone's chimney and was now standing in the hearth, peering into the front room.

A small section of the wall leading into the prison had been removed, large enough for one person to walk in and out of. A torch rested in a bracket on the opposite side of the antechamber, and a low-burning lamp sat on an unoccupied table along with two empty plates and a set of tin mugs. A couple of chairs and a pail in the corner were the only other fixtures.

There was no one in sight.

Chapter 9

WE WAITED FOR AS long as we dared, listening for any sign that the jailers might be coming back.

"How many guards are usually down here?" I whispered, peering through the hole in the wall.

"Two or three."

I placed my lantern just inside the opening and stuck my head out to get a better look. "Where is everyone?"

Mouse shrugged. "How should I know?"

On the left was a hallway leading to the first set of cells. "I'm going to check it out."

Mouse grabbed my arm. "Do you think you should?"

"We don't have time to sit here waiting for someone to show up."

He reluctantly let go and followed me into the guard station.

There was a door on the right I hadn't noticed from inside the well. It had a small sliding window about head high. At least for a grown man, it would have been head high; for me, it would have required standing on my tiptoes. Thankfully, both were closed.

"Where does that go?"

"That's the only way out of here," Mouse said. "Except of course . . ." He nodded back toward the hole in the wall.

We didn't have time to waste. Dawn was coming, and if we hadn't escaped the compound by then, odds are we never would. Leaving the open shaft behind, I skirted the outer edge of the room, making my way for the hall on the left, which led to the cells.

Mouse stayed on my heels. He kept a nervous eye on the door. We stopped at the corner, and I peeked around the other side. There was no one there, just an empty corridor with doors on either side. I motioned with my head, and we stepped into the hall.

Keeping to the shadows, we started into the prison. The stone was cool to the touch and the smoke from the torches was barely enough to cut through the stench of dirty bodies and overflowing chamber pots. All the doors we'd passed were shut. Did Rockslide really have that many prisoners, or did they simply leave them that way? I didn't hear any noises coming from the other sides, and I doubted Kore was one to keep people on a permanent basis. That would have meant supplying food.

"Where do you think the pickers are being—"

"This way," Mouse whispered, taking the lead. "Kore likes to keep prisoners in the back, as far away from everything as possible.

It's scarier back there."

Mouse led us through the corridors of the prison network. It was much larger than I'd expected. Had this been one of the main penal compounds for Aramoor in its early years? How had Rockslide managed to claim the old barracks for themselves?

It must have had something to do with those *favors* Reevie and Sapphire had spoken of after the Guild meeting. Some of the tribes had managed to find a way to be useful to the aristocracy, earning a waiver from patroller incursion. Unfortunately, we weren't one of them, which meant we couldn't afford to lose a single picker, let alone our entire team.

Mouse stopped in front of me, and I almost tripped to avoid hitting him. The hall had come to an end with only a single passage leading off to the right.

At this end, the prison looked like it had been carved straight out of the rock, perhaps expanding an existing cave. The smell of decay was even stronger there.

Mouse turned and raised his finger to his lips, though I didn't need the warning. I could already hear voices coming from somewhere down the next corridor. I peeked around the corner and found the jailers. Four of them. Why so many? There had only been two plates on the table at the guard station, and other than our pickers, all the other cells appeared to be empty.

Two of the largest boys had their backs to us; the one on the right held a cudgel. The other two seemed to be preoccupied with something on the floor, but I couldn't make out what, since the first two were standing in the way. It also didn't help that the single torch on the wall behind them was throwing shadows across the two on the floor.

One of the larger guards finally moved, and I realized the two on the ground weren't guards at all. They were our pickers.

"Fight, you worthless pieces of faerie dung!" the boy on the left hollered, waving his arm in the air.

"Kick him!" the guard with the cudgel shouted. "No, go for the face! The face, I said!" The guard jabbed the picker on the right, and the frightened kid lunged at the other picker's face.

Both boys were crying.

Mouse pulled me back behind the wall. "Kore lets the guards play with the prisoners. It gives them an incentive to sit down here." He drew his dagger. "What do you want—"

Before he could finish, I was already around the corner. I didn't even bother drawing my weapon. I kept to the balls of my feet to soften my approach, picking up speed as I went. Four steps . . . Three. Two. I leaped into the air and kicked both boys straight in the back. They flew over the two pickers and landed headfirst on the other side.

I landed on my back and quickly flipped to my feet.

"Get behind me," I said, and the two pickers scrambled to their feet.

I took a few steps back and raised the hood of Jayden's cloak to shield my face.

Behind me, Mouse released a high-pitched squeal. I glanced over my shoulder in time to see him charging up the hall, swinging his short dagger like a madman.

I raised my hand. "No."

His battle cry fizzled and died as he skidded to a halt behind me. "What? I was going to help."

"Stay with the pickers." I turned and waited for the two Rockslide boys to make it to their feet. The one on the left drew a long dagger from his waist. The other fumbled over to retrieve his cudgel.

"Who are you?" the guard with the dagger demanded, straining to see my face. "How'd you get in here?"

"Who is he?" Mouse blurted out, moving closer. "You better pray you don't find out. If I was you, I'd throw down my weapons and beg for mercy."

The two boys tensed, but neither attacked.

"What's your business here?" the taller boy on the right asked, holding his cudgel in front of him but staying out of reach.

"I've come for my people."

The two guards looked at each other, confused.

"Your people?" The guard with the cudgel looked at one of the doors a few feet away, where I could hear faint voices on the other side. "They're rejects. They ain't nobody's people."

The guard with the dagger edged forward. "Why don't you step into the light? Are you afraid to show us your face?"

"Yeah," the shorter boy on the left said, puffing out his chest as he, too, took a bold step forward. "You scared or something?"

I drew my sword slowly from its sheath, letting the metal sing as the tension built.

"Oh, you've gone and done it now," Mouse said. "You've made him mad. He's gonna gut you like a fish and wear your teeth for a necklace."

The two boys actually took a step back. Even my pickers moved away.

As if on cue, I stepped into the light and pulled back my hood.

As soon as the light reached my face, both boys stiffened, eyes wide and mouths gaping like fish.

"You're . . . you're—"

"That's right," Mouse said, glee in his voice. "You've raised your sword against Death's Shadow."

The guard on the left dropped his dagger. "I thought you was dead."

"Dead?" Mouse laughed. "How do you kill a shade?"

The boy on the right released his weapon as well. "Please don't kill us."

Both of the boys were trembling. They kept their gaze on the hilt of my sword, not willing to look me in the eyes. I still found it amazing how unnerved my eyes made people, especially in firelight.

"We'll do whatever you want," the shorter boy pleaded. "We'll do anything."

"I want you to release my people."

"Yes, sir." The guard grabbed a ring of keys from his belt and rushed to unlock the door. His hands were shaking so bad, he could barely find the right key.

When the lock finally snapped, the boy pulled the latch and opened the door.

The pickers inside stumbled past their jailers and ran to my side.

"Protector, we knew you'd come!" one of the girls said as she joined the others behind me. "I told them you'd save us, but they didn't believe me."

I looked at Mouse. "Take the pickers back to the entrance."

"What about them?" Mouse asked, pointing his dagger at the frightened guards.

"We'll lock them in one of the cells."

Mouse grinned. "Yeah, that's a good idea. When they come to get the pickers in the morning, they'll find their jailers instead."

"Wait!" the guard with the keys blurted out. "Don't leave us here. Please, take us with you."

Mouse raised his knife and started for the two boys. "You heard him. Get in the cell before I open you up and make you play with your insides."

The guards backed toward the open door, trying to keep away from the small boy with the crazy look in his eyes. I was starting to get a little worried about him myself. Apparently, he'd picked up some bad habits from his time in Rockslide.

"Please, don't leave us here," the taller boy said, echoing his comrade's earlier plea. Both were on the verge of crying. "We don't want to die."

"Wait." I pointed at the guards. "What did you just say?"

The taller boy gulped and took a step forward. "We don't want to die."

"Die? I said I wasn't going to kill you."

"Don't listen to them," Mouse said as he kicked the shorter guard in the shin, causing him to hop up and down. "Now get in there. And give me those keys."

"Hold on, Mouse. I want to hear what they have to say." I looked at the guards. "Why do you believe you're going to die?"

The shorter boy with the keys looked at me like I'd asked the silliest question he'd ever heard. "If a guard ever loses their prisoner, they're expected to take the prisoner's place."

I turned to Mouse. "Is that true?"

Mouse looked at the guards and ground his teeth. "I suppose."

"You suppose, or you know?"

He hesitated but finally nodded yes.

"So, if you let the pickers go, they will execute the two of you tomorrow instead?"

Mouse smiled. "Right fittin', if you ask me." Several of the pickers agreed.

I looked at the guards. Neither one moved. They stood there with desperation in their eyes, and as much as I wanted to see justice carried out for what they'd done to my pickers, I couldn't bring myself to leave them there to be executed. More importantly, something I hadn't thought about until now: if I left the guards there, they'd reveal who it was that had snuck into the compound, and I didn't want to give Kore any more clues than I already had.

Taking the keys from the shorter boy, I walked over and locked the door back in place and turned to Mouse. "Bring them with us."

Chapter 10

BACK AT THE GUARD STATION, I ordered the two Rockslide boys to sit at the table while Mouse directed the pickers up the rope and into the storage room above. It took a while, since most of the pickers didn't have the experience, or the upper body strength, to make it up the rope with any kind of speed, especially given their weakened condition and the beating they'd taken before arriving at the compound. It was a small miracle that none of them fell during the climb.

I stayed behind to keep an eye on our prisoners, but it seemed the threat of being left in one of the cells was all it took to keep the two boys in line. They were as yielding as a stalk of wheat in a summer breeze. Their clothes, even though somewhat threadbare, were in better shape than half our ragtag group. They even seemed to fit. Most of our kids wore whatever they could find: shirts and pants that were too long, too short, or too full of holes.

"What're your names?" I asked the taller boy on the left.

The boy kept his eyes on the top of the table. "Melvin." He jabbed a thumb toward the shorter boy. "That's Koal."

Koal fidgeted in his seat but, like his friend, didn't look me in the eyes.

We sat a moment longer as I gave our pickers a little more time to get up the rope, but as soon as the grunts and groans had faded from the open well behind me, I stood. "Your turn," I said, pointing at the hole in the wall. "In you go."

The boys hopped to their feet and scurried into the old well.

I grabbed my lantern from where I'd left it and relit the wick using the torch by the door before following the boys up. Instead of focusing on whether or not the rope would hold or the thrumming pain in my chest as I pulled myself up, I thought about Kore and what his reaction would be in the morning when he came to collect the rejects for execution and found that they, along with their jailers, had vanished into thin air.

Kore might think that his guards had set the prisoners free, but that would be hard to justify, considering the only door leading in and out of the cells was locked from the inside. I was still pondering over how the Rockslide chief would respond when the hole above me came into view. Mouse was waiting with the others at the top. I climbed out and placed the lamp on a nearby barrel in order to start hefting up the rope, but I stopped at the sound of eager voices behind me.

I turned to find the entire line of pickers stuffing their pockets with food from the shelves. Some didn't bother to make it that far and crammed the food in their mouths.

"Stop," I said. "Put it back." The hungry kids looked at me like I was crazy. "I don't want anyone to know we were here. We clean out their stores and it won't take much to figure out how you escaped."

"He's right," Mouse said, pointing at the shelves. "Put it back." Mouse waited until he thought I wasn't looking and quickly unloaded his own trouser pockets.

I felt guilty as I watched the kids slowly return the goods, but we couldn't take a chance on Kore figuring out how we had escaped.

Behind me, the Rockslide guards stood quietly near the barrels, keeping their distance from everyone else. I motioned them over. "Melvin. Koal. Haul the rope up."

The two guards quickly retrieved the rope from the well and untied the other end from the two barrels of pickles. Once free, I closed the trapdoor and had the two boys help me shove the heavy shelf back into place. It moved much easier with three of us.

Mouse re-coiled the rope and handed it to Melvin to carry. He gave the tall guard a harsh look but didn't bother offering his normal round of threatening.

After making sure everything was left as we had found it, including the floor where the dust had been disturbed, I cracked open the door leading out to the dining hall and listened for any sign that the cook had begun readying the first meal of the day. I had no idea how much time had passed while we were below, but it had to be close to dawn.

The dining hall was quiet, so I opened the door, and we started across the room. Melvin and Koal kept to my heels. Behind them, Mouse and the pickers brought up the rear.

I'd barely made it as far as the first table when a loud crash rang from the kitchen ahead on the right. "Faerie farts!" someone shouted from inside.

Everyone froze.

I quickly blew out the lantern and turned to wave everyone down, but they'd already dropped to their stomachs. I motioned for them to hide, and the pickers scurried like rats to get to the far side of the room behind the tables.

I could hear a piece of flint being struck, and pretty soon a small light blossomed from inside the kitchen. I peeked over one of the tables to get a better look.

A tall, wiry girl lifted a couple of pots from the floor that she'd knocked over in the dark, then worked her way around to the main cooking area. She hung the lantern on one of the rungs beside a stone hearth, and with a long piece of kindling she lit from the lantern's flame, she ignited the cooking fire.

Mouse crawled up beside me. "What are we going to do?" he whispered.

I pointed forward. "If we keep to the back wall where it's darkest, I think we can make it around without her noticing."

Making it to the end of the tables wasn't too difficult. However, to get to the door, we were going to have to cross about twenty feet of open floor with nothing but shadows and our luck to keep us from being seen.

I glanced at the kitchen. The cook's back was to us as she placed several pots and pans across the counter. We couldn't wait any longer. "Go," I whispered to Mouse, and held my breath as the first of the pickers left the protection of the tables and started crawling across the floor.

I wanted to urge them to move faster, but any noise from us might have alerted the cook. A few more cabinet doors being opened and shut on our right, and the pickers picked up speed. They looked like a line of sugar ants scurrying toward a piece of leftover fruit.

By the time Mouse reached the door, the last of our kids were just making their way across the open room. He stopped and turned. *What's he waiting for?* I raised my arm to wave him on, and a door on the other side of the room opened.

The pickers dropped to their stomachs once again.

I peeked over the table to see a figure heading in the direction of the kitchen. Could this get any worse? So far, we'd run into someone at nearly every turn.

"Is that you, Dillweed?" the cook shouted from behind one of the ovens. I couldn't tell if the title was meant to be derogatory or if that was actually his name.

"Yes," the newcomer replied. The short, chubby boy yawned and rubbed his eyes as he made his way into the kitchen and grabbed a fresh apron from off the rack.

"You're late. Again." The taller girl looked like she was ready to club her assistant with one of her rolling pins. "Where's Sprout?"

"He's coming. Kore had him up making a late-night snack. He

slept in."

Great, I mused, *now we have more coming.* I motioned for Mouse to keep going, keeping a careful eye on the cook and her assistant as they went about their chores.

Mouse pulled on the latch and slowly opened the door. It made a couple of rusty squeaks, but the clanging of pots from the kitchen easily covered it.

I was last in line as the pickers scrambled for the exit. Behind us, the door on the far side of the room opened once more, and the kids in front of me all but dove through the exit. It must have been the other assistant. I didn't wait to find out. I pushed Koal and Melvin forward and quickly slipped through the door. I didn't have time to replace the lamp, so I carried it with me.

Mouse was waiting on the other side. "I think it would be best if we go around the back of the barracks this time, over by the wall. It'll take longer, but it's less traveled."

I looked up. The moon wasn't there, and it wasn't because it'd been covered by a cloud or that the fog was too thick to see it. It was because it had already set. I could see the first hint of greying in the sky. "Fine. But hurry. We're running out of time." Mouse started to turn, but I grabbed his arm. "And don't wait for me. I'm going to go get the coat we left under the stairs. I don't want to leave any trace of us being here."

"Do you know where you're going?"

"I'll retrace our steps."

Mouse nodded and raced to the front of the picker line. "This way."

I watched the small group vanish into the thinning fog before turning to head back the way we'd originally come. I hadn't made it halfway down the beaters' barracks when it hit me that I'd forgotten something.

Jayden was still sitting in the meat shed, tied to the pork barrel, dried tears caked to his face. I laid the lantern amongst some of the other tools and untied his hands. His entire body was shaking as I removed his gag.

"Please," he cried. "Please don't leave me here."

"I'm not." I grabbed a couple of nearby sacks and stuffed a reasonable amount of meat into them, not too much to be readily noticeable. I wasn't quite as worried about anyone finding food stolen from the shed like I was from the storage room where the trapdoor was located. "Come on. We're getting out of here."

The barracks' windows were no longer lit, and the compound was as silent as a burial ground. I stopped long enough to collect my coat from its hiding place under the staircase, and then we sprinted across the open yard toward the gate. The fog was thicker by the wall, but I could still make out the turret at the top, so I knew we were at least heading in the right direction. Up ahead, I could hear footsteps, so we slowed. I hoped it was our pickers and not the watch, but in this fog, we wouldn't find out until we were on top of them.

Sure enough, the former prison guards appeared out of the mist in front of us. Koal yelped, and Melvin quickly grabbed the boy's mouth.

"What was that?" someone on the wall above us asked.

I pushed the two guards over against the wall and found the

door leading out in the process. Mouse and the rest of our pickers scampered over to see what was going on. He sneered when he saw Jayden.

"Do you see anything?" another voice above us asked.

"No."

"Best check it anyway."

I panicked at the thought of the watchers on the wall coming down and shoved Mouse toward the door. Thankfully, it was still unlocked. He opened it and quickly hopped back in and shut it. The look on his face let me know we'd chosen the wrong time to try getting out.

We had a patrol passing outside the wall, another one coming down the stairs from the inside, and us stuck in the middle.

"Why is it always me that has to go check on everything?" someone grumbled, about halfway down the turret's staircase.

My mind raced as I tried to think of what to do. There was no way we weren't going to get caught. I could hear muffled voices from the other side of the door as the two on patrol were just walking by. I could also hear the squeak of the stairs from whoever it was coming down off the wall. Half our pickers looked ready to bolt.

In a last act of desperation, I snatched Mouse's dagger from his hand and threw it as hard as I could in the opposite direction of where we were cowering. It hit the wall about twenty feet farther down.

"Who's there?" the watcher called as he rushed down the steps and ran in the direction of the dagger.

I turned and waved at Mouse to go. He stuck his head out the door, and as soon as the patrol had gone, he directed the pickers through the wall and into the fog-laden street beyond. Jayden was the last through the door. I locked it behind him and tucked the watcher's keys into my pocket for safekeeping. With one last look up at the wall, I turned and melted into the fog with the others.

Chapter 11

THE HARBOR BELL ECHOED out its seventh ring by the time we reached the old warehouse district. I had never been happier to see the abandoned buildings than right then.

After retrieving my other sword and Reevie's satchel from the alley adjacent to the Rockslide compound, we spent nearly an hour trying to get through their territory without being seen. It took even longer to navigate the city's streets. Not only was our trek slowed because of injured pickers, but I did my best to steer us clear of the higher-trafficked areas near the marketplace, while at the same time keeping us out of other tribes' territories. Not an easy task.

By the time we caught our first sight of the Granary, many of the pickers broke into a full run, no doubt hoping to find some leftovers from breakfast. They hadn't eaten since breakfast the previous day.

Nor had I, come to think of it.

Jayden, Melvin, and Koal stayed close to me, nervous eyes scanning the buildings ahead. After seeing the way their former tribe treated its guests, it was no wonder their knees were knocking as we approached the front doors.

Normally, I might have fretted over whether the three boys could be trusted, but having learned how Kore rewarded failure, I doubted they had any intention of showing their faces at Rockslide again. Still, I would need to assign a few kids to keep an eye on them.

Reevie and Bull stood at the head of the greeting party, Bull with a wide grin and Reevie with his arms crossed and a scowl on his face.

"What do we have here?" Reevie said, giving the guards and watcher a thorough looking-over. "You leave to get eleven pickers and come back with fourteen. How does that happen?" He looked at me and cocked his brow. "Where'd they come from?"

The three boys stared at their feet.

I handed Reevie back his satchel. "From the Rockslide compound when I snuck in and broke our pickers out."

Reevie choked. "Yellow fever! You did what?" He smacked his forehead with the palm of his hand. "What little brains the Creator gave you must have fallen out your ears. Better go find them, because when Kore realizes what you've done, he'll send the full force of their beaters against us."

"He's not going to find out. The only people who saw us were these three right here." I pointed at the cowering boys on my right. "The only thing Kore's going to discover is that their prisoners—which were set to be *executed,* I might add—have vanished in the middle of the night."

Reevie closed his eyes and visibly slowed his breathing until the veins on the side of his head shrank back to their normal size. "Still, why'd you bring them here?"

"Where else are they going to go?"

"They can take a dip in the bay, for all I care. We can barely feed the ones we have."

"Would you prefer I turn them loose to get nabbed by their own people?"

"Sounds like justice to me."

"And what happens when they inform Kore who it was that slipped inside his compound?"

Reevie clenched his fists. "Fine. Take them inside. I think Cook is getting ready for lunch, anyway. But afterward, we need to talk."

I nodded, then headed for the front door, the three Rockslide boys close on my heels. A couple of steps from the entrance, Tubby leaped out the door and growled, his Flesh Eater mask strapped to his face.

All three boys screamed. The two guards took off running around the side of the building, and Jayden dropped to the ground and curled into a ball, whimpering in the dirt.

I could hear Reevie laughing behind me.

I crossed my arms, attempting to look stern. "Tubby! That's

not helping."

The enormous boy laughed. "I scared them."

"Yes," I said with a heavy sigh. "Yes, you did. Now take off the mask and go get ready for lunch."

Tubby strolled back inside, his quivering shoulders betraying the fact that he was still laughing. He passed Mouse, Petal, and Squeaks on his way in, who were giggling just inside the doorway.

"Don't encourage him," I scolded.

Mouse just smiled and shrugged, then led the others inside.

I bent over to help Jayden back to his feet. "He's gone. You can get up now." The boy was shaking like a drunkard after a three-day binge. "Don't worry, he's not going to eat you. He doesn't do that anymore . . . at least not unless someone tries betraying us," I added.

I turned to Bull, who was listening to Reevie moan about the lack of provisions. "Here, take Jayden inside and show him around, will you? I need to catch Melvin and Koal before they take Reevie up on his suggestion and jump in the bay. They're probably half-way to the docks by now."

I took off running around the side of the building, my legs feeling as though on the verge of collapse. This was going to be another long day.

I found the two boys hiding in an abandoned warehouse closer to the water and talked them out. By the time we made it back, lunch was already over. Not that there had been much to it: a biscuit left over from a batch we'd picked two days prior, a slice of meat so thin you could see through it, and no cheese. Dessert was a single apple slice with the rotten parts cut out. I was hoping to see a little more substance for the evening meal, what with the new meat I'd liberated from Rockslide.

Mouse ran by, and I grabbed his arm. "I'm leaving you in charge of our new guests. Find them something to do."

"Love to," he said with a mischievous grin.

I left the table and crossed the main room to the door leading down to our chambers, wondering the whole way if I'd made a mistake in leaving Mouse in charge of the newcomers.

"Tubby!" I heard Mouse shout behind me. "Get over here and greet our new guests!"

I just shook my head and kept walking.

Reevie and Bull were sitting quietly around the table, waiting on my arrival. They already had a cup of the watered ale poured for me.

"So, what happened?" Reevie asked, leaning back in his seat to get comfortable.

After downing a long gulp, I unstrapped my swords, tossed them on my bed, and filled them in on my adventures from the previous night. The story might not have been all that entertaining, what with the lack of a good sword fight, but Bull seemed to enjoy the bit about me punching Jayden in the face.

Reevie smiled. "I wish I could see their faces when they go down to the cells and find the entire place . . . Wait. How would they even get in? You said you took the pickers and guards up through the hole. The doors would still be locked."

Bull laid his glass down and smiled. "I guess Kore will have to break down the door and search every cell in the entire dungeon."

Reevie chuckled. "And with you pulling the rope back up and placing the shelf back over the trapdoor, they aren't going to have the first clue what happened. They'll be talking about this for—"

The door at the top of the stairs opened, then shut, and a single set of boots started down.

"Have you heard the news?" Sapphire said, stopping at the bottom of the steps to let her eyes adjust. "An entire group of reject prisoners vanished from the Rockslide prisons last night, and no one's got a clue what happened." She looked directly at me and crossed her arms. "All right. What'd you do?"

"What do you mean, what did *I* do?" I stared into her bright azure eyes. "Why do you assume it has anything to do with me?"

"Experience," she said with an all-too-knowing look as she joined us at the table. "It always has something to do with you."

I answered her with a wry smile. I couldn't believe word had spread that fast.

"They're saying the cells are haunted, and now half the tribe won't step foot in them. Others are saying it's some sort of dark magic. Apparently, Kore has decreed that no one should speak of it, so of course everyone is. Each tribe has their own version of what might have happened. Some are saying that ghosts of formerly executed rejects have returned to claim their retribution, or it's the work of dark faeries who found their way back into Aldor. Oh, you'll like this one," she said, smiling at me. "There are even reports of Death's Shadow returning from the underworld to seek justice for what was done to him at the Pit. It seems a cook's assistant swears he saw your shade passing through the dining hall."

By the time she finished, I was laughing.

"I couldn't make this up if I wanted to," she said.

I finally got control of myself enough to take another sip from my glass. "What does ol' Weasel Face have to say?" Of course, I knew he wouldn't be saying anything, since he was probably green in the face at present, hiding in a fish barrel on his way to the Blue Isles. I was curious how the members at the Temple were reacting to their chief's mysterious disappearance.

"I don't know," she said. "He's been holed up in his room ever since the battle at the Pit. No one's seen him for the last few days." She pursed her lips, trying to keep from smiling herself. "No doubt he's too terrified you're going to show up and strangle him in his sleep to care about a bunch of rejects, anyway. When word came back that your body hadn't been recovered in the wreckage, he put the watchers on high alert. Been that way for the better part of the week."

I laughed again, and Sapphire gave me a hard look. "What aren't you telling me?"

"Fine," I said, "you got me. I might have had something to do with the rejects' disappearances. Although I can't believe you've already heard about it back at the Temple. It just happened last night."

"It's the tribes we're talking about," Bull said. "Word travels faster than an archer's arrow."

I nodded, then proceeded to once again tell of our daring rescue, leaving nothing out. By the end of the story, Sapphire's arms had slipped from their folded position, and her face had softened considerably, almost to the point of grinning.

"And you still have the keys to their compound?"

"I do." I pulled the ring out from my jacket pocket and laid it on the table between us.

She stared at them while running her hands down the long blonde strands of her braid. "Those could prove extremely valuable."

"I'd say," Reevie said. "But right now, having a way to enter their compound isn't all that important, unless we plan on doing so in order to raid their food stores."

A spark of interest flashed in Bull's eyes, Sapphire's as well. "That's not a bad idea," she said. "It's definitely a way to keep the kids here fed while you—"

"No." I needed to put a stop to this spark before it turned into a fire. "I have no intention of stealing from one group of kids to help another. That'd make us no better than Avalanche, which, if you've forgotten, was how Hurricane ended up getting ambushed in the streets and I ended up in the Pit."

Bull looked confused, and I could see his wheels turning. I knew where this was about to go. "But didn't you just bring back some food from Rockslide?"

"Yes, but swiping a few pieces of meat is hardly the same as sneaking in and wiping them clean."

"We wouldn't have to take *all* of it," he said with a sheepish grin.

I rapped my knuckles on the edge of the table.

"Fine," he said. "No raiding."

"Then what do you plan on doing?" Reevie asked. "You've already seen the books. We aren't going to last another week at this rate. I hope you enjoyed those biscuits we had for lunch, because you're going to be eating them until there's too much mold to cut off, or the maggots take over. Then we might be eating the maggots."

I shivered. "I get the picture."

"I don't think you do. If you did, you wouldn't still be bringing home more strays every time you go into town. In fact, you need to stay at the Granary until we figure out what we're going to do to keep from starving to death. Clearly, our picking days are limited. Most of the pickers have decided they'd rather join the watch after what they just went through."

"Can't very well blame them," Bull said, shifting uncomfortably on the stack of crates he was using for a seat.

"I can try talking to Spats and see if he'll be willing to change his mind about taking them in at the Temple," Sapphire said. "We need to replenish our members, anyway. We lost quite a few during the Pit battle."

"No need," I said. I had thought to keep my involvement with Spats's reassignment quiet, at least for now, letting everyone believe he'd left out of his own cowardice, but we were running out of time and options, not to mention food. "The reason you haven't seen Spats since the Pit is because he's not there."

Everyone turned.

"Not where?" Sapphire asked.

"He's no longer at the Temple."

"And how would you know that?"

"Because I might have made him disappear as well?"

No one said a word. I could hear the floorboards over our heads creaking from those walking around up top.

Reevie leaned forward. "What do you mean, you made him disappear?"

"I mean, I snuck into the Temple and kidnapped him from his own bed, then—"

"And how did you do that without the Guard seeing you?" Sapphire shot back. "Forehead's been standing watch over that stupid door for the last five days."

I grinned. "I have my ways." I didn't tell them it was Forehead who had let me in or offered to loan me his knife to put an end to Spats in the first place.

Sapphire snorted. "So, I've been beside myself for days, worried about why Spats wasn't coming out and what he might do when he did, and he hasn't been there this entire time?"

I offered her a smile in return. "At least not for the last couple of nights. Sorry, been too busy saving pickers to get around to telling anyone. Honestly, I'm surprised no one figured it out sooner. How long were you going to wait before checking in on him? He could have been dead and rotting in there, for all you knew."

"He's not, is he?" Bull asked. "Lying in there with a knife in his back, getting all smelly?"

"No," I said, surprised he'd even asked. Although if I'd been any other Upaka, that would have been a safe assumption.

"Then where is he?" Reevie demanded, growing more anxious by the second.

"I put him on a ship heading for the Blue Isles." I wiped some strands of hair out of my eyes and smiled. "You'd be surprised how costly it can be to hide a stowaway. I believe the deckhand said something about hiding him in a fish barrel in the lower galley." I chuckled. "He'll be nice and ripe by the time he finally reaches port."

"Talk about smelly," Bull said, and burst out laughing. The rest of us joined in for a brief moment.

"So," Reevie said, doing his best to regain his composure, "I guess that means we can relocate the rejects to the Temple and get them out of the Granary?" There was more than a little hopeful enthusiasm in his voice.

"That might not be as easy as you think," Sapphire said. "Hurricane might not have been as tough on rejects as some of the other tribes, but it doesn't mean they will want them just moving in."

Reevie nodded. "She's right."

"And what are we going to do about finding a new chief?" Bull asked.

Everyone turned and looked at me.

Chapter 12

"NO," I SAID FIRMLY—and hopefully for the last time—as I walked alongside Reevie, Sapphire, and Bull. Behind me, the long line of rejected kids slithered through the outskirts of the old city and up the brick drive toward the Temple's gates.

I was more than a little anxious about the greeting we'd receive from those inside. We needed this to work. The Granary wasn't big enough to handle all those we'd taken in. It also didn't have the fortifications that the Temple did.

"I told you, I have no intention of being the new chief of Hurricane. In fact, I can't think of anything I'd like less. I'd rather have my toenails pulled off one at a time than have to be stuck inside these walls." I adjusted my black Guard vest up on my shoulders.

I wanted those inside the Temple to remember I'd been part of Hurricane, too. Hopefully, the black vest and blue armband would be enough to remind them.

The warning bell started to ring as Toots peered over the wall, his head barely cresting the top, the feat most likely achieved by standing on a crate. His eyes bulged as he stared out at the crowd gathering in front of the gate. As soon as he caught sight of me, he gasped.

"Open the gates!" Sapphire shouted up at the watchers.

"What . . . what's the password?" Toots called down nervously.

Sapphire took a step forward. "Open the gate, Toots, before I climb up there and throw you off!"

The little watcher's mouth gaped even further. "I . . . I can't let you in without the password. Spats's orders, you know that."

"Spats is no longer chief of Hurricane," she said.

Eight more heads popped up over the wall, Forehead being one of them. Why had he left his post? Was no one guarding Spats's chambers?

"What you mean, he ain't chief?" Toots asked with a little more backbone now that one of the Guard was there.

"Because he's no longer here," I said, stepping forward to stand beside Sapphire.

"I thought you was dead," Toots whimpered.

"How do you kill a shadow?" I asked, sighing inwardly. If the tribes were going to continue to use Reevie's made-up name for me, might as well put it to good use.

Toots looked at Forehead, confused, but Forehead kept his

mouth shut, so he called back down to us, "Why you think Spats ain't here?"

"Have you seen him since the Pit?"

Toots looked at the other watchers. They shook their heads. "No. But everyone knows he's been in his room, planning."

Forehead shifted nervously as he looked down over the wall. He knew Spats wasn't there, but he clearly didn't want to be the one to tell the rest of the tribe why. And I wasn't going to break that confidence.

"Go have a look," I said. "We'll wait."

"But be quick about it!" Reevie shouted, limping up beside us. "We don't have all day, and my feet are killing me."

Toots looked at Forehead.

Forehead glanced over the side. "I'll go." He sounded almost relieved. He was probably tired of standing in front of Spats's room, knowing it was empty and not being able to tell anyone.

Everyone waited in silence for Forehead to return. Those on the wall stared down, gripping their clubs and pokers and slings. Those on our side carried no weapons; many were too tired to stand, some even needing to be carried.

"What happens if they don't open?" Bull whispered, joining the rest of us at the front.

"They'll open," Sapphire said. I could almost hear her teeth grinding.

A small commotion from the other side let me know Forehead was returning. Toots and the rest of the watchers disappeared from the top for a moment. Soon enough, Forehead was back on the wall.

"Spats is gone. His room's empty."

Anxious murmurs spread down the line of watchers.

"Now open that gate!" Sapphire demanded. "I'm getting hungry."

"Who's all those kids?" a second member of the Guard asked, his head appearing above the wall alongside Forehead.

"They're the new members of Hurricane," Reevie answered, thumping the ground with his walking stick. "Now, do you want me to quit treating your wounded, or are you going to open that gate?"

"They look too sick to be members," a watcher on the left called out. "Look more like . . ." He stared down at the long line of kids behind us. ". . . like rejects, if you ask me."

"That's because we are rejects!" Bull shouted up, pulling back his sleeve and brandishing the X on his arm.

I shook my head. "You could have at least waited until they'd opened the gates."

Murmurs and hushed conversations trickled down the line of heads on top the wall. Some of the watchers turned and shouted to those gathered behind them on the inside of the gate that the kids wanting in were rejects.

"We can't let rejects in here," Toots said. "It's against Guild law."

I'd had about all I could take at that point. "We're all rejects, you idiot! We've all been barred from society. We are the unwanted street sweepings of Aramoor. Now open that gate before I break it down." I needed to at least look like I was going to make good on my threat, so I turned and shouted back down the line. "Flesh Eater!"

Around the bend, I could hear the heavy thuds of Tubby's feet as he came running from his place near the back of the line. He roared as he charged the gate, leather mask halfway strapped to his face. Those on top screamed at the sight of the monstrous cannibal, scurrying off the wall as fast as they could.

Tubby pounded against the gate, and I used the distraction to scale the wall. A couple of watchers were cowering on the makeshift scaffolding as I swung over the top. One squealed when he saw me and tried jumping off the guard station, but I grabbed him by the seat of his pants before he could and pulled him back up against the wall.

"Calm down. I'm not here to hurt you," I said, pushing him toward the gate. "Now help me free the bracer."

The other watchers, still on the wall, ran down the stairs behind me and joined the growing mass of Hurricane members below, most holding weapons, looking ready for battle. With the watchers' help, I released the rope holding the crossbar and spun the wheel. Surprisingly, no one challenged me. Then again, maybe it wasn't so surprising. I was Death's Shadow risen from the depths of the Pit, after all.

With the bracer gone, Tubby's forceful pounding swung the doors open. Both sides stood there staring at each other. You could have cut the tension with a dull butter knife.

Tubby moved back beside Reevie, Sapphire, and Bull, while Forehead and the rest of the Guard stood at the front of Hurricane.

I had to do something before some fool called for a charge.

Grabbing the rope from the bracer, I swung off the scaffolding and dropped between the two contending parties.

"Spats is gone," I said. "Which means his rules are gone. The way he ran things is gone."

"And that's a good thing," Sapphire shouted. "He was an idiot!"

There were a few nods and half-chuckles on Hurricane's side.

"Spats also bought into the lie that just because you're small, or not as strong, or perhaps injured, that you don't deserve to be a member of a tribe. I say he was a coward and a nincompoop. Look at Bull here." I pointed to my right. "He was injured and thrown out of Avalanche, and then rejected by Spats and Hurricane. Any of you want to come challenge him in a fight and see how worthless he might be?"

Bull drew his bludgeon and took a step forward.

No one on the Hurricane side moved.

"And what about those deemed too small or weak? Mouse! Get up here!"

The little picker came running. He'd been hiding somewhere in the middle of the group.

"Mouse here was thrown out of Rockslide." I neglected to mention it was for pinching food. Mouse pulled a dagger from his belt and stood next to Bull. I guess he thought I was going to offer him up as a challenge as well. "Mouse happens to be one of the best pickers I've ever seen. Just because he's small doesn't mean he's useless."

I let what I'd said sink in a moment. "Hurricane should be a tribe who opens its doors to those looking for somewhere to belong, and as long as you abide by the rules and are willing to work, you should be allowed to stay." I pointed at Bull once again. "Just because he has a mark on his arm doesn't mean he has no worth. In fact, you should take pride in that mark. It means that despite all odds, you've managed to overcome. It means you're a survivor." I choked down a wave of emotion. Why was I getting so worked up? I was starting to *sound* like a chief, or a commander about to lead his troops into battle. I gritted my teeth and promised myself once more that I was *not* going to become the next chief of Hurricane.

I pointed at the Guard. "Get me Spats's branding iron."

No one moved.

I drew one of my swords, and the front line of Hurricane took a step back. "Well, what are you waiting for?"

Toots took off running through the crowd without looking back.

It wasn't long before the little watcher was pushing through the ranks toward the front, carrying a small metal rod about the length of my forearm, and no thicker than my first finger with a wooden grip on one end. The brand was a little different from the ones I'd seen from the other tribes. It had two thin pieces of metal welded into the shape of an X, but unlike the others, this one also had a circle around the outside of the X.

I sheathed my sword as Toots cautiously walked over to where I was standing and handed me the rod. I noticed he immediately tucked his hands up the sleeves of his tunic, evidently afraid I was going to use it on *him*.

Like always, the metal was sizzling. Each tribe generally kept their brand on a pedestal of coals that was stoked every day. I wasn't very sure about the ritual behind it, since I'd never actually seen it performed, but apparently, it remained heated for everyone to see as a deterrent. One look at the brand and I was sweating, and it wasn't because of the heat.

Reevie left the others to join me in the middle. "What are you doing?"

"You'll see."

"You're not about to do something stupid, are you?"

I smiled.

"What you plan on using it for?" Toots asked nervously.

"What do you think you're doing?" Sapphire said, marching over to put in her two coppers' worth.

Forehead left those gathered on the Temple's side and joined the group as well, too curious to stand back any longer. "Who's the brand for?"

"I'm going to prove to you and the rest of Hurricane that having a mark on your arm doesn't make you somehow less than anyone else."

The calloused bulge on the front of Forehead's forehead lifted as he realized what I was about to do. "Maybe this isn't such a smart thing."

"Have you lost your flaming mind?" Sapphire asked. "What's that going to prove?"

I lifted the red-hot brand, and Toots dashed behind Forehead and out of arm's reach. I took a step toward the Hurricane side and pointed at the blue piece of material on my arm. "You see this? This says I'm a member of Hurricane." I pointed at my vest. "You see this? This says that I'm a member of the Guard. And this," I said, holding up the brand for all to see. "This says that I'm also a reject. Not because people deem me to be, but because I choose to be." I took a deep breath and stuck the heated end against the inside of my left wrist.

At first, I didn't feel a thing, then it felt like someone was cutting off my hand, slowly sawing it off with a blunt blade. I bit down on my tongue to keep from crying out. My skin sizzled like fatback over a fire. I had no idea how long I needed to hold it there, so I tried counting to five. I only made it to three and a half before the brand dropped from my fingers.

Everyone stood there, watching in silence. The silence was louder than one of Tubby's roars. My head spun.

"Oak poison! What did you go and do that for?" Reevie said, looking like he would have slapped me upside the head if I'd been close enough to reach. "That's going to take weeks to heal, you ignorant clod. What if you've permanently damaged it?" He reached into his carry sack, pulled out a small pouch, and loosened the strings, pouring a couple of pinches' worth of dried herbs into my palm. "Eat it, now," he demanded, still shaking his head.

I dutifully chewed whatever he'd given me. It numbed my tongue, but it did little for the pain.

I picked the brand back up from where it had fallen, the metal still a dark red. I turned to those inside the gate and held up my arm. It burned. The warm breeze stung against the skin, and I clenched my teeth. "Who challenges my right as a member of Hurricane?" I kept my arm lifted high, making sure everyone could see the now glowing mark on my wrist. "You see? I bear the mark of the reject! Does anyone contest my right to be here?"

"I do," Reevie mumbled behind me, "for being too thick-headed."

I ignored him and waited for anyone to step forward. "Just because I have a mark on my arm doesn't make my life any less valuable than yours. I'm proud to be a reject. We should all be proud to be rejects." I turned and looked at Forehead, who was standing the closest. "What about you?"

"What?" The taller guard took a step back.

"Are you proud to be a reject?"

Forehead stared at the brand in my hand with a blank look. "I guess?"

"Was that a question or a fact?"

"Huh?"

Okay, this wasn't getting me anywhere. I needed someone to say something and get this ball rolling or I might have just mutilated myself for nothing. I turned to Reevie. "Are you proud to be a reject?"

"Not if you're going to try sticking me with that poker, I'm not," Reevie shot back.

I rolled my eyes and looked at Sapphire. "Are you proud to be a reject?"

"Yes!" she shouted, so forcefully that it startled me backward a step or two.

I smiled and looked at Toots. "What about you?"

Toots looked at Forehead, then at Sapphire. Something in her face had him stepping forward. "Yes!"

"How about it, Forehead?" I asked, hoping now that he'd caught on to the momentum. He was a member of the Guard, one that many trusted. I needed to get his acceptance. "Are you proud to be a reject?"

Forehead suddenly drew his sword and held it above his head. "I'm proud to be a reject!"

Finally! I turned to the rest of Hurricane. "What about you? Are you proud to be called rejects?"

"Yes," they said, some with enthusiasm, others not quite sure what was going on.

"I can't hear you." I said, pointing at them with the steaming brand. "Are you proud to be called rejects?"

"Yes!" they shouted back.

"Re-jects! Re-jects! Re-jects!"

I turned to find Bull standing beside Forehead, pumping his fist in the air as he continued his chant. "Re-jects! Re-jects! Re-jects!"

Forehead joined him. Pretty soon, the rest of Hurricane followed suit, chanting along. Those outside the gate joined in as they slowly started to move into the compound. "Re-jects! Re-jects! Re-jects!"

Those inside the walls slowly began to mix with the newcomers, all still chanting. "Re-jects! Re-jects! Re-jects!" It didn't take long before I couldn't tell one group from the other. Even Tubby managed to make it inside the gate without complete hysteria. It helped that he had taken off his mask and was carrying Mouse on one shoulder and Petal and Squeaks on the other.

"You sure know how to work a crowd," Bull said with a heavy wallop to my back that made my breath catch in the back of my throat.

"You sure know how to make my life miserable," Reevie added, grabbing for my hand. He held it up to inspect the damage, clicking his tongue as he studied the melted flesh. "I'll need to see you in the infirmary right away if we're to get that swelling down and make sure you don't end up with some kind of blood poisoning. Wouldn't that be just like you to go do something stupid to help others and end up getting your hand chopped off?" With that, he turned and limped his way through the crowd toward the main building, leaving me to stand in silence.

"I thought it was rather touching," Sapphire said, once Reevie was out of earshot. "Absurd," she added with a wink, "but touching."

"Touching. Yep, that's me," I said with a forced grin as I clenched my teeth and broke into a slow jog, heading for the infirmary. I hoped Reevie had some sort of salve in there for the pain, because whatever he'd given me, it wasn't enough.

Chapter 13

"HAVE I TOLD YOU how amazing you are, Reevie?" I said, whimpering as he plastered cooling balm on my burnt wrist. "You're my favorite healer." I leaned over and patted his cheek with my good hand.

He brushed it away. "That's just the medicine talking," he said, tightening the lid on the jar of light-green goop and placing it back on the shelf.

"Yeah, probably," I admitted. Whatever vile concoction he'd slipped into my drink after we got to the infirmary had the room spinning with colors. "You're my best friend, you know. My best friend in the whole . . . Look at that!" I stared at my left hand in wonder. My palm was as wide as a sheet of paper, with five, or was that seven, little nubs protruding from the end. I tried wiggling my fingers, but they were too stubby to bend.

The room spun to the right, and I grabbed my head before it rolled off my shoulders. "What did you give me?" I smacked my tongue against the roof of my mouth, not able to feel it.

"Tellareen mushrooms," Reevie said, chuckling. "About the only thing I can think of that will slow you down long enough to get some rest."

I stood from the cot and stumbled over to where Reevie was reorganizing one of the shelves, grumbling about idiots. I grabbed his shoulders, mostly to keep from pitching over on my face. I smiled at my best friend. He looked tired and worried, and I needed to cheer him up. "You know what? I don't care that you have a wonky leg," I said, shaking my head fervently to make sure he got my message. "I like you the way you are. You're worth a hundred . . . no . . . a thousand of the other . . ." *What was I trying to say?*

My knees started quivering, and I laughed. "I seem to be fall . . ." I grabbed for Reevie, but he was suddenly standing on the other side of the room, and I hit the floor. "Owww!" The room spun like a flicked coin on a table, and I suddenly felt as though I was tumbling down the Rockslide well. I looked up. Why was Reevie just standing there smiling?

"Come on," he said. "Let's get you into bed." His voice sounded strange, as though talking through a door. I could understand the words, but they seemed muffled.

Suddenly, I was moving, and Sapphire's face appeared beside me. She seemed to glow. Her smile was magnificent, and she smelled like . . . Well, I wasn't sure what she smelled like, but it was nice. "You're so pretty," I said. "Have I ever told you that before?"

Sapphire looked at Reevie. "What's wrong with him?"

"Tellareen mushrooms."

"Oh."

"No, I mean it," I said. "You're the prettiest girl I've ever seen. You wanna hold my hand again?"

Sapphire chuckled.

I tried reaching for her hand, but my arm didn't want to move. "I can't . . . I can't seem to rea . . ." Her hand disappeared, then her arm, then the room. The last thing I saw was her smile before the darkness took her from me.

I opened my eyes. The light pouring in from the window above me had me squinting. Pain rushed in, flooding my mind but clearing my thoughts. I looked around, wincing as I moved my left arm, noticing it had been wrapped. My hand and fingers had returned to normal size, which I guess was a good sign.

"What happened?" I asked, trying to sit up.

"Careful." Reevie's face appeared on my right. He grabbed me under my arm and helped me sit up.

I dropped my legs over the side of the cot and cupped my head with my hands. It felt like someone had mistaken it for an anvil. "I think I'm going to be sick." I looked up. "No, I'm definitely going to be sick."

Reevie shoved a pail under my mouth just as my insides erupted. By the time I finished, I felt about as weak as I had after my run-in with Wildfire on my first day in Aramoor.

"I'm going to kill you," I moaned.

Reevie chuckled. "Sorry about that," he said as he left me to hobble over to his desk at the back of the infirmary. "It was the only way I knew to force you to sleep." A couple of books were stacked on the seat of his chair, lifting him high enough to see the papers on top. He picked up a quill and started scratching away as I continued to hover over my very smelly pail.

He paused and looked up. "You haven't slept a full night since the Pit. Clearly, it's begun to affect your mind." He pointed at my bandaged wrist.

I looked around the room. It wasn't spinning as before. "How long have I been out?" My stomach growled on cue. "Did I miss supper?"

Reevie continued scribbling away at the parchment on his desk. "You've missed a couple of suppers."

"What?" My head shot up faster than it should have, and I grabbed the pail and dry-heaved. "How long have I been asleep?"

"A day and a half."

"What!" I hopped to my feet and nearly toppled over. I grabbed the edge of the cot behind me and slowly sat back down. "How's that possible? No one sleeps for a day and a half, unless they're old as dirt or about to die." I looked at my bandage. "I'm not dying, am I?"

"No, you're not dying."

"Then why was I asleep for that long?"

"Because I might have given you a few too many mushrooms, which required a larger dose of the tonic." He quickly lowered his eyes back to his work.

"So, it's your fault."

He looked back up and pointed his quill at me. "Hey, just be thankful I had some tonic for you." His glare had me thankful he was on the other side of the room.

"You're awake. Good."

I turned to find Sapphire walking into the room, carrying a bowl of something hot. Steam seeped over the rim. "We were really worried," she said, laying the bowl on Reevie's desk.

"She's been sitting by your bed for the last day," Reevie said, leaning forward to get a look at what was in the bowl.

"I have not."

My cheeks warmed. Vague memories of right before everything went black tickled my mind. Had I said anything stupid?

Sapphire sat down on the cot beside me, and I quickly shoved the stinky pail up under it.

"I blame it on the mushrooms," I said, trying to turn my head to the side so I didn't breathe directly on her and make her gag.

She smiled, her cheeks pinking just a little. "You didn't do anything that requires an apology. You were a perfect gentleman."

"Gentleman?" Reevie laughed. "He tried grabbing your hand. If he hadn't knocked off when he did, I thought he was going to confess his undying love."

My whole face felt like it was on fire. If he kept laughing, I was going to throw my pail of puke right at him.

Sapphire took my injured hand and gently squeezed. "Don't listen to him. I thought it was very sweet."

Sweet? I sighed and pulled my hand away.

"I've spent the last day and a half looking over Hurricane's books," Reevie said. "That and listening to you talk in your sleep."

Sapphire wore a wry smile. She must have also been around to witness my mushroom-induced discussions.

"What did I say?"

"Mostly nothing we could make out," Sapphire said, but the way she kept glancing at Reevie made me think she was keeping something back. I didn't ask, hoping the matter would get dropped altogether.

"So, what's happening with the tribe? Have they killed each other yet?"

"Surprisingly, no," Reevie said. "Sapphire's been able to keep everyone in line for now."

"There was one scuffle during mealtime," she said, "when some of the Granary kids got in line in front of the Hurricane kids, and the Hurricane kids didn't like the idea that the rejects were eating first."

"But," Reevie interjected, "after she ordered all of them to spend their meal sweeping the back walkways, they decided that eating was more important than complaining about what place they had in line. Haven't heard a peep from them since."

"Might be good to rearrange the sleeping quarters," I said. "Put an equal number of Hurricane and Granary kids together, force them to get to know each other."

"Good idea," Reevie said.

"They won't like it much," Sapphire added, "but better now than later. The longer we wait, the harder it will be."

"And if anyone argues," Reevie said, looking up with a smirk, "we can make them share a room with Tubby."

All three of us laughed at that, though I quickly stopped since it made my head feel like it was about to split open.

"How about the injured?" I asked.

"We've emptied one of the storage rooms in the back," Sapphire said, "and turned it into a secondary infirmary for those with more serious needs."

Reevie laid his quill down. "Some of the worst cases, those missing arms or legs, will take months to heal, if they survive at all. It's going to be a long and painful road back, so it'll be better to give them their own space than to bed them down with everyone else."

I nodded, half-expecting the dizziness to be there to greet me, but thankfully, it didn't. "Anything else happen while I was . . . napping?"

Reevie stared out the window to his left and pursed his lips. "Don't think so. It seems all the other tribes can talk about is the mysterious vanishing of the Rockslide prisoners."

"I hope you've told our people not to say anything."

Sapphire nodded, tightening the ribbon at the bottom of her blonde braid. "We did, especially after the Granary pickers began mingling with the Hurricane pickers."

Reevie huffed. "Tales of their rescue spread through the Temple faster than a bad rash. We told them not to talk about it beyond the gates." He snickered.

"What?" I asked.

"Well, Sapphire might have mentioned something about the fact that if anyone did get caught talking about it to anyone outside the Temple, Death's Shadow would pay them a little visit one night and make them disappear."

I groaned. "Why would you go using me as a way to threaten the tribe?"

"Why not? It works."

Sapphire smiled. "Another bit of good news is that the Hurricane pickers have taken the new Granary pickers under their wing, teaching them the ropes. Hopefully, that will help with rations."

"Mouse has declared himself the honorary head of the pickers," Reevie said with a smile. "If anyone questions his claim, he refers them to your little speech about how he was the best picker you'd ever seen."

"And if that doesn't work," Sapphire cut in, "he simply calls on Tubby to back him up."

I laughed. I couldn't help it. Mouse was a scoundrel, one you just couldn't help but like.

"We need to cut more blue armbands," Reevie said. "Reinforce that we are all Hurricane."

"Already done," she said. "I had the fixers sew some more with some of the material we had laying around. They aren't pretty, but they'll work."

Reevie nodded. "Good."

"Am I the only one who thinks that wearing identifying armbands while they are in the market seems . . . I don't know . . . foolish? I've never actually gone on a hunt with our pickers, but wouldn't the patrollers and shopkeepers be looking for that sort of thing?"

Both Reevie and Sapphire shared a baffled look. "How could you have been living with us this long and not know the answer to that?" Sapphire asked. "They don't wear them while they're in town picking. That would be stupid. They only carry them to identify themselves if ever questioned by other pickers."

"Oh." That certainly made more sense than running around town with blue bandages tied to their arms.

"We only wear them outside the Temple when it's for something official," Sapphire said.

No one spoke for a time, seemingly content to stare at the wall or the floor, or in Reevie's case, the bowl of soup on his desk.

Reevie finally scooted his chair back, pushed the papers in front of him out of the way, and pulled the bowl closer. "Guess we need to discuss the zyntar in the room."

"What?" My head must have still been fuzzy 'cause I had no idea what he was talking about.

"Spats," Sapphire said.

"Or lack thereof," Reevie amended while trying to swallow his first spoonful. He looked up from the bowl. "So, he's really gone for good?"

I nodded, still trying to clear the remaining cobwebs from my mind. "We won't be seeing Spats again."

"Now what do we do?" Sapphire asked.

I looked at Reevie. "What normally takes place when a tribe loses a chief? What happened when Spats became chief?"

"Don't look at me. I wasn't around when that happened."

"That was different," Sapphire said. "Spats was given the position by the former chief."

"You mean his brother, Kerson."

She nodded. "There was a formal ceremony at the Guild Hall where Kerson passed on his title as chief to Spats, but I don't know what happens when a chief up and disappears. That's never happened since I've been here."

"Word's going to spread," Reevie said. "No stopping it. I guess we'll have to wait and see what happens."

"Until then," I said, "we need to act as normal as possible. Make it look like we have nothing to hide, that nothing has changed."

"Hopefully, the new armbands for our pickers will help deter the other tribes from attacking," Reevie said. "'Cause we're going to need all the help we can get. Apparently, Spats wasn't exactly the most proficient bookkeeper." He walked around to the front of his desk and opened one of the larger tomes. "It appears our illustrious leader had been lining his own pockets for some time by skimming off the top."

"I thought you said that the tribal chiefs were allowed to do that."

"Not to this degree," he said, jabbing the page with his quill. "It's no wonder the Temple's in such rough shape."

"So, we're not doing as badly as you thought?"

Reevie scoffed. "No, we're doing worse." He stared at the figures on the page a moment longer, then struck the top of the table with his fist. "Stupid, faery-loving, redheaded weasel!"

"What's the problem?"

Reevie looked up. "The problem is, I have no idea where the

money's gone."

Chapter 14

I SPENT MOST OF THE DAY underneath my favorite tree between the main building and the front wall, watching the Hurricane members as they scurried from one location to another. Those from the Granary smiled or waved when they saw me. Those from Hurricane sped up, trying not to look, or pretended they hadn't seen me altogether.

Periodically, I found myself staring at Egla, the faerie goddess whose glory had dwindled down to nothing more than a naked statue in an empty fountain. She *was* beautiful. Unfortunately, every time I caught myself admiring her, I also couldn't help but vividly picture her end. Eaten by the very creatures she had created. Her beauty had clearly meant nothing to them.

"I thought I'd find you here," Sapphire said with a sneer as she crossed her arms, letting it be known that she didn't like me staring at the naked woman.

I looked up and smiled, then took a bite of the apple I'd been working on for the last hour. The sun was almost center high. "The fresh air is helping me get over Reevie's mushrooms. Besides, I couldn't stand being cooped up any longer."

"I know what you mean," she said, resting her hand on her sword. "I get edgy whenever I get stuck inside. I don't know how you and Reevie did it, living in that room under the Granary. I'd have gone crazy."

"In a way, it feels like home. I was born and raised underground, so I guess it doesn't bother me as much."

She sat down beside me and leaned against the tree. "So, what was it like living with the Upaka?"

"What do you mean? I *am* Upaka."

"Yeah, that came out wrong. Sometimes I forget that . . ." She passed me a sideways glance. "Never mind. To us, the Upaka are kind of like faeries."

I looked at her, a little dumbfounded. "Why would you say something like that?"

"Hear me out. The name *Upaka* strikes fear into most, not because anybody has ever seen one but because all they have to go on is rumor. Like if you ever see an Upaka, it's the last thing you'll ever see. That this secret sect of assassins hides in a place so deadly, not even the White Tower dares enter. Growing up hearing that, it tends to stick with you."

Hearing that, I actually felt proud of my heritage.

She stared at me a moment. "What's it like to live underground? Is that why you're so pale? Is that why your eyes are like that? How'd you bathe?"

"First of all, when I said I lived underground, I didn't mean we dug holes in the dirt and slept there. We're not moles."

She chuckled. "No, you'd need a few more whiskers for that." She tickled up under my chin.

I swatted at her hand. "The Lost City is beautiful. Where we live, there are entire buildings underground, tunnels wide enough to fit the Temple's dining hall in, underground rivers with waterfalls."

Sapphire's eyes widened as she listened.

"And as for my fair skin and eyes . . ." I shrugged. "I don't know. It might have something to do with living there."

She stared at me for an uncomfortably long moment. "I think your eyes are stunning. And scary. Mostly intriguing."

"Thanks. I think."

She smiled, and we turned and quietly sat there staring at Egla.

Finally, she sighed. "Reevie wants to see us. Something about the missing money."

I finished off the last bite of apple as I stood, then threw the core as hard as I could, watching it soar over the wall.

Sapphire was already halfway back to the main building by the time I caught up. I sneezed as we passed the dining hall. The smell of pepper was so strong, I couldn't help it, which usually meant Cook was running low on ingredients to flavor the stew. I grimaced.

We crossed the wide porch in front of the main building, passing a couple of the Guard who were milling about, seemingly with little to do but stare out at the lonely wilderness that was the Temple's gardens.

"Don't you have somewhere to be?" Sapphire asked. The Guard members scattered in a hurry, each heading in a different direction.

We were going to have to start organizing duties for the tribe. Idle hands tended to get into trouble, my mother used to say. My chest tightened at the thought of her, and I quickly forced it down.

I needed to train both the Guard and the beaters. Our battle outside the Avalanche compound had shown me how inept they were. The Guard had some training, probably thanks to the lessons Sapphire had received from her father, but they were a far cry from being proficient.

We walked through the foyer and down the central corridor toward the back. I couldn't help but admire the way the corridors and rooms seemed to flow together, the decorative etchings and engravings in the wood, the painted mosaics of the stone tiles on the floor. There was no need for murals. Each wall seemed to be a mural unto itself. The light from the overhead skylights was enough to illuminate the way without the need for torches. It truly was a remarkable piece of architecture. I wondered why it had been left to fall into ruin.

We might have been one of the poorest of the tribes, living the farthest from the picking grounds, but with a place like the Temple, it didn't always feel that way.

We passed Spats's former quarters, and one of the guards,

whose name I didn't remember, stiffened to attention. Reevie kept at least one guard out front at all times to make sure no one sneaked in and plundered the place.

We rounded the corner and stopped in front of the infirmary. Sapphire stood there waiting until I got the hint and opened the door for her.

Reevie was still sitting behind his desk, scribbling in one of the many ledgers he had stacked within arm's reach. He had two chairs laid out in front of the desk, but neither I nor Sapphire took them.

"Have you even moved from that spot since we were last in here?" I asked.

"Someone seems to be in better spirits," he said, finally laying the pen down and stoppering the ink jar. "I have something to show you." He blew across the page he'd been writing on and stood. Limping around to the front of the desk, he grabbed a book off the top of a small stack on the right. "Let's go."

"Go where?" I asked, following him and Sapphire out of the infirmary and back up the hall. We stopped in front of Spats's old office. The guard on duty saluted with a fist to his chest, then promptly unlocked the door and opened it for us.

Table lamps and candles had already been lit, mingling with the colored light from the stained-glass windows at the side. Reevie walked over to a large chest at the foot of Spats's bed and unlocked it with the ring of keys he pulled from his pocket. "This is where Spats had been keeping the money he'd stolen from the tribe's coffers."

"So, you found it, then," I said. "Good. Because the smell coming from the kitchen right now says we need to give Cook some of it for provisions. I thought I was going to choke to death just walking by the door."

"Yeah, that would be nice," Reevie said, "but the problem is there's *no* money here. It's gone."

I joined Sapphire at the chest and looked inside.

"What do you mean, it's gone?" she asked. "Where'd it go?"

"The only thing left behind was a record, logging the outgoing payments to some unknown source. Apparently, our beloved leader had been siphoning funds for some time in order to pay someone off." Reevie raised his hand. "And before you ask, no, I have no idea who he was paying or why." He looked at the little journal he'd taken from the chest. "There's no mention why, only the dates and amounts."

"That's not good," Sapphire said.

"Clearly," I added, then offered her a smile when she crossed her arms. "Sorry. I'm just tired of everything being so negative. Can't we get some good news around here for once?" I pointed at the logbook. "How often was the money going out?"

"Every two weeks, from what I can see."

"How much was he paying?" Sapphire asked.

"Three gold pieces."

"Three gold!" Sapphire looked like she was about to punch someone. Both Reevie and I took a step back to make sure it wasn't us. "What in faerie fire was he paying that much for? That's more than a week's haul. We can barely put food on the table, and he's been giving away gold like it poured from a fountain? We've got kids in here who are wearing repurposed rice sacks just so they aren't walking around naked. How long has this been going on?"

"Ever since he took over as chief, apparently," Reevie said with a nervous gulp.

"Could this be Guild dues?" I asked.

Reevie shook his head. "No. Those payments are met at the end of the year."

"How are they figured?"

"A set percentage of that year's profits, from what I can see. Keeps the tribes on equal footing. Those who make more pay more, and those like us who are barely scraping by pay much less. But the percentage remains the same for every tribe."

It was actually a fair system. Those that made more couldn't complain about others not paying enough, while those paying less couldn't balk at those who earned more.

"And when was the last of these three-gold payments made?" Sapphire asked. "How much time do we have before the next one is due?"

Reevie flipped through the pages and read the last entry. "The end of this week."

"That's just three days away," she said. "What happens if we don't pay it?"

Both looked at me.

"Guess we'll find out in three days."

Reevie snapped the book shut. "We can worry about it tomorrow. Right now, I need to get some tinctures made and head over to the Wildfire compound." He looked about as happy as someone getting a tooth pulled. "I'm already a day behind for my weekly examination of Red's wounds." He blew the hair off his face. "I don't know why I ever agreed to help her."

"Because she probably would have ordered her beaters to kill us if you hadn't," I said.

"Yeah, well, there is that."

"I'll come with you," I said, "if she lets me." I hadn't been inside the Wildfire compound yet. I'd spent a couple of nights studying the location but hadn't had reason to go inside.

"Figured you'd have better things to do," Reevie said wryly, "like sitting around all day staring at naked faeries."

I glanced at Sapphire. Her eyes sparked, and not in a good way.

"It's my favorite tree. I can't help it that it happened to grow in front of a naked fountain faerie." Not wanting to argue the point, I started for the door. "I'll help you pack after lunch."

"Wait for me," Reevie said, leaving his desk to follow me and Sapphire out the door.

I could smell the dining hall from the porch as we stepped outside, and my stomach growled. As hungry as I was, though, I doubted I'd be able to tolerate the strongly peppered stew.

As predicted, lunch didn't last long. I barely managed a single spoon of the broth before my gut let me know it would be in my best interest not to take another. Instead, I opted for a piece of bread that had clearly been picked sometime the previous week, by the sharp taste and green mold I had to pinch off the crust. Thankfully, Reevie still had a few apples stashed away, which was exactly where we were headed.

Sapphire, on the other hand, went to check on Bull, whom she had left in charge of making sure the fixers had enough blue material and thread to use in the making of new armbands for the Granary kids. She said she'd check in on us before we left.

I spent the next hour helping Reevie pack what supplies he felt we would need, while he busied himself mixing herbs and tonics and balms for Red's wounds. Wildfire had their own version of a healer, but her skills didn't extend much beyond giving her patients a healthy dose of ale before cutting into them.

Reevie referred to her practices as barbaric and said that we should thank the Creator every day that we were blessed to have someone like him around. I agreed but wasn't about to inflate his ego any more than it already was.

"Hand me that bottle," he said, pointing at the jar of orange-brown powder on the second shelf.

I pulled it from the row and handed it to him. "What is it?"

He scooped out two spoonfuls and stirred them into whatever tincture he was making. "It's valu," he said, continuing to stir until the liquid in the cup was a pasty brown. "It relieves pain. The leaves are dried and crushed into a powder that can be brewed in teas or simply added to a cup of water. I also use it in my tonics," he said, holding up the cup, "as you can see."

I nodded, not really caring all that much about the application but giving Reevie a chance to gloat about his work.

"The valu leaves are found in the wetter regions around the Riverlands. The people who live there chew the leaves to lessen normal aches and pains, but when the leaves are dried and crushed, the powder becomes even stronger."

"That's interesting," I said, finding it anything but. I left him to his stirring and packed several rolls of clean wrapping into the two satchels. It was fun to watch Reevie get excited about his work, but there were times I needed to intervene, or he'd ramble on until the sun went down.

It didn't take him long to finish mixing in the rest of the herbs and pouring the finished tonic into a stoppered bottle for transport. Before we knew it, our travel packs were filled and ready to go. We told Sapphire not to expect us back until the next morning, since walking all the way across the city to Wildfire's compound and back would take the remainder of the day, not to mention the time spent tending to the injured.

The streets were full, which was typical near the end of the week as shoppers picked up items for the week's end, not wanting to do it on their days off. We made it as far as King's Way East before being stopped at the bridge leading into the main Merchant District as a single-sailed ship made its way down the Tansian River toward the bay.

It was the first time I'd seen one of the bridges raised. The ship's mast was tall enough to require raising the walkways. It reminded me of pictures I'd seen of ancient castle drawbridges being lifted to keep the enemy out.

It only took a few minutes for the ship to pass, but it took significantly longer for the horse-drawn pulleys to lower the wooden archways back into place. I paused halfway across the bridge to stare at the riverboat as it headed south toward the Bay of Torrin. It brought back memories of my time on the *Wind Binder*. I wondered how Captain Treygan, Ismara, and the rest of the crew were doing, and if they missed me. There were times I wondered if I'd made the right decision in coming to Aramoor, but now that I was there, I couldn't very well abandon those who needed me.

With a quick sigh, I turned and ran to catch up with Reevie.

We made good time through the shopping district, the newer clothing Mistress Orilla had helped us purchase keeping the patrollers from chasing us down the street. Although a few did keep a pretty close eye on the two unaccompanied kids as we made our way through King's Square.

"We should have skipped lunch and stopped by Master Fentin's," I said, keeping my pace slow, which today was more for my sake than Reevie's. "I could really use one of Mistress Orilla's sandwiches." My stomach grumbled on cue, clearly upset at me for not having thought of it sooner. "Maybe we can stop by on the way back, if it's not too late," I said, hoping Reevie caught the hint.

He didn't, or he was ignoring me.

"What's got you so preoccupied?" I asked.

He didn't even bother looking up. "Red."

"What about her?"

"I was supposed to have tended to her wounds yesterday, but instead, you up and branded yourself, forcing me to miss my meeting with her to tend to you. I'm just wondering how upset she's going to be."

I decided a sarcastic comment at this point wouldn't go over too well, so I kept my thoughts to myself.

We stuck close to the side streets where possible, as the main thoroughfares were far too crowded. North Avis was packed with carriages, costermongers, horses, and shoppers, so much so that not even the king could have moved the flow of traffic faster were he accompanied by a regiment of lancers.

Once through the Merchant District, we headed east another half hour, crossing through a section of the city that housed some of the newest and tallest buildings. It was hard not to stop and gawk at the way the sun glinted off the glass domes and gold trim. Wildfire was located on the northeastern outskirts of the business district. It wasn't on one of the main thoroughfares, but it was in one of the northern quarters, which meant a higher standard of living.

We stopped on the other side of the street from the Wildfire compound, up against a four-story stone-block building with a number of signs posted out front. The most prominent appeared to be a cobbler, since his was the only sign with an image carved and painted into the wood. The image was that of four unique styles of shoes, each pair individually colored, two men's and two women's.

I glanced down at my own scuffed brown boots and shook my head. I had to stuff the toes just to make them fit, but it was better to have them too big than too small.

"Quite the place they have here," I said, looking at a similar four-story building across the street. It wasn't anything like the compounds of Rockslide, Avalanche, or even the Temple. Instead of sprawling grounds with buildings and a wall, this was a single construct. It wasn't as new as some of the more prominent buildings on the north side of town, but it certainly wasn't shabby, either.

It had been built with the same light-colored stone blocks as many of the surrounding buildings. The windows were well cleaned and beautifully crafted with trimming that resembled vines growing in a circular pattern. The craftsmanship was exquisite. Not as elegant as what we had at the Temple but certainly better maintained.

I noted several open balconies across the front, each large enough to hold two people standing. They appeared to be more for aesthetic value than for function. The railings at the front were barely tall enough to keep people from falling.

The compound also lacked any outside fortification, but I had a feeling that its location was protection enough. It wasn't likely that another tribe would march its members straight through one of the most heavily patrolled sectors in the city and attack.

Reevie sighed as he stared across the street at the steps leading up to the front doors. "Hopefully, this will be one of the last times I need to visit." He looked at me. "You reckon she'll be mad that I'm a day late?"

"Only one way to find out."

Reevie gulped.

Three of the Wildfire sentries, who had been doing their best to look like simple shoppers, spotted us and started across the street.

By their relaxed posture, they must have recognized Reevie, but they slowed when they caught sight of my eyes.

"She was expecting you yesterday," a girl on the end said, sparing only a quick glance for Reevie before turning to me.

Reevie smiled. "Sorry, something important came up that I couldn't get out of. But I'm here now. Lead the way."

The girl stared at me, and for a moment, I thought she was going to make me stay behind, but eventually she turned and motioned for us to follow. One of the other sentries rushed ahead of the group and ran inside the building, no doubt to warn the others of our arrival.

We followed the guards across the street but were stopped at the foot of the stairs leading up to the front. "Disarm," the girl said.

I didn't like the idea of giving up my weapons, but obviously I wasn't going to be allowed inside with them, so I handed over my sword and my dagger, not bothering with the one I had tucked in my shoe. If they didn't take the trouble to do a proper search, that was their fault.

As soon as the guards felt it safe to let us pass, we started up the stairs. By Reevie's near-panicked expression, he was clearly still worried about his late arrival.

Knowing Red, it was probably justified.

Chapter 15

I WALKED ALONGSIDE REEVIE as we headed into the building, passing at least five guards on the way in and just as many taking up position within the foyer—each armed, each with their hands resting protectively on their hilts.

"Not quite the warm reception I'd envisioned," I said.

"Don't look at me," Reevie answered. "This isn't the kind of welcome I usually get. Clearly, you're the one they're here to see . . . or kill." He gulped. "Maybe this wasn't such a good idea after all."

I tugged down my left sleeve, making sure to keep the brand on my arm hidden.

Besides the guards, the foyer was packed with kids, with more still arriving. By the time I turned to get a look behind me, the doors leading out were shut and stacked with tribal members, at least three deep. The halls leading to other parts of the building were lined on both sides, not to mention the grand staircase up to the next floor.

I was suddenly feeling as though I'd been in this situation before, reminding me of the first day I'd arrived in Aramoor and the welcoming I'd received at the hands of this very tribe.

Even if I had been carrying my swords, I doubted I could have fought my way out, not with Reevie beside me. There were just too many of them.

The surrounding kids were eerily silent, like a pack of vultures circling, waiting for their prey to breathe its last before diving in to gorge. I was beginning to rethink my reason for coming in the first place. Besides getting the opportunity to see inside Wildfire, I wanted to form a stronger relationship between our tribes. I couldn't think of a better time to do that than when their chief was in need of our assistance, but looking at the welcoming, this might have been a very poor decision.

I wasn't sure what they were waiting for, but I took the opportunity to get a look at the room—the size, the height, the furnishings, the number of windows, doorways, halls, or any other avenues of escape available should we find ourselves on the wrong side of our host's rather unpredictable temperament.

Like the exterior, the spacious entry was clean. The tiled floors were not only swept but scrubbed to the point of reflection. The walls were lined with furniture, and not the cheaply made pieces you'd find in the lower quarters but the kind you purchased for the way they made you feel when you saw them and not for their use.

However, it wasn't the polished floors or the plush furniture that caught my attention. It was the overwhelming use of red. Red cushions on the sofas and chairs, red roses in the vases, red apples in the pewter bowls on the table; even the carpet running up the center of the staircase was a deep red, albeit a bit faded with use. The muted grey undertones of the walls, railings, and floor made the color even more pronounced. The entire room had a very dark and yet oddly sensual sort of feel, the way I imagined pricier brothel houses in the north quarter would look.

"I see our guests have finally arrived," a voice from the top of the stairs called down.

I turned, and there she was, red vest pulled tight over a loose-fit shirt as black as the waves of hair that hung to her waist. Her lips were painted as well, making her look at least five years older than she was, which from all accounts was sixteen.

"I must admit," she said, sauntering down the staircase. "I didn't expect to have the pleasure of Death's Shadow today. A rare treat." She stopped at the bottom of the steps and smiled.

The kids quickly parted, leaving an open walkway.

My hand brushed across where my dagger had been, forgetting I'd given it to the guards before entering. "What are friends for?" I said, returning her smile with one of equal insincerity.

She cocked her head. "We are friends now?"

I shrugged. "*Friends* might be a little strong. How about *good neighbors*?"

"Yes, *neighbors* will do nicely. So," she said, looking us both over, "to what do we owe the pleasure of your company this fine afternoon?"

"Hang it all, Red," Reevie blurted out. "We're here to see to your wounds; you know that."

Red never broke her smile, although I noticed a couple of her guards reach for their weapons. "Do I? Is that something I know?" She turned to those standing nearby as if looking for an answer. "From what I remember, *yesterday* was when you were to be tending to my wounds. Yes, I distinctly remember that, since I was forced to cancel a very important meeting with Senator Bracken just to facilitate your visit." Her smile slipped.

"It was my fault," I said. "I took ill yesterday, forcing him to delay until I was back on my feet."

Red stared at me. "I hope it's nothing catchy. I'd hate to think you came all this way just to pass your disease off to me."

"I'd never allow that," Reevie said, crossing his arms. He looked offended.

Red walked down the open aisle left by the kids and stopped just in front of me to study my face. "You do look pale. But you've always looked pale. And those eyes." She took another step closer and ran her finger down the side of my face. "Those strange, beautiful eyes." Her face was so close, I could feel the warmth of her breath on my cheeks.

I thought she was about to kiss me when she finally let go of my face and took a step back, clearing her throat. "What's everyone gawking at? Get back to work!"

The room exploded with kids. They ran down the halls, up the stairs, out the doors, knocking each other over as they fought to make themselves scarce, not wanting to be caught within eyeshot of their chief now that her cheeks had turned the color of her lips.

She took a deep breath and released as she looked around the now empty room. "That's better." A couple of her black-vested Guard stood to either side of the entrance, waiting to be called. "Let's get this over with," she said, starting back up the stairs. She used the railing, this time to not put so much weight on her leg.

Reevie and I followed her up. Like the main foyer below, the corridors were richly decorated: dark wood tables with vases of red flowers, crimson and gold draperies, thick runners down the center of the halls. It reminded me of the rooms the Guild used for its meetings.

On the fourth floor, we followed a long hallway to a set of ornate doors, where two guards stood watch outside. One look from Red and they had the doors open before she arrived.

"Wait outside," she said to them as she entered the room.

As soon as Reevie and I had made it through the doors, the guards shut them behind us. Looking around, we were clearly in her personal chambers. Thick red pillows could be seen everywhere. They covered the enormous four-poster bed at the back. They were strewn across the sofas and chairs. There was even a large pile lying in front of the hearth. The glow from the fire added to the room's intimacy.

I turned to compliment our host on her lavish decorations and nearly swallowed my tongue as she brazenly dropped her vest to the floor and took off her shirt. I quickly spun back around, my cheeks flushing brighter than the pillows.

"Don't be such a prude," she said. "How are you going to tend to my wounds if you can't see them?"

Gritting my teeth, I turned back around. She was now lying on her back on the bed. Thankfully, she had laid her shirt across her chest. Still, it didn't make my hands sweat any less.

"Hand me your pack," Reevie said, giving me a harsh look as though I were embarrassing him. He started pulling items from the satchel and laying them on the table beside her bed. One of the vials held the tonic he'd been mixing before we came. He arranged everything in an orderly fashion on the table, then looked at me. "Well, don't just stand there. Remove her bandage."

With an exasperated huff, I walked over to the bed and started unwrapping the dressing from her upper arm, just below the shoulder. I did my best not to look her in the eyes, still feeling more than a little embarrassed by the situation. It wasn't like I hadn't tended to wounds before, but Red had a knack for making everything uncomfortable.

"What's wrong, Grey Eyes?" she asked as I slowly peeled back the blood-soaked bandage. "Are you intimidated by my beauty?"

I wanted to punch her in the arm but held my tongue instead. The wound on her arm was deep and red around the edges, which told me it still had some infection but Reevie's medicines were fighting it off. The skin had already closed from where the blade had pierced her, but it was going to be a while before she would be back to full fighting capacity.

"How does it look?" she asked, raising her head in an attempt to see.

Reevie pushed her back down. "Stop moving; you'll tear it open." He grabbed a small container and handed it to me. "Here, rub this over the wound. But carefully."

I nodded, took the opened jar, and scooped out some of the pale-green paste with my fingers. It was cool to the touch but smelled like stall mucking. It was the same paste he had used on my brand, not to mention the injuries I'd sustained during the Pit battle, allowing my wounds to heal faster.

"Be gentle," Red reiterated with a cheeky grin.

Being *gentle* was about the last thing I wanted to do. I wanted to plaster it across her face. With a sigh of resignation, I carefully applied the goo, making sure to give it a nice, thick coat.

"That feels nice," she said, not able to hide the slight wrinkling of her nose at the smell. "Who would have thought an assassin would have such a soft touch?" She grabbed my hand when I started to pull away. "It hurts down here as well. How about rubbing some more of that stuff right here?" She pressed my hand to her side just above her waist. "Yes," she said, looking deep into my eyes, "that's the spot."

I jerked my hand away, and she laughed.

Even Reevie chuckled, although he tried not to show it as he put a new dressing on the wound below her shoulder. I stood back to give him plenty of room to work and less chance for her to flirt.

"Alright," Reevie said, finishing with the bandage, "let's see the leg. And don't think I didn't notice you limping on it as you came down the stairs."

Red looked at me, then slowly undid the buttons on her leather pants. She whimpered as she leaned forward to pull them down, then collapsed back on the bed. "It hurts too much. You'll have to do it."

Reevie gulped as he leaned in, then took a step back and looked at me. "You do it. I, uh . . . I have to get the balm ready." He quickly scooted to the table and pretended to shuffle some of the vials around, leaving me to undress our very troublesome patient.

I shook my head, wondering if perhaps getting a look around the inside of her compound was really worth all this effort. Life as a healer was certainly not in the books for me, at least where Red was concerned. With a deep breath, I grabbed the waist of her pants and pulled them to her knees, leaving her with little but a pair of linen drawers, which stopped short of the tight wrapping around her thigh.

If she giggled even once, I was going to give her a matching hole on the other side of her leg.

Carefully, I unwrapped the layers, each bearing a wider circle of blood until at last I reached the leg itself. It was by far the worst of the injuries. I could see where the sword had been thrust completely through the side of her leg. She winced at my touch.

"Your hands are cold!"

"Sorry." I blew on them before angling her leg enough for Reevie to get to.

"You're not staying off this leg like I told you to," Reevie chastised.

Red rolled her eyes. "I don't have time to stay off my leg. I've got too many things I need to do."

"You won't be doing anything if I have to cut your leg off because it rotted."

Red snarled, her hands balling tight, but she didn't say anything.

Reevie rubbed her leg with some clear liquid that smelled strangely of licorice before applying the same pale-green paste to both the entrance and exit wound. He then used a fresh roll of dressing and rewrapped the leg.

Once he finished, she pulled her pants back up and rebuttoned them, never once complaining about any soreness. "Well, are you two just going to stand there and stare at my chest, or are you going to turn around so a lady can put her shirt back on?"

"If I see a lady, I'll let you know," I mumbled as we turned. Reevie kicked me in the shin. By the time the pain had subsided, Red had finished with her shirt and was limping around us for the door.

"Now for the others," she said.

"Not so fast." Reevie walked over to the table and unstopped the flask of tonic. "You need to drink this."

"No, I don't. We have other wounded that need your help."

"I'm not helping anyone until you drink this. You need it to heal. That paste isn't going to be enough."

"That stuff tastes terrible. Took me an entire day to wash the taste out of my mouth last time."

"I can't help the way it tastes. Do you want to get better or not?"

Red stared at him a moment. "Fine!" She walked over and snatched the bottle from his hands and took a good-sized swallow. "Satisfied?" she asked, thrusting the flask back in his arms.

Reevie nodded with a smile and limped back to the table to repack his bag.

Chapter 16

WE FOLLOWED RED out the door and back down the hall. She turned down the closest corridor and stopped at the first door. I could already feel something in me change, a hollow ache that let me know a piece of me was missing.

My magic was gone, which could only mean one thing—

Red opened the door. "You decent?"

A chubby, dark-haired boy was sitting in a chair in front of the fire, reading a book. He looked up and, catching sight of me, leaped from the chair and ran for the bed, diving underneath. It was the same short, dark-haired boy Red had taken with her to the Guild meeting. The same boy Red had been overprotective of during the Pit battle. It was also the same boy who was somehow keeping my magic from working.

"Get out here, Po! They aren't going to hurt you!"

"Yes, he will," a muffled voice called out from under the bed.

"No, he won't!" She looked at me. "Go on. Tell him."

I sighed. "I'm not going to hurt you."

"There, you see?" she said. "He's not going to hurt you. Now get out here, or *I'll* hurt you!"

Po's head poked out from under the left side of the mattress, eventually followed by the rest of him.

"Get over here and let the healer take a look at you."

Keeping a close eye on me, Po reluctantly slid one foot in front of the other. Reevie met him at the chair and motioned for the boy to take a seat. I stayed by the door, not wanting to scare him any further, considering I was the reason the side of his jaw was purple and green in the first place. If I hadn't knocked him out during our battle at the Pit, none of us might have survived.

Red joined me as Reevie opened his satchel and pulled out the first container. "Have you heard about Rockslide's disappearing prisoners?" she asked.

Reevie half-choked and turned it into a passable cough, but I managed to keep my face blank. "Yes, very strange. I heard they vanished in the middle of the night. Even the guards were missing."

"They say the doors were locked from the inside, and by the time they managed to chop their way through, there wasn't a trace of them."

"What do you think happened?" I asked, curious what rumors had been spreading.

She crossed her arms. "Don't know. Doesn't make sense, if you ask me. How does a group of unarmed rejects manage to walk through solid stone? And where are the guards? How is it not a single person saw them?"

"Maybe the guards felt sorry for them and set them free?" I said, hoping to steer her toward something at least remotely plausible.

"Fat chance," she said with a firm shake of her head. "If they'd set them free, Kore would have killed them for sure. Besides, like I said, the door was locked from the inside." She clicked her tongue and looked at me. "What does Spats think about it? For that matter, why are you still at Hurricane? From the way Spats was acting at the Pit, I got the distinct impression he was trying to get rid of you."

I looked at her and smiled. "I'm not that easy to get rid of."

She stared at me a moment, lips puckered, clearly trying to read something off my face. "How much is Spats paying you?"

I was a little surprised by the question.

"Whatever it is, I'll double it. Come work for me. Both of you."

Reevie stopped applying his salve to Po's face and turned.

Since Spats hadn't been paying us in the first place, getting double of nothing wasn't all that enticing; however, having another tribe bid for you was quite flattering. "We have too many people who need us in Hurricane," I said. "We can't just up and leave."

Red nodded, but the narrowing of her eyes said she was a little put out. "At least tell me you'll consider it."

"We will," Reevie blurted out a little too easily.

"If you'll answer something for me," I said.

She nodded.

"Tell me how it is that you've managed to claim an entire building in the north quarter without a single patroller raiding this place."

Red chuckled. "Favors."

"What kind of favors?"

"The kind you don't speak of."

"Like what, killing off an opponent?" I asked, trying to lighten the mood.

She didn't say anything, and my smile disappeared. I guess if I thought about it, I didn't exactly have the right to be judgmental. After all, it was what I had been trained to do.

Reevie finished up with Po's bruised and cut face. The dark-haired boy remained curled in his seat, peeking at me from around the side.

"Where to next?" Reevie asked as Red opened the door. Two of the guards I'd seen in the foyer were waiting for us in the hallway, along with a girl I hadn't seen. She stood head and shoulders over me and Reevie, and carried a small satchel of her own.

"Now we take you to see the rest," Red said with a passing glance at the taller girl on the end. "And take Nia with you. Hopefully, she can learn something useful while you make your rounds."

Reevie looked at Nia, and she smiled timidly. "How much training have you received?"

Nia looked at Red.

"Not enough," Red said as she walked down the hall.

Reevie blew out his lips and nodded. "Fine, but don't get in my way."

Nia nodded.

I looked at the guards and gestured back down the hall in the direction of the stairs. "After you."

By the time Reevie and I had been through the injured—those with wounds serious enough to keep them from work but not serious enough to be branded as rejects—the sun had long since set, and my stomach was letting me know I was an idiot for not having eaten Cook's peppered broth before we'd left.

We reached the bottom landing of the foyer and started for the front doors, still being escorted by the same two guards who'd been with us all day. Our packs were all but empty, having dispensed most of what we had brought with us.

I hated using such limited resources on another tribe when we had need of them at home, but Red had spared our lives at the Pit, so in a way, we kind of owed her. Of course, if I hadn't come to her rescue, she wouldn't have been around for us to owe. I guess it all depended on how you looked at it. For my part, we needed allies and not enemies, so if using some of our resources helped with that endeavor, then so be it.

"I'm not looking forward to the walk back," Reevie said, shifting his pack higher on his shoulder. "We should have asked Red to spot us a carriage ride or something. It isn't like she doesn't have the gold."

"Wait," Red called out behind us.

Reevie and I stopped and turned. Reevie gave me an embarrassed look when he saw Red walking out from one of the back halls. "Do you think she heard what I said about the carriage?" he whispered.

"I've had a room prepared for you for tonight," Red said, "as well as a hot meal."

Reevie's head shot up. "Supper? Lead the way."

Red turned and started back toward the same hall she'd exited from.

"Be careful with that leg," Reevie scolded. "I don't want my food to go cold 'cause I'm having to re-dress your wound."

Red growled but slowed her walk nonetheless. She stopped halfway across the foyer and turned. "Well, are you coming or not?"

Reevie and I were hardly in a position to refuse her hospitality—not that either of us would have after the offer of food—so we followed along. My mouth was already watering, but I didn't like the idea of spending the night here. I couldn't help but think Red was up to something. Or maybe this was her way of enticing us to join Wildfire.

We passed a few kids on the way, most steering toward the wall to allow plenty of room for their chief. Up ahead, a lanky girl with a white apron that hung to her feet was busy running a duster over a beautifully carved mirror on the wall. The frame was fascinating, each side a reflection of the other. At the top were two dragons sitting in a regal pose, facing each other, while their unrealistically long tails wound down the sides and bottom of the frame.

"Tell Cook we'll take our dinner in the blue room," Red said to the cleaner. The girl bowed and took off running, her head bouncing up and down like a new rider sitting their first saddle.

I looked at Reevie and mouthed: *Blue room*?

Reevie shrugged, and we continued around the next corner, where Red was waiting in front of an open door for us to catch up.

"In here," she said.

It was painfully obvious why it was referred to as the *blue* room. Blue checkered tiles ran along the outskirt of painted white oak floors, butting up against textured walls colored with an even deeper shade of blue. Even the ceiling was blue. If not for the long white beams that ran overhead, it would have been difficult to tell where the walls ended and the ceiling began. Not surprisingly, the table decorations were blue as well: plates, bowls, and saucers trimmed with various shades of blue etching; dark-blue napkin holders at each setting, even pale-blue stained goblets with gold trim to drink from.

It was incredible and ridiculous all at the same time.

"Wow!" Reevie exclaimed, his mouth gaping wide enough to toss a whole apple in. He limped over to the closest table against the wall and stuck his hand inside a bone-white bowl filled with blue flower petals. He turned and looked at me. "I think we need to consider doing some favors as well."

Red laughed and took her seat at the head of the table. "Please, sit," she said, beckoning us to join her. "I hope you like stuffed pheasant."

"Stuffed pheasant?" Reevie looked positively faint.

"No idea," I said. "Never had it." I took my seat on Red's right, and Reevie sat on her left.

She smiled. "Then you're in for a real treat. No one knows how to prepare a more savory bird than Cook. I don't know what kind of spices he uses, but one bite and you'll never want to stop eating."

"As long as it's not pepper," I said.

Reevie almost spat his drink, quickly wiping his mouth with his dirty shirtsleeve instead of the nice linen cloth beside him.

Red looked at me funny. "Whatever he uses, I promise it will change your life."

She wasn't wrong.

The meal started with baked apples covered in a sweet sauce that left a pleasant aftertaste of cinnamon and cloves. The pheasant was served with a cranberry sauce that had my eyes watering with pure joy. I'd never tasted anything so delicious. Not even Master Endle's honey tarts could measure up. Afterward, we enjoyed a warm bread pudding, cooked with raisins and plums. By the time we were done, I was ready to join Wildfire on the spot.

Red dabbed at her mouth with her napkin, looking rather pleased with herself. She dropped the napkin on her plate and leaned back against her cushioned seat. "Just think, if you came to work for me, you could be enjoying meals like this every week. We could use a proper healer around here, and having Death's Shadow by my side would be worth its weight in gold." She stared at the two of us a moment as if expecting an easy victory, especially after such an elaborate meal, but when neither of us caved, she lifted her goblet. "Anyway, something to think about. You don't have to give me your answer right away." She held out her glass. "To new beginnings and, hopefully, new partnerships."

I joined Reevie in holding our glasses in salute, very carefully clinking mine against Red's and Reevie's. "To new beginnings," we said.

After the meal, Red showed us to our room.

"I hope you don't mind sharing," she said. "The flue in our other guest quarters was clogged and smoked up the room when we tried to light the fire."

"No problem," I said. "Reevie and I are used to sharing."

Reevie nodded, staring wide-eyed at the comfort of the chambers. The bed was large enough to fit Hurricane's entire Guard or possibly one very large Tubby. Reevie eventually collected himself and took a stroll around the room. He wiped a finger across the top of a nearby table. "It'll do," he said, as if he'd ever stayed in a room half as nice.

"Good. Then I'll bid you a pleasant night," she said. "I'll have someone wake you for breakfast. I hope you like smoked sausage."

Reevie looked like a fish gasping for air.

Red smiled. "See you in the morning." She left and shut the door.

"Did she give you a key?" I asked Reevie, who was busy testing the firmness of the mattress.

He shook his head.

I grabbed the chair sitting in front of the desk on the left and placed it up under the door handle. "Guess that'll do." The last thing we needed was for someone to sneak into our room in the middle of the night and slit our throats.

"Did you hear that?" Reevie said, staring blank-faced at the door. "Smoked sausages." He looked at me. "Maybe having more than one tribe wouldn't be so bad."

I didn't answer him other than to cock my brow.

"You heard her; she said she was going to pay us. And smoked sausage for breakfast."

I plopped down on the edge of the bed, enjoying the noticeable spring. "What about all the kids at the Temple who depend on us? Half of them are rejects. Wouldn't they stand to benefit more from your help than the tribes that threw them out in the first place? What about Sapphire and Bull? Are we going to just leave them to deal with our mess? And what about Tubby and Mouse and Petal and Squeaks and—"

"Hey," Reevie said, "I never told you to bring all those people home. In fact, I remember telling you not to. But do you listen to me? No." He scooted over to the edge of the bed and let his legs hang over the side. "Now look at us. Left with the responsibility of feeding an entire compound of kids, without the coin to do it." Reevie slapped the top of the mattress. "I should have listened to my better senses," he said, "and never gotten involved. This is what I get for trying to help you. My life was so much simpler before."

I couldn't help but chuckle. "Your life was boring and lonely. Finding me was the best thing that ever happened to you, and you know it."

Reevie huffed.

"You wouldn't be able to live with yourself if you left the kids at Hurricane to fend for themselves while you lived in luxury, eating sausages and pudding."

There was a long pause. "I could try."

"I know you, Reevie. You'd be as miserable as me if we switched tribes."

Reevie crawled to the opposite side of the bed, pulled back the thick comforter, and hopped in. "I'm sure I could learn to live with it," he said, then pulled the blanket up over his head.

I stared at the lump under the comforter, wondering if Reevie would actually do it. Reevie might talk tough, but in the end, he usually did what was right. I pulled back the covers on my side and crawled in. I hoped this was one of those times.

Chapter 17

THE NEXT FEW DAYS PASSED without incident, apart from a small kerfuffle in the barracks when a couple of beaters caught Mouse sneaking into their room and snooping around their belongings. Sapphire was forced to get involved when Petal and Squeaks ran to tell her that the older kids were trying to toss Mouse over the wall.

She confined him to his room for three days, where he was forced to live on nothing but bread and water, which, under the circumstances, might have been preferable to the peppered broth the rest of us had to endure. On the third day, she released him with a strong scolding and a warning that if he was caught stealing from anyone else in the tribe, he'd be forced to leave.

"He got off easy if you ask me," Bull said with a grunt as he slowly walked the perimeter of the room, taking his time to fiddle with a collection of spearheads Spats had lying on one of the shelves in the corner. "Cutter would have cut off his hand."

I grimaced from my seat on the sofa beside Sapphire. "Good thing we aren't Avalanche and I'm not Cutter."

Reevie nodded, his eyes on a large tome in his lap, its hard binding reaching from one arm of his chair to the other.

"He won't do it again," Sapphire said, sparing a hesitant glance at me as she spun her dagger in her hands. "At least, I hope not."

"Mouse is the least of our worries," Reevie said. "It's a new week and still no word about our lack of payment."

"Isn't *no* news a good thing?" Bull asked, finally joining the rest of us by taking the seat next to Reevie's.

"Normally, but I'd rather know who it is we owe, and why, than sit here in the dark." Reevie snapped the book shut and dropped it on the floor. "I hate not knowing."

"How are the supplies looking?" Sapphire asked, studying the growing pile of discarded books beside Reevie's seat. "How are we doing for food?"

Reevie groaned. "Have you missed the last five days' meals? I'd say our morning gruel and afternoon broth speaks for itself."

Bull made a sour face.

"The pickings have been slim the last couple weeks," Reevie said, then looked at me. "The few gold coins you snatched from Spats's chest when you kidnapped him have already been used. If we don't come up with some other way to get some more, we're going to starve to death."

One look and I knew what he was referring to.

Sapphire must have spotted it as well. "What aren't you telling us?"

"What do you mean?" Reevie tried to play it off, but his attempt to evade the question could have used some work.

"I know you're hiding something." She pointed her dagger at Reevie. "What is it?"

Reevie blew out his lips. "Fine. Red might have offered me and Ayrion a position at Wildfire."

"Of course, you said no, right?" Bull said, more statement of fact than question.

Reevie looked at me.

Sapphire tried reading my face, but I kept it in check. Years of training to not show emotion gave me an advantage. I was Upakan. She wasn't going to break me.

She turned and looked at Reevie. Her face tightened.

"What? They had smoked sausages and bread pudding. And she offered to pay us double what we were getting paid by Spats—"

"Which was nothing," Sapphire said sharply.

"Well, she didn't know that."

"Maybe it's not such a bad thing," Bull said, causing everyone to turn. He was the last person I would have expected to hear an affirmation from. "We need the coin, don't we?"

"We need them more," Sapphire shot back.

"Maybe we can rent them?" Bull said.

I honestly hadn't considered that option before. "Bull might have something there." I looked at Reevie. "Maybe you could sell your services temporarily. You're already doing it for Red as a payment for not killing us. Perhaps, once she's fully healed, we could come to an arrangement where you made ongoing visits for a certain fee—"

"And smoked sausages," Reevie added with a hungry smile. "We can't forget the sausages."

"We could also do the same for some of the other tribes," Bull added, clearly excited that one of his suggestions had actually sparked some interest.

"I'm not about to step foot in Cutter's domain," Reevie said.

"Or Kore's," Sapphire added.

"But I bet Noph wouldn't be averse to the idea," I said. "I'm sure Sandstorm could benefit from having a skilled healer making random visits."

"Yes," Reevie agreed. "I know for a fact neither tribe has a capable physicker. You already saw Red's medicine girl. More of a mutilator than a healer, if you ask me. No wonder Red's so desperate to have me. I bet they'd pay out the nose for my services. And with that kind of gold, I can purchase more books on healing and medicinal herbs."

"All right, slow down," I said. "Don't get ahead of yourself. There's no guarantee either of them will accept such an offer, and if they did, we have no idea for how much."

"My father was a physicker, and he charged well for his services."

"That's a thought," Sapphire said, a positive glimmer sparking in her eyes as well. "What if we offered Reevie's services to more than just the tribes?"

"What do you mean?" Reevie asked.

"I'm sure there's plenty of people living right here in the Maze who could benefit from having a physicker nearby. Most of them can't afford the rates that the healers in the north quarter charge."

A knock at the door brought the conversation to an abrupt halt as we all turned.

"Who is it?" Reevie asked.

"It's Muriel. I have news."

Muriel was the tribe's birdkeeper. She tended the pigeon coop, making sure the birds had clean water, food, and a roof that didn't leak. No one else wanted the assignment. The idea of scooping bird poop was not high on the cleaners' list of desired duties. Muriel, however, enjoyed it. She loved her birds.

"Is it good news or bad news?" I asked jokingly, or somewhat jokingly. "Because I don't want to hear any bad news."

Sapphire kicked me in the leg and shook her head reprovingly. "Be nice."

"Open the door," Reevie said, "so we don't have to keep shouting."

Bull chuckled.

Muriel slid the door open and peeked inside.

Her brown hair looked like the birds had used it to nest in. Her clothes were dirt-stained, and there was the unmistakable odor of pigeon dung clinging to her skirt and long sleeves. Was she sleeping in the coop with the birds?

"You can come in," Sapphire said softly, trying to coax the little girl into the room.

Muriel nodded and stepped through the door. In her hand she held a small rolled-up piece of paper. "It just came in from Wildfire." She held out the paper to the first person she came to.

"Don't hand it to me," Bull said.

"Here." I leaned forward. "I'll take it."

Muriel gave it to me, curtsied, and then left.

"Phew." Bull waved his hand in front of his face. "Someone needs to give that girl a proper dip in the horse trough. She stinks almost as bad as Tubby when you first brought him home."

Sapphire glared at the blond-haired boy, and he shrugged. "Well, maybe not quite as bad. It's no wonder she doesn't have any friends."

"There was a time, not too long ago," Sapphire said, "when I remember you not smelling so pleasant, and we still took you in."

Bull sighed. "Guess you're right."

Sapphire looked at the missive. "What's it say?"

I unrolled the small parchment and read it aloud. "A meeting of the Guild. Fourthday at noon."

Reevie closed his book, concern on his face. "What do we do?"

I held the note in the palm of my hand. "We all knew this day was coming. We couldn't keep Spats's disappearance a secret forever."

"Maybe you were too hasty in getting rid of him," Reevie said.

I looked him in the eyes.

"Okay. Maybe not."

"Getting rid of that redheaded weasel was the right thing to do," Sapphire said with a nod in my direction.

"Fine," Reevie acquiesced, "but it still doesn't deny the fact that his disappearance has left us with a very large problem. We have a tribe without a chief."

"What are we going to do about the meeting?" Bull asked.

"The only thing we can do," I said. "We go."

Chapter 18

"HOW DID I LET YOU talk me into this?" Reevie asked, nervously studying the enormous cylindrical building across the street. It was one of four similar structures set up to form a perfect square, with long covered walkways that stretched between, allowing those inside to pass from one to the next. Reevie waved hesitantly at some people on one of the catwalks who seemed to be waving at anyone below.

"You've lived in Aramoor your entire life and you've never been here before?" Sapphire asked.

"Why would I? It's not like Spats ever invited me to come along to one of these meetings." He stared up at the incredible height of the building and gulped. "In fact, I think I'll just stay down here with Tubby and keep a lookout."

"Tubby's coming with us," I said, following Reevie and Sapphire back to where the gigantic boy stood at the corner, enthralled with all the people walking by.

"Like it or not," Sapphire said, "we have to go in there and represent Hurricane."

"And when they ask where Spats is?" Reevie asked.

"We tell them the truth. He disappeared sometime after the battle at the Pit and hasn't returned."

I looked up, noting the position of the sun. "It's noon. We need to get up there before they start without us." I turned to make sure Tubby understood what we were about to do, but he was too busy playing with his cloak. It wasn't much more than some thick curtains Sapphire had found in one of the abandoned buildings near the wharf.

The material was far from fine, but it was long enough to hang to his knees and wide enough to pull closed at the front. "No," I said sharply, trying and failing to get his attention. "It doesn't go on your head. Sapphire, can you help with this?" Tubby had pulled the back of his cloak up over his head and was attempting to take it off.

Sapphire tugged the material back into place while I held his arms. We hoped it would be enough to hide the fact that the rest of his clothes were about five sizes too small. We had also strapped a sword to his waist, in hopes it would give him the appearance of a personal guard escorting some nobleman's children. Unfortunately, it took the entire walk from the Temple to the north quarter to convince Tubby to quit playing with the weapon.

I turned and looked at Reevie, his outfit nearly as embarrassing as Tubby's. He was dressed in Spats's old Guild meeting clothes, complete with yellowed trousers, white top, and blue silk vest with its frayed brocade cravat, both of which were on the wrinkled side and quite faded with age. He was the only one of us small enough to fit into the clothing. We hoped it would help sell the idea that we were more than just a small band of street rats.

"You ready?" I asked.

"No!" Reevie stated.

"Good. I'd be worried if you were." I nodded to Sapphire. "Lead the way."

We stepped out of the shadows and headed across the street to the first building. I was more nervous this time than my first visit, which had ended with me fighting in the Pit. This time, we were walking in completely blind. We didn't even know what outcome we were hoping for, other than hoping that they let us continue running Hurricane.

With Tubby bringing up the rear, the crowds parted naturally, giving us plenty of room. No one wanted to get too close. He stood head and shoulders above everyone else, and even though he tended to stick out, I thought his presence at the meeting would outweigh the risk.

We headed up the open stairwell, keeping to the outside edge as it wound its way toward the upper levels. Every so often, I would stop to give Reevie a chance to rest his leg. Each time he looked over the side at the shrinking heads of the people in the lobby below, his hands would grip the rail even tighter.

"Quit looking down," I said. "You look like you're going to

faint."

"No, I don't," he protested.

"It's not that much farther," Sapphire said. "We're getting off on the next floor."

If Reevie was this frightened going up the stairs, I was scared to see what he'd do when he found out we were going to be walking across one of the sky bridges. I'd purposefully not told him about it while on the street, just in case he refused to go in.

We stepped off on the next landing, and Sapphire started for the bridge. Tubby was behind me, seemingly fixated on everything around him. His curiosity at all the people, the buildings, the stairs, even the bridge ahead, was a little intoxicating. I couldn't help but smile at his wide-eyed wonderment as his head darted back and forth, taking it all in.

"I'm not going out there!" Reevie said behind me. He pushed his back up against the balcony wall that fronted the bridge and scrunched down.

"Get up," Sapphire said. "People are starting to look."

Reevie shook his head adamantly. "I don't care. You didn't say anything about going out there."

Some of those walking by slowed. The last thing we needed was Reevie making a scene.

"His first time across the bridge," Sapphire said with a fake smile to a couple who had stopped to see if everything was all right. They nodded as though they'd seen it before, and kept going.

"Reevie, get up." I leaned over and grabbed one of his arms, but he pulled away. "You're the one who said you wanted to come," I pointed out. "You said you hated always being left out.

Well, now's your chance. The bridge is perfectly safe. Hundreds of people walk across it every day. It's been here for over a thousand years."

"Yeah, that's what worries me."

I ground my teeth. "Get up, or I'm going to have Tubby pick you up and carry you."

Reevie shot me a cutting look. "You wouldn't dare."

"Watch me. Every moment we sit here drawing attention to ourselves is another moment we could be caught by the patrollers. I don't plan on going to the dungeons today, so pull yourself together and let's go. The meeting's probably already started."

With shaky legs, Reevie finally stood. I kept one arm around him for support—and to make sure he didn't change his mind and try running.

"Close your eyes if you need to, and I'll make sure you get across."

Reevie followed my advice and closed his eyes as we started down the covered walkway. I kept him on my right. It was closer to the glass but away from the prying eyes of those we passed. Since his eyes were closed, he was none the wiser.

Most people ignored us as they walked by, much the same as it was on the city streets. No one wanted to look anyone in the eyes as they passed, either too busy getting to where they were going or too worried that if they did look, they would have to smile or, Creator forbid, offer some sort of greeting.

Little more than halfway across, a couple of kids jerked free of their parents' hands and ran for the window. The girl tripped on her brother's feet and ran headlong into Reevie, spinning him around and throwing him up against the glass.

"What happened?" Reevie asked, his eyes opening on reflex. He froze, his face twisted in horror as he found himself staring down at the street far below. His mouth started to open. This was about to get ugly.

I reached for Tubby's arm. "Quick, grab Reevie."

Tubby yanked Reevie off the ground and threw him over his shoulder just as Reevie released an ear-piercing scream that had everyone in the covered walkway turning.

"Make way! Make way!" I shouted. "Sick kid coming through!"

Sapphire cleared a passage through the crowd as we ran for the opposite end of the bridge leading into the next building. One look at the three of us charging down the walkway and people scrambled to get out of the way.

Reevie's scream had faded by the time we made it into the next building, but his face was as pale as a clean-pressed sheet, and his forehead was slick with perspiration. "Put him down over here," I told Tubby, waving him to the side of the corridor. I grabbed a rather expensive-looking vase from a nearby table, dumped the arrangement of flowers onto the floor, and quickly thrust it into Reevie's hands.

As soon as Reevie's feet hit the floor, he bent and heaved. Those who had stopped to see what all the fuss was about quickly changed their minds. Sapphire stood to the side, facing the oncoming traffic. "Nothing to see. Touch of elevation sickness; that's all."

Reevie's face was still milky by the time he finished heaving, but at least the perspiration had stopped. He didn't speak, but he did manage a nod to let me know the worst had passed.

Once the retching had died down, we headed for the next set of stairs and started up. Reevie clutched his vomit vase to his chest, not willing to release it. His legs were shaking so much that I kept one arm around him for support.

We made it to the third landing, and I immediately recognized the colored patterns in the hallway runner. The swirls of gold inside the teal were mesmerizing.

By the time we made it into the long corridor, Reevie's legs had strengthened enough to walk on his own, and he set the vase of spew on one of the tables as we passed. I felt sorry for the poor worker who would find it.

"How is the Guild able to afford rooms in a place like this?" Reevie asked, his voice weak.

"I asked you the same thing," I said curiously, "and you told me it was because of the side jobs they took for the nobility."

"Yeah, well, I never pictured it being somewhere like this. Then again, after seeing how Wildfire lives, nothing should surprise me." He glanced down at his wrinkled vest and cravat and tried straightening them as best he could. It was a wasted effort, and he eventually gave up.

Ahead, I could see the double doors on the right leading into the Guild lobby. They were open, and no one was mingling around outside. I didn't need to guess whether Red was in there or not. I could already feel my magic beginning to wane, which meant Po was with her. "They must have started without us," I said.

"Not surprising," Sapphire said. She was the first through the door, followed closely by me and Reevie and Tubby. The antechamber was empty as well, all except for a scrivener who sat stiffly at his desk to the left of the doors leading into the main assembly room.

It was the same older gentleman who had been there on my previous visit. In fact, he was wearing the same green suit and feathered cap.

"You need to first sign the . . ." The old man didn't finish, too preoccupied with gawking at Tubby, who hovered over his desk to see what the man was doing.

I looked at Tubby. "I want you to stay here with this nice gentleman while we go inside."

The old man wheezed; his head tilted backward as he stared up at the giant.

"Best not to scare those inside unless we have to. I'll call if we need you." I pointed to a sofa on the far side of the room. "Sit over there for now. If you hear me shout your name, though, I want you to come running."

The huge boy grinned and nodded.

"Good. Now remember. You aren't to leave that sofa unless we call you."

Tubby nodded once again, then plopped down in the middle of the couch. He sank nearly to the floor as the ropes under the cushions stretched almost to the point of giving.

I walked back over to the desk. "Did you sign us in?" I asked Sapphire.

She nodded and adjusted the sword at her waist.

My hand naturally felt for my sword as well. I could also feel the two knives I had sewn into the lining of my coat pressed against my chest, not to mention the dagger in my boot that was strapped around my calf. I looked at the scrivener. "Who's inside?"

He pointed at the book. "You can see for yourself."

Why didn't I think of that? I leaned over and read off the names above ours: "Noph plus two, Red plus two, Kore plus two, and Cutter plus two. Looks like everyone's here."

I looked at Reevie. "Just so you know, there's a large window on the back wall that looks out over the city. I'm warning you now so you don't have another fit. Hopefully, the curtains will be closed, but if they're not, try to keep from looking in that direction. We can't afford to have you losing it in front of the others."

Reevie took a deep breath and nodded.

"No turning back now," I said, and started for the door.

Sapphire grabbed my arm and pulled me to a stop. "Who's going to sit in Spats's seat?"

"I hadn't thought about that. I guess we should let Reevie, since it's hardest on him to stand with his leg."

"Whoever sits in the chair is the only one allowed to speak," she said.

"Then I think I prefer to stand," Reevie said.

"You're the one who knows the books," I added.

Reevie pointed at Sapphire. "Well, she's the one who actually runs the day-to-day operations."

I looked at Sapphire, and she shook her head. "Don't look at me. You're the one they revere."

I chuckled. "How are we going to go in there and demand our

right to Spats's position when the three of us can't even decide who's going to sit in his chair?"

We all stood there staring at one another in silence.

A throat cleared behind us, and we turned.

The old man at the desk smiled as he lowered his quill. "Perhaps all three of you should sit in the seat."

I looked at the others. They seemed to be mulling the idea over as well. The bookkeeper made a good point. We did each possess a strength the others did not, and we worked better together than apart.

"I agree," Sapphire said. "We each fill a role that's needed."

Both Reevie and I nodded.

"So," Reevie said, looking at the two of us, "who actually sits in the seat?"

We all shrugged at the same time.

Chapter 19

THE OLD SCRIVENER opened the door, and we stepped inside. As soon as we did, my magic disappeared altogether.

Sapphire, being the only girl in our group and the tallest of us, took the center. The arguing coming from around the corner stopped as soon as we stepped into the main room.

All heads turned to watch as we skirted the sitting area and made our way to the large table at the back. Reevie mumbled something under his breath, probably having to do with the fact that the curtains to the back window hadn't been pulled completely. I hoped he could hold himself together long enough for us to make it through the meeting. The last thing we needed was for him to have another attack, vomit on Kore, and start a tribal war.

"What's he doing here?" Cutter shouted, hopping from his seat. He drew his blade and pointed it straight at me. "Kill him!"

I was completely taken aback as Cutter's two guards drew their swords and charged across the room. Not one of the other chiefs did anything to stop them. Not even Red.

I shoved Reevie into Sapphire's arms and drew my own sword, meeting the two older boys head on. Without my magic, I felt as though I was fighting with only one arm, but with my training, that was still an advantage.

The first boy lunged, swinging for the top of my head in what is probably the most overused opening attack a fighter can make, and one of the easiest to defend against. I didn't even waste my time lifting my sword to block. I simply spun to the left and kicked the boy in the back of the knee. He went down just as his friend swung for my chest.

I deflected his blade with my own, then kicked him between the legs as hard as I could. He squealed and dropped to his knees. Behind me, Sapphire had already disarmed the first boy I'd sent to the ground and was keeping him prostrate on the carpet with the tip of her sword.

"Get them!" Kore shouted, and his guards ran to aid Cutter's.

Coming there to vie for Hurricane's seat was looking like a really bad idea. I needed to end this quickly before it got any worse, so I turned and yelled, "Flesh Eater!"

A roar sounded from the next room, followed by a high-pitched squeal—no doubt the old scrivener—as the doors burst off their hinges and Tubby came flying into the room, bedpost club in hand. Apparently, he'd anticipated our needs and had already strapped on his mask.

Cutter screamed at the sight of his former Pit champion and dove under the table. Kore slunk behind his chair, and Red, Noph, and the rest of the guards ran to join him on the opposite side of the table. Kore's guards didn't get much farther than Spats's seat before running to hide behind a large upright cabinet in the corner.

The two downed members of Cutter's protective detail curled into balls on the floor, both too scared to even move. The one whose fruit I'd just squashed was openly crying, his hands cupped between his legs.

Tubby ran straight for the table, and by the look in his eyes, if I didn't stop him, he was going to start dispatching chiefs one by one.

I hesitated. That might not have been such a bad thing. However, the last thing the tribes needed right now was more chaos. "That's enough," I shouted about the time the huge kid had reached Red's chair.

Tubby lowered his club and slowly backed away.

"Things have certainly changed from the last time I was here," I said.

When they saw that I was keeping the giant flesh-eating monster at bay, three of the four chiefs stood from where they'd been hiding behind the table.

Cutter remained under it.

"You can come out now," I said, leaning over to get a look at the Avalanche chief. Apparently, Cutter had managed to purchase, or abscond with, another one of his wide-brimmed hats. This one seemed a little worse for wear, having been crushed between the top of his head and the bottom of the table. "I promise no one will get eaten today. That is, if you're willing to act in a civilized manner."

Cutter crawled out from under the table and stood just behind Noph.

"Go wait for us over there," I said to Tubby, indicating the sitting area. It took very little prompting from me, considering the large boy had already been eyeing the trays of snacks and pitchers of drink on the tables. "Help yourself."

He happily obeyed.

I grimaced at the sight of the two doors behind me, one still clinging to life by a single hinge, the other sprawled on the floor about three feet into the room. The old bookkeeper was standing at the entrance, peering in. When he spotted me looking, he quickly disappeared back around the corner. I hoped he wouldn't call the patrollers.

By the time I'd turned back around, the other chiefs had retaken their seats and coaxed their guards out of hiding to stand behind them—all but Cutter's. Those two were still lying on the floor at my feet.

I motioned to Reevie and Sapphire, and we walked to Hurricane's spot. I could feel Reevie's effort to keep his gaze away from the large window on the right as I moved Spats's seat and we stood in its place. I couldn't believe no one had asked about—

"Where's Spats?" Noph finally said.

Sapphire spared a quick glance at me before addressing the Sandstorm chief. "We have no idea."

"What do you mean?"

"I mean, we haven't seen him since he abandoned his tribe at the Pit and made a run for it."

"That was weeks ago," Red said, glaring at me and Reevie. "Why didn't you tell me that the other day when you were at Wildfire?"

Kore leaned forward. "Why were they at Wildfire?"

"None of your flaming business," she said, turning her attention back to us. "Why didn't you tell me Hurricane didn't have a chief? Is that why you turned down my offer?"

"What offer?" Kore asked.

"To come work for me."

"You offered them a place at Wildfire?" Cutter asked incredulously, as though the very thought of me and Reevie joining Wildfire was the most absurd thing he'd ever heard.

"Why would you want them to work for you?" Kore asked. He pointed at Reevie. "And who is this, anyway?"

"He's our healer," I said.

Kore looked at Red. "Are you sick or something?"

Red's mouth tightened, and she reached for her dagger. No one besides me and Reevie would have noticed that she reached for it with her right hand instead of her left. "You want to test your steel and see how sick I am?"

Kore sneered but remained in his seat.

It was a good thing he didn't decide to take her up on it. With an injured arm and leg, she was hardly in a position to defend herself.

Cutter scooted to the edge of his seat. "If Hurricane has no chief, then I demand the right of acquisition."

"No!" Kore shouted. "That right is mine. Spats owes me a debt that he hasn't paid off yet. Hurricane is mine."

Sapphire, Reevie, and I all looked at one another at the same time. Guess we knew who those payments were going to. But why was Spats paying so much coin to Rockslide?

"And what debt could he have been paying to you?" Noph asked. "Spats owes me substantial winnings for our wager at the Pit."

"And what about me?" Cutter said. "Hurricane still hasn't paid for their attack on my compound."

"Our young grey-eyed friend there already settled that debt in the Pit," Noph pointed out. "Wasn't that the whole reason we were there in the first place? A fight to see who took the blame."

"No one won!" Kore said. "He let Flesh . . ." Kore stopped, suddenly remembering the former Avalanche champion was sitting not twenty feet away.

Everyone turned to look at the seating area, but Tubby didn't notice. He was busy washing down a mouthful of pastry with a half-filled pitcher. He produced a loud burp as he set the jug on the table and wiped the frosting from his mouth with his sleeve.

"He let him out of the Pit," Kore continued, not quite so loud as before, "which was the reason for the battle. Seems to me that Hurricane owes us all."

Noph pursed his lips and looked at the three of us. "He makes a valid point. One could say that it was your actions that caused the riot."

Noph's lack of support was unexpected. The couple of times I had talked with him, he seemed to be the voice of reason within the Guild. He had even gone so far as to say he respected me, but now it seemed as though an advantage had risen that he couldn't pass up, and he was jumping on board the wagon with all the others, a wagon that seemed to be heading straight for the Temple.

"And I blame Spats," I said, figuring if the others were able to throw blame around, I might as well get my two coppers in. "I was betrayed by my own chief, which left me with no other option. Every person in that arena was cheering for my death. What else was I supposed to do? Besides, if everyone believed the battle to be solely my fault, then why would Red offer me a position at Wildfire?"

Red glared at me, clearly not wanting to be dragged into the middle.

"Because she's a girl," Cutter said, "and too stupid to know any better."

Red hopped to her feet, her sword appearing in her hand before she'd made it all the way up. I was surprised she didn't topple over from her injury. "Come over here and say that to my face, you coward, and I'll cut off your arms and legs and toss what's left out the window."

With both of Cutter's guards lying unarmed on the other side of the room, Cutter didn't budge, but if looks could kill, Red would have been nothing more than a pile of scorched bones.

"So," I said, taking a moment to study the faces, "let me get this straight. You're blaming me because I took pity on a kid who'd been so badly treated that his hair had grown completely around his face, and his backside was crusted over with what looked like weeks of unwashed dung?"

Red's face turned green, and Noph held his hand up to his mouth. Kore, however, showed no sign of emotion at all, and Cutter actually smiled.

"Seems to me that I'm being used as an excuse to get your hands on another tribe's territory. But that would destroy all the tribes."

The table quieted momentarily, all eyes on me.

"And how do you figure that?" Kore asked, his thick forearms pressing against the table.

"Because it would lead to a shift in power," Reevie said. I was surprised it had taken him this long to speak up. He was never one for being shy when it came to speaking his mind, especially when he knew he was right, or at least thought he was right, which tended to be about half a dozen times a day.

"Avalanche is in one of the poorest sections of Aramoor," Cutter said, his face stuck in a permanent sneer. "The rest of you are living high on the hog; it's Avalanche what deserves those territories."

"Avalanche doesn't deserve anything," Sapphire said, matching Cutter's disdain with her own. "You've been stealing our stuff for years, and clearly it hasn't helped you any." She scanned the table. "We didn't come all this way to see who gets to chop us up. We came to make sure Hurricane still has a seat at this table."

"There is no Hurricane without a chief," Kore said, "which means—"

"Exactly," Sapphire interrupted. "Hurricane needs a chief, and it has one."

Cutter shook his head. "What are you talking about? You just said that your chief is missing, which means Hurricane has no chief."

"We are its chief," Sapphire said.

"We who?" Cutter pushed the brim of his hat higher on his forehead.

Sapphire pointed to the three of us. "We are here to vie for chief."

"You want to fight each other for the right of chief?" Noph asked.

Red scooted forward in her seat, a flicker of excitement in her eyes.

"No," Sapphire said. "All three of us will share the position of chief."

Kore looked at the others. "That doesn't make any sense. You can't have three chiefs. Each tribe only gets one. One vote for each tribe."

"We won't have three chiefs," Reevie said, taking over from Sapphire.

"But you just said—"

"It will still be considered a single seat. One chief but with three voices. We still only get one vote, but while each of you get to make that vote for your own tribe, it will take the three of us deciding together for ours."

"Sounds inefficient, if you ask me," Noph said. "What happens when you can't agree?"

"Majority will win," I added, feeling proud of ourselves at the way we were handling the situation. For the moment, it seemed to be working. "Which is another reason why dissolving Hurricane would prove a greater problem for the Guild than having us here. There's a reason why the Guild has five tribes instead of four. Without that offsetting number, you'll never get anything passed. You'll end up with a split vote. And that's not considering the battle that will take place just to see who gets our territories. A battle that will likely make the one at the Pit look like a tavern brawl."

No one spoke for some time, each considering my words.

"You can't just claim the right of chief because you want it," Red finally said. I could tell by her tone, she wasn't liking the idea of losing me and Reevie, but I had a feeling she liked the idea of one of the other tribes claiming our territory even less. "There has to be a majority decision by the Guild, followed by a price of admission."

"What kind of price?" I asked. That was the first I'd heard anything about a price.

Noph cleared his throat. "The price is determined by the Guild, each member exacting their own." He scooted his seat back from the table. "Which means the rest of us have a decision to make." He turned and looked at the three of us. "We will give you our answer next week."

Both Sapphire and Reevie looked about as anxious to leave as I was as they fidgeted from one foot to the other. Not knowing what else could be said that hadn't been already, we turned and headed for the door. I had no idea if there were any ceremonial procedures for leaving the meeting other than just walking out, but I had a feeling if there were, the rest of the Guild would be more than happy to overlook it just to get us out of the room.

"My apologies for the mess," I said to the old scrivener on the way out, and I ordered Tubby to lift the fallen door and at least lean it back against the wall. The old man shrank at the sight of the enormous boy. Once finished, Tubby smiled and waved, then followed us into the hall.

"I can't believe that worked," Reevie said as we trudged down the long corridor back toward the bridge. "Wait!" He grabbed my arm and stopped, his face turning pale. "That means . . ." He gulped. "That means I'll have to keep coming back here." He looked like he was about to faint. "Which one of you idiots talked me into this?"

Chapter 20

THE NEXT FEW DAYS trudged by. Like waiting for a pot to boil, the days just didn't seem to want to move. Reevie and I spent most of each day at the Temple but returned to the Granary every evening. It was nice having the place to ourselves once again, although at times, I must admit it did feel somewhat lonely.

Routine kept me going. I would wake, stretch, run through my exercises, eat, and then walk with Reevie to the Temple, where he would spend his time either organizing the infirmary or poring over books in Spats's old office. I, on the other hand, spent my time whipping our beaters and Guard into shape, focusing on martial defense training.

We didn't have much in the way of weapons, so my first order of business was to teach them how to use a staff and a pair of short sticks. The Temple was surrounded by trees, which gave us plenty of limbs to work with.

Once we'd cut and carved enough wood so that everyone had a staff of their own, I taught them the proper way to hold it. I taught them how I'd been instructed, starting with the basics and the routines I'd been expected to rehearse hundreds of times a day until they were ingrained.

Of course, with my magic, I hadn't needed the repetition like the rest of my fellow trainees. I'd only needed to perform the maneuvers once, and my body could automatically repeat them. But, not wanting to cheat my way through, I'd spent hours every day running the routines like the rest, a choice which had proven extremely valuable, considering the times my magic had been stripped from me.

After our first afternoon of training, a quarter of the beaters had ended up in the infirmary, passed out from dehydration. After a harsh scolding from Reevie, I changed our time of practice to the mornings, when it was cooler. Unfortunately, that meant either I woke earlier in order to get from the Granary to the Temple, or I stayed at the Temple to catch a little more sleep.

I wouldn't say the beaters had made great improvement by the end of the week, but they were at least able to make it through the routines without dropping their weapons.

"Protector!"

I stopped my work with one boy who was having a hard time

remembering how to place his feet and turned to find Muriel running down the path.

The little girl stopped in front of me, out of breath. Her skirt was covered from the knees down in dried pigeon poo, almost as though someone had picked up a brush to paint a snowy landscape and gave up about halfway through. "Protector, I have a message." She handed me a small piece of rolled paper. "One of the birds just brought it in."

"Thank you."

Muriel smiled but remained where she was as I opened the parchment, read what was inside, then rolled it back up and stuck it in my pocket. "It appears we are to have company this afternoon."

"Do you need me to send a reply?"

"Not this time."

Muriel nodded and ran back up the path toward the back of the compound, disappearing around the side of the dining hall.

I turned back to the beaters, who had stopped their practice to see what was going on. "What are you looking at?" I said, smacking my hands together. "Back to work."

I released them early for lunch so I could take some time to freshen up, which included a quick bath and a change of clothing that wasn't sweat-logged and covered in dirt.

The cleaners brought a tub to my assigned room and filled it. It had been a long time since I'd enjoyed a decent bath, which basically meant soaking long enough for my skin to get wrinkly. I was busy scrubbing the dirt from my fingers when the door opened.

I yelped as both Reevie and Sapphire marched in. I grabbed the closest thing within reach—my work shirt—and covered my lower region.

"What's this about us having visitors this afternoon?" Reevie asked as the two walked over to the edge of my tub and stood there. Sapphire tried not to smirk, and I pretended not to notice.

"I was going to come tell you as soon as I got out of the bath," I said sharply, trying, and failing, to give them a hint that I didn't want them there.

"Who's coming?" Sapphire asked.

"Noph."

"Did he say why?" Reevie asked, still oblivious to the fact that I was sitting in a tub of water with nothing but my wet shirt to cover me.

"No. The message simply said to expect him around the third hour. Now, if that's all—"

"That's strange." Reevie looked at Sapphire. "Do you think the Guild has already come to a decision?"

"I doubt it," she said sarcastically. "They're probably still sitting there trying to decide whether to even close the meeting. And without a fifth seat, they might not be able to do that, what with it taking a majority decision."

"As lovely as it might be to sit here and discuss this," I said, "how about doing it somewhere else? I want to finish my bath."

Sapphire smiled. "No one's stopping you."

"What?" Reevie looked at the tub, then at Sapphire, and his eyes widened. "Oh, right. Sorry." He grabbed Sapphire's arm and pulled her toward the door.

"You sure you don't want any help?" she called back playfully.

"I'd rather be kicked in the groin by a mule," I said with a smirk.

I waited for the door to shut before wringing out my shirt and finishing my bath. By the time I got out, my skin was good and wrinkly, and the water murky. I quickly dried and dressed, keeping one eye on the door in case someone else decided to barge in. One thing was for sure: I needed to put a lock on that door.

I met Reevie and Sapphire for lunch. Bull was there as well, filling us in on what the pickers had managed to bring in over the last couple of days. Or, more to the point, what they hadn't. It seemed that ever since our admission of not having a chief, our pickers were being pushed further out of the market.

"We can't let them continue doing this," Reevie said, waving his spoon at each of us in turn. "If we can't pick, we won't survive long enough for the Guild to make up its mind."

"Then I guess we'll have to find a way to protect our pickers," I said, slowly sipping on the leftover peppered broth Cook had re-warmed. It was meals like this that had me contemplating Red's offer. "They're hardly ready for battle, but I think with the help of our beaters, we might be able to find a way to keep Avalanche off our backs long enough for the pickers to do their work. I'll talk with them this evening after our meeting with Noph and see if I can arrange some sort of escort."

"That's a good idea," Bull said with a nod, fishing out what was probably one of the only pieces of meat in Cook's kettle. He grinned at the unexpected find and immediately stuffed it in his mouth before any of us could snatch it from him. The rest of us sighed as we watched him slowly work the chunk of meat around in his mouth for a good two minutes before swallowing.

I was too depressed to finish mine, so I excused myself and went to see if Reevie had any more apples stashed away in the infirmary. After spending at least a quarter-hour searching through every container on the shelves and digging through the unlocked chests, I finally concluded that he'd either eaten them or hidden them to keep *me* from eating them.

Finally giving up my search, I left the infirmary to help Bull and Reevie clean Spats's old chambers. It was the best room in the Temple for hosting guests, especially guests who were used to living in places that had *blue rooms* and *smoked sausages.*

Once the room was set for our meeting, I walked Bull back outside. "Gather the beaters and line them up around the inside of the wall, near the gate. Place some along the pathway from the gate to the main building. I want our guest to believe we can defend ourselves."

"Should I have them carry their staffs?"

I nodded. "And make sure to put the bigger kids near the front. We want to set a good impression. Oh, and keep the rejects inside and out of sight, at least until we're guaranteed that Hurricane remains a member of the Guild council."

"Yes, sir," Bull said with a firm salute. "You can count on me."

"I wouldn't have put you in charge otherwise," I said with an encouraging smile. "And stop calling me sir. You're older than I am."

"Yes, s—" Bull caught himself just in time, then waited quietly for me to release him. Bull took his duties very seriously. Half the time, he acted like a captain in the Elondrian Lancers.

"Dismissed," I finally said, and the big blond-haired boy left to round everyone up. I wasn't sure if there was an official position for the head of the beaters. Sapphire was the head of the Guard. But did the beaters have one? I was going to have to confer with Sapphire and Reevie about it and see if we couldn't come up with one for Bull.

In fact, while we were at it, we needed to promote Mouse to head picker. After our excursion behind enemy lines, it was clear the little pickpocket was up to the challenge, and by the way the others looked up to him already, he might make a decent sort of leader.

The bells in port began to chime, signaling the arrival of a new hour. *One. Two. Three.*

The third chime was followed by another bell, louder and more distinct. It was the gatehouse bell, and by the exhaustive way it was being struck, it could only mean one thing.

"We have company!" I could hear Toots shout from the direction of the wall.

If there's one thing I could say about Noph, the boy was punctual.

I ran toward the gate. Behind me, Sapphire was coming down the garden path with what remained of the Guard, Forehead at the lead. By the time I reached the wall, Bull had assembled most of the beaters. We hadn't practiced how to stand at attention before, so most stood in *first position*, which was the basic fighting stance that began their practice routine. The kids looked angry, but the closer I got, I realized they weren't mad; they were just trying to look tough.

I almost laughed. What in Aldor had Bull told them?

"Open the gate!" I shouted up to Toots.

"You heard him!" Toots yelled in turn to those working the pulleys. "Get those doors open!"

"Prompt as usual," Reevie said as he limped through the Guard to stand beside me and Sapphire. He glanced at the wall and the kids standing in front of it. "What's wrong with them? They look like lunch agreed with them even less than it did me."

I chuckled. "I believe Bull might have gone a little overboard in preparing our beaters to welcome new guests. I get the impression he wants to scare our visitors into submission."

"I don't know about the visitors, but they're scaring me good enough. They look stark raving mad."

The bracer lifted and the gates opened.

A horse-drawn carriage and a Sandstorm entourage waited quietly on the brick lane outside the wall. Noph stepped out of the carriage and started for the gates, his silver-tipped cane in hand, clacking every third brick as he came. He was the epitome of a gallant fop, and dressed to show it, from the feather in his black hat trimmed with a wide purple ribbon to the elegant silver buckles on his shoes. He stopped a few feet from entering and bowed with a flourish. "As representatives of Hurricane," he said, addressing me, Reevie, and Sapphire, "do I have your permission to enter?"

I noted he didn't say the *heads* of Hurricane or *leaders* of Hurricane, but simply representatives. "The *lord* of Sandstorm is most welcome within the walls of Hurricane," I answered, receiving an awkward glance from Reevie and Sapphire as we took a few steps toward the entrance, "and we are honored by your visit." I hoped my escalation of his title helped keep him in a good mood. We were going to need his vote in order to gain admittance.

Noph didn't seem to mind. In fact, he smiled and bowed once more in acknowledgement. "I thank you," he said, walking over to greet us a little less formally with a handshake. "Now lead me to the wine before I die of thirst. The dust on these roads is unbearable." He patted down his tailored suit, unleashing a puff of grey powder and revealing that his lavender jacket was actually a shade or two darker than at first glance. Even the purple sash around his waist had faded slightly from the dust on the road.

"I think we can manage that," I said, gesturing back toward the main building. "If you'll follow us." I had no idea if we could accommodate him or not. Reevie had uncovered a couple of bottles of something Spats had stashed away, but I had no idea what they were or if they were any good.

The four of us headed down the garden path toward the main complex. Noph's escort kept a few steps behind, followed closely by Hurricane's Guard and a few beaters led by Bull. The whites of the beaters' teeth were still showing as they stalked behind us like a pack of wild dogs. I sighed. I had my work cut out for me.

"A beautiful day for a drive," I commented, a sad attempt at small talk to fill the silence.

"A bit warm for my taste," Noph said, "but the breeze has made it at least tolerable."

I nodded, not knowing what else to say, and before I could

come up with another topic of conversation, we were standing outside Spats's old office. One of the Hurricane guards standing in front opened it, and we headed inside. Two of Sandstorm's Guard and two of our own joined us inside but remained by the door as the rest of us headed across the room for the prearranged seating.

Noph didn't need prompting. He went straight for the long sofa and plopped down, resting his silver-tipped cane on his leg. "Now where's those refreshments?" he asked, looking around the room.

The rest of us took our seats. Reevie joined Noph on the sofa while Sapphire and I took the two chairs in front. Bull remained at the door.

"With our pickers being run out of the markets for not having a chief," Sapphire said, "I'm afraid our selection of refreshments is stale cheese and a glass of whatever this stuff is." She handed Noph the bottle and he read the label: LA VANCHE.

Noph pulled the cork and took a whiff, then nodded slightly and reached for a glass. "It'll do." He poured half a cup of the dark-red liquid and took a decent-sized gulp. With a quick swallow, he exhaled and sunk back into the sofa's cushions. "Much better."

"We were surprised to have received your message," I said. "Might I take it that it has something to do with our request for the title of Hurricane's chief?"

"Has the Guild already come to a decision?" Reevie asked excitedly, not giving Noph time to speak.

Noph grumbled. "The Guild can't even decide whether or not it wants to decide."

Reevie scratched his head.

"Without a fifth member to cast a vote, we find ourselves locked, and we will most likely remain locked on every decision from now on. Spats, as stupid as he was, at least gave us the ability to have a deciding vote that brought us to a majority. Unfortunately, his vote was always determined by whichever side had the best offer."

"You mean a bribe?" Sapphire asked.

Noph smiled. "I prefer to use the term *business acquisition.*"

"Seems a pretty good arrangement for Spats," I said.

"Yes, he did tend to enjoy pitting the two sides against each other in hopes of enlarging the pot. In fact, that bottle right there," he said, pointing at the La Vanche, "came from a case he acquired during such an arrangement." Noph waved his hand flippantly. "Not that I could blame him. I would have done the same if I were in his boots. But with Spats gone, that's left us with a vacancy that we can't afford to have." Noph let his cane tap the rug under his feet. "Just between us," he said with a wink, "what really happened to old Spats? Don't get me wrong. I'm not judging. To be honest, I'm surprised he hadn't *disappeared* sooner."

"We weren't lying," Sapphire said. "We have no idea where he is. I never laid eyes on him once we returned from the Pit. His personal Guard said that he was in his chambers and didn't want to be disturbed, but after several days without hearing anything, we finally went in and found it empty."

"Knowing him," Reevie said with a sneer, "he probably took off in the middle of the night, having realized his plan to see Ayrion die had failed. If I'd just betrayed the champion of the Pit and lost,

I'd probably leave the city as well."

"So, you believe he left the city?"

"Well, I, uh, I'm just guessing. Where else would he have gone?"

Thankfully, Reevie had enough sense not to turn and look at me.

Noph leaned back in his seat and raised his glass in salute. "Either way, I say good riddance to poor company."

"Not to be blunt," Sapphire said, "but if you didn't come to talk about the Guild's decision, what did you come for?"

"Ah, the quintessential Guard, right to business. You'll find, Miss Sapphire, that there is value to be had in the pleasantries of a shared cup."

Sapphire looked at me, her eyebrows hanging over her eyes in a way that said she had no idea what Noph was talking about.

"Perhaps I came to judge your capabilities in running this tribe," he continued, waving his glass at Sapphire. "The watchful guard." He shifted next to Reevie. "The learned scholar." Finally, he turned to me. "And the mortar that binds them together." Noph took another sip and nodded. "Yes, I believe Hurricane will be in capable hands, if the Guild so deems."

"Seems it would be in the Guild's best interest to deem it," Reevie said, fidgeting in his seat. "But somehow, I get the impression you're here to do more than just determine whether or not we can manage without Spats."

Noph drained the last of his drink, then took the bottle and refilled his glass halfway.

"He wants to know which side of the coin we will fall on when it comes to making decisions for the Guild," I said. Noph's smile said I was right. "He wants to know which way we will be inclined to vote if he decides to back us in our claim for chieftain."

Noph raised his glass to me with a nod. The older boy was fairly predictable. He didn't do anything unless it benefited him. He was also smart, which meant there was always more than one reason for anything he did.

"I have a question," Reevie said, grabbing a book from the stack beside his chair. He opened the journal and flipped to a specific page. "Do you have any idea why Spats would be making biweekly payments to Rockslide? We have records going back nearly a year where every second week, Spats pilfered Hurricane's coffers to send gold to Kore, and for the life of me, I can't figure out why."

Noph's cane stopped tapping as he leaned forward and rested his weight on it, lips pursed in thought. "Interesting. Obviously, there was an arrangement of some sort made. Do you know exactly when these payments began?"

"Last fall," Reevie said, flipping back through the pages. "The month of Kùma, to be precise.

"I can't think of anything off hand, but if I were to hazard a guess, I'd say it was protection money."

"Protection from what?" Sapphire asked.

"From anything—the patrollers, other tribes, mostly from him." Noph chuckled. "Kore tried the same with me when I first took over as chief. Basically, if you're willing to pay him, he'll forgo the pleasure of sending out his beaters to harass your pickers." Noph shrugged. "A legitimate business venture if you can find a tribe, or chief, who's too frightened to stand up for themselves."

"Which Spats most certainly was," Sapphire said, tightening her grip on the arm of her chair.

"His brother wasn't," Noph said. "When Kerson was in charge, it was Hurricane that the other tribes tended to pay tribute to. But let's face it: Spats wasn't his brother."

"Hardly," Reevie said, still holding his book in his lap.

"And if you want to get out of those payments, you'll have to be willing to stand up to Kore, which could mean a battle." Noph looked at me and smiled. "But I have a feeling you're up to the challenge."

"Kore has enough to worry about," I said with a hint of sarcasm, "what with prisoners disappearing right out of his dungeons while he sleeps."

Noph's eyes narrowed as he studied my face. "Yes. Quite the uproar, I hear. It seems as though Kore has sworn his tribe to secrecy, but when people start walking through walls, word tends to get out."

No one said anything for an uncomfortable amount of time before Noph finally stood. "This has been enlightening. A profitable visit." He downed what was left of his drink and set the glass on the table. "Next time, we'll have to do this at Sandstorm." He smacked his tongue a couple of times, letting us know our quality of refreshments wasn't up to the standards he was used to. "That is, if there is a next time," he added somberly before walking to the door.

Outside, we picked up the rest of Sandstorm's Guard as they

patiently waited for their chief on the front porch. By the time we made it through the garden and reached the gate, we had picked up the rest of our Guard as well, along with a number of beaters, who, thankfully, had given up snarling at our guests and had opted instead to simply stare at them.

"If the vote were to happen today," I said to Noph as we passed through the open archway of the Temple wall, "how do you see it turning out?"

Noph stopped and looked at the three of us. "Cutter is a definite no. He craves your territories too much to want you in. Kore, on the other hand, could be persuaded if the right offer came along." Noph turned and started for his horse-drawn carriage. "I guess we'll see how skillful of a negotiator you are." He climbed in, and the Sandstorm delegation made its way back down the brick path, leaving the three of us to ponder his words.

Chapter 21

"ANY WORD BACK FROM KORE?" I asked, walking into Spats's old office to join Reevie and Sapphire. I shut the door behind me.

"Back already?" Reevie asked, looking up from the desk.

"Already? It's been three hours." I'd been all the way to the Granary and back, fetching supplies Reevie needed for the infirmary. Now that we no longer housed the rejects at the Granary, we were slowly moving most of our medicinal supplies over to the Temple.

"Three hours?" Reevie laid his quill down and looked at the stained-glass window on the side. "Has it really been that long?"

I sat down in one of the chairs facing his desk and placed the bag of herbs and bandages beside it.

Sapphire wrinkled her nose from the seat next to me. "You stink. When was the last time you bathed?"

I raised my arm and took a whiff but didn't smell anything noticeable. "Before our meeting with Noph. Why?"

She wrinkled her nose again. "That was four days ago."

I shrugged. "I've washed my clothes since then. Doesn't that count?"

"Not if what you put in them stinks like you." She leaned over the edge of her chair. "You sure you don't need help scrubbing your back? My offer still stands."

I gritted my teeth, and she laughed.

"Quit picking on him, Sapphire," Reevie said. "He's too easy a target."

"I know. That's why I do it."

"And yes," Reevie said, looking at me, "to answer your question, we have heard from Kore. A bird flew in not an hour ago." He held up a small rolled piece of paper.

"What did it say?" I asked.

"I don't know. I was waiting to read it till you got here."

"He better say yes," Sapphire said. "The Guild is supposed to give us an answer this week, which only gives us a couple of days to make Kore an offer."

Reevie opened the rolled missive and cleared his throat. "First, it says the Guild will be meeting on Seventhday at noon to discuss our inquiry, and second, the chief of Rockslide will be happy to listen to any and all proposals we care to make." Reevie laid the paper down on his desk and looked up. "Guess Kore knows why we're coming."

"We still have no idea if there's anything Kore'd be willing to take in compensation for voting in our favor, though," Sapphire said.

"Preferably something other than our coin," Reevie added, jabbing his pen in my direction. "You have to make it clear to him that we don't have the gold to continue whatever arrangement Spats made with him a year ago."

I sighed. "I'm sure that'll go over well. 'Oh, and by the way, Kore ol' buddy, we can't keep paying you, so please vote for us.'"

"You don't need to be smug about it. I was just saying."

Sapphire bit into one of the few remaining apples Reevie had been saving and chomped down. I had to find out where he was hiding them. "Maybe he'd be willing to accept something else."

"Like what?" Reevie asked. "We don't have anything of value he'd want."

"Maybe he'd be willing to accept a trade of favors?" she said.

"That's an idea," I said, grasping at ropes I knew weren't there. I looked at Reevie. "We could offer your services as a physicker. I could tell him we'd be willing to make a trip over there once a month to tend to any specific needs they have."

"I'm not going anywhere near there!" Reevie said, smacking the top of his desk with his fist. He looked like he was ready to stab me with his pen. "Volunteer yourself if you want to volunteer someone."

"What other options do we have?" Sapphire asked. "We're barely surviving as it is, and if they completely reject us from doing any picking, we'll starve to death. Right now, nothing should be off the table." Her face hardened. "A week more of Cook's broth and I'd sell one of you for a leg of meat."

"One of us?" Reevie looked appalled.

Sapphire cleaned under her nails with the tip of her knife. "Well, I'm too valuable to be sold."

Reevie and I shared a glance. Apparently, at this point, we were desperate enough to take any deal.

"Perhaps we judged Spats too quickly," Reevie said, looking rather forlorn as he stared at the open ledger in front of him. "Maybe it was something like this that led him to make his deal with Kore."

I nodded.

"The problem still remains that we have nothing to offer Kore in return," Sapphire said, finishing off the rest of the apple and tossing the stem in a nearby pail.

"Maybe he can be persuaded by reason," I said.

Both Reevie and Sapphire looked at me and laughed.

I shrugged. "We have to try."

"Do you have everything you need?" Sapphire asked, taking a step back to give me one last good looking-over as we said our goodbyes just outside the Temple gate. "I still wish you'd let me come along in case there's trouble."

"If there's trouble, then we don't need to have all of us in it. If something happens to me, Hurricane will do just fine with you and Reevie leading them."

"At least take Bull or Forehead with you."

"Or Tubby," Reevie added.

"No. I'll be fine. Bull needs to be here setting up escorts for our pickers. I work better alone anyway; you know that."

"Stubborn oaf," Reevie grumbled under his breath, then limped forward and gave me a quick hug. "Don't do anything stupid." He slapped his forehead. "Wait! What am I saying? Look who I'm talking to."

I smiled. "Don't worry about me. Just focus on getting ready for that meeting on Seventhday."

Sapphire took a step forward and planted a soft kiss on my cheek. "Just make sure you're back for it."

It was the second time she'd kissed me but the first time it felt like it meant something. "I will" was about all I could get out before I turned and headed down the brick lane toward the old merchant district.

Meeting with Kore was risky. Meeting at the Rockslide compound was even more so. And going alone was plain lunacy, but we were too desperate to do otherwise. The more injured among us weren't receiving enough food to help with the healing. We'd lost our first patient yesterday, and I couldn't sit around and watch as one by one, the rest followed.

Kipp's death had hit everyone hard, especially Reevie, who had spent the last couple of nights with the boy, giving him every concoction he could think of. Kipp had been injured pretty severely during the battle at the Pit, and as much as Reevie tried to save him, it wasn't enough.

The walk across Aramoor seemed to take no time at all, which normally would have been a good thing, but since the life of all the kids in Hurricane depended on me knowing exactly what to say by the time I got there, fast was not beneficial. Before I knew it, I was standing outside the Rockslide walls, no closer to figuring out what to say than when I'd started.

The wooden gate to the former lancer barracks opened, and I found myself facing off against what looked like the entire Rockslide army. Kore stood at the front like an Elondrian commander without the horse. He wore his typical green leather vest over a black sleeveless shirt that revealed arms thicker than my legs, each forearm wrapped with a leather guard. He looked ready for battle, standing head and shoulders above the other kids, even his own Guard.

"Quite the welcoming party," I said with a nervous grin. I wasn't sure what the protocol was for making an appearance at another tribe's front door, so I offered the same formal greeting Noph had given to us. "As chief of Rockslide, do I have your permission to enter?"

Kore turned and looked at those standing nearby, then back to me. "What?"

I sighed. "Should I come in, or do we talk here?"

"This way," Kore said. His beaters parted as he turned and headed back toward the main building at the center of the compound.

I followed hesitantly.

Walking through the throng of beaters reminded me of my march from the Justice Hall in the Lost City to the whipping post outside, my fellow Upakans all gathering to watch. I kept my head held high, not daring to show fear. My hands never strayed more than a finger's width from the hilt of my blades as I waited for the inevitable vision to spring to life.

None showed, which was a good sign, as long as Kore didn't have someone like Po working for him. So far, though, I hadn't felt any disturbance with my magic.

The compound looked different in the light of day, and without the heavy blanket of fog, I was able to better judge where all the buildings were. They were all similar in design: square walls of old stone and wood-shingled roofs.

Kore led me inside the main building. The floors, ceiling, and rafters were solid oak. It wasn't visually attractive like the Temple or comfortably elegant like the stone-block building housing Wildfire, but it was practical, sturdy, and would stand up against attack. It was the perfect location for someone like Kore. The perfect place for anyone wanting to shield themselves from outside incursion, should their actions provoke it.

I followed him past an open stairwell and down a long corridor that ended at a wooden door, which he opened before motioning me inside. I noted Kore had no guards posted outside what appeared to be his office. Maybe he didn't feel it necessary, considering he was taller, stronger, and no doubt meaner than any other member of the tribe, and anyone stupid enough to break into his office wasn't long for this world.

"Take a seat," he said, pointing to a stool in the center of the room.

I walked over and sat down.

Like Spats, Kore's decorating tended to lean toward violence. Weapons of all shapes, sizes, and uses lined the walls. Mounts of wild animals stared down at me from above. He even had a full-size brown bear erected near the back, its jaws open and paws reaching into the room as if ready to strike at a moment's notice. Unlike Spats, though, I had no doubt that these mounts were Kore's own kills and not something he had purchased in the markets for the purpose of making himself look more manly. He apparently enjoyed his hunts. How he found the time to enjoy them, I had no idea.

I suddenly felt very small, sitting on my stool as Kore loomed above me. It was clear that the position was to humble the one sitting in it, and to frighten them into agreeing with anything Kore had to say. I now understood the reason for the dark stain in the middle of the seat.

Instead of sitting himself, Kore proceeded to circle me. "So, what is it you wished to discuss? My time is short, so be quick about it."

I guess idle pleasantries were out of the question, let alone something to rinse the dust from my dry throat. "I'm here to find out what it will take to secure your vote on Seventhday."

"More than what you've got, that's for flaming certain." He walked over and pulled a long two-handed sword down from its rack on the wall to my left and lifted it high enough to stare down the blade.

It was of decent craftsmanship, recently whetted, and even

though there were several scrapes from use, the steel had maintained its shape. Kore slowly walked around behind me. My hand slid toward the hilt of my own blade when I lost sight of him. I purposefully didn't turn, relying solely on my magic for warning.

Eventually, he circled back around, stopping in front of me long enough to take a few practice swings.

"Surely there has to be something we can offer that will prove of value to you." I knew it was a long shot, but I had to try. "Like you said, we don't have much in the way of coin, but perhaps we can find something else of equal or greater value?"

Kore lowered the sword. "I'm listening."

Reevie was going to kill me. "As you know, we have a rather skilled healer at our disposal, which we could make available to you, say, once a month?"

"I have my own healers," he said.

"Yes, but none of them can claim to be a true physicker. Ours has studied under the tutelage of his father since he was old enough to talk, and his father was a renowned physicker here in Aramoor."

Kore grinned. "And what's to stop me from just taking him?"

"A battle you aren't prepared to lose."

"Lose?" Kore laughed, deep and menacing. "To Hurricane? A rowdy group of half-starved, half-dressed ragamuffins?"

"It won't be just Hurricane. If the other tribes believe you are making a move on our territory to expand your own, they will be forced to get involved, and the end result will make the Pit look like a simple disagreement between friends."

Kore's earlier laughter withered as he paced in front of his desk.

"Don't look at this vote as something you can gain," I said, "but rather something you can hinder."

Kore turned back around, a flash of curiosity in his eyes.

"Hurricane's a buffer." I tried using Noph's logic. "We are also the one thing keeping Avalanche from taking over the entire southern region. Sure, we don't have the richest picking fields, but allowing any one tribe to hold that much land would be dangerous because it would allow them to expand. And with Avalanche already encroaching on Hurricane's territory, they would have the greatest advantage. What do you think will happen if Cutter manages to spread across the entire southern half of the city? Do you think he'll be satisfied enough to stop there?"

I could see the wheels turning in Kore's head as he continued to pace. He finally stopped and sat on the edge of his desk. "There's a flaw in your logic."

"Oh? And what is that?"

"Cutter is loyal to me. He will do what I tell him to."

Kore's arrogance was going to get him killed. Cutter wasn't the kind of person who took orders, unless he could use it to his own advantage later on. "Are you willing to take that kind of chance?"

"Better to trust the enemy I know than the one I don't," he said, pointing his sword at me. "And I don't trust you."

"You don't have to trust me to realize my value and the value of having a fifth tribe on the council. Right now, you're split, which means any future meetings would be pointless. Vote for us, and I promise you a fair hearing of both sides."

Kore seemed to ponder my offer for a moment. Perhaps this was going to work. It had to. It was in everyone's best interest. Kore finally stood. My hands clutched to my pants leg. This was it.

"Time's up," he said, and started for the door.

I was confused. "What?"

"Best you were on your way."

Was he needing more time to think about it? I was hoping to have gotten an affirmation from him before I left. "Do I have your word you will at least consider it?"

Kore didn't say anything as he led me down the corridor and back out to the main lobby. Why wasn't he saying anything? If he didn't want to do it, he could have at least told me as much. We passed the open staircase and were nearly to the front door when Kore stopped and put his fingers to his lips.

The whistle was sharp and clear.

Before I could even turn around, the entire entranceway was filled with beaters. Kids rushed in from every hallway, from outside, from down the stairs. I was reliving Wildfire all over again. By the time I had drawn my sword, two rows of beaters stood between me and Kore. He was clearly smart enough not to want to get close enough for me to use him for leverage.

I was completely surrounded.

The kids watched, weapons up and ready for a signal from their chief. There was fear in the eyes of the closest, whether of me or Kore, I didn't know.

"What is this?" I demanded. "I'm here under a guise of truce to meet."

"Like I said, I don't trust you. And those I don't trust, I get rid of."

Surely Kore wasn't stupid enough to think he could get away with this. "The Guild will hear about this. My people know where I am, and if I don't return, they'll know who to blame during the council meeting."

Kore laughed. "The only reason the Guild is meeting is because your chief up and disappeared. What's one more going to do? Seems you have an epidemic of disappearing leaders over there. Just another reason why Hurricane should be disbanded and given to those who'll actually know how to run it."

"Who? You? A chief who can't even hold on to his own prisoners? Seems like you have an epidemic of disappearing people right here."

Kore's eyes burned. "Lies!" he shouted. "Lies created by the other tribes to belittle me. Take him below!" he ordered with a wave of his sword that nearly decapitated a couple of beaters who'd gotten too close. "Let him see firsthand how secure our dungeons are."

I tightened my grip on my sword, but even with my magic, I could see this was a losing battle. There were far too many of them, and I knew I wouldn't make it out alive if I tried to fight, so I slowly lowered my weapon and waited for them to take me away.

It wasn't like I hadn't already expected it.

Chapter 22

THE CELL DOOR CLOSED behind me and the lock snapped into place.

"I want guards sitting outside this cell all night," Kore said. "And if anyone so much as gets up to pee, I'll have both your heads."

I almost felt sorry for the two kids picked to remain behind.

Kore walked over and peered through the bars at the top of the door. "Enjoy your stay . . . *Death's Shadow*," he said with a mocking sneer. "It won't be a long one."

No need to guess what he meant by that.

His personal Guard followed him out, and I was left to lean against the cold stone wall and ponder yet another mess I'd managed to get myself into. The two boys sitting outside my door appeared too afraid to even talk, leaving me to my thoughts. In the distance I could hear the door leading out of the dungeons slam shut.

As frustrated as I was, I was thankful Sapphire and Reevie hadn't talked me into letting them come as well. Someone needed to represent Hurricane at the Guild meeting tomorrow. I could already hear the names Reevie would call me when I didn't make it back.

The fact that I was locked away inside the Rockslide dungeon was a pretty clear indication as to which way Kore's vote was leaning. Still, in all likelihood, the vote would be split. That was the most positive outcome we could hope for at this point. Although I wouldn't be too terribly surprised if Red decided to switch her vote to no in hopes of getting her hands on me and Reevie.

I closed my eyes for just a moment, and the next thing I knew, I was being awakened to the sound of raised voices on the other side of the door. I had no idea what time it was or how long I'd been asleep. Long enough to drool, evidently. I'd used my arm as a pillow, and by the time I made it to a sitting position, I felt a thousand pinpricks rush into my fingers. I must have been lying on it all night.

A silhouette overshadowed the bars at the top of my door, letting me know I had company.

"I hope you found your accommodations to your liking," Kore said. "I hear you Upakans are used to sleeping underground." He laughed. "I just wanted to let you know that I'm off to deliver my vote. Not that it will be all that necessary, since I have a feeling neither your girlfriend nor your crippled healer is going to be in attendance."

I stood and stumbled for the door, my feet still half asleep. "What are you talking about?"

"If there's one sure way to stop a vote, it's to have the ones we're voting on never show up."

"You wouldn't dare openly attack another tribe like that," I said, hitting the door with my shoulder. It didn't budge. "You'll incite a war."

"I'll incite nothing of the kind. Like you said, the Guild is split, and it will be in everyone's best interest to look the other way. Once I'm through with your friends, I'll be back to finish with you. I'm going to make an example out of you, hang your head from our wall. No one will dare mess with Rockslide again." He walked back down the stone corridor, his laughter echoing behind him as he went.

"Kore!" I shouted, and rammed the door again, then once more for good measure. I screamed my fury and kicked the stone wall. Pain shot through my foot, and I limped around the cell for a good five minutes, trying to think.

I should have never come. Desperate or not, it was a stupid move. Korc wasn't going to budge. He believed he had all the cards. He still believed Cutter was going to simply hand over our territory because he asked. I balled my fists and screamed as if it would somehow help, then slunk down in the corner.

I heard a noise in the hall and spun. Something flew past the door's tiny window. There was a shout, followed by a grunt and what sounded like someone hitting the stone. I hopped to my feet and peeked out.

The two guards were lying unconscious in the hall. One right in front of the door, the other a few feet away.

"It's about time!" I hissed. "What took you so long?"

Mouse's head popped into view, followed quickly by Bull.

"It took us a while to get in," Mouse said. "It's not so easy without the fog."

"Quick," I said, shaking the door, "get me out of here. Sapphire and Reevie are in trouble."

"Hold on." Bull pulled out a set of keys from one of his trouser pockets and worked the first into the lock. It wouldn't turn. It took four tries before he managed to find the right key. The lock clicked and I opened the door.

"Those keys we took the last time we was here came in real handy," Mouse said.

"Here." Bull handed me a cape, a green armband, and a sword. "Mouse managed to lift these from one of the barracks last night. If we can keep our heads down, we might be able to sneak out of here right under their noses."

I looked at the two guards on the floor while strapping on my sword. "Wake them."

"Wake them?" Bull cocked his head. "We need to get out of here."

"Not again," Mouse said with a huff.

I flung the cape over my shoulders. "I'm going to give them the choice, at least."

Bull shrugged and proceeded to slap the two boys hard enough to jolt them back to consciousness. He grabbed each and yanked them to their feet.

I stood in front of both. "I'm going to give you the same choice I gave your predecessors a couple of weeks ago. You can either come with us and join Hurricane, or you can stay and hope Kore will be in a good mood when he gets back. Your choice."

The boys didn't need to even take a moment to consider. "We'll go with you," they said simultaneously.

"Good. Let's go."

"Go where?" the boy on the left asked. "We won't make it up the stairs without getting caught."

"We aren't going up the stairs," I said, letting Mouse finish tying off my green armband.

"Then where are we going?"

"You'll see," Mouse said, and he took off down the stone corridor back toward the guard station at the front. I grabbed one boy and Bull grabbed the other, and we charged after him.

We reached the guard station and found Jayden waiting for us. I looked at Mouse, and he shrugged. "He volunteered."

"This way," Jayden said, heading into the hole in the wall at the bottom of the well. "Hurry."

It was hard for me to imagine this was the same boy I had knocked out and tied to a barrel inside the meat shed the last time I was there. He held the lantern as the others started their climb toward the top, Mouse in the lead. I was the last one up. Climbing seemed to go much quicker this time with only the five of us instead of an entire team of injured pickers, and it helped that my own injuries had begun to heal.

Once inside the kitchen storage room, we pulled up the rope, shut the door, and slid the shelves back into place, dusting around the edges to make sure we didn't leave any noticeable prints.

"We need to hurry," Jayden said, walking over to the door leading into the dining hall. "Cook will be preparing for lunch soon." He reached for the handle, and it opened before he could turn it.

"Cook!" Jayden squealed, acting as though he'd seen a faerie.

Mouse scooted back behind Bull, hiding his face.

She looked at the five of us and lifted a large wooden spoon. "What do you think you's doin' in here? Stealin' my supplies? I'll boil the lot of ya!"

"No!" Jayden said. "Uh, Chief wanted us to fetch him some fresh fruit for his trip to the Guild. You know how he gets on an empty stomach."

She pondered a moment, then raised her spoon once again. "Go on! Get out of here. If I catch you's in my food again . . ."

Jayden raised his hands. "We're going, we're going. I'll be sure to tell Chief how accommodating you were."

The girl grunted and blew her brown bangs out of her face as the rest of us took off for the side door and headed out into the small courtyard in back of the beaters' barracks.

"Phew!" Mouse said. "That was a close one." He patted Jayden on the back. "Quick thinking back there."

With Jayden in the lead, we kept together as a group, which seemed a lot less conspicuous than walking around by ourselves. It helped that we were each wearing our green armbands. We crossed back behind the barracks and circled around to the door we'd used the last time we'd come. Using Jayden's keys, we made it through and disappeared into the buildings on the other side.

Narrowly escaping was starting to become a habit. It wouldn't be long before my luck ran out. Then again, if Reevie were there, he'd say it was my lack of luck that kept landing me in these messes in the first place.

"Which way, Protector?" Bull asked.

"We need to get to the Guild." I placed my hand over my eyes and looked up. "We still have at least an hour before the meeting."

"Then we've got some time," Bull said.

"No, we don't. Kore's going to stop the meeting by killing Sapphire and Reevie before they get there."

"How's he going to do that?" Mouse asked. "He doesn't know where they are."

"No. But he knows where they'll be. My guess is he'll try it somewhere near the Guild."

"But there's too many people," Bull said. "The streets are crowded this time of day. Too many witnesses."

"You're right," I said and took off running down the street. "Which leaves only one other place: inside."

Chapter 23

THE WIND ON MY FACE drowned most everything out. I couldn't even hear the sound of my own feet or of those following me. All I could hear was the pounding of my heart as I willed my legs to go faster.

We reached the towering white stone buildings where the Guild held its meetings, and after quickly searching the surrounding street for any sign of our people, we untied our armbands and headed inside. I left Jayden behind to keep watch below in case Sapphire and Reevie showed up late, and to let them know they were in danger. Jayden kept his hood up so as not to be spotted by any of Kore's beaters.

We moved through the crowd and joined a large group of kids

who were being escorted up the winding staircase to the upper levels, no doubt on their way to one of the catwalks to enjoy the view. I was already winded from our run across the northeast quarter, but my blood was pumping so hard, I barely noticed. As nice as it was to be able to hide amongst others our age, the group was taking its sweet time getting up the stairs.

Two landings shy of the one we needed to get to, the entire group stopped as their instructor proceeded to give them a lesson on the history of the building. I tried leading our small group around them, but they were taking up most of the stairs, leaving only enough room for those coming down.

I spared a quick glance over the side of the rail. Still no sign of Reevie or Sapphire. We needed to get past these kids.

"What are we going to do?" Bull asked.

"Leave it to me," Mouse said, then disappeared into the group in front of us.

"What's he doing?" one of the Rockslide jailers asked.

"I reckon we'll find out soon enough," I said. I'd barely gotten the words out when someone ahead of us squealed, then another, and another. Within moments, the stairs erupted into panicked screams as the herd of kids stampeded up to the next landing.

"Come on!" I shouted to those behind me, and we charged after them, but instead of getting off at the landing, we kept on going up to the next level, where I found a rather devious-looking Mouse waiting at the top. "What did you do?"

He pulled out his belt knife. "I urged them to get a move on."

"We need to get out of here before the patrollers are called." I left the landing and headed straight for the catwalk, jogging across without sparing even a single glance out the glass. As soon as I reached the other side, I turned to see how close the others were. Bull was the only one still with me.

Frantically, I searched the bridge and spotted Mouse and the two Rockslide beaters back near the beginning; each kid had their nose pressed to the glass, staring in wonder at the streets below.

"Come on!" I hissed. Every moment we waited could be the difference between our friends being alive or dead. Mouse grabbed the other two by their shirtsleeves, and they raced to catch up. I noticed that the flower vase on the table beside me, the one Reevie had used the last time to catch his retch, had been replaced. "You can look later," I said. "We've got to find our people."

We left the landing and started up the next set of stairs till we reached the floor with the teal-and-gold runner. The farther we went, the more I worried. Something was wrong. I could feel it in the back of my mind. "This way."

We charged down the long corridor, stopping at each adjoining walkway to listen. Still no sign. Had Kore managed to get to them before they made it into the building? They could be lying dead in some alley, and I'd never find them. I stopped at the third crossing, and a faint noise caught my attention. "Did you hear that?"

The others strained to listen.

Mouse shook his head. "I didn't hear—"

This time, the muffled sound was louder, a definite shriek, followed by a voice I recognized all too well. "You gut-festering, canker-spreading sons of—"

"There!" I shouted, pointing down the right hallway.

"That sounded like Reevie," Bull said, chasing after me, ears pricked to see if we could hear which room it was coming from.

Another scream, this time from a girl, led us to the third door on the left. I flung it open and rushed inside, sword drawn.

The room was identical to the antechamber outside the Guild Hall, except this one seemed to be decorated in bodies. Five boys and one girl lay sprawled across the floor, none of whom I recognized. Three weren't moving. All were bleeding.

In front of me, five beaters with swords, bludgeons, and daggers were backing Sapphire into the wall. On the left, another group had Reevie in the corner, stomping him with their boots as he cried for help. Kore was nowhere to be seen. And where was Tubby?

"Bull, help Sapphire!" I shouted, and tore across the room. Reevie had stopped screaming, his body limp, but the beaters continued to kick.

I didn't give them time to even turn before my blade was sliding into them. It happened so fast, they barely had time to scream before collapsing to the ground, writhing alongside Reevie.

I knelt beside my little friend and felt his chest, then checked his mouth for air like he'd shown me. He was still breathing, but it sounded raspy. I wondered how many ribs had been broken. His face was swollen where their boots had connected. I started to move him, but a cry from Sapphire had me turning.

One of the beaters had stabbed her in the side with a knife. By the time I'd picked up my sword to help, she'd broken the kid's wrist, pulled the blade back out, and rammed it into his chest. With Bull's help, they finished off the rest of the beaters.

Mouse and the other two guards stayed near the door. Mouse had his little dagger out and ready, but for all his blustering, he was clearly too frightened to help.

I lifted Reevie and carried him over to where Sapphire was slumped against the wall.

"Where were you?" she demanded, biting down against the pain. She pressed her hand to her side to try stemming the bleeding.

"Sorry. I got here as soon as I could."

"We found him locked in Kore's dungeon," Mouse said, navigating around the fallen Rockslide beaters.

"And where were you?" she asked.

Bull grabbed a clean cloth from Reevie's satchel and pressed it against her wound. "We were breaking him out."

I looked around the room. "Why were you two here alone? Where's Tubby?"

"I left him at the Temple to protect the others since no one else was there," she said with a stern look at Bull. "I don't understand what happened. Who attacked us?" She glanced at the closest of the fallen, but none of them were wearing their armbands.

"They're from Rockslide," I said. "Kore told me this morning that the best way to stop a vote was to get rid of us."

"The vote." Sapphire grabbed Bull's shoulder and tried to stand. "We've got to get in there."

I grabbed her carefully around the waist and helped her to her feet. "You need to have this wound looked after." Unfortunately, the person in charge of doing it was lying on the floor unconscious.

"We need to tell the others what Kore just did," she said, ignoring my statement as she started for the door.

"How are we going to prove it?" Bull asked. "Kore wasn't here. None of these kids are wearing armbands. It'll be our word against his, and he'll just deny it."

"I think us showing up looking like this will be enough to sway the council that what we say is true," I said. "And maybe with any luck, Kore will even agree to vote our way if just to keep from looking bad."

"Well," she asked, "what are we waiting for?"

I lifted her shirt and pulled the red-stained cloth from the wound. Blood continued to seep from the hole, and I clicked my tongue. "We can't go anywhere until we get this tended to. You could bleed to death right here."

"No." She pulled my hand away and placed the cloth back against the wound, wincing as she did. "If we don't get in there before they vote, we'll all starve for sure."

"Blazes, Sapphire! Why do you have to be so flaming stubborn? Fine." I waved Bull over. "Here, take her."

Bull worked his arm around her back. Even Mouse attempted to help by keeping close in case she needed to steady herself by grabbing the top of his head.

"What about Reevie?" Mouse asked.

"I'm bringing him with us." I picked my friend up as carefully as I could. He looked as bad as I had the day Red had ordered Wildfire's beaters to make an example of me. The problem was, Reevie didn't have a *Reevie* to help him. All he had was me, and even though I had some basic field training for treating battle wounds, I was hardly qualified to do much more. If we made it through this, I was going to insist that Reevie begin training some of the other kids in basic field medicine.

The two Rockslide prison guards opened the doors as we neared. “What about them?” one of the boys asked, pointing at the bodies of his former comrades.

“Leave them.” It was one thing to sit outside my cell on threat of losing their head. It’s quite another for a gang of thugs to stomp a lame kid nearly to death. Those kids could wake up in the underworld for all I cared.

We left the room and quickly made our way down the hall. We had to get there in time for the vote. After what we’d been through, I wasn’t about to let Kore get away with this. The doors to the antechamber were open as usual as we stumbled inside. However, the doors to the main meeting room were closed, which meant they had already started without us.

The old scrivener rose from his seat when he saw us hobbling into the room. His eyes widened even further when he saw Reevie’s battered face and the blood seeping from Sapphire’s shirt.

“What happened?”

“We were attacked.” I looked at the doors. “Has everyone signed in?”

He nodded, glancing nervously behind us at the hallway we’d just entered from. “You didn’t bring that big boy with you, did you? We just got the new doors installed yesterday.”

I hadn’t noticed until he mentioned it. “No. He’s not here.”

The old man released a small sigh and walked over to examine

Reevie. "Should I call for a physicker?"

"How discreet are they?"

"Very."

I looked at Sapphire, and she shrugged, so I nodded. "But have them wait out here. We have business to finish inside first."

The old man winced as he stared at me over his spectacles. "Try not to break anything, will you?"

"I can't promise anything," I said, tightening my grip on Reevie as I headed for the door.

The scrivener quickly moved around in front as if afraid I was going to kick it in myself. Not that the thought hadn't crossed my mind. He opened one of the doors and we marched in, Sapphire leaning against Bull and me carrying Reevie. Mouse decided he'd rather sit in the antechamber with the old man than to be seen by Kore. The two Rockslide guards agreed.

Noph was the first out of his seat. "What's going on here?"

Red was the next up as she walked over to get a look at Reevie.

Kore got one look at me and was out of his seat as well. "How did you—" He looked at the others and quickly shut his mouth and retook his seat.

"We were attacked . . . again!" I said.

"By who?" Noph demanded as he and Red helped me lay Reevie down on top of the table. He was still unconscious. I wondered how long it would take the old scrivener to get the physicker.

"It was a pack of beaters."

Kore's face was red, his hands squeezing the arms of his chair.

He knew what was coming. I could see his mind racing as he desperately tried to think of what he could say to refute his involvement.

This was my chance. "It was—"

"This is ridiculous!" Kore protested. "For all we know, they could have had a run-in with the patrollers on their way here."

"You want proof?" Sapphire said through gritted teeth as Bull helped her into the seat on the end. "You'll find what's left of our attackers right down the hall. Take the first corridor to your left, then the third door on the left. Hard to miss the smell of blood."

Both Noph and Red sent one of their guards to check.

"Whose beaters were they?" Red asked, glaring across the table at Cutter.

"What are you looking at me for?" Cutter said with a sneer. "They aren't mine. If I'd have sent mine, they would have finished the job."

I looked at Kore, his eyes flaming. He looked like he was ready to spit nails.

"How do we know they were attacked by any tribe?" Kore said. "Were they wearing colors?

"No. They weren't," I admitted, noting Kore's slight exhale. "I don't know which tribe they belonged to, but clearly, someone didn't want us voting today." My head spun as I realized Kore had just handed us the vote. No one would dare vote no now and risk looking like the one who had sent the beaters after us. I wanted to lay the blame square on Kore's shoulders, but getting him to vote yes was more important.

The door to the main room opened and the two guards returned. "There's a healer out here," Toothless said as he retook his place beside Po behind Red's seat. The other guard found his place behind Noph.

I turned to Bull. "Take Reevie out there and stay with him."

"What about Sapphire?" he asked, glancing her way.

"I'm not leaving until we get a vote," she said, sweat pouring from her forehead. Her cheeks were as pale as mine. "We nearly died today to be here for this, and I'm not leaving until it's through."

Bull lifted Reevie off the table and headed out the doors and into the lobby.

"Well?" Red said, looking up at Toothless. "What did you find?"

"She was right," Toothless said. "We counted almost a dozen beaters; no colors, though. I didn't recognize any of them."

"Neither did I," Noph's guard was quick to add.

Finally. We had leverage. I looked down at Sapphire and her blood-soaked bandage. It wasn't how we wanted to get it, but at this point, we couldn't afford to be choosy. I could have pushed the issue further and told them of my imprisonment at Rockslide, but keeping Kore guessing was probably going to serve us better in the long run.

Noph tapped the tip of his cane on the top of the table. "Very well. A vote is what we came here today to give, and a vote is what we shall have. I'll start by giving a yes." He turned and looked at Red, and I couldn't help but hold my breath. Hers was the one I was the most unsure of, and it was probably the most important. It would at least give us a tie and not a definite no. But she wanted Reevie and me, and I didn't know how far she would go to get what she wanted. At least, not in this case.

Red twisted in her seat and looked at each of us in turn: Sapphire holding the bloody cloth to her side, and me trying to support her. She stared into my eyes for what seemed the longest time, then a calculated smile crept across her face. "I vote yes." She turned and looked at Cutter, but Kore spoke first, although his declaration wasn't quite as emphatic as the first two.

"Yes," he said, teeth grinding as he stared at the top of the table.

"What?" Cutter turned, his face indicating something between utter shock and undeniable anger. His fingers tightened on the edge of the table. Kore had left him holding the bag. If he said no, the rest would suspect him of the attack. Cutter bit his lips but finally nodded, unable to say it out loud.

"Good," Noph said. "It's unanimous. Hurricane will remain as one of the Guild, and you three its chief, provided you are able to meet the purchase price."

Sapphire's head shot up. "Spats did that already."

"Spats is no longer here," Cutter said with a smirk. "You want to be chief, then you've got to prove you're capable."

"What's the price?" I demanded. Sapphire needed help, and we didn't have time to sit around arguing.

"Each chief sets their own price of admission," Noph said.

Hurricane was too broke to even feed its members; how were we going to afford to buy our way into the Guild all over again? "What kind of price are we talking about?"

"It can be anything, within reason," Noph said. "For example, I can't demand that you jump out the window there and sprout wings. Obviously, that's not physically possible. Also, I can't demand that you bring me a wagon of gold. Again, not within reason. Nor can any of us demand," he said, sparing a quick look at Cutter, "that you give up any of your tribe's territory. For my price, I require . . . a new hat." Noph grinned. "Preferably purple. Preferably unique."

I breathed a small sigh of relief. The request was at least feasible. "Fine, we accept," I said, trying to move the process along so I could get Sapphire to the physicker in the next room.

Red was next. She leaned forward in her seat and rested her arms on the table. "I require the services of your healer once a week for the next three months . . . if he survives," she added. I was surprised to see the concern on her face, which she tried covering with a smile when she caught me looking.

I nodded reluctantly, knowing the scolding I was going to get for giving away Reevie's services without first discussing it with him. But we didn't have a choice. "Accepted."

Sapphire groaned beside me in her seat as she struggled to stay upright.

Cutter leaned forward with a sneer, and my heart skipped a beat. I caught the gleam in his eyes under the brim of his hat.

"I want fifty pieces of gold."

The breath caught in my throat.

"What?" Both Noph and Red came out of their seats.

"That's absurd," Noph said.

"That's not even close to being reasonable," Red followed, eyes flaring at Cutter. "What did they ask of you when you took chief?"

Noph pointed the tip of his cane at Cutter. "His buy-in price was a pair of good daggers."

Cutter looked at Kore, but the big Rockslide chief remained silent, seemingly contemplating his own request. Not getting the support he was looking for, Cutter turned back around. "Fine. Make it thirty gold."

Was he insane? "We can't even put food on our tables," I said, my hands trembling. It took everything I had not to draw my sword and put an end to his stupidity right there. "How in Aldor are we supposed to raise thirty pieces of gold?"

Cutter smirked. "Not my problem."

"It will be in just a moment," Sapphire said as she tried drawing her blade. She made it only halfway out of her seat before collapsing against my arm, her breathing ragged.

"Bull!" We couldn't wait any longer. Behind me, Bull rushed into the room. To his credit, his club was in his hand. "Take her to the healer."

Sapphire tried to protest, but her eyes rolled up into her head and she slumped over in her chair. Bull quickly lifted her and hustled out the door.

I looked at Noph and Red, but neither said anything, their eyes on me. I shook my head. This was absurd. How were we going to raise that kind of coin? "Ten," I countered, not having any idea how we could ever come up with such a price.

"Twenty," Cutter shot back.

"Fifteen."

Cutter looked at me, then at the others. "And a pair of new daggers."

This was beyond ludicrous, but my options were limited, and it appeared that the others were no longer arguing for me. "Accepted," I finally agreed, basically knowing it to be an impossible task. How were we going to come up with fifteen pieces of gold?

Kore waited until last. He was also the hardest to read. His earlier anger seemed to have melted away, leaving behind an eerie sort of smugness that had the hairs on the back of my neck perking. It bothered me that I couldn't tell what he was thinking. Would he concede defeat and offer me a reasonable price as a truce to keep me from talking, or would he join Cutter in making things as difficult for me as he could?

"Well, Kore," Red asked. "What will it be?"

Kore didn't move. He didn't smile, didn't frown, didn't so much as twitch an eye as he stared at me from across the table. "Since your arrival in this city, you have caused quite the stir. The kid who can't be killed. You've earned the name Death's Shadow, championed the Pit, started a tribal war, survived Wildfire's beaters"—Red cleared her throat at that admission—"and have now set yourself up to become one of the new members of the Street Guild. So, I ask myself, what test could be worthy of such greatness? Unlike my fellow chiefs, who want something for themselves—a hat, a healer, some gold—I want something that is worthless to me but priceless to others, something that will underscore your true skills and worthiness to be a chief among the Aramoor Guild."

"Are you going to tell me what that is," I asked, "or do you just enjoy hearing yourself speak?"

Kore leaned forward and looked me in the eyes. "I want the royal seal."

I was too dumbfounded to speak.

Noph spat his drink across the table, stopping just shy of Red. "Are you insane? We said *within reason*! You might as well ask him to host the royal family for dinner."

Kore maintained eye contact. "The Upaka are known for their prowess, are they not? Are you saying you are not up to the challenge?"

He was goading me, pushing me to fail or, worse, admit defeat. It was one thing to attack my ability as a chief, but he went after my heritage. Flame him!

"He can't accept that!" Red said. "No one could. That's the stupidest thing I've ever heard."

I planted my fists on top of the table. For me, I didn't care if Kore asked for the legendary treasure of Kumala; it was all absurd. There was no way we were going to be able to pay this. It had been a long shot at best. Even still, there might be a way to use this to our advantage. "How long do we have?"

"He's baiting you," Red said. "No chief would ever be forced to take such a price."

"You'll be given till the harvest moon," Noph said, before any of the others could voice their opinion. The harvest moon marked the beginning of fall, which meant we had about three weeks.

"Then I accept . . . under one condition. I want our pickers to be allowed back in the market while we meet the Guild's price. We can't meet your demands and have to worry about our people starving to death at the same time."

"A reasonable offer," Noph said, looking at the others. No one objected. Not even Kore. And why would he? He'd just given me an impossible task. Noph slapped his cane on the table. "It's agreed. While you gather the price of admission, your members will be allowed to continue picking *without harm*." He said the last with a stern look in Cutter and Kore's direction.

Cutter appeared too delighted to care. He could see our failure looming, and his chance to get his hands on our territory.

"If there's nothing else," Noph said, "this meeting is adjourned."

I rushed out the door and into the next room, where the old scrivener and another man were kneeling over Reevie and Sapphire. "Pull your hoods up," I said to Mouse and the former Rockslide guards. "You don't want to be recognized."

They quickly obeyed. Mouse didn't have a hood, but he did have a knit cap, which he pulled down completely over his face.

The man working on Reevie and Sapphire wore the white robes of a healer. He carefully used his needle to stitch up Sapphire's side.

"How are they?" I asked, noting the wrapping around Reevie's head and arm.

"Time will tell. They are very weak." The healer finished his sewing, cut and tied the string, then turned again to Reevie.

"How did it go in there?" Bull asked.

I winced. "You don't want to know."

I looked at Reevie, but instead of being concerned over the extent of damage done to his chest and face, all I could think about was his reaction when he found out what I had accepted while he was unconscious.

He was going to kill me.

Chapter 24

EVEN WITH THE LOOMING deadline, the next two weeks seemed a nice reprieve from the constant threat of starvation hanging over our heads. With the pickers being allowed back in the market, we were once again able to start earning, which eventually led to something besides peppered broth. Of everyone, Muriel was the most relieved, as she had taken to sleeping in the pigeon coop to fend off those hungry enough to eat her birds.

Both Reevie and Sapphire had been allowed to stay at Wildfire until healed enough to be transported back to the Temple. Apparently, Red and Sapphire had remained surprisingly civil during their stay, mostly on account that Sapphire was too weak to fall for

Red's goading, and Red didn't find much sport in hassling an injured opponent.

It had taken Reevie two days before he'd finally opened his eyes. I checked in as often as I could, but with both Reevie and Sapphire out of commission, the daily running of Hurricane had fallen on my shoulders, which made finding time to figure out how we were going to earn our tribe's place in the Guild rather difficult. I didn't realize how much the two had done until they were no longer there.

By the time they'd healed enough to be transported back to the Temple, things had gotten pretty out of hand. Clearly, I wasn't well suited to running a tribe on my own. For example, without someone there to make sure the cleaners were doing their jobs, there wasn't a single floor anywhere in the Temple that wasn't covered in dirt, and the rooms were beginning to stink like a dung pile, as no one had been there to empty the chamber pots.

Sapphire came close to ripping her stitches as she dressed down those who'd let it get that way, which, to my dismay, included me.

Once Reevie healed enough to sit up in bed, he ordered the books of accounting be brought in for him to look over. I think I saw tears in his eyes right before he spewed out an entire string of new medical curses that had me running for the door.

But none of this compared to the reaction I received from my co-chieftains when they learned what I had agreed to for admission into the Guild. If Sapphire had been armed, I might have been laid up beside Reevie with a hole in my gut. As it was, I had to duck a few jars of herbs that she'd flung at my head. Reevie had been too weak to throw anything himself, but the names he'd decided I had earned were enough to make a grown man blush.

"So," I said to Master Fentin, "I decided it would be best for my own health to come help you in the shop today." I pulled a book off the shelf and ran the feathered duster over it. The dust floated into the air only to land on the unsuspecting book beside it, leaving me to wonder why I was wasting my time.

Master Fentin plopped down on the stool beside his desk and sighed. "You boys have a way of attracting trouble like I've never seen in all my years. And let me tell you, I've seen some trouble." He unhooked the wire-rim spectacles from the bridge of his nose, blew on the glass, then wiped them with his handkerchief. "I could write a volume of novels from the stories you tell." He replaced the spectacles and stared at me over them. "Yeppers, I'd be a wealthy man if I were to sell such works of fiction."

"But it's all true," I said, peeking out from behind my shelf. "I'm not making it up."

Master Fentin smiled, then picked up a book from the pile beside his stool, read the cover, and tossed it on one of three other piles on the other side. He wasn't looking as stiff today, and his cane was used more to point out items on the shelf that he wanted me to move rather than merely support his weight. Reevie's mix of herbs and tonics must have been working, but nothing could hide the wrinkles on his face. He was old. Really old. At least sixty.

"Seems to me," he said, "that instead of spending the afternoon helping me clean my shop, you should probably be at home figuring out how you're going to get out of this mess you've managed to conjure for yourself."

I blew out my lips. "I know. But after spending the last two weeks looking after Reevie and Sapphire, not to mention making sure our tribe has enough to eat and clothes on their backs, and ensuring the safety of our pickers, overseeing the training of our beaters, and quelling the constant fighting amongst the tribe members, I had to get away to clear my head." I peeked through the shelves. "Besides, I like coming here. I like the smell of the books." I lifted a thin hardbound up to my nose and took a whiff, then sneezed. I'd forgotten to dust it first.

Master Fentin chuckled. "Guess I can't blame you. There's been plenty of days I've wished to be anywhere else but here." He watched the people on the street outside as they walked past. There was a sadness in his eyes I didn't recognize. "There was a time when the shop would have been filled with customers, but with each year, there seem to be fewer." He tried to mask his concern as he stood and moved around to the other side of his desk and started rummaging through the return pile.

"Why aren't people coming like they used to?" I didn't want to upset him further, but I wondered if there was something that I could do to help. Not that I didn't already have enough on my plate.

Master Fentin walked over to the front window and looked out. "This used to be one of the most-shopped districts in Aramoor," he said, "but it seems most of the more prominent stores have moved to the island, leaving those of us on the outskirts to wither."

I also couldn't help but wonder if the lack of shoppers had something to do with the state of the shop itself. Even with my and Reevie's occasional help, the place was looking rather dingy—the books were older with signs of wear and age, the shelves were in need of repair, a few more decent reflector lamps couldn't hurt, and having looked through his ledgers, it was obvious that Master Fentin wasn't the most meticulous when it came to recordkeeping. I wasn't a bookkeeper, but I could tell just by looking that there was a big difference in the chaotic placement of his figures all over the pages compared to the neatly logged rows and columns in Reevie's books at the Temple.

Unfortunately, there wasn't much I could do. I had to think about Hurricane. If I didn't come up with the price for Guild entrance, I'd be condemning an entire tribe of kids to a slow death. Most of the older ones would probably end up in the salt mines.

"You two look like you could use a break," Mistress Orilla said as she stepped out from the door at the back of the shop that led up to their personal residence. "I made some sandwiches, if you're hungry."

I caught Master Fentin's eye, and we both smiled. Leaving the duster propped against the book I'd just finished cleaning, I raced the old shopkeeper to the back.

I won. But only because I took a shortcut and slid under the table at the back instead of going around.

"Is that your new outfit?" Mistress Orilla asked, looking at my scuffed clothes with folded arms.

I looked down at the wear around my knees and the dark-red splotches on the front of my shirt, where I'd tried washing out the blood after our battle at the Pit. "Afraid so," I admitted with a nervous gulp. "Hard to keep them clean with everything I've been through." It wasn't like I had a second set available every time some new battle arose.

She clicked her tongue but eventually stepped aside and allowed me to pass.

The food was delicious, the company even better. Master Fentin and Mistress Orilla might have been old, but I found their friendship comforting. And even with the growing concern from the lack of business, I felt safe there. In some ways similar to how I had felt back at the Lost City before my banishment. They felt like family, or at least what I thought family should feel like.

I spent the rest of the afternoon helping Master Fentin tidy up the front half of the shop. The other half would have to wait for another day. Most people would have been annoyed with all the cleaning, but I found the work relaxing. The repetition kept me focused as I would pull a book, dust the front, dust the back, blow the side, then repeat the process.

Time passed quickly, and before I knew it, I was saying my goodbyes to Master Fentin and Mistress Orilla, hoping to get back to the Temple before supper. Master Fentin locked the door behind me and pulled the shades as I brushed the dust off my clothing. A strong breeze carried the dust down the street, preventing me from sneezing.

I took a moment to look for any lingering patrollers. Not seeing any, I started down the sidewalk. I'd barely made it past the first awning when I spotted a couple of boys watching me from an alley across the street. They moved back into the shadows to hide, but not far enough to keep me from noticing some green material sticking out from one of their pockets. I quickly looked away, hoping they hadn't realized that I'd seen them.

Clearly, Kore was keeping an eye on me. Or maybe they'd been sent to finish me off once and for all. I raised my hood and started south down Meadow Way, glancing back every so often to make sure they were still following. Instead of continuing toward the Temple, however, I headed due east and led the three boys on a wild-goose chase.

Back and forth, I wove through the crowded streets, never letting myself get too far ahead to lose them. No matter how long I let it drag out, the beaters never seemed willing to give up, sticking with me all the way to the riverfront. Finally, I managed to climb under one of the bridges until they passed, giving me a chance to turn the tables.

I followed them for a couple of blocks until they realized they'd lost me. At the corner of Birchwood—beside a cobbler whose leatherworking was strong enough to overpower the smell of the river—they huddled to discuss what to do next.

Being too far away to hear the conversation, I had to content myself with studying their body language. From the expressions on their faces, they didn't seem pleased at all. In fact, they seemed frightened. The tallest of the three took one more look around the busy street, then motioned the other two on. Apparently, they were giving up the chase and going home.

I started after them. By the time they'd reached the top of the Merchant District, they were no longer glancing over their shoulders to see if I was following. The three boys stayed away from the main avenues, keeping mostly to the alleyways between, some of which ran as long as the streets themselves. Behind us, the sun was beginning to set, and the way ahead was cut in shadows, which was perfect for me.

They crossed North Avis and into an adjoining alley on the other side. I followed. I didn't get much practice stalking these days, and honing my skills was always a welcomed distraction. The passageway was dark and ran quite a long way before reaching the next street up. There were piles of garbage and stacks of crates lying haphazardly on either side of each doorway we passed, giving me ample room to hide as I closed the distance.

I kept to the sides of the buildings where the shadows were darkest. The beaters in front continued in single file up the alley, which made what I had planned all the easier. My steps were silent—a practiced discipline I'd learned during my training—not that it mattered, since the taller boy in front seemed to be carrying on a one-sided conversation with himself. His rather boring tale of taking on two Sandstorm beaters at once masked any noise I could have made.

I moved up behind the last boy in line and placed my hand over his mouth, wrapping my arm around his neck with a hard squeeze. It didn't take long before his jerks stopped and I slowly lowered him to the ground, dragging his unconscious body off to the side.

The second boy wasn't much taller than me, but he was rather on the chubby side, with very little neck to grab hold of. So, I doused a rag with some ether I had left over from Spats's kidnapping and quickly worked my way up behind him. I'd taken to carrying the ether with me ever since the Pit. In one sweeping motion, I stuffed the rag over the boy's mouth and pinched his nose.

His flailing was never heard over the first boy's rambling.

Unfortunately, the boy was too big for me to pull to the side, so I left him where he was. The alley was dark enough not to see him, anyway.

The first boy was still talking about his heroism when I moved up beside him. "That's quite the battle," I said, doing my best to sound impressed.

The boy smiled. "It was." He turned and looked at me, and I punched him in the face. His feet flew out from under him, and he went down hard. His head hit the side of a barrel and sent him rolling. Dazed, he flipped over, wiping the blood from his mouth, looking for his friends.

I kept my hood raised. "I see you've been following me," I said, lowering my voice as much as I could without it cracking. "You should know better than to trail a shade. There's a reason they call me Death's *Shadow*."

The boy didn't say a word, his hands shaking. A dark stain appeared on the front of his trousers. I was almost too embarrassed for the kid to continue.

"If your prison couldn't hold me, then what do you think the three of you were going to do? I'm an Upaka. I make people disappear for a living." I made a point of looking around the darkened alleyway. "As you can see, your friends are gone, and you'll be next if you don't answer my questions."

The boy whimpered but nodded emphatically.

"Good. Why were you following me?"

"Ch . . . Chief told us to."

"And why would he do that?"

"I . . . don't know?" The boy recoiled as if expecting his lack of knowledge to be followed with a swift kick to the face.

"How did you know where I'd be?"

"We didn't. Chief, he sent several teams out. We're all supposed to be looking. My team just happened to be the first to find you."

"And what were you to do if you did?"

He looked up and swallowed. "We were to report anything we saw."

Kore must have been wanting to keep an eye on us to see whether or not we were managing to make any headway in reaching the Guild's demands. I wasn't sure why he would care, considering the price he'd set. The king's royal signet. A wagon of gold might have actually been easier. My problem was now he would know about Master Fentin's shop.

I looked at the boy, not sure what to do with him. I couldn't keep bringing home strays, and these hadn't done anything that could lead to their executions. In fact, they'd probably go back and claim they never saw me. I pulled one of my shorter blades from under my robe and leaned over, letting the tip press against his nose. He started to cry.

"If I ever see you near that shop again, I'll cut out your eyes and make you eat them."

The boy's face went white.

"Now close your eyes."

The boy whimpered even louder but eventually obeyed.

As soon as he did, I melted back into the shadows and disappeared down the alley.

Chapter 25

TWO MORE DAYS had passed, and the pending deadline was weighing heavy on us all. Reevie and Sapphire had finally healed enough to be let out of bed, not that we could have stopped them had we tried.

Today was the first meeting we'd conducted since my imprisonment.

"Finding a purple hat isn't the problem," Reevie said from behind his counting desk in what we were now calling the chiefs' study, not wanting to remind ourselves of its previous owner. "The problem is your rash stupidity. What kind of toe-fungus idiot lets Kore goad them into agreeing to steal the royal seal?"

I melted into the sofa and sighed. "How many times can I say I'm sorry? It wasn't like I was thinking straight. Blazes! I would have agreed to steal the king himself if it would have meant ending the meeting sooner. All I could think about was the two of you dying in the next room." I pondered that thought a moment. "So, in a way, this is your fault."

"What?" Reevie's head shot up, quill gripped tightly in his right hand.

"Sure, if you hadn't gone and gotten yourself beaten up, you could have stopped me from agreeing." I smiled, expecting him to take what I'd said as it was meant—a joke.

He didn't.

"And if you hadn't gone and gotten yourself thrown in Rockslide's dungeon, I wouldn't have." He threw his quill at me but only managed to stain the rug in front of the sofa where it landed.

"And if the two of you don't shut it," Sapphire said with a harsh grunt as she retrieved the quill and placed it on a table out of our reach, "I'm going to wallop you both." She gently touched the area where she'd been stabbed, then lay back down on the other end of the sofa, her legs stretching far enough for her feet to reach my waist. "The fact is, we're neck-deep in this mess. Doesn't matter how we got here. Only matters how we dig ourselves out."

"And if we only have till the harvest moon, then we've already lost half our time," Reevie said, as though we didn't already know that. His sharp glare at me clearly said he was laying sole blame at my feet.

"Sorry. I was a little preoccupied with keeping you alive."

"Let's start with what we can manage on our own," Sapphire said.

"Yes, like volunteering my services for the next several months?" Reevie said, his scowl deepening. Lately, he seemed to be in a foul mood, even more than usual. I had a feeling it was because Reevie didn't like being tended to. He prided himself on his independence. The thought of others having to take care of him while he recovered had clearly put him on edge.

"That, at least, is one thing we know we can handle," Sapphire said with a smile. "I can have Bull send out some of our pickers to find an appropriate hat for Noph."

I shook my head. "I tried that a week ago. Nearly cost us three of our kids. The type of shops that would sell a hat worthy of Noph's attention are the type of shops that can afford a patroller on duty. The first boy we sent was nabbed before he made it out of the shop, but with the help of a couple pickers standing watch, he managed to escape. The second boy never made it inside. One look at him and they didn't let him through the door."

"We need to try something," Reevie said.

"If you do," I said, "send what's-his-name. The tall, lanky one. String Bean."

"You mean Willis?" Sapphire asked.

"I guess. I don't know his real name."

"Why him?"

"Because his height makes him look old enough to get inside without the owners running him out for not being accompanied by an adult. Oh, and we'll need to find him some better clothes. It doesn't matter how old you look if you walk in there with tattered trousers and bare feet."

Sapphire nodded. "I'll see what we can do."

"Which brings us to the final two items," Reevie said. "Fifteen pieces of gold and the royal seal."

"Don't forget the two daggers," I added sheepishly.

Reevie scowled. "Yes, we wouldn't want to forget those, would we?"

Sapphire stared up at the intricate woodwork that covered the ceiling. "Even if some wealthy benefactor showed up at the gates today and handed us a bag of gold, there's no way we're ever going to get our hands on the king's seal. We'd be better off trying to figure out how to sneak these kids out of the city before the other tribes descend on us and claim our territory for themselves."

"We can't not try," I said.

Reevie leaned forward, pushing the book he'd been scribbling in out of the way so he could rest his arms on the table. "Not even Mouse could sneak into the royal palace. The only way to get in is to breach the gate, and the only way to get to the gate is to cross that ridiculously high bridge." Reevie shivered. "And the only way to get across the bridge is to pass through the bridge's gate, which happens to be guarded by two towers' worth of Elondrian Lancers."

"From what I heard," Sapphire said, "the last thief that tried looked like a pincushion after a volley of arrows rained down on him from the guard stations. So, unless you want to look like a porculus with two or three dozen quills sticking from you, I'd suggest finding an alternate route."

"And, of course, like I just said," Reevie pointed out, "there isn't one. And we're right back to where we started . . . up the bloody pus creek without a paddle."

Sapphire tapped my side with her foot. "What's got you so preoccupied?"

I raised my head. "What do you mean?"

"You have that look in your eye."

"I do? What look?"

"The look you get when you're about to do something stupid. Something that usually pulls the rest of us in with you."

"I'm sure I don't know what you're talking about."

Reevie huffed. "Well, let's see if we can refresh your memory. You get yourself beaten up the first day you arrive in Aramoor, forcing me to have to take you in; then you try to set the Avalanche compound on fire, causing Hurricane to take the blame and landing you in the Pit; then you release Flesh Eater and start a tribal war, after which you bring him home and nearly scare everyone out of their wits. You house a band of rejects, which leads to a mass influx of injured street kids looking for a place to live. You sneak into the Temple and manage to make the head of Hurricane disappear, forcing us to go before the Guild. You then decide to have a face-to-face with Kore, which leaves you imprisoned and me and Sapphire nearly killed on our way to the Guild meeting. Then you take it upon yourself to accept the most ridiculous price any chief has ever been forced to pay, all but guaranteeing us to lose the tribe. And . . ." He looked at Sapphire. "And I don't even remember what we were talking about."

"We were talking about the look on Ayrion's—"

"Protector! Protector! Come quick." A loud knocking on the door had Sapphire sitting up on the sofa. I recognized the voice.

"Come in, Mouse."

The door opened and the little picker raced inside, out of breath. "Protector, you're needed out front."

"Great. What's Tubby done this time? Did he knock down the south wall? Did he accidentally pull someone's arm off? I told you to quit wrestling with him. He doesn't know his own strength."

Reevie chuckled.

"No. You have a visitor. And she looks upset!"

"She?" I stood and started for the door, Sapphire and Reevie on my heels. "What have we done this time? Must be something bad if Red's crossing the entire city to see us."

"It's not Red," Mouse said, hurrying to keep up, his shorter legs being outmatched by ours. "It's some old woman."

I looked at Reevie, and we picked up our pace, practically jogging through the garden to reach the front gate. Why was it closed? I shouted up to Toots. "Open the gate!"

Toots, in turn, shouted orders to the watchers.

Bull met us before they'd managed to get the door opened. "What's going on?"

"Apparently, we have a visitor," Sapphire said.

"An old one," Mouse pointed out.

The gate opened, and Mistress Orilla stood waiting on the other side. She was alone, and it was clear she'd been crying. My heart pounded in my chest. Something had happened to Master Fentin. Had Kore sent more beaters looking for me?

I was the first through. "Mistress Orilla. What's wrong? What happened?"

"It's Fentin. They've taken him."

"Who's taken him?" Reevie asked.

"The patrollers."

"Why would the blue capes take him?"

"He's been arrested for harboring criminals."

"Criminals?" I was shocked. "What criminals?"

"He's been charged with being in league with the tribes."

"How did the patrollers find out that he was helping street kids? Did they say who accused him?" It had to have been Kore. I was regretting not having disposed of those beaters instead of just threatening them. Still, the way their leader had soiled his pants, I couldn't believe they'd been brave enough to rat me out.

She shook her head, still sobbing. "I don't know. I was returning from the meat market when I found the door open and the shop . . ." She wiped her eyes with her kerchief. "There were books everywhere, entire shelves overturned. Here," she said, pulling a parchment from her bag and handing it to Reevie. "This was nailed to the doorpost."

Reevie looked at the document. "It's a proclamation that on the authority of Lord Gerrick, the owner of this shop is being charged with harboring fugitives and is being sentenced to ten years in the salt mines."

"The salt mines?" Bull paled.

"How did Gerrick find out about Master Fentin in the first place?" Reevie asked. "No one even knew we were there."

A tingling sensation worked its way up my back and wrapped its chilly fingers around my neck. "I think it was me."

"You think what was you?"

"When I left the shop two days ago, I noticed I was being followed by a couple of Rockslide beaters. I gave them the slip, then cornered them in an alley and threatened that if they ever tried following me again, I'd make them disappear like I had the jailers."

Bull puckered his lips. "Yep, that would do it."

I looked at Mistress Orilla, embarrassed by what my actions had caused. "I'm sorry. I didn't know they would do something like this." I looked at Sapphire. "How did Rockslide get patrollers on this side of the city to arrest Master Fentin in the first place?"

Sapphire shrugged. "They have powerful friends. I'm sure an anonymous tip from Kore to the right person, and Lord Gerrick would be all too happy to make an arrest. You know how much that pig-sucker hates us."

"Remember," Reevie added, "he's the one who tried to run you over with his carriage. The one you humiliated."

My cheeks flushed. "Don't remind me."

"Kore did this on purpose to keep us from getting the Guild's payment," Sapphire said, her dagger suddenly spinning in her hand. "I'm sure of it."

"She's right," I said. "This couldn't have happened at a worse time. Any ideas?"

"Don't look at me," Reevie was quick to say. "If this is Gerrick's doing, we're all in pus-oozing hot water. Unless we manage to change his mind—which would be about as likely as Cutter deciding to give *you* the fifteen pieces of gold—Master Fentin will most likely be shipped out on the first boat to the Isle of Delga."

I balled my fist. This was all my fault. I had to fix it. "Then I guess we'll just have to change his mind."

"You did just hear me say how likely that was, right?"

"Yes."

"So, how exactly do you expect us to change his mind?"

"By convincing him that it's in his best interest."

"And how do you plan to do that?" Sapphire asked with the same crazed look that the rest of them were giving me.

"By doing what I do best."

"Getting us into trouble?" Reevie asked.

I smiled. "No. Embracing my heritage."

Chapter 26

"THAT'S HIS HOUSE," Sapphire said, pointing to the last home on the corner before the road circled back around to Bay Street. "That is, if you want to call it a *house*," she said with a hint of disdain. "More like a massive waste of space. Why would anyone want to live in something like that?"

She gripped the limb above her for balance as she leaned over to peek through the leaves. The slim but sturdy white oak we were sitting in across the street gave us the best view of Senator Gerrick's home and kept us from being spotted by the mounted patrollers, who seemed to pass by every few minutes. Apparently, those living in Bayside had no issue with paying extra for the privilege of keeping a constant patrol of their streets.

Gerrick's residence was the largest along the bay. A four- or five-story structure stood at the center with several offshoots, along with two outbuildings, probably housing the staff. There was also a carriage house, which looked to include a small stable, and over a dozen guards surrounding the place.

The guards didn't wear the crimson and gold of the Elondrian Lancers, but by the way they carried themselves, they could have. Instead, their uniforms were white with royal-blue accents. Perhaps they were on loan from the palace as a personal favor. Who knows, maybe all the senators were given such protection. All I knew was that it was going to make my job that much more difficult.

Even though the estate was larger and far grander than those of Magistrate Sirias's in Oswell, the man my father and I had been contracted to remove last year, the grounds were quite small. In order to fit as many homes as possible into Bayside, it was obvious that each estate was required to work within a confined parcel of land. The limited space meant most of the homes grew upward instead of out, making them seem like miniature castles, complete with bulwarks, towers, and parapets.

Lord Gerrick's home was no exception.

I stared at the grand monstrosity blocking my view of the ocean and found myself agreeing with Sapphire. Why would anyone want to live in something that big? "Gerrick probably has to use a map just to find the privy."

Sapphire laughed, then wrinkled her nose. "Eww, thanks for putting that image in my head." She stared at the twelve-foot wall surrounding the estate before turning to give me a thoughtful look. "So, how do you plan on getting in there?"

I set my jaw as I stared across the road. "Carefully." We were high enough in the tree for me to see over the wall, so I took that opportunity to sketch a basic layout of what I could see of the home, garden, outbuildings, yard—what little there was—and guards on duty.

Once I'd captured what I could on paper, we climbed back down and left the mansions of Bayside behind, making our way back to the Temple to prepare.

"How long do you think we have before they take Master Fentin?" I asked her as we jogged down Bay Street in front of the shipping yards.

"They aren't likely to leave in the middle of the night. Most ships embark at first light."

"So, if I don't find a way to set him free tonight, I won't get another chance." I would have liked to spend two or three nights scouting the place—getting a better idea of where the buildings were located, what they were being used for, where the doors and windows led, the rotation of the guards, and a host of other minute details—but Master Fentin didn't have time. As much as I wanted to charge the gates right then, getting arrested alongside Master Fentin wasn't going to help anyone. The cover of darkness would be my greatest ally.

Unfortunately, I didn't have the gear available that my father and I had during our contract in Oswell. I really needed a grappling hook. I was either going to have to come up with some sort of substitute or manage to do without.

We made it back to the Temple in good time and met with Reevie and Bull to discuss my upcoming adventure.

"Are you planning on going like that?" Reevie asked, sitting at his desk.

"Like what?" I looked down. "Dressed? Would you prefer I went in the nude?"

Sapphire giggled as she sat in the chair opposite mine in front of the desk. "That would scare anyone into submission."

I sneered, if only to keep from chuckling.

"I think he means do you plan on wearing something a little more . . . inconspicuous," she said. "Tan trousers and a white tunic are hardly a good disguise."

"It's all I have. You got a better idea? One that doesn't involve me running around naked."

"You could wear the black cape we stole from Rockslide," Bull said, leaning against one of the bookshelves on the left side.

I shook my head. It was obvious none of them had ever tried climbing a wall before. "I'd rather go naked. A cape is too constricting, too easy to get snagged on unexpected objects."

"Paint," Reevie spurted out. "You could use some of Sapphire's face paint."

The last time I'd seen her wear it was during our battle outside the Avalanche compound. Come to think of it, she might have worn it at the Pit, but I couldn't remember.

Sapphire twisted in her seat. "That's a good idea. Instead of wearing a white shirt, which is sure to be spotted in the moonlight, I could paint your chest and back. In fact," she said with a sly wink, "I could paint all of you."

"Over my dead body."

"I've got a spare set of long underpants you can have," Bull offered. "You could paint them."

"There," Reevie said, "you see? You don't need to run around Aramoor naked after all. You can run around in your underpants." He leaned back and roared, nearly toppling his chair. He grabbed the side of the desk to keep from falling.

The other two joined in.

"This is hardly the time for jokes," I said, smothering my own laughter. "Master Fentin's life is on the line."

The room quieted.

I looked at Sapphire. "How fast does this stuff dry? We only have the day. I don't want to go running around town leaving a trail of wet paint."

"It's a special mix my father taught me. Dries quick. You'll see."

Reevie laid his quill beside the ink jar. "Seems we have plenty to get ready for, then. Best we get to it."

We needed the afternoon to assemble whatever gear we had available. It reminded me in a way of my time in the Lost City, of how my mother would help my father prepare for his contracts. How she would read over the list while he organized his travel bags. My chest ached, and I found it hard to breathe as the memories flooded back. I missed them terribly.

By the time I'd made it to Sapphire's chambers for my painting, the sun had already begun to set. Sapphire held a sly smirk as I stood in her washroom, half-naked, waiting to be slathered in paint. Bull's underpants hung in the corner from where she had painted them earlier in hopes of having them dry by the time I put them on.

"Where's the brush?" I asked.

"There isn't one," she said, a smile creeping across her face. "I use my hands." She quickly stuck them into the bucket of black paint, then rubbed them across my shoulders. I jerked slightly at her touch. It was cold at first, but the longer she rubbed, the warmer her hands became. The smell of the paint was strong and acidic. It burned my nose at first but eventually calmed.

Sapphire's strokes were slow and smooth, and I found myself closing my eyes and enjoying the feeling of her hands. My skin tingled on contact with each new layer, her touch sending bumps down my arms. She didn't say anything as she worked, which made the experience even more alluring.

It took a while. She spent extra time on my chest and stomach, but she finally managed to cover every inch of my arms and torso. I looked at myself in a mirror and smiled. "This might actually work."

"Now for your face." She carefully applied the paint, but instead of simply adding streaks and lines like she did to hers during the battle, she covered the entire thing, even into my hairline.

The paint was sticky at first, and as it dried and hardened, I found it rather uncomfortable, making my movements stiff. It eventually split around the elbows and wrists, anywhere a joint could bend and force the paint to separate. I looked in the mirror and almost took a step back. I looked positively hideous. The black paint made my grey eyes even more feral.

I loved it.

"This is great," I said, trying not to get too excited. "Reminds me of a time while I was on the *Wind Binder* and we bathed a group of refugees in flour water. By the time we were done, they looked like walking corpses."

Sapphire wrinkled her nose. "And why would you do that?"

"We did it to frighten the living Pits out of a band of river pirates who were trying to commandeer our ship. I've never seen grown men dive off the side so fast as when they saw those white bodies come up out of the ship's hold."

"I haven't heard that story before. You'll have to tell me sometime." She took a step back and admired her work with a proud grin. "You do look scary, though." She glanced down at my waistline. "Sure you don't want me to do the rest of you?"

"I'm sure," I said.

Sapphire grabbed Bull's underpants off the line and tossed them to me. "These should be dry by now."

Sapphire turned around to give me some privacy while I put them on. They were still a little tacky and quite stiff, requiring me to bend and stretch in order to loosen them up. But after a few knee-bends and a short bout of hopping up and down, I felt I was ready, or at least as ready as I was going to be, wearing a leathery second skin.

Sapphire opened the door and stuck her head out in the hall. "He's ready."

Reevie and Bull stepped in to get a look. Bull's eyes bulged, and Reevie actually recoiled, taking a step toward the door. "You look terrible," he said.

I smiled. "Thank you."

"Scariest thing I've ever seen," Bull agreed. "Maybe even creepier than Tubby's mask. You look like some kind of tar monster with glowing eyes." He walked over and touched the paint on my arm. "Talk about having a thick skin," he joked. "I wish I could be there to see the look on Gerrick's face when you show up."

There was a knock at the door. Sapphire opened it, and Mouse walked in, holding a thin rod of metal in his hand. "I found this in . . ." One look at me and he screamed at the top of his lungs and fled, but instead of running out the door, he ran straight into it, knocking himself backward and dropping the hook onto the floor.

"Mouse, it's me," I said, holding up my hands. "It's Ayrion."

Mouse rubbed his forehead where he'd planted it against the edge of the door and looked up. "Protector?"

I smiled, and he shrank back even further.

"Yes, it's me. Now, what's that you brought?"

Mouse leaned over and picked up the object. "It's the end of an old pruning hook I found in one of the storage rooms. I overheard you mention something about needing a grapple, and I figured it might come in handy. See?" he said, spinning the metal around so it hooked the back of his neck. "It can catch things."

I took the tool from Mouse. The tip of the old pruner reminded me in a way of a hawk. The thick end curved sharply to a point, much like the bird's talons. It wasn't all that heavy, which would make it easier to throw, but it was missing the other two teeth a normal grapple would have, which would make it harder to catch its grip. Regardless, it was better than nothing.

"Thank you, Mouse," I said, offering him an encouraging smile. "This is exactly what I was looking for."

Mouse beamed and then dashed out the door, clearly not wanting to be around the scary tar creature any longer than he had to.

"Have you got everything you need?" Sapphire asked.

"I don't know about everything I *need* . . . but I've packed what we have."

"Hopefully, it'll be enough," Reevie said, unease in his voice. "Are we sure there isn't another way to help Master Fentin besides sneaking into Gerrick's home? What if we snuck into the patrollers' office and broke him out like you did with the pickers?"

"I considered that. But I had a way in that time, and the patroller cells are going to be better guarded than Rockslide's. If by some twist of fate we managed to get in, we'd never get back out without a fight, risking Master Fentin's life in the process. Besides, even if we managed to get him out, he and Mistress Orilla would never be able to go back home again. They'd be left with nothing. You know how much that shop means to them." I shook my head. "Our best option is going to be forcing the senator to have Fentin released."

"And what makes you think he's going to do that?"

I raised the pruning hook like a weapon. "I'm not going to give him a choice."

Back in the chiefs' study, I gathered my bag as I readied myself for what was coming. I hadn't eaten all that much for supper. I never felt hungry just before a mission, my nerves always overcoming my appetite. This time was no different. Even more so since the stakes were so high.

"The sun is almost down," Sapphire said, walking in with a

half-eaten apple. "It dropped below the buildings in the old market at least a half hour ago."

I nodded and gave the rope I had tied to the pruning hook one final tug. "It'll have to do."

On the way to the main gate, the kids we passed stopped to stare. Most froze, eyes filled with fear. Some shrieked. A few took off running back toward the main building. I couldn't blame them. I was gruesome enough to frighten the faeries themselves if I happened to come across one.

At the gate, I received a few lackluster words of encouragement and one somber hug from Reevie. If I didn't know any better, I would have thought that they didn't actually expect me to return. I started down the brick drive toward town, carrying my pack in my hand so the strap didn't rub the paint off my shoulder.

It was a strange feeling, walking around town in nothing but underpants. Not that it was the first time. My arrival in Aramoor had left me in somewhat the same predicament. Except this time, it was by choice. I had to keep looking down to reassure myself that I wasn't naked and that the paint would keep me from being seen. Still, I felt on edge. I didn't have the first clue how I was going to pull it off.

No Upaka would have taken a contract like this without suitable preparation. The reason my people remained so effective wasn't our training, which was extensive; it wasn't even our prowess, which was formidable; it was the methodical preparation we used to accomplish our missions. We didn't do anything halfway. We also didn't take a job we didn't already know we could handle. We planned for everything.

"No one plans to fail," I could hear my instructors say, *"except those who never plan to succeed."*

My problem was that the world outside the Lost City didn't seem to operate in the same way. Ever since coming to Aramoor, I'd been forced to jump from one bad situation to the next without any opportunity to plan. The fact that I had made it this far was sheer dumb luck and magic. And here I was, once again running headlong into the unknown.

The buildings to either side of me cast long shadows across the streets, the moon barely peeking above the rooftops. I melted into the darkness as though I were part of it. At one point, a group of sailors passed by on the same side of the street and never realized I was there. I stood against a tree with my pack behind me and watched as they strolled along, unaware of my presence. I was rather enjoying this new sense of invisibility.

It didn't take me long to get through the Maze, cross over the Tansian, and pass beyond the shipyards. I kept to the backstreets, only crossing the main thoroughfares when there was no other avenue to take. Even then, I limited it to the sides of buildings where the shadows were darkest. Once I reached Bayside, I kept behind the sculpted shrubberies and undergrowth that fronted most of the residents' yards.

I stopped on the opposite side of the cobbles from Gerrick's estate and climbed the same tree Sapphire and I had been in earlier that day, just to see what I could of the patrol on the other side of the wall. It wasn't promising. Even from across the street, I could see a cluster of guards near the front garden.

This was it. Master Fentin's life was in my hands, and I couldn't let him down. I waited for the next mounted patrol to pass and then climbed down. *Here goes nothing*, I thought, and raced across the street.

Chapter 27

BY THE TIME I REACHED the corner of the twelve-foot stone wall surrounding Gerrick's home, my heart was pouning like a razorback with a mouthful of kiskis weed. According to Hobb, it was a plant that grew in the deeper regions of the Slags, and apart from its rather bitter taste, it was a strong stimulant that left you hungry and looking for someone to kiss. Hence the name. It had been outlawed in Oswell for its addictive nature.

I wouldn't have minded a little right about now, just to take the edge off.

I took a deep breath to steel my nerves as I peeked around the corner to see if the way was clear. Nothing but the wall and a walkway around it. The guards patrolling the outer perimeter were still on the opposite side of the house. I had timed how long it took them to make a full rotation, which only gave me a few minutes to make it up and over before they rounded the back corner and spotted me.

I followed the wall down the left side of the estate and stopped beside a section that I'd marked on my paper, indicating shrubs on the inside that were tall enough to hide behind. I pulled my makeshift grapple from the bag, unwound the rope, and tossed the metal hook up. As soon as it reached the top, I gave it a tug, hoping to snag the backside of the lip.

It didn't, and I jumped out of the way to keep from getting clubbed on the top of the head as the grapple plunged back to the ground. Quickly, I grabbed the hook and tried again, giving another sharp pull just as soon as it swung over the top. This time, it stuck.

I didn't have time to test how secure it was, so I donned my satchel and started up the rope. The wall seemed taller now than it had from my perch in the tree across the street. A fall from this height might not kill me, but it could certainly break a bone if I wasn't careful.

Three-quarters of the way up, the hook slipped, and my fingers clamped down on the rope as I struggled not to move, afraid the grapple would give way altogether and send me hurtling to the bottom. Angling to the left, I quickly scanned the path leading around to the backside of the wall. The guards would be coming around the far end at any moment. I had to hurry.

Carefully, I pulled my knees to my chest and locked my feet around the rope, using them to balance as I slowly stood and reached for the top. My fingers barely scraped the edge. I wasn't close enough. I grabbed the rope again, locking my feet higher, then slowly pushed myself up. My fingers found a firm grip around the stone, and I pulled myself up just as the guards walked around the corner.

I flipped over and laid flat against the top of the wall as I tried frantically to pull the rope up before the guards arrived. The top of the wall was barely wide enough for me to lie on without falling, which forced me to hang one leg over the inside to keep my balance as I hoisted the rope up. My hands were sweating as I pulled, the footsteps drawing closer. With one last swift jerk, the tail end slid over the top and dropped harmlessly onto the other side.

I didn't move, still holding the metal hook in my hand as I listened to the footsteps pass below. I didn't know which was louder, their boots or my heart. Soon enough, their footfalls disappeared as they rounded the far corner.

I released a sigh of relief that left me a bit lightheaded, then turned to study the small yard on the inside of the wall. Most of the guards were at the front, where the torchlight was the brightest around the garden. A couple stood at the back, but as far as I could tell, there were no guards patrolling the side of the estate where I was—another reason I had chosen this section to climb over.

All but two of the windows on this side of the house were dark, their curtains drawn. I placed my hook on the top of the wall and slid over the side while no one was looking and lowered myself halfway down before dropping the rest of the way. Once on the ground, I freed the grapple and stuffed it back in my sack before making my way around the back of the shrubbery to the first opening.

The only trees available for cover were at the back of the estate, leaving nothing but a well-manicured lawn between me and Gerrick's home.

Everything was quiet. Even the guards gathered at the front kept their conversations to a minimum, no doubt to keep from disturbing the senator's rest.

Directly across from where I knelt was the side entrance to the estate. It jutted out from the wall about six to eight feet, like a small enclosed veranda tacked on to the side of the home.

From its roof, it couldn't have been more than a three-foot jump up to the balcony on the second floor. I had no idea which room that particular balcony belonged to, but since it had remained unlit, I doubted it was one of the family rooms. However, from *that* balcony, I stood a good chance of reaching the one above it on the third floor where a light had just been extinguished a few moments before.

It had to be one of the bedchambers. I hoped it was Gerrick's.

On my hands and knees, I started across the narrow strip of grass between the outer wall and the covered entrance ahead. The grass was thick and dry, the evening dew not yet settled.

I tried to imagine what the Temple must have looked like with its yard covered in grass. If we ever managed to make it through the Guild's testing and found a way to get our feet back under us, perhaps we could think about planting some more greenery, even if just around the walkways. I knew my spot by the fountain could definitely benefit from having something softer to sit on.

With luck, I made it across and up against the side of the house. Thick vines of ivy growing up the light-grey stone made it easier for me to remain hidden. For a brief moment, I considered scaling the vines and even grabbed a handful, but when they easily ripped away from the wall, I decided to stick with my original plan.

Keeping a close eye on the guards at the front, I eased my way around the covered entrance. No light was coming from inside, just a single torch resting in a bracket just outside the door.

On the far side, I looked up at the roof. It was too high to simply grab and pull myself up, so I used the house's wall as a kick-off to gain some leverage. Not wanting to make the jump carrying my satchel, I unhooked it and tossed it up on the clay tiles ahead of me. With a quick burst of speed, I ran straight at the wall.

My foot caught the lower stone encasement, and I kicked off, leaping sideways into the air and catching the edge of the gutter. What was left of the paint on my hands after my climb up the rope kept my grip strong, allowing me to pull myself up the rest of the way without slipping.

At the top, I rolled over and took a moment to catch my breath. I smiled at the dark splotches on my palms. I was going to have to use paint more often. The tiles pressed against my bare back, making me thankful for the extra layer of skin. Flipping over, I slipped my satchel on and made my way to the peak.

Other than the occasional movement by the guards up front, the place was quiet. I was surprised they didn't have anyone patrolling the inside of the wall. I guess with those on the outside, they didn't figure there was much cause.

All the better for me.

The deep shadows under the overhang kept me hidden as I stood to get a better look. The balcony was low enough for me to grab the bottom of the rail, and with one good hop, I managed to pull myself up and over. The doors leading inside were closed and the curtains drawn, so I couldn't see what the room was being used for. But that was fine, since I didn't intend to go in anyway.

The next balcony I needed wasn't going to be so easy. It was not only the next floor up but the next room over, at least a span of ten feet between them. It was too high to reach by jumping, and the wall was too flat to scale by hand, so I pulled out my homemade grapple and uncoiled the rope. I was going to need to be careful. Painted or not, swinging from one balcony to the next was going to leave me exposed to any of the guards who happened to look my way.

Judging the distance, I wrapped the end of the rope around my hand so I didn't accidentally throw it along with the hook. With the balcony railing keeping me from swinging the rope to get a stronger toss, I was forced to hold the hook by hand and lob it at the next balcony over. The intricate pieces of the decorative lattice making up the center of the railing were too narrow for my hook to fit through, which meant I needed to catch the guardrail at the top for this to work. Taking a moment to steady myself, I flung the hook.

It flew upward with an arc and landed over the top. I released a short sigh of relief and pulled on the rope to make sure it was secure.

It held.

Satisfied, I climbed out onto the edge of the balcony. My hands were shaking. It was one thing to start up a grapple from the bottom, giving me plenty of time to test the grip. It was quite another to simply step off a balcony and hope it held. I didn't want to think about all the ways my very motion could cause the hook to slip and me to fall. And from a third-floor height, I was certain to cause permanent damage.

I swallowed nervously and took one last tug on the rope to assure myself it was at least momentarily fastened. With nothing else left for me to do, I took a big gulp and stepped off.

The wind caught my hair as I flew from one balcony to the next—warm, inviting, but a sharp reminder that at any moment I could plunge to my death. The rope reached its length and whipped me back toward the balcony I'd just left. Before it made its second rotation, one of the guards up front left the others and started my way.

Blazes! I didn't wait for the rope to slow. As fast as I could, I started up, hand over hand, desperate to reach the balcony before the patrol spotted a black tar creature hanging from under his master's window. My hand reached the lip around the outer edge of the floor, and I pulled myself up.

Clinging for dear life, I squatted against the outside rail. I didn't have time to climb over. I barely had time to raise the rope. I watched in silence, waiting to see if the guard would notice.

He did.

He stopped directly under the balcony and looked up. My heart sank. It had all been for nothing. I bit my lip, hard. This was why taking the time to plan a mission was so important: it didn't leave you acting impulsively or, in my case, sitting on the edge of a balcony in my underpants, open and exposed for all to see. The guard didn't move. He just sat there staring. Why wasn't he doing anything? I wondered if I should try hitting him in the head with the grapple, then dismissed the idea as utterly ridiculous.

Before I had a chance to come up with a plan for when he sounded the alarm, the guard turned and walked away.

I couldn't believe it.

Bless Sapphire and her paint. He hadn't seen me. Apparently, he'd just been looking at the balcony. I was going to kiss her if I made it out of this alive.

As soon as the guard disappeared around the back of the house, I swung over the side of the rail and made my way to the double doors.

Taking a moment to stuff my grapple back in my satchel, I pressed my ear against the glass pane and listened. No sounds were coming from the inside that I could tell, so I tested the handle. It wasn't locked. Clearly, the senator wasn't too worried about intruders reaching him on the third floor.

But I wasn't just any intruder. I was Upakan.

As quietly as I could, I pulled the latch and slid the door open, taking my time in case the hinges squealed. I opened it just wide enough to squeeze through, then slid it back into place. I didn't want to take a chance that a gust of wind might slam it against the wall.

I hardly made it three steps into the room when I stepped on something with my bare foot and almost yelped. The pain was sharp but eased quickly. The light from the moon allowed me to see that I'd gotten the wrong chambers. Unless, of course, Senator Gerrick was in the habit of playing with dolls.

I picked the carved wooden soldier from off the floor. The lancer was tall and proud. He wore his uniform well and carried a somewhat crooked halberd at his side. Unfortunately, this soldier's polearm had just lost its tip, since it was buried partway in my foot.

I shook the head of his spear from the bottom of my heel and laid the little wooden man back down. I had to pay more attention at where I was placing my feet. As quietly as I could, I snuck across the room, skirting the bed altogether as I made my way toward the door. The only other balcony that had been lit had come from the next room over. I reached the door and turned the handle when a soft grunt behind me had me dropping to my stomach and rolling against the wall.

Ropes grinding under the mattress and a thump on the floor let me know that whoever had been in the bed was no longer there. I didn't budge. Rapid footsteps padded across the rug back toward the balcony doors. I turned to see what was happening.

A little girl with long wavy hair that hung halfway down her nightdress grabbed a stuffed doll from a chair near the door before making her way back to her bed. She hopped in and crawled under her covers, with her doll squeezed against her chest.

I waited until her breathing slowed before leaving my spot. I moved over to the door, opened it, and slipped into the hallway beyond. It was empty, and I couldn't hear any noise from the little girl's room, so apparently, she hadn't seen me.

I glanced up and down the hall for guards. It was empty. None had been posted outside the family's sleeping quarters, not that I was too surprised. I wouldn't have wanted men sitting outside my bedroom door listening to me, either. Apart from the occasional flicker from the sconces on the walls, no other noises could be heard.

Elaborate murals with rich frames of gold lined the walls, between which were pedestals holding statues of people, animals, and objects, all sculpted with such realism that it was hard not to think they were watching me.

Senator Gerrick's home made Wildfire's building look positively commonplace.

One statue in particular stuck out above the rest. A naked gentleman with curly hair held the severed head of a strange beast in one hand and a sword in the other. His scowl had me worrying he might hop off his pedestal and come after me.

I crept down the marble tiles, passing one statue after another until I finally reached the next door. I pressed my ear to the wood, but other than the occasional groaning of the building itself, all was silent. Unlike the last door, though, this one was locked.

A sudden *clang* from down the hall had me spinning. There were guards inside after all, and by the sound of his sword bouncing against his leg, he was heading right for me. I tried the handle once again, hoping I just hadn't applied enough pressure the last time.

It didn't budge.

Frantically, I slipped out from the inset doorway and looked for somewhere to hide. The guard was already passing the little girl's bedroom. I pressed myself up against the wall and eased my way down the corridor and away from the guard. The man's boots echoed off the tile behind me, growing louder with each step.

With nowhere else to go, I climbed up onto one of the pedestals and hid behind the sculpture of a vicious-looking cat, which, as mercy had it, was as black as me. I slowed my breathing as I got down on all fours and positioned my body to match that of the creature's. I placed my arms behind the cat's front paws and my feet behind its back, holding my stomach high enough in the air to not be seen underneath.

The guard stopped just outside the senator's door. What was he waiting for? Was he delivering a message? I didn't hear a knock. Was he expecting Gerrick to come out and pat him on the head and tell him what a good job he was doing?

Move on already!

As if hearing my thoughts, the guard turned and started down the hall in my direction. I closed my eyes and listened, counting down the steps, but they never slowed. He passed without so much as a sideways glance. It wasn't until the echo of his boots had gone that I convinced myself to crawl out from behind my large feline protector. I scratched behind its ear before climbing down. *I owe you one, my friend.*

Back outside the door the guard had been staring at, I opened my satchel, digging around for my pick set, one very similar to the set I'd lost the day I'd arrived in Aramoor.

I placed the bump key in first, along with the pick, and used the mini hammer to lightly tap the lock into place. And with a sharp turn of my wrist, the door opened. I took a deep breath. I couldn't believe I'd made it this far. Quickly, I stowed my picks and slipped inside the senator's bedchamber.

Chapter 28

THE ROOM WAS ABOUT what I expected from a wealthy aristocrat: enormous, overly furnished, and entirely too stuffy. But that could have been the work of the small fire crackling in the hearth. The stone and marble helped keep the interior of the home cooler even during the month of Èldwin, but not enough to need a fire.

Loud snoring was coming from the bed on the left side of the room. I couldn't tell if it was the senator or his wife. Either way, I quietly worked my way around the room, sticking to the outer wall as best I could. Now that I'd made it inside Gerrick's bedchamber, my planning had reached its end.

I stopped beside a large dresser in the corner and stared at the bed and the two lumps on it. The longer I stared, the angrier I got.

The thought of poor Master Fentin being snatched out of his shop, thrown in prison, and awaiting the salt mines had me reaching for my dagger. I knew what I wanted to do. I wanted to walk over there and stick a knife in him. Unfortunately, my father had raised me differently. Worse, I needed the . . . How had Sapphire put it?

I needed the *pig-sucker* alive.

The two occupants took up half of the bed, one lump on the right side, and one on the left. With the amount of space separating the two, they might as well have been sleeping in different beds. I stared at the bulges, hoping to determine which was Senator Gerrick's, but they were too similar to tell.

The problem was, there was only one of me, and I couldn't exactly hold them both down at the same time. Which left me with only one option.

Quickly, I dug in my satchel for the bottle of ether. I was going to need more soon, as much as I had been using it of late. After dousing one of the cloths and replacing the bottle, I lowered myself to all fours and crept toward the bed, the loud snoring covering any noises I might have made. I maneuvered around a nightstand—the top littered with empty vials, several glasses of water, and a stack of books—and pressed myself up against the side of the mattress. I rose to my knees and peeked over the top just as the lump on my side of the bed sucked in a blaring inhale.

It wasn't Gerrick. It was his wife, and she sounded like she was about to suck the canopy curtains right off the top of their bed. One thing was for certain: I wasn't going to have any problem getting her to take a deep breath.

I waited for the next big intake. The silence let me know it was going to happen at any moment. I raised my cloth, glancing briefly across the bed to see which way Gerrick was facing. As luck would have it, his back was to me, no doubt trying to block out as much of his wife's racket as possible. Maybe that was why he always seemed to be in such bad spirits. Lack of sleep will do that to you.

Before the thought had time to finish, the woman's mouth ripped open, releasing a garish roar that would have sent a mountain cat running for its lair. I thrust the rag over her face and she nearly swallowed it whole, gagging only once before returning to a somewhat normal pattern of breathing, the snoring having stopped altogether. I was about to remove the cloth and check to make sure she was indeed still alive when the lump on Gerrick's side of the bed sat straight up.

I dove to the floor and slid under the bed.

"Finally," I heard him mumble, then the mattress groaned and everything went quiet.

I decided to leave the cloth where it was, not wanting to risk exposing myself any more than I had to. Hopefully, it didn't do any permanent damage.

With nothing under the bed to stop me, I slid from one side to the other and peeked out from underneath. Gerrick's arm was hanging partway over the mattress, but it wasn't moving, so I crawled out from under the bed, dagger in hand.

Steeling my nerves, I stood.

Gerrick's eyes were open. He shouted when he saw me, tangling himself in his blankets as he tried to wrestle them off. Too startled to shriek, I leaped on top of him. He flung one arm up to take a swing, but I pressed my blade to his throat, and he went still.

"Don't move or I'll slit you from ear to ear."

The senator didn't so much as twitch. For a moment, I was afraid I'd gotten the wrong room. The man under my knife didn't have a single hair on his head, and I remembered Gerrick with a full head of hair on our last acquaintance, when he had nearly run me and Laris down with his carriage. His thick, well-groomed beard made it look even stranger.

There was a knock on the door. "Senator? Are you all right?"

I pressed down on the dagger. "Be careful what you say. It might be the last thing you ever do."

Gerrick's cheeks were flush with rage. "I'm fine. Go back to your post."

I waited. When it appeared the guard had followed the senator's command, I turned my full attention to Gerrick.

"Do you know who I am?" the senator hissed. "I'm Lord Gerrick, and you've picked the wrong house to burgle this time. I'm going to find every person you've ever known, every person you've ever loved, and I'm going to make them suffer. Now get off of me!"

"Oh, good," I said. "For a moment, I wasn't sure I'd gotten the right house."

"What?" Gerrick looked confused, as if the very thought of anyone coming after him was beyond impossible. "Who sent you? Striffus? It was Striffus, wasn't it?" Gerrick tried to shift positions, but my blade kept him from doing so. "How did you get past my guards?"

"I climbed in the window." I didn't tell him I climbed in the wrong one.

Gerrick glanced at the balcony doors on the left side of the room. "Impressive." He looked at me. "So, what's he paying you? Whatever it is, I'll double it."

"Begging doesn't become you, senator."

"I'm not begging!" Gerrick snapped. "I'm negotiating. There's a difference." His eyes were fierce, but the sweat on his forehead told a different story. Then again, his bedchamber was as hot as a faerie's armpit.

Gerrick attempted to turn and look at his wife. "Luiza?"

"She's unharmed," I said, doing my best to sound threatening. "For now."

"Go on, then," Gerrick said. "What are you waiting for? Do what you came here to do. Just leave my family out of this."

I was momentarily taken aback. From the one encounter I'd had with the man, not to mention the gossip, I knew him to be a heartless swine who cared for nothing but himself. Apparently, he still retained enough of a soul to worry about what would happen to his family.

"I'm not here to kill you," I said, but quickly added, "not that I won't if you give me reason."

Gerrick nodded, his shoulders relaxing slightly. "I believe there's room here for a deal," he said. "You tell me which senator paid you, and I'll forget this ever happened."

"A moment ago, you promised me double."

Gerrick gritted his teeth. "Fine."

I tightened my grip on my knife. "No one paid me."

Gerrick's brows lowered, concern creeping across his face.

"Then what do you want?"

"I want you to tell the patrollers to let Master Fentin go."

"Who?"

"What do you mean, *who*? You have a man arrested today and you don't even know who he is? You ordered the patrollers to seize Master Fentin because you believed he was harboring street kids."

Gerrick looked me in the eyes and sneered. "Clearly, I wasn't wrong."

I pressed harder, drawing blood. "Master Fentin's done nothing to deserve this."

"Yes, I remember something about that now," Gerrick said, his smirk vanishing but the fire in his tone still burning strong. "I received word from a reliable source that one of my constituents was breaking the law—"

"He was giving food to starving children!" I hissed, my hands shaking in anger. "I don't call that breaking the law. I call that common decency. And for that crime, you sent your goons to grab him, tear up his shop, and haul him off to the salt mines? I've half a mind to finish you right here. Maybe the next senator they put in your place will be a little more reasonable."

Gerrick smiled. "Yes, and by then, I'm sure your friend will have already suffered for his crimes."

"Not if you give the order to have him released."

"And what incentive do I have to make this happen?" Gerrick asked, once again attempting to steer the conversation.

"How about I don't pull your tongue out through your neck?"

Gerrick thought a moment. "And what's to stop you from doing that anyway as soon as I agree?"

"My word."

Gerrick laughed, at least, as much as he could afford with my blade to his throat. "Anyone tell you you're a terrible negotiator?"

"You're the one with the knife to his gullet; I'd say I'm doing fairly well."

Gerrick's wife stirred from the other side of the bed, diverting both our attentions. The adjustment hadn't been enough to dislodge the ether-soaked cloth, though, and soon enough, we were back to staring each other down.

Gerrick replaced his sneer with a wry grin, making me even more apprehensive. "The art of a successful negotiation is to know who holds the better hand, and right now, I seem to be holding all the cards."

"How do you figure? Your life is in my hands." I glanced over at the wide lump on the other side of the mattress. "In fact, your whole family's life is in my hands."

"If you had it in you to kill like that, they would most likely already be dead. No," he stated, rather confidently, "you need me more than I need you. I didn't get to where I am by cowering to threats. Besides, I know an opportunity when I see it." He looked at me as if trying to read my face. "Or maybe I'm wrong. If so, kill me, and what happens to your precious Master Fentin will be on your head."

I held his gaze, my jaw tight enough to make my teeth hurt. Gerrick was right. I had no intention of killing his family. In fact, the very thought turned my stomach, which only left one other option. "You mentioned an opportunity?"

A gleam appeared in the senator's eyes. "Clearly, you have a gift that needs to be utilized. There're very few I know who could have made it in here as you have without being seen. That's a valuable skill that could make us both a lot of gold."

"I don't care about gold. I want you to release Master Fentin."

"Then it appears, for the time being, we could be of use to each other."

"What do you mean?"

"I have something I want that only someone with your ability can get me, and you have something you need that only I can provide. I suggest an exchange of services."

I lessened the pressure of the blade. "Go on."

"Senator Striffus has taken something from me, and I want it back. If you can get me this item, then I will draw up a writ of pardon for your shopkeeper."

"I don't have time for that. The ship to Delga could be leaving at any time."

"Then I guess you'd better get a move on. Dawn will be here before you know it."

"I can't break into someone's house in the middle of the night without proper planning. Too many things could go wrong."

"Isn't that exactly what you just did?"

"I don't even know where this Striffus person lives. I don't know what his house looks like, how many guards, what kind of access to the inside. I don't even know what I'm looking for. It can't be done."

"Then I guess your Master Fentin has put his faith in the wrong person. That's what he gets for trusting street rats."

My hand slipped, and a thin line of red appeared under Gerrick's chin.

His eyes flared, but he kept his mouth shut.

"Whoops. I guess us street rats are a clumsy lot." I stared down at the senator, wracking my brain for another solution. But none came. Gerrick was right. Flame him! I wasn't going to start killing his family to get the pardon, which meant I needed him more than he did me. "This Striffus, what is it he supposedly took from you?"

"A ring. It's been in my family for five generations."

"So, how did Striffus get his hands on it?"

Gerrick cleared his throat. "That's none of your concern. The only thing you need to worry about is getting it back." He glanced at the balcony doors. "And if I were you, I'd be quick about it. Dawn can't be too far off."

"Where does he live?"

"As it happens, today's your lucky day," Gerrick said with a wide grin. "Striffus lives next door. Our families have been neighbors for nearly a hundred years."

If the man hated his neighbors that much, why didn't he just move? I would have asked, but I was afraid he would tell me, which would waste valuable time. "What's the ring look like?"

"It's gold and bears the crest of a black jaguar."

"Like the one in your hallway," I said, thinking of the stature I'd hidden behind earlier.

There was a moment's pause. "How do you know what's in my hallway?"

I bit my tongue. *Idiot!* "Who says this is the first time I've been here?"

It was Gerrick's turn to look surprised.

I smiled. I couldn't believe I hadn't thought to say that earlier. If he thought I could come and go as I pleased, Gerrick would be less likely to try stabbing me in the back by reneging on our deal.

"Where's he likely to keep this ring?"

"As close to him as possible."

"Which room is his?"

"If you were to look straight across from my house to his, you'd spot his room on the second floor, third from the front. If you can make it in here, you shouldn't have any problem getting over there."

My decision was already made, but I didn't want to appear too desperate. "Fine," I said, after pausing a moment to consider. I slid off the bed, keeping my knife where it was. "But I want a written pass to get through your gate and back." I knew I wasn't going to have time to sneak back out the way I'd come, make it next door, sneak in the same way, find the ring, then sneak back in over here before the sun came up.

Gerrick nodded, and I motioned for him to stand. I didn't bother checking on his wife. Instead, I followed him over to his desk, my knife at his back. He lit the candle on top and wrote a quick note, which he signed. He turned and handed me the parchment. "This should get you by the guards."

I read it to make sure it didn't say something like *Kill the bearer of this note.* If he thought I was illiterate, he might have attempted it. Surprisingly, it simply read, *Allow safe passage to the bearer of this note*. Apparently, Gerrick wanted this ring pretty badly.

"Seal it."

Gerrick took the note, heated some wax, and punched it with his seal before handing it back over.

I clutched the paper in my fist and started for the door, stopping only long enough to remove the cloth over his wife's face and grab my satchel. For a brief moment I pondered the idea of using the note as a way to free Master Fentin, then quickly disregarded it. All the note had said was to let the bearer pass. Even with the senator's official seal, it didn't say anything about freeing Master Fentin. It didn't even mention Master Fentin's name, and I couldn't take the chance of going down to the patroller's office and wasting what precious time I had just for them to turn me away.

"Good luck," Gerrick said behind me.

I turned.

Gerrick smiled, and it was anything but friendly. "I see a long and prosperous future ahead for us."

Chapter 29

IT TOOK ME A WHILE to navigate the maze of corridors inside the senator's home, but I finally managed to find the grand staircase leading down to the front doors. I was halfway to the floor before the two armed guards standing watch realized that the black, half-naked creature moving toward them wasn't just a figment of their imagination.

"Hold there!" the taller man on the right shouted. Both drew their weapons and rushed across the marble foyer to stop me. I hoped the torches anchored at the sides of the staircase gave enough light for them to see me waving Senator Gerrick's note.

"I'm on urgent business for the senator," I said, trying to sound as formal as possible.

"Don't you move," the second guard demanded as the two men

pulled to a stop in front of me. He was shorter than the first but thicker in the chest and arms. Both men maintained their distance, their swords at the ready as they were clearly trying to figure out what they were looking at.

"I told you, I'm on an errand for Senator Gerrick. See?" I shoved the parchment at the shorter guard, since he was the closest. "Read it. But hurry. The senator said that it's urgent."

The shorter guard snatched the paper from my hand, then walked over to the torch to get a better look. "He's telling the truth." The guard held up the parchment. "Has the senator's crest and all." He stepped over and handed me the paper.

"And what are you supposed to be?" the other guard asked, his brow set as he looked me over. "What are you all dark for?"

"To keep from being seen," I said, trying not to sound like I was mocking the ridiculous question. These guards were clearly not hired for their wit.

The guard looked me over one more time, then pointed toward the front with his sword. "Best be on your way, then."

I nodded and followed the two men across the foyer to the doors, which the taller one opened.

The courtyard and garden standing between us and the gate were filled with armsmen. "Walk with me," I said to the two guards, "so I don't have to explain this all over again."

The taller of the two nodded to his partner. "Go ahead; I'll keep watch here."

The shorter rolled his shoulders. "Fine. Come on."

I followed him down the stone path leading through the garden and out to the front wall. My escort seemed apprehensive at having me so close and kept his steps fast, as if trying to get away from me. The men in the courtyard turned to see what was happening. A couple even reached for their blades.

"Stand down," my escort said with a wave of his hand. "He's on assignment by the senator."

The guards released their swords but kept a close eye as we passed.

My escort repeated the same instructions to those standing on either side of the gate.

I stopped long enough to address those on watch. "I'll be back before the sun comes up. Don't attempt to hinder me or you'll have Gerrick to answer to." Just the mention of the senator's name and the guards opened the gate without question. "Oh, you might want to inform your patrolman about me as well. I'd hate to have to kill him because he mistook me for a common thief."

I didn't wait to see their reaction as I took off at a jog toward the next home over, sticking close to the wall. The stars were still bright in the sky, and the moon was beginning its slow descent over the bay, which meant I didn't have a whole lot of time.

I turned down the narrow walkway between the wall surrounding Gerrick's estate and the one surrounding Striffus's. They were both the same height and close enough for me to easily jump from one to the next, which left me with an idea.

Spinning my satchel around to my back so my hands were free, I took a moment to judge the distance between the walls. I wasn't going to have any room to get a running start, but if I did this right, I really wouldn't need any. I backed up against Gerrick's wall and pushed off, taking one good stride before leaping at the opposite wall. I kicked up and off, turning as I headed straight back toward Gerrick's side. My foot hit the stone, and I kicked up and back toward the second wall, rising high enough this time for my hands to grab hold of the top.

Quickly, I scanned the inside for guards before swinging over. I didn't have time to use my grapple, so I hung as far down as I could, then dropped to the other side next to a small sapling that was barely tall enough for its uppermost branches to reach above the wall.

This yard was even smaller than Gerrick's, barely a stone's throw between the wall and his home. More like a stone's toss, and only if you didn't put much effort behind it. I ducked down beside the wall when I heard footsteps and soft voices coming my way.

A couple of guards passed me as they walked down the crushed-rock path leading around the side of the house. One of the men carried a torch, but the light wasn't strong enough to reach all the way to my hiding spot beside the sapling. The men were too engrossed in their conversation to have noticed me anyway. Something about one of the new serving girls over at the Wooden Leg. Whatever they were discussing had one of the men slapping the other on the back.

As interesting as the debauchery might have been, I had more important things to worry about. My thoughts drifted to Master Fentin lying in a cell, alone and frightened, knowing he was going to be shipped off to the salt mines. I wondered if he was cursing the day he'd ever met me.

The guards turned the far corner of the house, and I slid out from the wall. There were several windows lining the second floor, even a couple of small balconies, but only one large enough to have a full two-door walk-out. I headed straight for it. Unlike Gerrick's estate, this one didn't have the handy side entrance that jutted out from the house, but it did have several pillars that ran from the ground to the underside of the balcony, not to mention decorative stone blocks that protruded from the main wall far enough for me to get the tips of my fingers around.

I wasn't going to need my grapple there after all.

Desperation drove me forward, and I grabbed the first stone and started up. It reminded me of how much I had enjoyed climbing Howling Gorge, and my free climb up the Black Hills lagoon during my time with Captain Treygan and Ismara on the *Wind Binder*. I glanced down, half-expecting to see the deep cerulean waters of the Shemoa River below, and realized I was barely eight feet off the ground. With a shrug, I continued.

It didn't take long to reach the top of the balcony, which was good, because I could hear more voices behind me. Quickly, I leaped from the wall and grabbed the stone lip of the railing and swung myself over just as another set of guards rounded the corner of the house. Surely, it couldn't have been the same two men who had passed me earlier. If the senator's house was even half the size of Gerrick's, which it was, it would have taken them much longer to make a full loop.

The three men weren't wearing guard uniforms. They looked more like pantrymen. Most likely part of the cooking staff, getting ready to prepare breakfast. Another strong indicator that my time was running out.

Racing across the balcony, I tried the door. It was open. No one seemed to lock their balcony doors at night. Then again, during the summer and early fall months, most left them open to catch the breeze.

I couldn't hear anything from inside. Either the senator and his wife—if he had one—weren't much for snoring, or I had the wrong room again. I hoped for the former as I slipped inside and gently slid the door shut. The room was silent. No fire in the hearth cracking and popping, no snorts or grunts from the bed, only the wind gently vibrating the door behind me.

I took a moment to let my eyes adjust.

The bed was on the left side of the room, but before I started rifling through the man's belongings, I needed to make sure I was actually in the correct bedchamber.

Keeping my hand on my blade, I crept over to the bed. There was a single lump near the center. What was it with these rich people and their gigantic beds? Was it a symbol of status? The wealthier you were, the bigger your bed? If that was the case, Gerrick and Striffus were indeed very wealthy men.

I peeked over the mattress but still had no way of knowing if it was the senator. He looked about the same age as Gerrick, with a thick mustache that curved down to the chin and out toward the sides of his face. I could only assume that it was indeed him.

Striffus snorted and turned over, and I nearly yelped as I dropped to all fours. After several long minutes with no other movement, I finally peeked over the bed.

His back was to me.

I crossed the room, sparing a glance out the balcony doors on the way by, noting that the stars didn't seem quite so bright. I had to hurry. Two long dressers against the right wall caught my attention, each lined with an array of random objects. The perfect spot to place a ring, I thought.

Frantically, I scoured the tops of the dressers. Both were filled with knickknacks, collectibles, various pieces of junk that I doubted Striffus actually used or even wanted. There were pendants with family crests, brooches, necklaces, several stacks of rings of various sizes, but none of them had anything that resembled a large black cat. I doubted half this stuff was even Striffus's. I couldn't imagine why the man was collecting all these heirlooms. Perhaps he had won them in a game. By the rather large stack of winnings, he was pretty good at it.

The minutes slipped away as my earlier anxiousness turned to desperation. I raided every drawer, but other than discovering piles of neatly folded clothes, I was no closer to finding Gerrick's infernal ring than when I'd first stepped foot in the room.

Had Gerrick sent me on a fool's errand? What if Striffus never had Gerrick's ring? It wouldn't make much sense to go to the trouble of giving me a signed document to get back into Gerrick's estate if he wasn't expecting something in return.

No. Gerrick knew what I was capable of. He wouldn't have sent me over there carrying a writ of passage with his seal if he didn't at least half-expect me to be able to accomplish the task.

I left the dressers, having scoured his entire collection of rings twice. Gerrick's wasn't in the lot. I looked around the room. Where would I hide a ring if I . . . My hand reached for my neck on instinct, forgetting I had left my father's ring back at the Temple.

That's it!

An image of Red suddenly came to mind, standing there inside the Pit with my father's ring out for all to see. I could see Striffus doing the same to Gerrick.

I marched across the room for the bed, passing the balcony doors once more. This time, the stars were all but faded, and the sky had shifted from black to a deep grey. The boats could be setting sail at any time.

Striffus lay quietly in the center of the bed. His chest rose and fell in rhythm, letting me know he was still asleep. He was no longer on his side but had turned to his back, his blankets tucked all the way to his chin. I hoped the senator wasn't a light sleeper.

There was no way I could reach him from where I was standing. I was going to have to get on the bed with him. I laid my satchel on the edge of the mattress and slowly crawled up on top, letting my body sink into the thick cushion. I didn't want to make any sudden movements that would shift the balance and wake the senator.

Once I had sunk as far as the stuffing would allow, I pulled out what was left of the bottle of ether and the cloth. I'd used quite a bit on Gerrick's wife. I hoped what was left would be enough. I pulled the cork on the bottle and upturned it, doing my best to hold my breath as I did. I remembered how strong this stuff had been the day of the street battle outside Avalanche's compound when Reevie had chucked a bottle of it at me, thinking I was another Avalanche beater.

The folded rag was feeling good and damp, letting me know I had soaked it enough, so I raised the bottle to cork it.

"Ahhh!" Striffus, having suddenly woken, flung his arms out to the side and knocked the bottle out of my hand, spilling part of what was inside across the mattress and my underpants. The room started to spin. I turned, feeling the ether's effects. No! This couldn't be happening. I had to stop the senator. I had to get that ring. I stumbled forward and threw myself on Striffus, muffling his screams with my rag.

Everything went black.

Chapter 30

BY THE TIME I CAME TO, a swath of grey light was worming its way through the glass panes of the balcony doors.

"No!" I sat up and the room spun. Striffus was lying beside me, his snores nearly as loud as Gerrick's wife's. I looked down, feeling something clutched inside my hand. I thought it was the bottle of ether, but that was lying over near the side of the mattress where I'd dropped it. I opened my hand and found a gold ring with the crest of a black cat at the center. I must have managed to pry it from Striffus before the ether took over.

I couldn't remember doing it. I couldn't remember much of anything after I'd landed on the senator. Behind me, the rising sun said I was probably too late to do anything about it anyway.

How could I have been so stupid? Leaping from the bed, I shoved the ring in one of the outside pockets of my satchel and recorked the bottle of ether before tossing it in the bag as well. I opened the balcony door and took a deep breath of fresh air, then I exhaled and took another. My head was pounding, but the spinning had lessened.

I shut the door behind me and crawled over to the rail, looking through the decorative spindles to see where the guards were. The sun hadn't risen, but the grey fingers of dawn had already inched over the tops of the buildings to the east.

With a close eye on the guards at the front of the estate, I climbed over the railing, grabbing hold of the protruding stone on the side of the wall, and started down. About halfway, I released and dropped onto the soft grass beside one of the pillars. I crouched up against the wall and scanned the yard to see if there were any other guards near the back of the house.

I didn't see any.

What was I going to do now? Black paint only worked at night. If any of the guards were looking this direction, they'd spot me for sure. Six bells sounded from the harbor, ringing out the new hour. If Fentin's ship hadn't left already, it was sure to be setting sail at any time.

With the ring tucked safely in my satchel, I lay down on my stomach and started to crawl, inching my way toward the sapling I'd hidden behind earlier. Part of the paint on my chest and stomach rubbed off in the wet grass, leaving a tickling sensation on my skin as I pressed myself as close to the ground as I could manage.

Somehow, I made it across the yard without anyone noticing

and hunkered down beside the sapling and its leafy branches. The tree was far too thin for me to climb, and had I tried, it would have snapped in half before I made it even partway up the wall, which left me reaching for my grapple.

I unwound the rope and spared a quick glance toward the front of the house to see if anyone was looking before tossing up the hook. It reached the top with a clang, and a couple of the men turned. I hunkered down, doing my best not to move as I kept a tight grip on the rope, hoping my paint might still be enough to mask me in the shadows.

The rope was taut in my hands, and I kept it that way as best I could, worrying that at any moment, the hook would slip and come crashing down on top of me, alerting everyone to my presence. I waited for what seemed an eternity before the men finally shrugged and turned back around, and I started up the rope. If I could just make it to the top, it wouldn't matter if they saw me or not. I could simply hop over.

Near the top, the hook shifted, and my stomach knotted. Thankfully, it didn't come completely loose. I didn't even bother looking to see if the guards had noticed as I scrambled the rest of the way up.

My fingers latched on to the stone at the top, and I frantically pulled myself up, clutching the grapple in my arms so it didn't fall back inside Striffus's yard. I couldn't believe I'd made it this far without being seen, and not wanting to risk it now by standing up and leaping to the next wall, I simply lowered myself between the two and dropped.

My feet hit the bottom, and I turned to find one of Striffus's guards standing there. He hit me in the face with the butt end of his staff, and I felt something in my mouth give as I slammed into the wall. Pain exploded inside my head, and I spit blood along with several teeth.

I screamed, and everything shifted.

Once again, I was back on my feet between the two walls. Without a moment to lose, I leaped to the side and dodged the guard's swift jab. My vision had saved me from capture or, worse, losing my teeth. I turned and faced the man. He bore the same orange-and-brown livery as the guards watching over Senator Striffus.

Both senators must have employed guards to walk the same route. Unfortunately, I happened to drop on top of the wrong one. The guard swung again, but with plenty of warning, I sidestepped and grabbed his arm, throwing him off balance. I kicked his leg out from under him, and he landed on his knees. Before he had time to realize what had happened, I kicked him in the side of the face. It wasn't enough to knock him unconscious, but it was enough to stun him and guarantee he wouldn't be getting back up too soon.

The sun was already rising over the buildings.

I left the man wallowing in the dirt and ran for the front gate, pulling Gerrick's note out for the guards to see. Not that they needed much reminding. Who would forget running into a half-naked boy wearing nothing but black paint? The guards opened the gate, and I ran through the garden, across the courtyard, and up the stairs to the front doors. The two out front saw me coming and quickly opened the doors.

"Did you complete your errand?" the shorter one asked as I flew past.

"Yes," I called back over my shoulder as I ran for the stairs. I hoped I didn't run into any of the staff on my way to Gerrick's room. I doubted the guards would have relayed a message to them that I was working for Gerrick. I shivered. The very thought of me working for the man who had thrown Master Fentin in prison had my stomach turning.

It took a while to get my bearings, which led me down the wrong corridor the first time, only to backtrack before I spotted something I recognized. The last time I'd come through there, it had been pitch-black, and even with my eyesight, things looked different in the daylight. I stopped in front of the senator's room and put my ear to the door.

Nothing.

I tried the handle, but it was locked. No surprise there. I pulled my picks out of my bag and stuffed them into the lock. It didn't take long before I heard the *snap* and replaced them and opened the door. Slipping inside, I gently shut it back in place, listening for the soft click. The room was brighter this time, but the corners were still cast in shadow.

I started for the bed. Gerrick's wife was still breathing deeply, not having woken from the ether.

"You're late."

I jumped, realizing the voice was behind me.

Gerrick was sitting in a chair on the other side of the room. He had either miraculously grown a full head of hair while I was gone or had donned a rather realistic-looking wig. The fire had died out, and it didn't look like the senator had attempted to stir it. I wondered if he'd been sitting there the whole time. If a stranger broke into my bedchamber in the middle of the night and startled me out of my sleep with a knife to my throat, I wouldn't have gone back to bed either.

"Did you get it?"

I reached into the pocket and pulled out the ring, holding it up for the senator to see.

He came to his feet with a wide grin.

I didn't have time for pleasantries, and at that point, I didn't even care how desperate I looked as I rushed across the room and shoved the ring into Gerrick's hand. "Now, where's that pardon?"

Gerrick took a moment to admire the ring, walking over to the balcony doors to get a better look from the light spilling through the crack in the curtains. Behind me, the senator's wife stirred but soon enough was back to her snores. I hoped I hadn't done any permanent damage to the woman from the amount of ether I'd given her.

"Did anyone see you?" Gerrick asked, placing the ring on his right hand before turning to look at me.

What he was really asking was did anyone see me coming and going from his residence. "No." I wondered if Striffus would think it had all been some elaborate nightmare when he woke. I'd taken any clue of my passing with me. "But I'm sure when Senator Striffus wakes and realizes the ring is gone, he's going to figure it out. Not to mention if he sees you wearing that around town," I said, pointing at the ring.

Gerrick smiled. "Good. I want him to realize that nobody steals from me and gets away with it."

As interesting as this game between Gerrick and his neighbor was, I needed that writ. "You have your ring. Now give me the pardon."

"It won't matter now. The boats were scheduled to set sail at first light."

I pulled my blade from my satchel, my blood pumping so loud in my ears I could barely hear anything else. "You promised me a writ of pardon. Now give it to me, or I'll take your ring and the finger it's on."

Gerrick's smile never dipped. "Fine." He walked over to his desk and started scribbling on a piece of parchment. He finished by folding the paper and reached for his seal.

"Wait! I want to read it first." Knowing Gerrick, he'd probably written something about grabbing me and throwing me on the ship alongside Master Fentin. Then again, that might not be the worst thing. At least then I could find a way to help him.

Gerrick handed me the parchment. It read: *By order of Senator Gerrick, Master Fentin is to be released from custody. All charges dropped.* And it was signed at the bottom.

I thrust the parchment back at him to stamp his seal in wax on the back. Not bothering with pleasantries, I grabbed the missive and rushed out of the room. I ran through the corridors, not caring who I might run into, stopping only long enough to snatch a few small decorative items off one of the tables on the way out. It was the least the senator owed.

The guards saw me coming and opened the doors without question. I ran down the stairs and straight for the gate. Again, the guards outside opened the gate without a word, no doubt believing I was on another time-sensitive mission for the senator.

I ran down the street, not caring one whit about my black paint or my half-naked condition as I cut through the shipping district. Dark thoughts flooded my mind. Thoughts of poor Master Fentin stuck in the salt mines, forced to do hard labor until he died, had my legs moving all the faster.

Ahead, white sails peeked over the buildings in front of the harbor. The road leading to the docks was filled with sailors. Those heading away from port moved at a brisk pace with a spring in their step, many walking in the general direction of the lower brothels. Those on their way down to the water weren't quite so energetic. I pushed and shoved to make it through.

"Hey, watch it," most said until they got a look at me, then they simply moved aside. I was tempted to pull my knife and start sticking people to get them to move out of the way. I could only hope that the large number of men and women on their way to the docks meant that all the ships hadn't sailed yet.

I broke through the crowd and charged down the boardwalk. There were several ships still in port. But there were also a number already in the bay, setting sail.

I ran down the gangplank, staring up at the ships I passed, trying to see if there were any noticeable markings that would tell me where each ship might be heading. I stopped a couple of sailors to ask, but one look at me and they made a hasty retreat.

The main office building was just ahead. If anyone would know which ship Master Fentin was on, it would be there. I rushed through the door, sailors cursing when they saw me, some making the sign of an X on their chest and spitting off to the side.

"Has the ship going to the Isle of Delga left yet?" I asked the attendant at the desk, who looked up from his papers and yelped.

"Has the prisoner ship to the salt mines left?" I repeated. "I have a pardon for one of them signed by Senator Gerrick himself."

"The salt mines?"

"Yes," I said angrily, "the ship taking the prisoners to Delga. Has it left yet?"

The room was busy enough to drown out some of my shouting, but those in the lines on either side turned to see what the commotion was about.

I didn't have time to be embarrassed. "Why are you just standing there?" I shoved the senator's sealed parchment in the man's face. "See! I have a writ of pardon for one of the prisoners. It was signed by Senator Gerrick. Can someone please tell me if the ship has left?"

"Sorry, son," an older sailor sitting on a bench behind me said. "That ship left port about an hour ago. I'm afraid you're too late."

"What?" He couldn't be right.

"They already left," the sailor said.

My mind went blank. I didn't know what to say. This couldn't be right. Perhaps he didn't understand what I'd asked. "No. I'm talking about the ship taking the prisoners to the salt mines." I walked over to the man and handed him the parchment. "See, I have a pardon. I . . ." I looked around the room. By now, everyone was turned in my direction.

"I'm right sorry, son." He handed me the parchment back. "Afraid it ain't gonna do ya much good."

I was lightheaded. I couldn't tell if the room was spinning or if it was me. I stumbled for the front door. Those coming in saw me and moved out of the way. How could this have happened? How could I have gone through all of this just to be told I was too late? How was I ever going to face Mistress Orilla again?

A stabbing pain tore into my chest, and I stumbled out the door and retched. The pain didn't let up. It didn't even have the courtesy of killing me and releasing me of the guilt. Tears streamed down my cheeks. I couldn't stop them. What's more, I didn't care. I had failed him. I was too late. Master Fentin was going to die in a salt mine because of me.

I slowly trudged my way back up the boardwalk, almost hoping one of the haulers would run me over or accidentally knock me into the water. Maybe the Creator could spare me the pain and let me be crushed between a piling and one of the ships. It would be no less than I deserved.

I don't remember much of what happened after that. I have no recollection of leaving the port or walking through the city streets. I have no idea how many people I scared or patrollers I might have run from. All I knew was the next time I blinked, I was standing in front of Master Fentin's bookshop.

The door had been partially ripped from its hinges and was hanging awkwardly to the side. I heard a noise coming from the inside. "Master Fentin?" I ducked under the broken door and ran into the shop. How had he gotten out? Had they released him? The inside of the shop was dark. The front faced due west, and the sun hadn't risen high enough to reach the windows.

There was a thump near the back steps leading up to the personal residence.

"Master Fentin? Mistress Orilla?" I ran through the rubble and upturned shelves. It had to be him. I reached the back and quickly dove to the ground as a thick club flew over my head and hit the shelf behind me, scattering a row of books that the patrollers hadn't already seen fit to destroy.

Thanks to another vision, I was back on my feet before the boy had a chance to realize he'd missed. There were three of them, and the one with the club wore a patch on his right sleeve up near the shoulder that bore the Rockslide logo. I recognized him as one of the three boys who I had spotted across from the bookstore some days back.

My fists tightened, and I dropped my carry bag, but not before pulling my knife. "I told you what would happen if you came back here. How dare you show your face in this shop again!" I looked down at a large knapsack lying at their feet. It was filled with Master Fentin's books. All reason fled and rage consumed me, the heat of it threatening to scorch me to the core of my being. Not only had they been responsible for having Master Fentin arrested, but they had the audacity to walk into his shop afterward and pilfer it.

The boy's eyes widened, fear setting in as he recognized who he was standing in front of. I dropped my knife. I didn't need a weapon. I wanted to feel their flesh in my hands: each snap of the bone, each pop of the joint, each blistering strike that would leave jaws wobbling, teeth flying, and kids screaming in pain. These were three beaters who'd never step foot in this shop again.

By the time I was finished, all three were writhing on the ground. The longer I stared, the angrier I got. It wasn't enough to simply break a few bones. They deserved much worse. With that thought at the front of my mind, I leaned over and grabbed my blade.

"Ayrion?"

My hand froze halfway to the first boy.

"Ayrion, is that you?"

I spun around, accidentally knocking a couple of books off the shelf as I did. "Master Fentin?" My mouth gaped. It couldn't be. I dropped my knife and raced across the book-strewn floor and grabbed the old man, nearly knocking him off his feet.

"Master Fentin! You're alive!"

Chapter 31

I DIDN'T WANT TO LET GO. I couldn't. I held the old man as tight as I could, my face planted in his chest as tears burned my eyes.

It was wonderful.

"How did you make it off the ship? They said I was too late." I finally released my grip and took a step back, holding up the sealed parchment that was somehow still clutched in my right hand. "See? I got you a pardon."

Master Fentin stared into the distance, completely unresponsive.

"What happened?" I asked, anxious to know how he had escaped.

There were tears in his eyes as he stared at the wreckage.

"It's all my fault, Master Fentin," I said, overwhelmed with guilt. "I'll help you rebuild."

Master Fentin hobbled farther into what was left of his shop. Leaning over, he grabbed his cane from where it lay against a shelf on the left side, no doubt dropped in the scuffle with the patrollers. He grabbed his chest as he stood.

"Are you hurt, Master Fentin? What did they do to you?"

He waved me off and started slowly toward the back of the shop, stopping every so often to glance down at the piles of books lining the floor.

I waited near the front as he made his rounds, wanting to give him a moment to himself. Something was wrong. Master Fentin didn't seem himself. It wasn't as though I expected him to act like nothing had happened, but surely he felt some relief at not having been hauled away with the rest of the prisoners. Maybe it was seeing his shop in such a state.

"I can help you fix—"

Master Fentin squawked, and I ran to the back. "What's wrong?"

"Who are they?" he asked, jabbing his cane at the Rockslide beaters.

"Looters," I said, kicking the biggest boy in the arm. He didn't move.

"What happened to them?"

"I made sure they'd never loot here again."

Master Fentin stared at them a moment, then leaned over to get a closer look. "They're not . . ."

"They're alive," I said, but only because Master Fentin had

walked in when he did. "I've half a mind to turn them over to the patrollers, though. It'd serve them right."

"No!" Master Fentin exclaimed, a mix of anger and fear on his face as he quickly straightened. "I never want to see another patroller again." He turned and headed for the stairs leading up to the living quarters. "Orilla?" he called out, then looked at me. "Is she . . . They didn't take her, did they?"

I walked over and placed my hand on his arm. "No. She's safe. She's staying with us at the Temple." I looked around at what remained. There was little Master Fentin could do at this point, and the pain on his face let me know he needed to be anywhere else but here. "She'll want to see you," I said, trying to steer him toward the front. "Let me take you to her. Reevie will want to see you as well."

Master Fentin didn't budge from his spot.

"Please, you don't need to be here. Let Reevie take a look at you. In fact, you and Mistress Orilla can stay with us until you're feeling better."

"What about them?" he asked, staring down at the injured kids.

"Don't worry about them. When they wake, I have a feeling the only thing they'll be concerned about is getting back to the safety of their own territory."

Master Fentin didn't nod or acknowledge what I'd said at all, but he did allow me to lead him to the front of the shop without protest. I think even he knew that seeing his bookstore in its current condition wasn't doing him any good. I grabbed my satchel on the way to the front, and we left, stopping only long enough to push the broken door back into place.

Master Fentin roused enough to ask the younger couple who owned the shop next door if they would keep an eye on his place.

They seemed hesitant at first, the wary glances and standoffish behavior saying they must have witnessed Master Fentin's arrest and didn't want the same happening to them, or it could have just been me, standing there in my underpants, covered in black paint. Whatever the reason, they did eventually agree.

It was a slow, quiet walk back to the Temple. Master Fentin needed to lean on me for support most of the way. With my current state of undress and paint, I kept us to the back alleys and side streets, away from the traffic of the busy thoroughfares. A million questions flooded my mind, but the vacant look on Master Fentin's face let me know that my questions could wait.

Our route added quite a bit of time to our journey. Whenever we came across an old barrel or pile of crates, Master Fentin would stop to sit, grabbing his ribs each time, and again on the way back up. There were bruises on his face, and his lip was split. The old man must have put up quite the fight.

By the time we reached the Temple's gates, it was well into the afternoon.

Master Fentin didn't seem all that interested in where he was, his eyes barely leaving the brick path in front of him. There was more than physical damage ailing the old man. I couldn't imagine what he must have gone through.

"The Protector's back!" Toots shouted from the top of the wall as he rang the warning bell and ordered those inside to release the bracer.

"Fentin!"

The gate had barely opened before Mistress Orilla pushed her way through the watchers and ran out to meet us. Reevie, Sapphire, and Bull were right behind her. She wrapped her arms around her husband, causing him to moan, and her to release her grip.

"Ayrion, you did it!" Reevie wrapped his arms around me. "How did you manage it? I can't believe you got him out."

"I won!" Bull said gleefully. He looked like he'd just picked a pocket filled with gold. "The Guard bet me the meat from our stew this week that you wouldn't be able to pull it off." Bull was beaming from ear to ear. "Never bet against the Protector."

"That's a terrible thing to bet on," Sapphire said as she walked over and planted a kiss on my cheek.

Bull looked at Sapphire and sheepishly lowered his head. "Sorry."

"Fentin, are you all right?" Mistress Orilla looked him over.

"They roughed him up," I said. "Possibly a broken rib or two."

"Fentin?" Mistress Orilla put her hand to the sides of her husband's face and forced him to look at her. When he finally did, she smiled. "We're safe. There's no need to fear. Everything will be fine." She kissed his forehead.

Master Fentin started to cry. "The shop. They've destroyed it."

"We can fix it, Master Fentin," Bull said. "Don't you worry."

"Come, my love." Mistress Orilla turned and led him toward the gate. "Let's get you inside so Reevie can take a look at those ribs."

Fentin nodded.

Reevie directed us back to the infirmary, where Bull and I helped Master Fentin onto one of the longer cots. He wanted to lie down, but Reevie told him it was best if he remained seated while he checked his back and sides.

After a lengthy inspection, Reevie determined that the ribs didn't appear to be broken, just severely bruised. He mixed a tonic of willow bark, mandrake, and valu, and made sure Master Fentin drank the entire cup. Master Fentin grimaced at the sour taste, but in the end with Mistress Orilla's encouragement, he managed to get it all down.

Reevie wrapped Master Fentin's chest to help support his breathing and ordered for a bowl of soup to be brought in. The old shopkeeper looked like he was ready to tip forward off the cot.

"Let's take him to the study," I said. "It'll be more comfortable there."

"He can use the sofa," Sapphire added. "It's softer than the cots in here."

I grabbed Master Fentin's right arm while Bull grabbed the left. Together, we managed to get him to his feet and down the hall. Once inside the chiefs' study, Sapphire stuffed a few pillows on the right side of the sofa, and we lowered him as gently as possible.

Master Fentin released a slow exhale and held his ribs as he sank into the cushions. "Whatever you gave me seems to be working." He offered a half-smile to Reevie.

Reevie beamed.

While we waited on the soup, Bull used his pocketknife to slice up one of the apples on Reevie's desk and handed a piece to Master Fentin.

"Thank you," Master Fentin said, and nibbled on the slice.

"So, how did you do it?" Reevie asked, pulling up a seat. The rest of us joined him in a half-circle around the sofa. Mistress Orilla sat beside her husband.

Sapphire pointed at my chest. "And how did you manage to do that?"

I looked down at the strip of paint that had been rubbed off by my belly crawl across Striffus's yard. I'd almost forgotten I was sitting there in my underpants. "I need to wash this stuff off."

"That can wait," Sapphire said. "I want to know how you managed to get Senator Gerrick to change his mind."

"Senator Gerrick?" Master Fentin tried to sit up but winced and lay back down. "What does Gerrick have to do with this?"

"He's the one who had you arrested," Reevie said.

"But it's my fault," I added.

"How could it possibly be your fault?" Mistress Orilla asked, looking as confused as Master Fentin.

I went on to explain how I'd been followed from the shop the last time I was there, and because of our conflict with Rockslide, it seemed Kore had sent word to Gerrick that someone in his district was harboring street rats. "And Gerrick took it upon himself to have Master Fentin arrested."

"Which leads me back to my question," Sapphire said. "How did you manage to change his mind?"

For the next quarter-hour, I relayed my harrowing adventure from the previous night, not leaving anything out, except maybe the bit where I accidentally dosed myself with ether. I wasn't about to tell them that I'd taken a nap in Senator Striffus's bed while he was still in it.

By the time I finished, there wasn't a closed mouth in the room, and everyone was on the edge of their seats—except Master Fentin, who was more than happy to enjoy the tale from the comfort of the sofa's cushions. Sadly, my ending was rather lackluster. No shouts of excitement or slaps on the back for encouragement. In fact, most were left scratching their heads.

"Wait a minute," Bull said. "If you didn't manage to save Master Fentin, then how did you"—he looked at Master Fentin—"save Master Fentin?"

"I don't know," I admitted. "After they told me I'd arrived too late, I walked back to the bookshop, where I found the beaters. After I took care of them, I turned around, and there was Master Fentin standing behind me."

Everyone looked at the old shopkeeper.

"Well, Fentin?" Mistress Orilla said, shaking his leg with her hand. "What happened?"

Master Fentin took a deep breath, then exhaled with what sounded like a painful wheeze. "After the blue capes arrived at the shop, they took me to the patrollers' office and locked me in a large room with several other prisoners. From what I could tell, they were all headed for the salt mines. I tried telling the patrollers they'd gotten the wrong man, and that this was a mistake, but they just laughed."

His hands were shaking, so Mistress Orilla laid hers on top. He looked at her and nodded, taking another deep breath. "They never did tell me what I was being charged with." He paused a moment as if trying to remember something. "Some of the other prisoners didn't take too kindly to me insisting that I didn't belong there. In fact, it caused such a stir amongst those in the cell that a fight broke out." He grabbed his ribs. "The patrollers had to pull me out just to keep them from killing me. I can see why some of those men were being taken to the mines. Nothing more than savage beasts, if you ask me. Don't want people like that walking the streets of Aramoor."

"So, it wasn't the patrollers who did that to you," I asked, pointing to the wrapping on his chest.

Master Fentin shook his head. "No." Then he reached up and felt the back of his head. "Although I did get a good whack on the head by one in the shop." He smiled. "But I gave him an even worse wallop with my cane."

I chuckled. The old man had grit.

Master Fentin lowered his cane. "Where was I?"

"They moved you to another cell, dear."

"Right. I spent the rest of the night in my own cell, alone. Don't think I've prayed that much since I was a young man." He shivered. "Longest night of my life."

Mistress Orilla patted her husband's leg, and he laid his hand on hers.

"By the time the stars had faded from view, they came for me. Two blue capes escorted me out of the cell and threw me in line with the other prisoners and marched us all down to the port where we were to be loaded onto the first ship bound for Delga. I was halfway down the dock and getting ready to board when one of the patrollers came and pulled me out of line. Without saying why, he unlocked my shackles and told me I was free to go. By the look on some of the other prisoners' faces, I thought another fight was about to break out."

"So, they just let you go without telling you anything?" Reevie asked.

Master Fentin suddenly straightened with a wince. "I almost forgot." He reached into his trouser pocket and pulled out a folded piece of parchment, which he handed to me. "The patroller said I was to give this to you."

I took the paper. "To me?"

Master Fentin nodded and rested back against the cushions. "He said I was to give it to the little white-eyed mongrel that fancied climbing in people's windows at night." He shrugged. "I had no idea what he was talking about."

The parchment was sealed with wax, but the seal had no visible markings. It looked like it was simply pressed with a cork.

I broke the seal and read the note.

"Well?" Sapphire asked, practically leaning over my chair to get a look at the paper. "What's it say?"

"It says, *I look forward to a long and fruitful partnership.*"

Bull scratched the top of his head. "What do you think that means?"

I squished the paper in my hand, feeling nauseous. "It means Senator Gerrick owns us. I'm going to be forced to be at his beck and call. As long as he has something to hold over my head, he knows I won't have a choice."

"Maybe we're looking at this the wrong way," Reevie said.

"Maybe we should look at this as an opportunity."

My fingers tightened around the paper. I knew where he was going with this, and I didn't like it.

"What is it that the other tribes have that we don't?"

"Money," Sapphire said.

"Food," Bull added.

"Common sense," I groaned.

Reevie gave me a scolding look. "They have sponsorship. They have ties to the aristocracy. And if we were to have the same, it could lead to us having everything you just said we were missing—money, food, even better clothing. This might be the break we've been looking for. We might get a senator of our very own."

"You act like that's a good thing," I said.

Sapphire shifted, a hungry look appearing on her face. "It could be."

Except they weren't the ones who would be forced to deal with Gerrick. I was. "I guess we'll find out," I said, not wanting to argue the point. "But right now, Senator Gerrick is the least of our worries."

"What do you mean?"

"I mean we have less than one week to meet the Guild's demands. If we can't produce the required price, then there won't be a tribe here for Gerrick to profit from."

Reevie sighed, his earlier excitement melting from his face like hot candle wax. "Good point."

"How are we going to raise fifteen pieces of gold?" Bull asked, wearing the same downcast expression.

"At least on that, I might have us covered," I said, attempting to keep a straight face.

Everyone turned, watching in silence as I grabbed my overstuffed satchel off the floor and emptied its contents. Their eyes bulged as gilded candlesticks, painted platters, miniature statues, and at least one decorative vase came rolling out.

I shrugged with a wry smile. "I might have pilfered a few things on my way out of Gerrick's. Reckon he owes us this much for what he put us through."

The others nodded, no one saying a word as they stared at the small fortune lying at their feet.

Reevie's smile reappeared.

"That still leaves us with the king's seal," Sapphire said. "And no one gets into the palace without an invitation."

"An invitation?" Master Fentin lifted his head, his spectacles tilting enough for him to adjust. "You have one."

I shared a befuddled look with the others. "We have what?"

"An invitation. Haven't you heard that the king has recently announced the opening of the throne to the people of Elondria?"

Mistress Orilla's head popped up. "That's right. We received the notice a couple of weeks ago. Can you imagine being able to walk right into the throne room and meet the king and queen?"

Master Fentin pursed his lips. "I have a few things I'd certainly like to get off my chest."

I looked at Reevie and Sapphire. Both had the same excited look on their faces.

This might be it. Our way in. I started to laugh.

"What's wrong with you?" Reevie asked.

"I was just thinking. If Kore hadn't tried to stop us from meeting the Guild's demands by arresting Master Fentin, and if I hadn't snuck into Senator Gerrick's house to save him, we would have never found something worth selling, and we would have never heard about the palace opening its doors. So, in a way, if we pull this off, we'll have Kore to thank for it."

"I'll be sure to send him a thank-you," Master Fentin said with a yawn, grimacing as he prodded the wrapping around his chest.

"Come, Fentin," Mistress Orilla said as she stood. "We need to get you into bed."

Master Fentin yawned again, and I joined him. It hadn't really dawned on me until then that I'd been up all night as well, and my bed was calling. After helping Master Fentin and Mistress Orilla to one of our empty guest rooms, I headed straight for mine and what would be a long soak in a very hot tub of water. I hoped the paint wouldn't prove too difficult to remove.

Chapter 32

AFTER A MUCH-NEEDED night's rest, we found ourselves back in the chiefs' study discussing strategies. Master Fentin was feeling a little better, and he and Mistress Orilla agreed to stay a few more days so Reevie could keep an eye on him. There wasn't much they could do about the shop now, anyway. Not until his ribs had healed enough to move about. I had already promised him as much help as we could afford.

"It's the only chance we have," I said to the others, scratching at my arm. I'd spent part of the night soaking in a hot tub of water, trying to scrub the paint off. Reevie had laced it with some sort of concoction to help it come off easier, and for the most part it had worked, but it had left my skin raw. I lifted my sleeve to scratch a little harder, then noticed my brand was showing and quickly lowered it.

"It's certainly a risk," Mistress Orilla countered.

"I still don't like it," Master Fentin said, wagging his head as he tapped his boot with his cane. "Wish I'd never brought it up. Too many things can go wrong. The palace is like an island. If you were discovered, you'd never make it back across that bridge." He shook his head, tapping the bottom of his cane with his foot. "I tell you, I just don't like it."

"Unfortunately," Reevie sighed, "we don't seem to have much of a choice at this point. Either we get the seal or we starve. Without Guild membership, Hurricane won't be able to pick. In fact, I'd lay wager that before the end of next week, more than one tribe will be at our doorsteps, demanding their claim to our territory."

"Kore wants our territory, no doubt to keep Cutter from getting it," Sapphire said.

I scooted forward in my seat. "Either way, it doesn't matter. I have to get the ring this week."

"You'll have to get it tomorrow," Mistress Orilla said.

"What? Why tomorrow?"

"Because that's the only day the palace is open."

I sank back in my chair.

After a short but glum silence, Reevie spoke. "Let's say by some twist of fate, luck actually decides to shine on you tomorrow and you manage to make it not only through the gates, but into the palace itself. What then?" He looked at the others. "Have any of you been inside the palace before? Does anyone know where the king would keep his seal?"

"Wherever he signs his documents, I guess," Sapphire said.

"Like his study?" Bull blurted out, looking pleased with himself for having thought of it.

Reevie's jaw tightened. "And does anyone know where that study is? For that matter, do we even know where the throne room is? What if the ring isn't in his study? What if he's wearing it? Do any of you . . ."

"Fine," I said. "We get the point. It's a hopeless mess."

"It's more than that," Reevie added. "The palace is a city in itself. This isn't like climbing into Gerrick's bedroom window and pilfering some keepsakes. This would be like trying to search every room in every house in Bayside."

"So, what are you suggesting?" I asked, throwing up my arms in frustration. "Are you saying we shouldn't even try?"

"No. I don't know. I just don't want to see you get caught. If you're hauled off to prison or, more likely, executed for breaking into the palace to commit thievery, then what happens to the rest of us?"

"The same thing that happens if I don't try. You starve."

Reevie sat back in his chair, grumbling under his breath. "My point exactly."

"I doubt the king will be wearing the signet," Master Fentin said, stopping the rhythmic tap of his cane. "The signet is rather large, and probably uncomfortable to wear. However, if the goal is to make your way around the palace, I might have something that could help."

"What is it?" At this point, I'd take any amount of help I could get.

"I have a couple of historical books written on the construction of Aramoor. One of them, I believe, specifically describes the royal palace. There might even be a diagram or two depicting what it looked like back then. It couldn't have changed too much." He hesitated. "I doubt it tells you where the king's study is, but at the very least, you'll know something about the layout."

"That would be extremely useful," I said.

Master Fentin scratched the top of his head. "I don't know why I didn't think of it sooner. Guess I'm just getting old." His smile suddenly faded, and he sank back into the sofa cushion despondently.

"What's wrong?" I asked.

"After what the patrollers did to the shop, I have no idea where the book is."

The short-lived glimmer of hope in everyone's eyes winked out.

I looked at Reevie. "Do we have enough to hire a carriage across town for Master Fentin? He doesn't need to be walking that far, and he's the only one who stands a chance of finding that book."

"We have a few spare coins I've been saving for an emergency."

"Good. I'd say this qualifies." I looked at Bull, frowned, then turned to Sapphire. "Do you think you could find us a carriage? You're the best-dressed of us. If I were to send Bull out there, he'd likely frighten them off."

Bull looked down at his threadbare clothes and grunted.

"I can manage the carriage," Mistress Orilla said. "Leave it to me."

I turned to Sapphire.

She nodded, already anticipating what I was going to ask. "I'll go with her."

"Good. We also need someone to hock the items I grabbed from Gerrick's. If we show up with a bag full of wares, I'm sure Kore and Cutter will complain that we didn't complete the task. There's at least fifteen or twenty pieces' worth in there, don't you think?"

"More," Reevie said, "depending on who you take them to. I didn't see any specific markings on the items that would indicate they belonged to Senator Gerrick, so they should be easy to sell."

I nodded as though that had been my intention all along, when in truth I hadn't given two flips of Sapphire's blade as to whether they'd been marked when I grabbed them. "Fine," I said, clapping my hands on my knees. "While Master Fentin and I look for that book, see if you can find a buyer, and with any luck, we'll be one step closer to saving Hurricane. And maybe, just maybe, we won't all starve to death."

Sapphire groaned. "Sure, all we need to do is sneak into one of the most heavily guarded places in the Five Kingdoms and steal one of the most highly regarded royal artifacts. And if we somehow manage to do that, we get to eat. Lucky us."

Bull looked like he was going to be sick.

"Way to dampen our spirits, Sapphire," Reevie said, standing from his chair. "Best we get to it, then. Half the morning's already gone."

As I helped Reevie pack our sack load of treasures, Mistress

Orilla and Sapphire walked into the old merchant district to purchase a buggy. When they returned, Sapphire agreed to accompany Reevie and Bull into town as they met with a couple of vendors our tribe typically did business with, vendors who didn't worry with where the goods came from as long as they were marketable.

The ride across town was rather pleasant. It was my first time in a buggy. It was clearly only made to seat two, but three would fit if you didn't mind getting a little squished. It wasn't a full carriage with a top and decorative siding, more of a glorified cart with padded seats, but it certainly beat walking. The horse trotted along at a comfortable pace, the driver attentive to the pedestrians, unlike Gerrick's drivers, who seemed to find running people down good sport.

I spent most of the time eagerly anticipating getting my hands on a blueprint of the palace. Having a guide like that would be worth its weight in gold. I just hoped I had enough time to study it. The palace was larger than most cities, and finding possible locations for the king's study was going to be extremely difficult.

The driver pulled up beside the shop, and we all got out. Mistress Orilla paid the man with the rest of the coin Reevie had given her. We couldn't afford to pay him to wait, so the man tipped his hat and snapped the reins.

While Master Fentin stopped to chat with the young couple next door and explain that his arrest had all been a big misunderstanding, I followed Mistress Orilla into the shop.

"It's dark in here," she said, grabbing one of the lanterns hanging on the wall behind the front desk.

I found the light from the windows rather adequate. The sun had risen high enough to reach the front, and its rays were slowly crawling across the floor like a line of turtles, each wanting to be the first to reach the shelves.

Mistress Orilla found a striker, and the shadows within reach of her lamp fled all the more. By the time Master Fentin finished his conversation with the neighbors, Mistress Orilla and I had managed to light most of the lanterns hanging around the shop, illuminating the darker recesses where the sunlight was unable to reach.

"What a mess," Mistress Orilla said as she stumbled over a small pile of books on her way across the front.

"Aye," Master Fentin agreed with a downcast look, "this could take a while."

The place was in chaos. Books strewn everywhere. Shelves overturned. It wasn't to say that it was ever in perfect order, but at least you could walk from the front to the back without hindrance.

"Do you at least remember which shelf the books had been on?" I asked. "Maybe it hasn't been thrown too far."

Master Fentin stood for a bit, nibbling on his lower lip. Finally, he pulled out his spectacles, placed them on the bridge of his nose, and started forward. "I think I had them with the books on architecture near the back. Or maybe they were lumped in with the historical references." He shook his head. "It's been so long since I purchased those books, I'm not sure."

I groaned. "Do you remember the names of the books, at least?"

He stopped beside a small pile, slowly attempting to straighten crumpled pages. "You know, I don't recall."

I bit my lip as well.

"You might try the back wall on the right," he finally said. "Books that haven't been requested in some time tend to get stuck there."

I nodded and started for the back.

The books in the far corner hadn't received the same amount of attention from the patrollers as those near the front. In fact, the shelves appeared mostly untouched, which was made even more apparent when I sneezed and a cloud of dust lifted into the air. Master Fentin wasn't exaggerating when he said these books were rarely touched. They were in clear need of a good dusting. I waved my hand in front of my face, hoping to drive the cloud away, but there wasn't much farther it could go.

The last shelf butted up against the corner wall. Mistress Orilla and Master Fentin rounded the second-to-last shelf and joined me in the aisle, bringing the light with them. Mistress Orilla held up the lantern. She appeared to be looking for a hook on the wall to hang it, but not finding one, she simply scooted a couple of books on the adjacent shelf out of the way and placed it there.

We stood to either side of the lantern to keep from blocking its light. There was no order to these books, at least none that I could find. A set of judicial regulations regarding the collection of taxes sat beside a thin volume of Cylmaran poetry. *Cylmaran poetry?* I chuckled to myself. Those were two words I'd never thought to hear in the same sentence. Next was a rather thick tome on the intricacies of court etiquette. I had half a mind to grab the etiquette book for reference, except it was as thick as my fist and I didn't have a month to read through it.

"Do you see anything?" I asked, having scanned each of the five rows on the shelf and come up empty.

Master Fentin didn't say anything at first as he slid his finger along the spines on the top shelf, mumbling as he read each one. He finally shook his head and took a step back. "Nope. Don't see anything yet."

Moving the lantern down, we continued on. Row after row, we scanned the spines, but with no more luck than we had on the first shelf. By the time we reached the last of the untouched rows, I was sweating. Without some kind of guidance, there was no way in the flaming Pits that I was going to pull off this heist.

Mistress Orilla lifted the lantern, and Master Fentin released an exasperated sigh. "I'm sorry, my boy. It's been so many years, and my mind isn't as sharp as it used to be. Perhaps I sold them. I just don't remember."

I followed the two to the front of the shop, doing my best not to step on any of the books, which proved rather difficult, considering how many of them there were. Some I had to scoot out of the way or risk leaving my shoeprint on the covers. "Don't you have a record in your bookkeeping, or something, that lists what books you have here?"

"Ah, inventory was never my strong suit. When I was younger, I had a wonderful memory, though. I could tell you the name and place of any book in my shop."

Mistress Orilla snorted. "That was a *very* long time ago."

Master Fentin sighed. "Sadly, it's not what it used to be." He turned and slowly scanned the shop. "I'm afraid it's a hopeless cause. If the books are here, I don't see how we could ever find them in time."

The last remaining glimmer of hope I was clinging to was gone. Like a dandelion in the wind, I watched the seeds float away, knowing I would most likely never see them again. What was I going to do now? I'd been counting on those drawings to help me move around the palace. I gave the shop one last look around, then headed for the door. There wasn't much more that could be done here, and I needed to get back and pack whatever I might need for tomorrow. I stopped at the door and turned. "Are you coming?"

Master Fentin looked at his wife, then shook his head. "Now that we're here, I think we'll stay and clean up a bit. Besides, there's nothing quite like sleeping in one's own bed."

I nodded. Reevie wasn't going to be happy, but it wasn't like I didn't understand. I remembered my first couple of nights sleeping someplace other than the little cubby under the Granary. It had taken a while for me to adjust to the Temple's sleeping quarters.

I thanked Master Fentin and Mistress Orilla for their help and promised to send some of our cleaners over to lend a hand, that is, if we still had any cleaners left after the Guild meeting.

My walk across town was a gloomy one. Not at all like the carriage ride I had taken from the Temple to the bookshop earlier. Now, each pad of my shoes on the worn cobbles whispered of my upcoming failure.

Chapter 33

"YOU COULDN'T FIND one book that would help?" Reevie gave his hair a good tug. If he kept it up, his head was going to look as sparse as Bull's beard. Bull had been trying to grow one in for weeks without much success. It was sporadic at best, little more than patches of whiskers across his cheeks and chin. He looked like an alley mutt with mange.

Not wanting to repeat the bleak news all over again, I simply shook my head. It was hard enough saying it the first time, let alone with any semblance of determination. I needed to appear unconcerned, confident I could still pull this off. Besides, I was the one who'd agreed to the absurd requirement in the first place, so it was my job to get us through it.

I was Upakan, after all. We Upaka were masters of disguise. If anyone could sneak in and out of the palace, it was me. I sank into the cushioned sofa in the chiefs' study, releasing a heavy exhale as I did. Who was I kidding? I wasn't the master of anything. Except, perhaps, getting into trouble.

"What are you going to do, then?" Bull asked, standing to the side of the arranged seats. He said he didn't feel right sitting with the rest of us, as though a chief himself. After his second refusal to sit down, we finally gave up arguing and let him continue standing.

I took a moment to consider. I could have lied to him and told him I had it all under control. But I wasn't that good of a liar. "I have no idea."

Bull stared at me a second, then plopped down into the empty chair after all.

"On the brighter side," Sapphire said, lifting a thick purse from where it hung around her neck, "our errand in town went very well. We found a buyer for the items you picked from Senator Gerrick's."

"And we fetched a good price," Bull added.

Sapphire smiled. "Thirty-two gold for the lot."

I leaned forward, nearly tempted to snatch the purse. "Thirty-two gold?"

"It was worth more than that," Reevie said, "but considering who was selling it, we were lucky."

"Hey," Sapphire said with a sneer.

"Not you in particular," Reevie quickly amended. "I mean street kids in general. They had to know the items had been swiped."

Sapphire's eyes softened.

Bull snickered. "It also might have had something to do with the way Sapphire was gripping the hilt of her blade while the man considered his price."

Sapphire shrugged, but the corners of her mouth curled with what I thought was pride.

"That should leave us with enough left over to get Cutter's daggers and Noph's hat," I said.

"Done and done," Sapphire said. "We stopped by the haberdashery and the cutlers on the way back and found a hat Noph would probably like. Well, I don't know if he'll like it or not, but it was purple. And we found a couple of daggers for Cutter."

"I hope you didn't spend too much on them," I said.

Sapphire shook her head. "Nothing fancy, just durable."

"Good." Having that burden lifted off my shoulders was at least some relief.

"You need to start packing," Reevie said, shifting in his seat. "What are you going to take with you?"

"Whatever I can fit in my pockets."

Bull scratched at his uneven beard. "Why not take Reevie's carry bag?"

"Because the guards at the palace will probably search it," Sapphire said, clicking her tongue.

"Oh, I didn't think of that." He looked at me. "Guess you better take your overcoat, then. More pockets."

Regrettably, he was right. The coat would be one more headache I had to look forward to. We were still at the tail end of Èldwin, and the days were as hot as an Azmarian wasp pepper. But as long as I wasn't carrying any noticeable weapons, like a sword or bow, the guards were probably less likely to search my clothes than a satchel.

After the meeting, I went straight to the infirmary to start gathering supplies, the most important of which was ether. At least, what little was left.

"We're running low," I said to Reevie, who was busy looking for some clean wraps and a small bottle of strong wine in case I was stabbed or cut or shot. "Are you able to make more?"

"No. It would take too long. I have the mandrake but only a dash of hemlock, and tellareen mushrooms are hard to get this time of year. Even when we have the gold, vendors aren't all that willing to sell to someone my age." He handed me a small jar of herbs that he used for cleaning wounds, mostly willow bark and yarrow. "You'll have to make do, I guess." He pulled another jar off the shelf and poured some of its contents into a small vial and capped the end. "And take some of this. You never know when it might come in handy."

"What is it?" I pulled the cork to take a quick whiff.

"I wouldn't do—"

"Whoa!" I stumbled backward. My nose felt like it was on fire. My eyes watered so bad, I could hardly see Reevie standing there with his hand over his mouth. "Why didn't you warn me?"

"I tried to."

I looked for a label, but there was none. "What is it?"

"It's hartshorn. That'll wake a black bear in the middle of winter."

"I'd say." I wiped the run of snot dripping from my upper lip.

My eyes were still watering, but not so bad that I couldn't stopper the cork and stuff the little container into one of the inner pockets of my coat.

Reevie looked me over. "You think you got everything?"

I glanced down at the bulges in my jacket. "I think I have too much."

"Nonsense," Reevie said emphatically as he headed for the door. "You can never have too much."

I followed him out, but instead of heading to the dining hall, I returned to my room, where I promptly unloaded half of what Reevie had stuffed in my pockets. I couldn't afford to take this many supplies, not if I wanted to move about the palace freely. I did keep what was left of the ether, and a few of the clean wrappings and wine. I even kept the hartshorn. I figured if I ran out of the ether, the other might daze someone long enough for me to incapacitate them.

With two piles stacked neatly on my bed—one for taking, and the other for hiding to make it look like I was taking—I headed for the dining hall to join the others.

Our meal was consumed in silence, and it wasn't because the quality of the food had us stuffing our faces, more the fact that no one really knew what to say.

The entire hall seemed to have noticed our table's somber disposition, as the room held a stillness that wasn't usually seen during mealtime. Whispered conversations and anxious glances in our direction let me know that tomorrow's activities weighed heavy on everyone. The tribe knew what was at stake. I couldn't afford to let them down.

I lowered my spoon back into the bowl. "Think I'll turn in early," I said, not bothering to look at the others as I stood from the table.

"Good idea," Reevie added, clearly trying to sound encouraging. "Some rest will help clear your mind."

I nodded and left.

Rest was about the last thing I managed that night. Tossing and turning, I ran through a thousand scenarios of what might happen on the morrow, none of which ended with me getting the ring and making it out alive.

I'd barely managed to doze off when I was startled awake by a knock on the door.

"You up?"

I groaned. "I am now."

Sapphire walked in and sat on the edge of my bed. "Didn't sleep much, did you?"

I yawned and raised myself up on one elbow but made sure to keep my lower half under the covers. "Not really."

"Not at all, by the look of you. Are you ready?"

"Would it matter if I wasn't?"

"You sure you don't want me to come along?"

I hesitated. Actually, I would have loved the company, but I shook my head. "It'll be easier to move around the palace if there's only one of us."

"I don't think sneaking around that place is going to be easy, no matter who's there."

"True, but it'll be easier for me to blend in if I'm not worrying about someone else."

Her shoulders stiffened.

We sat there a moment longer without saying anything. Didn't really need to. Everything that needed saying had been said. All that was left was for me to eat a quick bite of tacky porridge and be on my way.

I started to pull back my covers and get out of bed but quickly yanked them back up. I'd forgotten I wasn't dressed. "Do you mind?"

She shook her head, then stood. "I'll save you a seat for breakfast." She left and shut the door behind her.

I waited to throw back my covers until I'd made sure she wouldn't invent some excuse to step back in, then got out of bed and quickly pulled my trousers on.

After slurping down the porridge, made palatable only by the minute hint of honey that had been stirred in for flavor, I packed the rest of my gear and met the others at the front gate. By the crowd gathering at the front, it looked like the entire tribe had shown up to see me off.

I stared at the ragged, dirty faces staring back at me, reminding myself why I was doing this, and why I had to succeed.

"Do you have everything?" Reevie asked for the hundredth time, like a fretting mother.

"Everything I can carry," I said with a soft pat to the front of my overcoat. I didn't tell him that half of his provisions were hiding under my bed.

"Good," he said with a curt nod, but I could see the concern in his eyes.

I turned to say something to Sapphire but was suddenly yanked off the ground and swallowed up by a pair of meaty arms.

I wheezed as the air in my chest was squeezed out. "Tubby. I . . . I can't breathe."

"Sorry." The huge boy lowered me back to the ground.

I took a moment to catch my breath, then patted him on the forearm. His shoulder was too high to reach. "I'll be fine. You obey Reevie and Sapphire while I'm gone."

He smiled mischievously.

"Are you armed?" Sapphire asked.

"Of course." I had a couple of blades stashed away in the folds of my coat. I wasn't about to walk in there without weapons.

"Do you want us to walk you there?" Bull asked. Our head beater didn't like me wandering off around the city without protection. He usually insisted on following me himself. Honestly, I think he looked for any excuse that allowed him to get out from behind the Temple's walls.

"No need. I'd prefer to go alone."

"If they take you, Protector," Mouse said, "I'll sneak in there and get you out. They don't call me *Mouse* for nothing."

"You'll do no such thing. If they take me, you'll need to help the others find a way out of the city before Kore and Cutter rush in."

"We'll fight them off," Mouse said.

"No, you won't. The safest thing will be to leave."

"And go where?" Squeaks asked in his high-pitched voice as he stood between Mouse and Petal.

I looked at Reevie and Sapphire. "See if Red or Noph will be willing to take in refugees. If not, you might need to leave Aramoor."

"But Aramoor's our home," Mouse said, looking astonished that I'd suggest such a thing.

"It's better than being scooped up by the Sil'foren Orphan Homes."

More than a few of the kids standing nearby trembled. Everyone knew that Sil'foren used the homes as a front for free labor for his warehouses. Many of the street kids had at one time been members of Master Sil'foren's labor force and had since run away, deciding that living on the streets was preferable to living there.

"We'll keep them safe," Sapphire said.

I nodded and smiled, doing my best not to appear too upset about saying goodbye for what could be the last time. With an emotional hug from Reevie, a firm handshake from Bull, and a punch in the arm followed by a soft kiss on the cheek from Sapphire, I headed out the gate.

"Wait!" someone up ahead said. "Are we too late?"

Master Fentin and Mistress Orilla hobbled down the brick lane to meet us. When they saw me, they waved. "Good. We caught you in time," Master Fentin said.

I ran to greet them. "You found the books?"

The older couple stopped in front of me as the kids inside rushed through the gate to see what was happening. Master Fentin shook his head. "Sorry, my boy, no such luck. We searched all night for a single reference, but to no avail, I'm afraid."

"We wanted to catch you before you left," Mistress Orilla said with a warm smile, "to wish you luck and offer you a ride across town."

"That's very generous." A carriage would certainly save me some much-needed time. Time I could put toward locating the king's study.

"Good," Master Fentin said as he turned. "Then let's be on our way."

I took a moment to look at those I was leaving behind, those I had grown so close to over the last couple of months. They were more than friends. They were family. And they were depending on me. So, with a very fake smile, I turned and marched down the lane, head held high for all to see.

Chapter 34

THE BUGGY RIDE ACROSS town saved quite a bit of time. The driver attempted to give us a smooth ride, but with potholes like the ones we had in the Maze, it was an impossible task. The jarring eventually lessened the closer we got to Bayside, signaling that my time was almost upon me.

I stared out at the blue waters of the bay as we passed the shipyards, hardly noticing the boats at dock or the crest of the waves moving in, or even the harbor bell chiming out the time. My mind was in a fog. My father would be ashamed by how unprepared I was for this mission.

Well, maybe not my father, but every other instructor in Clan Orpa would have been. The number one lesson they ingrained in us during our training was to always have a plan, and three more lined up in case that one didn't work.

I had no plan at all, other than to use the king's open-door policy to sneak my way into the palace. We passed Bayside and took the next road to the left, which ran alongside the wall separating the city from the bay. When I saw the spires rising in the distance, my hands began to tingle, the same way they had when I'd found myself facing Instructor Dorin's whips.

I looked across the seat at Master Fentin and Mistress Orilla. It was the quietest I'd ever seen them. Both smiled when they saw me looking, but there was sadness in their eyes. They were just as frightened as I was.

"You can stop here, driver," Master Fentin said, his hand pressed to his chest as he spoke. I knew the feeling. My own ribs were twinging as well. Reevie had done a thorough job of wrapping them earlier, which helped.

The driver pulled back on the reins, and the buggy came to a stop.

Ahead was King's Way West and the two guard towers stationed at the entrance to the bridge. On the other side of King's Way West, and a few blocks north, was the main barracks for the city. It was one of the only places in Aramoor I hadn't risked scouting during my overnight escapades. And for good reason. There seemed to be a never-ending supply of lancers flowing from the bridge to the barracks and back.

The armsmen held their heads high as they marched past. Uniforms bearing the crest of the crown and sun gleamed in the early morning light. They stood tall and proud. The city's patrollers certainly didn't display that level of regard for their own uniforms. Something about them made me smile. I think it was their kinship. A brotherhood of soldiers willing to lay their lives down for each other. In a world where it seemed that everyone looked out for only themselves, it was comforting to see a group of people who worked as one.

"You ready?"

"What?" I looked at Master Fentin, who had leaned forward to place his hand on my knee. My momentary distraction ended, and all my previous fears came rushing back in.

Taking a deep breath, I nodded and stood. I wasn't ready, but I didn't want them to know that. I even went so far as to give each of them a firm hug. Who knew; it might have been for the last time.

"You be careful, my boy," Master Fentin said. "Keep your eyes open and your head down."

Before I could answer, Mistress Orilla shoved something in my hands. "Here, take it with you. You'll probably get hungry during your search."

I didn't have to look. I could smell it. I smiled and stuffed the sandwich in the only inner pocket that wasn't completely filled with Reevie's necessities. My mouth watered, and I almost teared up, but I forced it down.

Master Fentin patted me on the back one last time, and Mistress Orilla kissed the top of my head. With a quick straightening of my coat, I moved to the edge of the buggy and stepped down.

"May the Creator guide you," Master Fentin offered solemnly, and the two retook their seats.

I waved as the driver turned the buggy around and carried the couple back the way they'd come. I stood there until they rounded the corner, no longer to be seen. I don't know if it was out of sentiment that I continued to stand there, or if I was just looking for any excuse not to turn around, but eventually I squared my shoulders, took a deep breath, and started for King's Way West and the growing line of pedestrians standing in front of the bridge.

Surprisingly, the line wasn't as long as I had expected, and I took my place at the end behind a young couple and their daughter. The little girl wasn't much older than ten, and quite unafraid of strangers, as she smiled and waved at me. She also didn't seem to be all that bothered by my eyes.

"What's your name?" I asked, trying to be polite.

She squeezed the somewhat worn doll in her arms as though wanting to make sure it was safe. "Eva."

"That's a pretty name."

She smiled, her freckled cheeks lifting. "What's yours?"

"I'm Ayrion."

She looked down at her doll, then back at me. "Naddi thinks that is pretty, too."

"Thank you," I said, not sure if I was to be addressing Eva or Naddi, so I took a moment to look at both.

"Have you come to talk to the king?" She raised her doll for me to see. "It's Naddi's first time."

I looked at the doll. Naddi's dress, which at one time had been a bright yellow with red roses, had faded to a soft goldenrod, and the once-bright flowers had transitioned from red to pink, an indication that the toy was well loved. "It's my first time, too."

"Don't be scared," she said. "Papa says he's real nice."

Eva's father turned around, and I took a small step back and lowered my head, making sure to keep a safe distance from the little girl.

The man looked me over, then scanned those standing in line behind me. "Who are you here with, son?"

"I'm, uh, I'm here by myself."

"By yourself?" The man sounded surprised. "This line is for people wanting an audience with the king." His tone seemed to portray a sense of urgency, as if afraid I might not have known where I was and had simply stepped in line out of curiosity.

"I know," I reassured him. "I hear he actually lets you talk to him. In person."

"Aye," Eva's father said with a curt nod, "but that's nothing to take for granted. Serious business, talking with the king."

"It is," I agreed, nodding as I prepared to deliver one of the lies I'd concocted the night before, "but my father's ill and needs help." The way they were looking at my eyes, they probably thought I was ill as well. "If I can't get him some medicine, he's going to die." I added an emotional sniff at the end, just like I'd rehearsed.

The man's wife took a step forward. "Where's your mother, dear?"

I wiped my eyes. "With the Creator, ma'am," I said, forcing my voice to crack slightly. I doubted they believed the king would get involved with something that trivial, but who was going to turn away a boy trying to help his dying father?

I felt a strong hand on my shoulder and looked up. The man attempted a comforting smile. "We'll say a prayer for him tonight, son." He looked at his wife. "Won't we, dear?"

His wife nodded. "Of course."

"Me too," Eva said with a bright smile. "And so will Naddi." She lifted the doll to look in her eyes. "Isn't that right?"

Naddi's head bobbed up and down, and Eva smiled.

"Thank you kindly," I said with an appreciative bow. I started to say more, but our conversation was cut short as we reached the two towers and the armed guards in front.

The bridge beyond was incredible, built completely of stone, and not the sort of rock one would see cobbled together on any city road, but blocks almost as large as those used to form the massive wall surrounding Aramoor. On either side were raised walkways wide enough for several people, along with crenelated lookouts affording a breathtaking view of the Bay of Torrin on one side and the mighty Shemoa River on the other.

The bridge was wide enough for at least four wagons, and long enough to make me wonder how anyone could have built something so high off the ground without it collapsing. It made the sky bridges at the Guild seem positively trivial.

"Turn out your bags," one of the lancers said as we moved up in line. I was thankful I'd left my bag at home. "What's in there?" The guard pointed at Eva's father's satchel.

Her father opened it for the man to see. "Just our lunch. It was a long walk here."

The guard took a look inside, then nodded. "Names?"

"My name is Fosner. This is my wife, Tula, my daughter, Eva—"

"And I'm Ayrion," I quickly added, hoping Eva's father wouldn't turn me in.

Eva's father looked at me for a moment, then finally nodded. I felt guilty about using them like that, but what choice did I have?

The lancer looked at me also, but I kept my head turned away just enough to keep my eyes from being seen. I tugged on my sleeve, making sure the brand on my wrist remained hidden.

The guard's stare seemed to last forever. If I'd had a hood on my overcoat, I might have been tempted to raise it. "*Act like you belong there, and others will believe it*," my concealment instructor would say as she'd walk through class, jabbing at us with her tapered rod. "*But always carry a sharp knife up your sleeve in case they don't.*"

I patted my arm, reassuring myself of the blade that was securely fastened.

The guard jotted something on the paper he was carrying, then motioned us forward. "Move along. Once you reach the other side, someone there will escort you to where you need to go. Next," he said, already motioning for those behind us to move forward.

I followed Eva and her family out onto the bridge. I could hear the guard behind me, demanding the next in line turn out their bags and present their names. I almost felt sorry for him. I couldn't imagine having to stand there all day, saying the same thing over and over and over again. Then again, I'd trade what he was doing for what I was about to do any day of the week.

Eva took off running for the side of the bridge. Hoping to take my mind off of what was awaiting me on the other side, I joined her at the edge to get a peek at the river below.

Eva's family soon followed.

"Amazing," Eva's father said, glancing over the side. "Simply amazing."

He wasn't lying. We were walking hundreds of feet over the river below. I hocked up a wad and spat it over the side, but instead of dropping, it blew up under the pylons. The wind was quite voracious from this distance. It reminded me of Howling Gorge, except without the eerie noises the wind would make when whipping through the rocky peaks.

I left the edge and joined Eva's family as we made our way to the other side. Ahead, there was a group of people waiting underneath the archway. I recognized a few of those who had been in line before us. The guards must have been waiting for the group to reach a certain size before escorting them in.

I followed Eva's family through the arches, taking a moment to stare up at the spiked beams of the gate overhead. The thought of it snapping loose and dropping on my head had my feet shuffling faster. However, the gate was soon forgotten as I crossed beyond the guard towers and took my first good look at the royal palace.

It was like nothing I'd ever seen before. I could catch a glimpse of the uppermost spires from any point in the city, but I was unprepared for what it was like to see them up close. Nothing could hold a candle to the magnificence of the royal palace. The intricate details and beauty carved into the stone itself was remarkable.

An open courtyard ahead led from the bridge and outer bailey to what looked like the main entrance. Lancers on horseback patrolled in formation across the cobbles, their horses in perfect step with each other. Almost like a parade. I'd never seen horsemen perform like that before. I remembered my brief time on a horse, traveling from the Lost City to Oswell. I had been lucky just to stay in the saddle. I couldn't imagine being able to make something so powerful obey like that.

I found myself wanting to try.

There were gardens to the right and left, each one splendid and lush despite the heat. Drooping willows and sculpted greenery set the perimeter, while vine-covered trellises and shapely trimmed floral displays filled the space within, leaving only enough room for the crushed-rock paths and the statue-lined fountains. The gardens were dotted with onlookers. I couldn't tell which were more colorfully arrayed, the flowers or the people admiring them. I'd rarely seen such fanciful outfits, even in town. These must have been the upper nobility. Snobs all, I was sure. I'd certainly never met any of them who weren't.

Along with the polished lancers and the gaudy nobles, there were scores of workers and staff scurrying around the courtyard from one building to another. Each wore their own set of uniforms. Some were brown with white trim, others black and gold. I saw a few with blue, and those working in the gardens wore green and white.

A thought took hold, the beginnings of a plan forming. The uniforms might work to my benefit if I could get my hands on one.

"This way," one of the lancers in front said, motioning us forward. Another group of people behind us had just made it across the bridge.

I stuck with Eva and her family as we strolled across the courtyard for one of the main buildings ahead. There was a nervous energy amongst those gathered. I could feel my heart picking up speed as we drew closer to the wide, arching tunnel that led through the front of the building and into what looked like an inner courtyard.

The mounted lancers, who stood between us and the palace, shifted position and split down the middle, leaving just enough room for us to pass between. I couldn't tell if it was for show or intimidation, but whatever the reason, it seemed to be working. I was impressed, but my palms were sweating.

We crossed through the tunnel and into the inner courtyard, completely surrounded by balcony-lined buildings, all facing toward the center fountain, which we had to skirt to reach what was clearly the central entrance into the palace itself. Unlike the naked faerie goddess who donned the Temple's fountain, this held an array of characters, mostly soldiers depicted in some great battle. I didn't know who they were fighting, but the scene portrayed their ferocity, both sides locked in an unending conflict.

Beyond the fountain were long white steps leading up to two enormous gold-inlay doors that were cut from white stone, and on either side of the doors stood a row of stone sentinels shaped from the same white rock. Each of the warriors was at least four or five times the size of an actual man. They stood at attention, halberd in one hand and shield in the other.

Looking up at them, it almost felt as though they were looking back, judging my worthiness to be there. I felt a flicker of bumps run down my arms as I scurried up the steps and into the open foyer beyond.

My mouth dropped, and I nearly collided with Eva's mother, who'd stopped in front of me. It was like stepping into some mythical realm. Senator Gerrick's estate, with all its lavish furnishings, looked like a broken-down hovel compared to what I was seeing. Gasps and excited chatter spread through the group. They were clearly as enthralled as I was.

The marble floors bore a myriad of designs, the most notable of which were the checkered tiles around the outer edge, like it was a large game board and we were the pieces. The vestibule was covered in exquisite architectural beauty: painted murals across the ceiling; pillars adorned with gold filigree; enormous vases that stood head and shoulders above me, each resting on stands of the same color and design; crystal chandeliers, their light reflected in the floors below.

It was beyond breathtaking. And daunting. I couldn't imagine the person who owned all of this being willing to take the time to even acknowledge someone like me, let alone actually listen to what I had to say.

"This way," the lancer urged. We were herded toward one of the open doorways on the left. Our steps echoed off the polished tiles as we moved to follow, no one wanting to leave the splendor of the place. But we weren't there to see the foyer; we were there to see the king.

Wait, I'm not here to see the king.

Quickly, I swept the vestibule, looking for any hint of where I might find the king's study. Unfortunately, it wasn't like they had a sign posted: THIS WAY TO THE ROYAL STUDY. As huge as this place was, some markers would be a good idea.

Apart from a stream of lancers, I couldn't make out anything of note. I did spot several more staff, dressed in black and white with gold trim, busy polishing the railings running up the grand staircase to the second floor.

I needed to get my hands on one of those uniforms. But how? For that matter, how was I going to sneak out of line long enough to look?

"Where're you going?" Eva asked as she caught me trying to creep toward the back of the line.

"I'll be right back," I lied, holding my finger to my lips. Everyone was too busy gawking at all the portraits and floral arrangements along the walls of the long corridor to notice me slipping between them. On the left were great windows looking out across the courtyard we'd just crossed. The morning sun reflected off the fountain, forcing me to squint.

We passed several branching corridors on the right, but only one had a potted plant large enough for me to hide behind. I slipped out of line. The people behind me kept me hidden from the lancers long enough to scrunch down behind the broad, angular leaves of the tall shrub.

I watched and waited as the procession made its way down the hall. Thankfully, the lancers hadn't seen me. Once the last of the group had passed, I slipped out to make my way back to the main foyer. If there was one thing I knew, the king's personal chambers wouldn't be on the first floor. That would be too easy to access, which meant I needed to reach the upper floors.

I rounded the corner and ran straight into a second company of lancers.

"Hey, you," one of the guards in front said, "back in line."

I ground my teeth. "Sorry," I said, keeping my eyes lowered. "I stopped to look at . . . this plant." I grabbed one of the shrub's longer stalks that was hanging out into the main corridor. "I, uh, I've never seen leaves this big."

"Move along."

"Yes, sir." I ran after the others, shuffling back into line. This was going to be harder than I thought. The corridors were simply too open, making it easy to spot anyone straying from the group. And these guards were clearly too well trained to miss it.

I wormed my way back to Eva and her family. "See? I told you I'd be right back," I said to Eva, doing my best to not let her see my frustration. Eva smiled and waved Naddi's arm at me to let me know her dolly was glad to see me as well.

The group chatted quietly as we marched along, pointing out one lavish decoration after another, but after a while, the earlier excitement died away.

The corridor opened into another large foyer, not quite as big as the first but every bit the size of the Temple's dining hall. On the right was a set of double doors, and the guards had everyone lining up behind them. The doors weren't quite as big as those from the main courtyard, but they were certainly fancier. They looked to be made of white marble, covered with intricate gold designs and edging. Just one small piece of the trim would keep

Hurricane fed for a couple of months.

Looking around, the only other way out was through the double doors ahead. There were guards stationed outside the corridor we'd just walked through, as well as where it picked up on the other side of the antechamber. There were also guards ahead, standing outside the double doors, and guards behind, moving us into place. I'd never seen so many watchful eyes. One thing was for sure: the chances of me sneaking away were slim to . . . well, it would be a cold day in the Pits of Aran'gal.

But it didn't stop me from trying.

The doors opened partway, and another couple at the front of the line walked through, then they closed once again. My legs felt wobbly and my forehead was slick. From the brief glimpse I got, I could tell the throne room beyond was massive.

If I didn't think of a way to escape, I was going to find myself standing before the most powerful man in the Five Kingdoms. I looked around once more, my hands visibly shaking. It wasn't like I could try fighting my way out. Maybe I could feign being sick and ask to leave. I looked at the lancers guarding the corridor. If I could make it past them, I could probably outrun them back to the foyer. But then what?

I guess if I was fast enough, I might be able to lose them in the corridors leading off the entranceway, but the entire palace would be alerted, making it even more difficult to move around unchallenged. I wrung my hands. I had to think of something.

I looked at the people behind me. I could try causing some kind of ruckus and sneak away during the commotion, but for a disturbance that big, it might cause the lancers to take action, and I couldn't take that chance. *Blazes!* Why was this proving so difficult?

"What's your name, and who are you with?"

"What?" I turned back around. It was the first time I'd noticed Eva and her family were no longer there. In fact, I'd been so preoccupied with trying to figure out how I was going to get out of line, I'd failed to notice how far in line we'd gone. *Flaming bunions!* I bit down on my lip. Reevie was rubbing off on me. What was I going to do now? I looked at the people behind me, hoping to find someone—anyone—I could reasonably claim to be with, but those closest turned away, not wanting to appear that they knew me.

With a nervous gulp, I turned back around, doing my best to not look the guard in the eyes, and if I did, only a quick glance in the hope he didn't notice their lack of color. "I'm here to see the king," I stated in as timid a voice as I could manage.

"Minors should be accompanied by an adult," the guard said, staring at me with a raised brow. "You shouldn't have been allowed in."

"But . . . but I've been waiting in line all morning, sir," I said, pitiful as a three-legged cat meowing for scraps. I placed my hand on my stomach. "I missed breakfast just to be here; probably won't get no lunch, either."

"Oh, let him in," one of the men behind me said; a couple of the others voiced their agreements as well.

I held a mournful expression, my head lowered to the side. If I could have conjured a tear or two, I would have. Just thinking about what was going to happen to my tribe if I didn't succeed was almost enough to jerk one out of me.

"Fine," the guard said, looking a little guilty himself. "Give me your name."

"Ayrion, sir."

"Where you from?"

"Aramoor, sir."

There was a man sitting behind the guard at a desk, jotting down my answers. He nodded, and the guard turned back around. "Step forward."

I took a couple of steps closer to the double doors. My knees had joined my hands, which were quivering bad enough that I placed them in my pockets. What was I going to do? My mind raced. I'd heard others in line talking about wanting their taxes lowered, or more patrols on the roads, especially in the outer regions. I heard one man and his wife speak of seeking justice for an abusive landowner whose property they managed. But none of these did me any good.

The doors opened, and the guard put his hand on my shoulder and pushed me forward. "You're next."

Chapter 35

A TALL, LANKY MAN stood just inside the doors, waiting for me. He was impressively dressed and wore a fluffy hat that reminded me of the old scribe who sat outside the Guild's meeting room and took roll. The only difference being that this man's uniform was crimson and gold instead of green, and most likely four or five times costlier.

The attendant looked me over, then took the slip of paper from the guard and read it quickly. As he did, I got my first good look at the throne room. It was enormous, even bigger than the open lobby at the front, if that was possible. The ceiling was at least three stories high, arching toward the center. It almost looked like the inside hull of a ship, just turned upside down.

The floor was hewn from green marble, each tile with its own set of white veins. A row of fluted pillars on the sides of the room, cut from the same emerald stone, formed a long corridor from where I stood to a set of steps on the far end that led up to the thrones.

My breath caught in my throat. It was the king and queen. "Holy gut rot." They were really there.

The man with the fluffy hat looked down at me with a startled expression, and I lowered my head.

I hadn't really thought they would be there. Sure, everyone had been saying they were taking their problems to the king, but I'd thought it was just a way of saying they were going to the palace and leaving a request in hopes the king would see it. I figured a royal scrivener would be the one taking requests.

My mind was racing. What was I going to say to them? The king and queen were too far away for a good description, and the longer I stared, the more nervous I became. I could see Eva and her family standing at the bottom of the steps, but I couldn't hear what they were discussing.

Needing something else to focus my attention on, I went back to studying the room. Apart from the main doors behind me, the only other way out was two doors on the opposite side of the chamber. One to the left of the dais and one on the right. Guards stood at both.

Sets of lancers flanked each of the pillars, and even more were around the base of the stairs where the king and queen sat. However, those guarding the platform were different from the rest of the lancers I'd seen so far. Their uniforms were black with some kind of white, or silver, emblem on the front. From this distance, I couldn't see what it was.

Light from windows lining each side of the hall streamed across the marble tiles, causing the white veins to sparkle. The morning sun backlit the crowd of nobles who'd clustered in between the columns, casually engaging in hushed conversations while no doubt enjoying the entertainment provided by us common folk. The half-smirks and disdainful glances had me fidgeting.

Just ahead, Eva and her parents bowed to the top of the platform where the king and queen sat and were escorted toward the door on the right. Having the petitioners exit a different way than we entered must have been to keep the foyer from getting overcrowded. I wondered which direction we would take back to the main lobby, and if there was a chance for me to sneak away there.

Someone grabbed my shoulder, and I jumped. "Follow me," the man with the fluffy hat said as he started across the room. The clicking of his shoes echoed in my ears, counting down the seconds before I was left standing in front of the royal family.

The nervous tremble in my hands and knees permeated every part of my body as I rushed to keep up. All thoughts of escape, the king's study, and the royal seal, had somehow vanished, my mind completely occupied by the two people seated on the platform ahead. What could I possibly say to them that wouldn't make me look like a complete fool or get me arrested?

The whispers to either side of the aisle increased as the nobles chattered about the lone boy being brought before the king without his parents.

Halfway across, I realized the emblem on the black-uniformed guards ahead was that of a bird, perhaps a hawk or falcon. Its wings were spread above, and its talons looked ready to strike. Something about those black uniforms and the way the men held themselves made them appear even more dangerous than the average lancer.

We reached the base of the steps leading up to the throne, and the man beside me cleared his throat to get my attention as he bowed toward the platform.

I quickly did the same, catching my first real glimpse of the king as I rose. He was younger than I had expected, maybe ten years older than my father. He had a touch of silver in his beard and around the sides of his head where his golden crown sat. His face was strong, but his eyes were kind. Something about them made me want to relax, but I didn't.

Beside him sat the queen. She was every bit as beautiful as she was regal. No silver in her hair, only long dark waves that ran halfway down her chest, covering the top of her green gown. She too had a strong bearing. She smiled, and her expression reminded me of the way my mother would look at me when she thought I wasn't looking. A kind look, almost loving.

"Ayrion of Aramoor, Your Majesties," the man beside me announced with another bow, pulling me from my examination.

I didn't know if I was supposed to bow as well, but I did just to be safe. By the time I had straightened, the man beside me had turned and started back across the room, leaving me all alone and feeling more exposed than I had ever been before. Not even standing in front of the Peltok had left me so unnerved. Not knowing what to do, I bowed again.

A couple of giggles from the nobles behind me let me know that perhaps that wasn't the proper decorum. I could feel the knot in my stomach tightening. I tried working my tongue around in my mouth, but it was as dry as shale. I couldn't think of a single thing to say.

"Well, Master Ayrion," the king said, a welcoming smile on his face, "what is it you wish to speak with us about? It must be urgent to have braved coming here alone."

My mouth opened, but nothing came out. I cleared my throat and bit my tongue, hoping the pain would be enough to refocus my scattered thoughts. It wasn't. "Yes, Your . . ." *What was it the man with the fluffy hat had called them? I should know this.* If you call a lord his lordship, then it would stand to reason that I'd call him . . . "Your Kingship."

More chuckles and a couple of bursts of laughter behind me had my face turning red.

"Your Majesty," a guard on the left whispered. He kept his eyes focused ahead.

"I mean, Your Majesty," I said with another bow, feeling utterly humiliated at this point. I spared a quick glance up at the platform. The king looked to be biting his lower lip in an attempt not to laugh, and the queen raised her hand to her mouth and coughed. It was one of the most delicate coughs I'd ever heard, like the wisp of a hummingbird's wings. "I do have something urgent I'd like to say, if you don't mind?"

The king leaned forward in his seat and nodded. "How could I refuse such a polite request?" He motioned with his hand for me to continue.

I grabbed the folds of my trouser pockets and squeezed. "I'd like to talk about the growing number of kids living on the streets."

The chuckling behind me faded rather abruptly. In its place, murmurs of approval spread throughout the room.

"Aye," a man said from somewhere on the left. "They've become a plague on our city."

A woman on the right responded in kind. "Thieving little creatures robbed Lady De'Witt not three nights ago, Your Majesty. Made off with a brooch that had been in her family for generations."

I cringed. Apparently, they'd gotten the wrong idea about what I was going to say.

It suddenly occurred to me that Lord Gerrick might have been in attendance today. I glanced behind me, but there were too many faces. I wondered if he'd recognize my voice. I doubted he would have recognized my face, considering I'd been wearing black paint. I looked up at the throne. "I think we should find a way to help them."

"Help them?" a man behind me on my right said forcefully, sounding quite bewildered. "Have you gone mad? They already help themselves at every chance they get, their little fingers snatching up everything that isn't tied down. I've seen more than a few purses cut right off the waist."

"My point exactly," I countered, turning around to address the man. "If you'd help them, we . . . I mean, *they* wouldn't need to resort to picking."

Several in the gallery looked puzzled. Of course, they didn't know what *picking* was. I hadn't known what it was either, the first time I'd heard it.

"That is what the orphan homes are for, young man," the king said. "Those that are without family should be cared for there. We set aside funds every year for such a purpose."

"Then you might want to set aside a little more," I said.

Gasps filled the room. I looked up at the king. Maybe I'd been too forceful. He didn't seem angered, though. At least he was listening. "What I mean to say is that most of the kids on the streets are there because they couldn't handle living in these so-called orphan homes. Most of the kids, especially the older ones, are hired out to the warehouses to line the pockets of those running the homes."

"That's preposterous," one of the more vocal men said, stepping to the front, his wife beside him. She was as skinny as he was wide. "I know for a fact that they are treated with the utmost care."

The king seemed to study the overly dressed man for a moment, then looked back at me. "This is quite the accusation you levy. Do you have proof of your claims?"

I couldn't very well tell the king I knew this because I lived with these kids. They'd probably arrest me on the spot. My hands squeezed the inner lining of my pockets so tight, I thought I might rip them. "I . . . I have a friend who lost his parents, Your Majesties, and was sent to one of these homes." It wasn't entirely a lie. I did have a friend who'd lost his parents. And I knew of others who'd been to the homes.

The king and queen listened intently.

"He said the home he was sent to has so many kids living in it that they were practically sleeping on top of each other. The rooms have no beds, so they are stacked in rows across the floor. During the winter, they're thankful for it because it keeps them warm enough to make it through the freezing nights. The owners keep the money they should be spending on coal or wood, and what little food they are allotted each day is barely enough to keep them alive, let alone give them the strength to work all day in the warehouses. After just a couple of months living at the home, I barely recognized my friend."

Most of the arguments and grumbling from the crowd ceased. Both the king and queen sat stiffly in their seats, each wearing a somewhat disturbed look.

"That is troubling indeed," the king said, thumbing his chin, "if true." He glanced at the queen, and she nodded. "We will look into the matter more thoroughly, Master Ayrion. I appreciate you bringing this to our attention. Was there anything else you wished to speak with us about?"

I was about to say no and excuse myself when I had a thought. "I did have one other concern, Your Majesties, if you don't mind."

"I wouldn't have asked otherwise," the king said.

I spared a quick glance over my shoulder at the crowd before bringing my full attention back to the platform. "My grandfather owns a bookshop in the lower Merchant District, on Meadow Way. Perhaps you've heard of it?"

The king and queen exchanged a brief look. "I'm afraid not," the king said with a polite smile.

I shrugged. "No bother. Doubt many have. Anyway, about a

week ago, an armed group of patrollers showed up at his shop and dragged him out into the streets in cuffs while they went through and destroyed his life's work. There wasn't a single book left standing. They ripped out pages, stomped on covers, and left the place in ruins."

After an uncomfortable silence, the king finally spoke. "You have me in suspense, son. What was his crime?"

I wiped my eyes. "They said he was being charged with harboring fugitives. But he wasn't, Your Majesties! He wasn't. He's the kindest man I know. He was giving scraps of leftover food to starving kids. But when my grandfather insisted he'd done nothing wrong, they threatened to take my grandmother as well."

Both the king and queen were leaning forward in their seats by this time. The king's hands tightened on the arms of his throne.

"They said his accuser was highly respected and not to be questioned. Next thing you know, he's being dragged to the port harbor cells, where he's scheduled to be shipped to the salt mines on the next transport. Where's the justice in that? He stood before no judge, no witnesses were called, only the word of one man. I went down to the docks to plead with the patrollers for his life and found that the man who had accused him had undergone a change of heart. Don't get me wrong, I'm thankful the man changed his mind, but what is my poor grandfather to do now? His shop has been destroyed."

"We will certainly look into this situation for you, Master Ayrion," the queen said sympathetically. "Won't we, dear?"

The king's knuckles were white. "Do you know the name of this man who accused your grandfather?"

I swallowed. "I . . . I do, Your Majesty—"

"Good. I demand you give it at once. Destroying a man's livelihood for feeding hungry children will not be tolerated. Not in this kingdom. Not if I have anything to say about it."

I glanced behind me once more, but no one came forward. No protests. No arguments. The room was silent. I almost hoped Gerrick was in the room.

"What is his name, child?" the queen asked.

"I don't want to say it out loud in front of them."

The king looked out at the nobles. "You have nothing to fear, I promise you."

"Please, approach," the queen said.

I froze. Was she wanting me to go up on the platform with them? I looked at the guards.

The queen must have sensed my hesitancy. "Yes. You can come up here."

"Let him through," the king said. And immediately, the black-clad guards shifted to allow an opening at the front.

I took a deep gulp and started forward. Once past the guards, I slowly scaled the steps to the top, bowing once again when I reached it.

"Who is this accuser who has given your family such grief?" the king asked.

I kept my head lowered so they didn't see my eyes. "It was Lord Gerrick, Your Majesties."

The king leaned back in his seat. He didn't say anything for the longest time, and I started to grow very uncomfortable as I stood there in front of the two most powerful people in all the Five Kingdoms. Did they not believe me?

The queen was the one to finally speak. "I'm sorry for your hardship, Master Ayrion. I'm sure we can find a way to rectify it for you." She looked at the king and cleared her throat.

The king shifted in his seat, clearly startled out of whatever he'd been considering.

"This is for you and your grandfather," she said, nodding at her husband. "It's not much, but it should help until we can look into this situation."

The king opened a jewel-crested box that was resting on a pedestal beside the throne. From where I was standing, I couldn't see what was inside, but when he turned around, there were several gold coins resting in his palm.

"Spend them wisely."

My eyes widened with excitement, but it wasn't the coins that had captured my attention. It was his ring. Was it the signet ring? I couldn't tell. All I could see was the gold band. I needed him to turn his hand over.

I took a step forward and reached out for the coins, but instead of simply lifting them from the king's hand, I took his hand in mine and proceeded to shake it, turning it sideways as I did to get a better look. "Thank you, Your Majesty. Bless you. My grandfather will be so grateful." The front of the ring didn't bear the royal crest. It did, however, cradle a rather exquisite ruby.

The king cleared his throat. "You might want to cover that up."

I looked down, and nearly choked when I realized my shirt cuff had slid up my arm, revealing my brand. I released his hand and quickly stuffed mine in my pocket, along with the gold. I wasn't sure what to do, so I bowed once again and stepped back, keeping my eyes lowered. "Thank you, Your Majesties, for your generosity." I didn't give them time to say anything else as I swiftly backed my way down the steps.

"It was a pleasure to meet you, Master Ayrion," the king said with a wry grin.

"I hope you'll come and see us again," the queen added.

I bowed once more. "I'd like that, Your Majesties. You have a very nice home." I bit my tongue.

"Yes, we are rather fond of it," the king added with a slight chuckle.

One of the guards on the right stepped forward. "If you'll follow me," he said, as though I had a choice. I bowed once more, then followed the guard toward the door on the right, the same one that Eva and her family had been ushered through earlier.

I took a deep breath as we neared the exit. The experience had left me somewhat lightheaded. I'd survived. More than that, I'd walked away with gold in my pocket. If only my family could see me now. Who in the Five Kingdoms could say they'd shaken hands with the king? My opinion of the nobility had shifted slightly after this meeting. Perhaps they weren't all a bunch of self-centered prigs.

Before I had a chance to ponder it further, I stepped through the door and found Eva and her family waiting on the other side.

"Ayrion!" Eva squealed, waiving Naddi's arm. "Did you see the king? Papa talked to him." She ran over and grabbed my hand, pulling me through the crowd to where her parents were quietly talking with a small group on the side. "The queen said hello to me and Naddi. She thought Naddi was very pretty." Eva held the little doll up for me to see.

"That's wonderful," I said, still in awe of the situation myself. "I'm sure Naddi was on her best behavior."

Eva crossed her arms, squishing Naddi in the process. "Of course she was. Curtsied and everything."

"That was very thoughtful of her."

"It was." Eva relaxed her arms. "I reckon we'll be on our way home now." She glanced mournfully around the waiting area. "I'll miss this place. I like it here. It's pretty."

I smiled. "I like it here too." I studied the small lobby and the two corridors leading from it. This entryway was much smaller than the one outside the throne room. Our group filled at least half the space, and I could only see two guards.

Apparently, they were more worried about those going into the throne room than those coming out. Which made sense. You never knew if any of those gathered might have been up to no good. But if they didn't attack the king and queen while standing in front of them, it was highly unlikely they were going to do so now.

With only two guards watching over the room, and both of them up near the front, I was left with a small window of opportunity.

And I planned on taking it.

Chapter 36

THE TWO LANCERS SPOKE quietly at the head of the group, standing just inside one of the two corridors leading off the atrium. Theirs looked like it headed back toward the main entrance. The second, near the back on the left, led in a different direction. I had no idea where it went, but since it was the only hallway not being watched, it was probably going to be my only chance of making a clean break for it.

As inconspicuously as I could, I worked my way through the crowd toward the back of the room. Everyone was chatting about what it had been like to talk to the royal family. The excitement they'd felt. The honor they'd been afforded. No one had a harsh word to say.

At the back, I waited behind a group of ladies who were busy discussing the lavish gowns they'd seen worn by the women of court. Unfortunately, the way they were huddled left half of them facing my direction, making it impossible for me to slip away without them seeing. I was racking my brain for a way to get them to turn around when the door leading into the throne room behind us opened and everyone turned. This was it. No one was looking.

I took two steps, and something grabbed my arm and pulled me to a stop.

"Where're you going?"

I turned to find Eva clinging to my jacket sleeve. "Go back to your parents," I said, pulling my arm free. "Look." I pointed toward the front of the group. "I think they're about to leave. You don't want them to go without you, do you?"

Eva's brows raised as she quickly glanced over her shoulder to make sure they hadn't left her. "What about you?" she asked, turning back around. She held her dolly up. "Naddi was worried."

I smiled and patted Naddi on her yarn-strung head. "I'll be along shortly. Save my spot, okay?"

Eva nodded with a smile and quickly pushed back through the people.

I watched until the legs of those around us had blocked her from view. I was going to miss the little girl and her family. They reminded me of what I was missing: my own family. For a brief moment, I wondered what Rianna and Jorn were up to.

The group of ladies behind me were still turned as they waited for whoever had just exited the throne room to walk over.

It was now or never. With one last look to make sure no one was watching, I dashed into the corridor.

The passageway was well lit, much like the antechamber we'd been waiting in. However, unlike the long corridor we'd taken from the main entrance to the throne room, this one had no windows, which meant it was an inner hallway and likely didn't have an exit.

I followed it past several doors, all closed. None of them looked grand enough to be considered the king's study, not that I knew what the king's study would look like, but I doubted it was any of these since I was still on the first floor and none of these had guards standing watch. Besides, I didn't have two or three weeks to spend opening every door I passed.

I needed to find my way back toward the main foyer. It was the only place I had seen that led to the upper floors. I reached a junction with branching corridors. The right led in the general direction of where I was wanting to go, so I took it.

A few steps in and a door on the right opened. In a panic, I grabbed a large vase of flowers off the table beside me and started forward, trying to look like I knew what I was doing. I don't know what possessed me to do it, but my quick thinking probably saved me as two men and a woman stepped out of the room, followed by a lancer.

Quietly, I moved to the far side, giving them as wide a berth as I could manage while holding up the flowers to cover my face. Neither the well-dressed men nor the woman gave me a passing glance. I couldn't tell what the guard was doing, since he was standing in the doorway and the others had blocked him from view.

As difficult as it was, I didn't turn around. The best thing was to keep going. I had to look like I belonged there, which meant acting like I knew what I was doing. The thumping of my heart grew with each new step.

The voices behind me had faded by the time I reached the next intersection, allowing me to breathe a little easier. I peeked around the corner and spotted a group of people passing in the distance. My excitement grew when I saw that the corridor to the right ended at a set of windows. In fact, if I were to guess, I'd say it was the same hallway we'd taken earlier, leading back to the main foyer. The group passing by was probably those I'd just left, including Eva's family.

I was on the right track.

Quickly, I continued down the corridor I was in. It looked parallel to the other hallway, and with less traffic. I felt optimistic it would lead me back to the main foyer.

Doors came and went as I scurried down the hall with my vase of flowers, all remaining closed, thankfully. I did hear people in the corridor behind me, so I hurried as fast as I dared without drawing attention to myself. These crazy flowers were getting heavy, and carrying them made it difficult to see where I was walking.

The hall I was in came to an abrupt stop, ending at another corridor and not the grand foyer I'd been hoping for. Heading right would have to take me back in the direction of the entrance. However, the sound of footsteps coming from that direction had me scrambling backward.

The floor vibrated with the sound of booted feet, and the clang of metal had me pressing myself up against the wall. I held the plant in front of me, hoping they didn't notice the floating flowers or the person holding them.

My palms were sweating as row after row of lancers marched by, their eyes fixed straight ahead, their arms swinging in perfect rhythm. It was awe-inspiring and terrifying at the same time.

I didn't twitch an eye until the last of the troop had passed. With a slow exhale, I lowered the flowers and peeked around the corner. No one was coming. This had to be the craziest thing I'd ever done. Now the question was, how was I going to make it up—

"Where are you going with those?" someone asked behind me, causing me to jump. "And why aren't you in uniform?"

I raised the planter and turned. My heart sank. I could see the white mantle through the flowers. Whoever the lancer was, he looked about my father's age, maybe a little younger, with strong features, accented by a well-groomed jawline beard. He was taller than most and filled out in the chest. Not a man I would want to meet in a dark alley after picking his pockets. "I, uh . . ." I had to think fast. "I was told that the queen requested a fresh arrangement for her chambers, my lord, but I seem to have gotten a little lost. And I, I haven't been assigned my uniform yet." I tried bowing, but I almost dumped the flowers onto the floor and quickly righted myself.

The lancer stared at me a moment, and I thought I caught the flicker of a grin through some of the taller stems. "First of all," the lancer said, "you do not address me as *my lord*. I'm an officer in the royal guard, not a member of the aristocracy." He almost seemed offended.

"I'm sorry . . . sir? It's only my second day. Please don't kick me out." I added a very realistic touch of fear to my words. "It took a great deal of effort on my father's part to get me this position. I can't let him down. Please. He's been sick for months, and I . . . Well, I don't know what will happen if I lose this position." I was all but crying by the end.

"No need for the tears, son," the lancer said, glancing around to see if anyone was watching. "We won't be kicking you out today." He took a step forward. "I'm Undercaptain Tolin. You can address me as such."

I bowed my head. "Yes, sir, Undercaptain." I paused a moment, trying to think of something else to say. "Is an undercaptain pretty important?"

The man chuckled. "Important enough, I guess."

"Are you the leader of the Lancers?"

"No. I told you, I'm an *under*captain."

"Oh," I said, as if I knew what an undercaptain was.

"Who've you been assigned to?" he asked, taking another step closer. "We need to make sure you get your duty uniform."

I had no idea who I could have been assigned to. It wasn't like I'd studied a reference on the palace staff. The only positions I was familiar with were those at the Temple, and I doubted they were anything like the ones here. I thought a moment. "I was assigned to the . . . the . . ."

"The butlery?"

"No, it's the . . ." I paused once again.

"The runners?"

My head shot up. "That's it. The runners." It's amazing how something as simple as letting someone finish your sentence can generate information.

"Well, follow me, and we'll get you a uniform."

"Shouldn't I deliver the flowers first? I can get a uniform later." I didn't want to go traipsing all over the palace if I didn't have to, but if the undercaptain was willing to escort me, I couldn't pass up the opportunity.

"Uniforms are stored on the first floor in the west wing," he said, stepping into the hallway that the troops had just passed through. Instead of turning right and heading back toward the main entrance, he turned left and took me deeper into the palace compound. "Stay close. It can get very confusing, navigating this place. Can't tell you how long it took me to eventually find my way around." He glanced back over his shoulder. "To be honest, there are times I still find myself looking up and not knowing where I am."

"You'd think they'd hand out maps."

"Hmm. An interesting idea."

I followed closely behind my tall guide, switching the grip of my planter from one arm to the other as we passed people on both sides. Pretty soon, my arms were too tired to keep changing positions, so I kept my head lowered instead, not looking at those whose paths we crossed. It seemed the closer we got to our destination, the busier the halls grew, people rushing to get from one place to another. As big as the palace was, it was no wonder many of these people were half-jogging down the halls.

With each new corridor, I was growing more and more thankful that I hadn't grabbed one of the bigger vases. We stopped only once. It was a particularly busy intersection, and the undercaptain took a moment to study both directions before finally taking the left avenue. We rounded the next corner, and he slowed.

"Here we are."

Most of the doors on this particular hall were open, as men and women in black-and-white uniforms entered and exited, carrying cleaning utensils or laden down with blankets, quilts, and sheets. Those farther down the hall carried trays of food and drink. My mouth watered as they passed, steam rising off their platters. If I hadn't been toting these crazy flowers, I'd have snatched a few of the loaves as they went by.

Undercaptain Tolin took a door on the left, and I followed him out of the busy hall. This room was filled with rows and rows of shelves, each one stuffed to the brim with linens and pillows and bedding. Master Fentin could have fit ten of his shops in the place.

"I have a runner here who needs a uniform, Master Trip," the undercaptain said to a short man behind a desk on the right. The man's head barely rose above the mountain of papers in front of him. The undercaptain leaned in to me and lowered his voice. "His name is Tripkin, but everyone just calls him Trip."

"Talk to Elfia," the man said as he waved us toward the back, not bothering to so much as look up. It appeared he wasn't going to say more, but then the clerk suddenly raised his head and shouted, "Elfia!" then went right back to his bookkeeping. I was glad I didn't have his position. His hair was about as unkempt as his uniform, and his bloodshot eyes spoke of little sleep.

Moments later, a young girl came flying down the center aisle. She was skinny, with straight brown hair that ran to the middle of her back. She had thick eyebrows that hung just below a purple headband. "What is it, Papa?"

Master Trip pointed in our direction, still not bothering to look up from his papers. "See to them."

The girl walked over, glancing at the patch on the lancer's shoulder. "What can I do for you, Undercaptain?"

"We need a runner uniform for my young friend here."

She nodded and walked over to stand in front of me. "Well, let me have a look at you."

She was taller than I was, but not by much. About the same height as Sapphire. "What's your name?" she asked.

"Ayrion."

"Well, Ayrion, are you going to put the vase down, or am I going to have to guess? Don't blame me if your sleeves are too short or your trousers too long."

This was exactly what I was trying to avoid. I stepped in front of the undercaptain to position myself so he couldn't look me directly in the face, then placed the plant beside a shelf filled with white sheets.

"There, that's better," she said, getting a good look at me.

I kept my head lowered, not looking her in the eyes.

"Shy one you have here," she said to the undercaptain with a soft chuckle, before raising my arms out to the side. The top of my brand was just poking out from the end of my sleeve, so I quickly turned my wrist.

She stood beside me and felt for my waist, comparing it with hers. "Yep, I should have something that will fit." With that, she took off down the aisle and disappeared about seven or eight rows in.

It wasn't long before she was returning with a pair of black trousers, a white tunic, a blue vest with gold buttons, and a fluffy blue hat with a gold medallion at the front. Apart from the color, the hat looked like something Noph would have worn. She also handed me a set of polished black calf-high boots.

I glanced at the clothes. "Where do I change?"

Elfia looked around the room as if not having thought that far ahead and pointed to the left. "Just change behind that shelf there."

"What?" I looked up, surprised, and caught her eye, every bit as brown as her hair. I quickly jerked my head back down. "You want me to take my clothes off out here?"

"Ain't no one caring what you have on under those pants."

"And if I'm not wearing anything under them?"

She cleared her throat. "Like I said, ain't no one caring."

"Go on, son," the undercaptain said. "If you're all that worried, I'll stand here and protect your honor." He winked at the girl.

Could this get more embarrassing? I trudged over to the shelf on the left and stepped behind. After peeking out to make sure no one was looking, I pulled down my trousers. It wasn't so much the fact that I didn't have on underpants; it was the fact that I had several weapons and vials all stuffed away in my clothes that I didn't want them seeing.

It was probably the fastest I'd ever changed. My mother would have been proud. Surprisingly, Elfia's choice for the trousers and tunic fit perfectly, and the clothes were rather comfortable. Not too tight. Not too baggy. Plenty of room for the dagger strapped to my arm. I took a couple of the vials from Reevie's stash, including the bottle of ether, and left the rest in my coat. There weren't enough inner pockets on this jacket to fit everything I'd carried, but I did make sure to grab the gold coins the king had given me, as well as take a quick bite of Mistress Orilla's sandwich, before placing what was left back in my jacket.

With a firm tug and stomp of my foot, I pulled on my boots. They were a bit snugger than I was used to. I placed the hat on my head, letting the top part hang down one side of my face, similar to how I'd seen others wear them. I didn't have a mirror, but I was sure I looked ridiculous. It was, however, the nicest set of clothes I'd ever worn.

Carrying my other outfit in my arms, I stepped out from behind the shelf. "What do I do with these?"

Elfia was standing there with a small canvas bag opened in her hands. "In here," she said, holding it out for me.

That'll be helpful, I thought. Once they were in, she tied the top with a string and wrote my name on the card that was attached to it, along with some random code made up of numbers and letters.

"What's that for?" I asked.

"That's so I can find them later."

"What do you mean, *later*?"

She tried pulling the bag from my hands, but I wasn't about to release it. "I'm going to shelve them for you until the end of the day. You can pick them up before you leave."

"I'd prefer to hold on to them now."

"You can't," she said, attempting another good tug, without

success.

"You can't very well run all over the palace carrying a bag of clothes," the undercaptain said. "You heard her. You can pick them up at the end of the day. Now let's be going."

I reluctantly relinquished the bag, knowing I'd probably never see my clothes again. If I did manage to get my hands on that ring, I wasn't about to take my time trying to recover my old clothes, Reevie's herbs or not; I would be trying to get out of there. The one positive aspect was that the change of clothes I was wearing was definitely much finer than the ones I was giving up.

"Good day, Miss Elfia, Master Trip," the undercaptain said with a slight doff of his leather hat as he headed for the door. I grabbed my vase and ran after him.

I followed the undercaptain back toward the front entrance, all the while attempting to memorize our route in hopes of finding my way back. But it was clear that it was a wasted effort. There were just too many twists and turns. Before I knew it, we stepped out of another long corridor and into the main foyer. We had come out directly behind the large rotunda holding the grand staircase.

We continued on around, my arms growing weary from holding my pretend delivery. We scaled the stairs to the second level and started down another long passageway. This one was just as grand as the rest, maybe even more so, with white marble floors decorated in gold and deep-blue triangular tiles.

"Thank you for your help, Undercaptain Tolin. Are you sure I'm not keeping you from other things?"

The undercaptain flipped his hand as if waving the notion off. "I was on my way to lunch, but I can grab something later."

My stomach growled in response. I had left my lunch in my clothes and was kicking myself for not having eaten it.

"Is the king's study anywhere near here?" I asked cautiously. "I've heard from some of the other runners that they get sent there quite often, and it might be good to know where it is."

"You're in luck," Undercaptain Tolin said. "We go right by there on our way to their chambers."

We climbed another set of stairs, taking the corridor at the left of the landing. It seemed each passageway was more exquisite than the last, with gold-inlay trim, mosaic tiles, and rich murals covering every inch of the ceilings. I didn't know how the guards and staff managed to keep their focus. No one seemed bothered by the fact that so much wealth was just sitting around for the picking. Undercaptain Tolin didn't seem to notice. I, on the other hand, was going to get a kink in my neck.

"That's the king's study," he said, pointing to a door on the left up ahead. It wouldn't have been hard to miss, what with the armed guards standing out front.

"Good to know," I said, shifting my plant far enough to get a better view as we passed. These weren't the regular white-garbed lancers I'd seen moving throughout the palace. They wore the same black uniforms as those in the throne room.

Neither of the men looked my way. In fact, they didn't even blink. They looked like a couple of statues themselves. Add a little grey paint and some bird droppings, and you wouldn't have been able to tell the difference. I smiled. "Why do those men look different from the other lancers?"

"Because they are part of the High Guard. They serve at the king's behest, and only his."

I glanced back over my shoulder. The street tribes had guards as well, but they were nothing like these. "Are you a High Guard?" His uniform already gave that answer away, but I didn't think it could hurt to ask.

The undercaptain smiled. "No. I like where I'm at. My duty is to protect all of Elondria, not just the king."

He was clearly proud of his position, so I left it at that.

We took the next junction to the right and followed it to where it ended at a set of beautifully engraved doors. These too had a set of guards out front.

"Delivery for the queen," the undercaptain said on approach. "Are they in?"

My breath caught in the back of my throat. What if the king and queen were in there? That hadn't even occurred to me. What if they recognized me? I turned to leave, but the undercaptain laid a hand on my shoulder and locked me in place.

The black guards took one look at the undercaptain and opened one of the doors.

"They are still in the throne room," the one on the right said, and stepped aside for us to enter.

I released a heavy sigh.

The room was quite large, set with a number of very plush-looking settees and sofas, intermingled with a few short tables and shelves overflowing with books. Every bit of space not occupied with books was filled with vases of brightly colored flowers.

"Where's the bed?" I asked, looking for a nightstand or something to lay the arrangement on.

The undercaptain laughed. "This isn't their chambers. This is just the sitting room outside their chambers."

I looked around. "They have a room just to sit in?" Seemed like a waste of space. "I don't see anywhere to set these."

"Then let's try inside. I'm sure you'll have a better chance of finding a free spot in there than out here. The queen spends most of her time reading. Takes great pride in learning new things."

I looked at all the books. It reminded me of Master Fentin's shop, almost as chaotic. How could anyone read that much?

We stepped inside the next room, and my mouth swung open. The room was like nothing I'd seen so far, and that was saying something. The floors were wood, painted and styled in such a way that each piece fit into some elaborately shaped artwork. The ceiling was painted with wisps of clouds on a soft-blue sky. Gold inlay decorated every inch as the ceiling arched and curved from one pillar to the next. It was like staring at waves in the ocean with the water cresting toward the columns.

Murals of trees and forest landscapes had been painstakingly inscribed onto the walls. All the furniture was white with gold trim and thick cushions, and the curtains surrounding the enormous four-poster bed were a rich-blue velvet. I looked down at my pathetic little plant. This thing was sure to look out of place.

"Be quick," the undercaptain said. "I don't want to be here when they get back."

I looked around the room, trying to find a place to stick my little arrangement, finally settling on the dresser, where I noticed a couple of displays of jewelry. I placed the vase down and quickly scanned the rings, but I didn't see anything resembling the royal seal.

"Good. Let's be on our way." Undercaptain Tolin was back at the sitting room by the time I turned around.

Gaining access to the rooms was proving easier than I'd expected. However, finding what I was looking for was not. We left the royal chambers and started back down the hall, passing the king's study, and continued until we reached the stairs leading down to the second floor.

I stopped at the top of the landing and grabbed the undercaptain's arm before he started down. "I want to thank you, Undercaptain, for all your help. I would never have been able to find my way this far without you."

He turned. "That's quite alright. I hope your father gets to feeling better."

"Yes, I'm sure he will. At the very least, he'll be happy to hear I managed to keep my job, thanks to you." I held out my hand, still keeping my eyes lowered.

He grabbed it and shook. "It was my pleasure." I waited for him to release, but he held his grip. I couldn't look up to see what was going on, but the longer he held, the more anxious I became.

"Son, I'm going to give you a piece of friendly advice my father gave me when I was your age. If you plan on working here, you're going to need to stand up straight. Timidity is expected in some situations, but this isn't one of them. When you shake someone's hand, you show them the respect of looking them in the eyes and squeezing like you mean it." He released my hand. "Now, let's try this again, shall we?" He stuck out his hand.

Blood and guts! What just happened?

I hesitated, but finally reached out and took his hand, squeezing as firmly as I dared without looking like I was trying to, then with a nervous gulp I raised my head and looked him in the eyes.

Chapter 37

THE UNDERCAPTAIN JERKED away and took a step back, grabbing the hilt of his sword. "You're Upakan."

My heart pounded in my chest. I almost took off running, but I had nowhere to go. "Yes, sir."

The big lancer looked up and down the hallway, as though worried that there might be two or three more of my people hiding in the shadows about to leap out and attack. He wasn't too far wrong. We usually were sent out in teams on larger jobs.

His hand remained at his side, but so far, he hadn't pulled his weapon. I had to make him see that I wasn't a threat before he ruined everything.

"Now you know why I keep my head lowered. One look at my

eyes and people usually run off screaming." I shook my head despondently. "I told my father this was going to happen. Getting a job in the palace was a terrible idea."

The undercaptain's brow rose. "There are more of you living here?"

"No."

"But you just said—"

"I was adopted. My father . . . Well, I call him my father. He's old enough to be my grandfather. I was given to him by a book peddler who'd found me wandering around some village up north during one of his trips to Syrel. At least, that's what he told me. I was too young to remember."

The undercaptain stared into my eyes a moment longer, then finally released his grip on his sword. "I guess if you had a choice, being a runner would be the most logical occupation here. For the most part, no one pays you much mind. Very few nobles would ever acknowledge your presence, let alone look you in the face." He rolled his shoulders. "When it comes right down to it, there are very few in Aramoor who know anything at all of the Upaka, other than rumor. The only reason I recognized you was that I've encountered one of your people before. But it has been a number of years."

"Really?" I said, my attention perked. "What were they like? I know so little."

"There's not much to tell. Although I will say that rumors of your people's prowess are not exaggerated. I don't believe I've ever seen such skill with a blade before, or since." His shoulders relaxed, but the calculated stare remained. "I'll be sure to check in on you from time to time."

I wasn't sure if that was for my benefit or his. I thanked him anyway, and he turned and walked down the stairs to the next landing, then disappeared around the corner.

What was I to do now?

Looking to see if anyone was watching, I left the stairs and started back the way I'd just come, toward the king's study. There were footsteps and chatter ahead, so I turned and pretended to be straightening some of the decorations on a long table on the right of the corridor. It was an older boy dressed in the same runner garb I was wearing, accompanied by a young lady in the formal black and white of the maid service.

I continued fiddling with one of the statues as though making sure it was aiming in the right direction. Neither said a word to me, and as soon as they passed, I grabbed a set of flowers from the table and moved the statue over so it didn't look too obvious that something was missing. This time, I found a vase that wasn't quite so heavy, and with a deep breath, I left the table and started toward the king's study.

The same two black-uniformed guards were standing out front. *Here goes nothing*, I thought. *Or, better yet, here goes everything.* I kept my head lowered on approach, thankful that my hands were occupied with the vase so they couldn't see how much they were trembling. I stopped a few feet in front of the guards and cleared my throat.

"Flow . . ." My voice cracked. I swallowed. "Flowers for the king's study," I said in as official of a voice as I could muster.

"Move along," the guard on the left said, not even giving me a second glance.

"But I have flowers for the king's study."

The guard on the right tightened his grip on his halberd. "No one enters the king's study without the king present. You know that."

Horse dung! "My apologies. I was under the impression he was back from the throne room. I'll return later." I turned and walked away, forcing myself not to look back, no matter how badly I wanted to.

I rounded the next corner and stopped. What was I going to do now? It wasn't like I could set a meeting with the king and search his room while he sat there watching. I wanted to chuck the flowers into the wall.

A door on my right opened, and I jumped to the side to keep from getting run over by a group of men and women in black robes. They weren't dressed like nobles, and I didn't recognize their attire as palace staff. Regardless, they paid me no mind and continued their discussions as they walked down the hall.

The door to the room they'd just exited had been left open a crack, and I peeked inside. It was empty, save for a few tables arranged near the center of the room, so I entered and shut the door behind me. It was clear by the stacks of paper strewn across each that they were coming back. Perhaps they'd gone to take a meal.

The room was rather splendid in its décor: crystal chandeliers, murals on the walls, and portraits of people long dead and gone. As with most of the rooms in the palace, everything seemed to be accented in gold. A grand fireplace rested against the back wall behind the tables, and on either side of the hearth was a row of windows that looked out over one of the inner courtyards. I could see a couple of stragglers passing below, some carrying buckets, others baskets of food. I placed the flowers on an empty stand in the corner and noticed a slight rustling of the petals.

I followed the breeze and found that one of the windows had been left open just a crack. I pushed against the window trim and it pivoted outward. I pushed a little more and stuck my head out. My heart fluttered. A small ledge ran directly along the outer rim of the building, just below the window. I couldn't see if it continued on around the corner, but I guessed it would. It was barely wide enough to fit half a boot on, but I'd scaled worse.

I climbed up on the sill and pushed the window open farther. It spun outward with a soft whine, opening wide enough for me to fit through. The room appeared to be on the fourth or fifth floor, certainly high enough to break half the bones in my body if I fell.

The sound of hurried shoes on the cobbles below echoed off the surrounding buildings, forcing me to remain perfectly still. I waited for them to pass, hoping that whoever they were, they didn't look up.

It wasn't the people walking through the courtyard I was most worried about but those staring out the windows on any of the surrounding buildings, especially the windows on the same level. Worried or not, the thought of reaching the king's study without fighting my way through his personal guard had me climbing out on the ledge before I'd given any thought as to how I was going to get back in.

If I managed to get the ring and return, what was I to do if those scriveners were once again occupying the room? One thing at a time, I told myself. From the hallway out front, I knew I was three or four rooms down from where the king's study was. I could only hope they were as empty as this one.

I left the window cracked only slightly behind me and pressed my stomach up against the stone, using the edge of my boots for leverage and whatever small grips my fingers could find in the mortar. Climbing was dangerous enough with unexpected wind gusts; doing it while wearing an uncomfortably new outfit could easily have me falling to my death. Thankfully, the inner courtyard cut away most of the stronger winds.

Carefully, I shimmied forward to the edge of the building and peered around the corner. More of the same. The courtyard continued another sixty or seventy feet, almost a mirror copy of the one behind me. Ahead, I could see the king's study, at least where I thought it was. It was hard to miss with the ornate balcony attached and doors leading inside. But I still had to cross three rooms to reach it, two with their own sets of windows and one with a smaller, less-decorated balcony.

With a deep breath, I put all other distractions out of my mind as I focused on getting around the corner of the building. One slip and there would be no coming back from the fall. I grabbed one of the larger stones on the other side and tested my grip. It seemed firm enough. I needed to make sure before releasing the one I was holding with my other hand.

Confident that I had a solid grasp, I released the other stone and wiggled my way around the other side. My foot slipped and my stomach leaped into my throat. More echoes of boots below, and I froze in place. I didn't dare look down. Even the smallest movement could garner someone's attention if they happened to be looking up.

The muffled conversation eventually faded, and I continued, eventually reaching the first set of windows. I waited at the side, listening closely for any noise from within. I didn't hear anything. Then again, that might just mean no one was talking loud enough for me to hear.

Carefully, I slid my head closer to the glass. The room inside was dark. It looked similar in size to the one I'd just left, flaunting every bit and more of the same rich furnishings. However, instead of several tables being organized at the center, this room held a variety of grouped seating areas along the walls, desks for writing, couches for lounging, and even a single step platform on the side with a diverse arrangement of instruments laid out on stands. It must have been some kind of formal sitting room for entertaining guests.

I pressed on, having to slow as I worked my way around a protruding section in the wall that must have been the chimney for the hearth. As I reached the room's final window, my foot slipped again, and I nearly swallowed my tongue as I grabbed the window trimming and yanked myself up against the glass.

My blood was pumping in my ears, and I forced down a couple of deep breaths to calm it. I looked down at my boots. The soles were thicker and wider, which under most circumstances would have been a good thing, but when trying to shimmy around the outside of a building on a small ledge no bigger than my wrist, it was anything but ideal. Stupid things were going to get me killed. Worse was the amount of scuffing they were receiving as I rubbed them up against the stone.

I wanted to laugh. Only someone as poor as me would care about scuff marks on his shoes when clinging to the side of a building for dear life. Using the outer sill for support, I quickly moved on to the next room. There were only three windows in this room, but there was also a private balcony at the end, and this time I could hear noises coming from inside.

Blazes! I glanced around the edge of the first window. How was I going to get—

The curtains in the windows were drawn. I couldn't believe my luck. Who could be inside and what could they be discussing that would have them blocking off all the windows in the middle of the day? I didn't have time to find out.

Quickly, I scooted past the first window, paying careful attention to my feet this time, not wanting to repeat my previous experience. Fortunately, the sun wasn't behind me, casting my shadow against the curtain for those inside to see. I reached the second window and worked my way around the next chimney, thankful that the stone edging for my feet had been sturdy so far. I made it to the other side and grabbed the sill on the next window to balance myself.

The curtain ripped open in front of me.

I squealed, both feet slipping this time as I desperately reached for the window, but my fingers only skimmed the surface. The man inside shrieked as I plummeted over the side. I didn't even have time to scream as I plunged to the cobbles below.

Suddenly, I was back on the ledge and reaching for the sill. With no time to think, I stepped off the edge and dropped before the curtain was opened. I caught the narrow rim I'd been standing on with my fingers. I hoped no one was walking through the courtyard at that moment. It was going to be hard to miss me now.

I hung there, my fingers burning. If I could work my way under the balcony, perhaps I could pull my way back up from there. Frantically, I reached out with my left hand and grabbed the next section of jutting stone farther down. Inch by inch, I swung my way over, using my extra-wide soles to feel for the grout between the stone. Any amount of weight that I could take off my fingers was going to help.

Pretty soon, I was up under the protection of the balcony. Its supports were low enough for me to grab hold, so I pulled myself up far enough to get my feet back on the ledge I'd been hanging from and worked my way to the other side. I'd never been so thankful for my visions.

I took a brief moment to catch my breath and give my fingers a chance to get the blood circulating again. But I couldn't wait long. I had no idea how long the king and queen would be in the throne room. I might already be too late.

The final room between me and the king's study was empty as well. But not just empty of people. Empty of everything. There were no sofas or chairs, no desks or tables, no platform with instruments, no paintings or mirrors to adorn the walls, not even a rug on the floor.

It was a strange sight, but in a way, it made sense. If I were the king, I wouldn't want a room sitting adjacent to my study, where people could potentially listen in on my private conversations. I bet the room on the other side of his study was empty as well. Not that I was going to take the time to look. Although I did notice that the room was an adjoining room. There was a door on the side that no doubt led into the king's study.

Excited by the prospect of reaching my destination, I tried pushing on the windows to see if I could get in. None of them moved. Other than smashing my fist through one, which would certainly alert the guards, I had no way of getting inside. So, with little other choice, I moved on.

I quickly skated past the empty chamber and peered into the first window of the place I'd been trying to reach all day. Bumps prickled my arms. No one was inside. The king must still be in the throne room. As fast as I could, I climbed past the windows and swung over the balcony rail. I squatted beside the door, taking a moment to look around at the surrounding buildings to see if anyone was watching. I wondered why the king didn't have guards standing outside these doors. Then again, who'd be crazy enough to try scaling the side of a building like this? I smiled and turned the handle.

It was locked.

I wanted to scream but instead grabbed my lockpick set from my pocket, and a few seconds later, I was inside.

The king's study felt different from the other rooms I'd seen. It lacked the opulence, seeming almost plain compared with everything else. The trim and molding were still accented in gold, but there were no murals on the walls or ceiling, no magnificent portraits of the king riding at the head of some grand charge, no enormous mirrors or decorative sculptures, and apart from the door leading out to the balcony there were only two other possible exits: a door at the front of the room, leading out to the hall, and the door on the right that led to the empty room.

From what I could tell, the only real furnishings were a wooden desk and chair on the far-right side of the room with a large standing armoire against the wall behind them; a couple of short sofas in front of the fireplace; a few seats in front of a wide set of inlaid shelves on the left side—each shelf holding a long row of books—and a single painting of what looked like a map of the Five Kingdoms on the wall directly in front of me. It was so large that I could see the Lost City from where I was standing on the other side of the room. Underneath the map was a selection of unique weapons laid out on display.

The one thing I didn't see was a single vase of flowers anywhere. No wonder the guards outside had looked at me funny.

I ran straight for the king's desk. If I were him, I'd want to keep the royal seal close to where it would be used. I scoured the top, but other than some scribbled-on parchment, an inkwell, and a few other knickknacks, my search turned up nothing, so I reached for the first drawer but stopped when I heard muffled voices just outside the door.

Faerie farts! This is just my luck. Not only do I find the king's study and make it inside without anyone knowing, but then someone shows up before I even get the chance to find what I came for.

I turned, looking for somewhere to hide. Apart from crawling up the chimney, the closest place available was the armoire behind the desk. *Please don't be locked.* I grabbed the handle, twisted, and dove inside, shutting it as I did.

I'd barely gotten the door closed when something grabbed my leg, and I screamed. I grabbed my mouth to stifle the noise.

"Who are you?" someone in the corner asked. Whoever it was, they were hidden behind several long overcoats.

I was too startled to answer.

"What are you doing in here?"

I took a deep breath, attempting to lower the thumping in my chest long enough to find my voice. "I'm hiding," I said, barely above a whisper. "What's it look like I'm doing?" I could hear raised voices in the room.

"What's your name?" the person whispered.

"I'm Ayrion. What's yours?"

The cloaks covering the person's face shifted to the side, and a boy about my age peered out. "I'm Dakaran."

Chapter 38

THE VOICES IN THE ROOM grew louder, and my curiosity over who this kid was vanished as I joined him behind the longer cloaks. Neither of us said anything else as we tried to listen to the conversation outside. Unfortunately, the layers of clothing and the armoire's thick doors muffled the sound, making it impossible to hear what was being said.

I recognized the deeper voice as the king's but didn't recognize who he was talking to. I hoped whoever it was didn't stay long. My knees were already wobbly from my climb over, and I really needed to stretch.

There was a spurt of laughter and another round of talking as the voices moved back toward the entrance. A door shut, and I leaned against the side of the dresser to see if I could hear anything.

It didn't sound like anyone was there. Had they gone?

Unless I planned on spending the rest of the day hiding in the king's closet, I needed to find out. I pushed through the clothes and put my ear to the door. Silence. After a few minutes, I turned the latch and opened, just a crack. I listened intently before finally sliding the door open farther and sticking my head out.

The room was empty.

I crawled out and took a moment to stretch. I could hear shuffling behind me, and the boy I'd been sharing the armoire with climbed out as well.

Dakaran was about my height, with dark-brown hair that was mostly straight but curled at the ends where they touched his shoulders. He had a nervous-looking face and flush-red cheeks, but that was probably from having spent the morning hiding in the king's furniture.

"So, why were you in there?" I asked. "Trying to get out of cleaning?" He wasn't wearing a uniform, at least not one that I recognized. "Wait. How did you get in here? The guards told me no one could get in without the king present."

The boy looked at me a moment, then crossed his arms. "Then how did you get in?"

"I, uh . . ." He had me there.

"How long have you been working here?" Dakaran asked, looking at my wrinkled uniform. "I haven't seen you before."

"I just started this week," I said, pulling my cap out of my pocket and placing it on my head.

He took a step closer. "What's wrong with your eyes?"

"There's nothing wrong with them," I said sternly. "What's wrong with your eyes?"

Dakaran looked startled. He rushed over to a small table beside the armoire, which held a water basin, towel, soap, and a mirror, and looked in the mirror. He finally turned back around with a huff. "There's nothing wrong with my eyes."

I smiled. "Good. There's nothing wrong with mine, either."

"Then why do they look like that?" he asked as he joined me in front of the armoire.

"Because they're special. They allow me to see when someone is lying."

The boy's mouth widened. "Really?" He took another step closer to get a better look.

I wanted to shake my head. This kid would have made an easy mark on the streets.

Dakaran finally took a step back and looked around the room. "You want to play find-the-rover? I'll hide first."

I shook my head. The poor kid was really hard up for friends. "I can't right now. Maybe later. I need to . . ." I tried to come up with something plausible. "I need to clean the king's desk. Make sure it's organized before he gets back." I walked over to the desk and opened the top drawer.

Dakaran watched me from the other side as I proceeded to rifle through the king's belongings. He had a curious look on his face, one that said he didn't exactly believe me, but wasn't sure enough to come right out and say it.

I looked up from my searching. "You want to help?"

Dakaran shrugged and moved around to the front.

"We need to take all the smaller objects, like rings and items tiny enough to fit in your hand, and place them in a drawer of their own so they don't get lost." It sounded logical, I guess, and Dakaran seemed eager to help, so I had him start on the bottom drawers.

I worked my way through the top drawer, but other than a decorative letter opener, a couple of wax sticks, a bottle of ink, and a spare quill, I had nothing to show for it, so I proceeded to the next one down on the left.

"What about this?" Dakaran asked. He held up a small letter opener.

"Sure, that can go in the top drawer as well." What part of "fit in your hand" did he not understand?

"And this?"

This time he was holding what looked like some kind of glass paperweight with a flat bottom. "Yeah, sure. That can go as well." This kid was really starting to get on my nerves. I'd barely made it through a stack of documents when Dakaran's voice rang out once more.

"What about this?"

I grabbed the drawer handle and squeezed, afraid if I didn't, I might strangle the kid and stuff him back in the armoire. I turned to find him holding a red jewelry box with gold trim and four peg legs.

"It's not small enough to fit in your hand, but there are rings inside."

"Rings?" I snatched the box from him and laid it on the desk.

Inside, there were several gold and silver jewelry pieces scattered around the velvet-lined box, but only one that grabbed my attention. I reached in and pulled out a large gold ring with an oval crest. The band was etched with flourish designs, and the crest held the image of a crown and sun, with its rays extending to the outer edge. This had to be it. "Yes, I think those can be placed along with the rest, but you can put the box back in the bottom drawer where you got it." I handed him the box.

"What about the ring?" Dakaran asked, looking at my hand.

"Why don't we play find-the-rover with it?" I suggested, looking around the room as though searching for a good place to hide it. "You get in there," I said, pointing back at the armoire, "and I'll go hide it. Whoever finds it the fastest, wins."

"Wins what?"

"I don't know. Just wins."

Dakaran looked at me a moment, then at the ring. "Fine. But I want to hide it first." He walked over and tried taking it from me, but I clamped down.

"No. I'll hide it first." I wasn't about to let go of the ring now that I'd finally gotten my hands on it.

"No. Let me do it."

We struggled for a moment, neither getting the upper hand. The boy's cheeks were growing even more flushed.

"Let me have it!" he demanded. "I want to hide it first."

I didn't have time for this. I balled my fist and—

The door to the study opened.

There was no warning, no talking in the hall, no sound from the guards, only the door opening and both of us standing there fighting over the royal seal.

The man standing in the doorway was wearing the white mantle of a lancer, but also the same type of insignia on his sleeve and chest that Undercaptain Tolin had, only more so, along with a red sash. "Who are you?" One look at the two of us fighting over the king's ring and he drew his sword. "Guards!"

I released my grip on the ring and shoved Dakaran behind the desk. "Stay there."

"He's Upakan!" The officer raised his sword and charged.

Why were they so upset over two kids playing in the king's study? I yanked my dagger from my sleeve, grabbed a waste bucket from beside the desk, and ran to meet him. The two men in black uniforms who'd been standing out front were just making their way into the study. The polearms they carried slowed them down. Not a weapon made for close combat.

The officer swung for my head, but with the aid of a vision, I dove to the right. The blade barely missed my shoulder, leaving the officer vulnerable on his left side. I spun and pummeled him in the head with the bucket. Paper flew everywhere, and the officer's eyes rolled up as he dropped.

I grabbed his sword and moved toward the center of the room to meet the next two. The first lowered his halberd and thrust. It was about the only useful maneuver one could make in tight quarters with such a long weapon. Using the unconscious officer's sword, I batted the spear away with little effort. The second guard swiped for my head over the first, forcing me to duck and retreat.

More cries for guards could be heard in the hallway beyond.

I needed to get that ring from Dakaran and get out of there.

The guards dropped their polearms and drew their swords, rushing me at the same time. Certainly more sensible on their part, but not so good for me.

With a quick fake to the left, I stabbed the first guard in the leg with my dagger while blocking the second guard's strike with my new blade. The first went down, but the second continued on. I sidestepped another thrust and kicked him in the leg. A crunching snap left him on the ground as well, and I stuck him in his sword arm for good measure.

By the time I made it to the desk, more guards were pouring in from the front. "Give me the ring," I said to Dakaran. "You don't want to be seen with it. Maybe I can use it to bargain for—"

A shout brought me around as more armed men tore across the room, all wearing the white mantles of the Elondrian Lancers. I grabbed the bottle of hartshorn from my coat and took a deep breath before yanking the cork and throwing its contents across the first wave of men.

Most dropped, grabbing their throats and gasping for air. I knew the feeling, like swallowing fire.

Even from where I was, the smell had my eyes watering.

"What was that?" Dakaran shouted behind me. "It burns."

"Stay there," I shouted back at him, and charged across the room to meet those I hadn't managed to douse. I struck down the next in line with a quick stab to his leg. The second received a deep cut across his sword arm and a solid kick between the legs. I parried the third's swing with my dagger and stuck him through the shoulder with my sword.

My visions were coming from everywhere now, and it took all my concentration just to keep up. A block here, a lunge and thrust there. I'd spin to the right, then duck and roll to the left. There had to be at least a dozen guards in the room by now, and they were driving me back toward the fireplace.

I was losing ground.

No matter how many I put down, more were filling their place, an endless supply of soldiers. My arms continued to swing as I blocked and cut and stabbed, but with each passing swing, I was being pushed farther back. Why had everything gone so wrong? I'd actually had the ring in my hands, and now it looked as though I was going to lose everything. Apart from jumping out a window, I had no idea how I was getting out of this room.

Then it hit me. The empty room adjoining this one.

I stabbed a guard in the forearm, and he lost his weapon. I swept the legs out from under another as I ducked and rolled to the left. I took a wide swing at the rest and made a dash for the desk to grab the ring.

I hadn't made it past the sofa when the adjoining door opened, and two rows of High Guard came rushing in. Right behind them was the king. The men in black uniforms grabbed the scared boy and carried him back toward the empty room before I could get to him.

"No!" I shouted. "Leave him alone! He didn't do anything!"

Anger and desperation opened something inside of me, and my magic poured out. I'd never delved this deep before, hadn't known I could. The visions took over, and so did my body.

Men dropped around me as I tried to fight my way to Dakaran. I couldn't let the king execute him. It wasn't his fault. I felt a burning sensation on my left arm, then one on my right side, but I was so focused on the fight and the magic that I barely slowed.

Both rooms were filled with guards. Magic wasn't going to get me out of this. I managed to stab a couple more men with my dagger before they wrestled me to the floor. The last thing I remember was a black-gloved fist driving straight for my face.

Chapter 39

INDISTINCT VOICES FILTERED into the back of my mind, slowly pulling me away from the peaceful darkness. ". . . waking up."

I leaped up and tried taking a swing at the first blurry object my eyes could focus on, but my hands had been bound.

"Hey! Watch it," a familiar voice shot back, as the person jumped backward to keep from getting hit. "You nearly took my head off."

Dakaran's face slowly came into view, a bit blurry but enough to recognize. "Where am I?" I asked, my head still groggy. I was having a difficult time keeping my thoughts together. "What happened? Did they get us?" My head suddenly started to throb, and I closed my eyes till it passed. My jaw was aching from where the guard had punched me. “Are we in the dungeon?”

“The dungeon?”

I opened my eyes. “I’m sorry I got you into this. I promise I’ll explain to the king that you had nothing to do with it.”

For some reason, Dakaran didn’t seem all that worried. In fact, he looked downright jovial. The poor kid was a few bricks shy of a wall. I took a moment to let the haze clear from my head before finally getting a good look at our prison.

It was the most luxurious cell I’d ever seen. It almost looked like the king’s bedchamber. I looked down and noticed plush velvet sheets under me. I also noticed I was missing my shirt and had a fresh dressing on my arm, around my waist, and even on my leg.

My head cleared rather quickly when I noticed the men in black uniforms standing along the far wall.

I looked at Dakaran. “What’s going on?”

“I’ll ask the questions,” someone behind Dakaran said.

Dakaran scooted out of the way, and the king stepped forward.

My breath caught in my throat. I tried getting up, and nearly stumbled to the floor in the process. “Don’t blame Dakaran! It wasn’t his fault. He didn’t do anything wrong. It was me. I’m the one who took the ring.”

“What ring?” The king looked confused.

“I, uh.” I looked at Dakaran, confused myself. Had he stuck the ring back in the desk? Maybe he wasn’t as dumb as he looked. “We were going to play find-the-rover.”

The king turned and looked at Dakaran. “Well, speak up. What’s this about a ring?”

Dakaran pulled his hand out of his pocket and held up the gold signet.

I whimpered, feeling suddenly lightheaded. Stupid kid. He could have at least lied about it.

The king took the ring and turned and looked at me, his face losing that calm demeanor I'd seen in the grand hall. In that moment, I could see the strength of a leader coming through, his eyes sharp as daggers. "Who were you sent here for, Upaka? Was it me?"

Great, one look at my eyes and everyone thought I was there to kill them.

"Don't think I don't recognize you from the throne room," the king said. "You had your opportunity there. Why didn't you take it? I'm guessing that story about your adopted father's shop was your way to get in?" The king's mouth tightened. "I'm impressed. You actually had the queen and me looking into the matter."

I didn't know what to say. I looked at the king, then at Dakaran, then at all the armed men around the room. I wondered if there was enough space under the bed to hide. "I wasn't sent here by anyone, Your Majesty. Except myself. I wasn't lying when I said that my father's shop had been destroyed by patrollers and that he'd been falsely arrested." I glanced at the king's guards. "Besides, if I wanted you dead, I wouldn't have done it in the middle of the throne room, with a hundred onlookers and a couple dozen armed guards standing between me and the exit."

The king opened his mouth, but before he could say anything, a door on the left opened and a lancer stepped in. It was Undercaptain Tolin, and he looked out of breath. "Your Majesty, I take full responsibility for this. The boy told me he was a new runner and was delivering flowers to your chambers."

"He was in my chambers?"

The lancer looked at a loss for words. "Of course, I never left him unattended, Your Majesty." The undercaptain glared at me with disappointment. The look hurt more than my arm. I couldn't tell if it was me he was disappointed with or himself. Probably both.

"Don't blame yourself, Undercaptain," the king said. "The queen and I were just as fooled by his lies as you."

"But I wasn't lying," I pleaded. Not exactly.

No one said a word as they waited for me to explain. Unfortunately, I was drawing a blank when it came to a credible story I could offer, a story that would tie all the previous ones up without conflicting. The easiest story to tell was always the truth. And so, that's what I did.

Mostly.

I might have left out that I was the head of one of the city's street tribes or that I lived in the now-vacant Temple of Egla, but I did tell them that I had broken in to steal the royal seal in order to keep my adopted father, Master Fentin, from any further harm. I told them how one of the street gangs was using Lord Gerrick to threaten my father. Apparently, they didn't appreciate the fact that we were helping some of their members leave the tribe.

"I'm sorry for trying to take the ring, Your Majesty," I said humbly, "but I just didn't see any other way. The threat is real, I promise. They proved it when they had my father arrested and destroyed his shop." I looked around at the distrustful faces. There had to be something I could say that would win them over. "I can take you there, if you don't believe me."

"I believe him," one person said. Sadly, that person was Dakaran, the very boy who'd been caught inside the king's study with me. "He tried protecting me. Even taking the blame." He turned and pointed directly at the king. "You can't deny you saw it."

I couldn't believe the kid's tenacity. Regrettably, it was likely going to cost us both our heads.

The king rubbed his beard in thought but eventually nodded. "Yes, I saw it. I also saw the way you fight. I've never seen anyone fight like that before, which seems to contradict what you've told us."

"But I did tell you the truth, sort of."

The king raised a single eyebrow, and I knew if I didn't explain, my next stop would be the dungeons.

I twisted my hands around where the rope was pinching at my wrists. "I wasn't found by a traveling book peddler like I told Undercaptain Tolin. My arrival in Aramoor was more recent. But everything else is true." The important stuff, that is.

The king stood there a moment with a stern look on his face, sparing a passing glance at the undercaptain. "You've left me in a difficult position, young man. How am I to trust your word, given the circumstances?" He looked at Dakaran. "And yet, actions do speak for themselves. And the way you tried coming to Dakaran's aid when you thought him in trouble says something about your character as well." He looked me over. "Besides, I have a feeling that if you had meant me or my son ill, there would have been little I could have done to stop it."

"Your what?" I looked at Dakaran.

Dakaran blew out his lips and crossed his arms with a huff. "Father! You weren't supposed to tell him that. Now he's never going to want to come back."

I was too stunned to care. "Your father's the king? Why didn't you say that earlier?"

"Because as soon as people find out who I am they treat me differently. You said you wanted to play find-the-rover. No one's ever wanted to play find-the-rover with me before."

I actually found myself feeling sorry for the kid . . . crown prince. He might have dressed in nice clothes, slept in soft sheets, eaten from fancy plates, but apparently, he was even more alone than I was. As bad as it was living on the streets, I at least had friends to rely on.

"Here's my proposal," the king said, looking me in the eyes. "Will you stand by what you say?"

I looked at Dakaran, and he nodded for me to say yes, so I nodded. "Yes, Your Majesty."

The king looked at Undercaptain Tolin as if trying to make up his mind, then turned back to me. "Fine. Then I will have the undercaptain, and a company of armed lancers, escort you home, and while he's there he can check into your story. If what you say is true, and he does find that you have an adopted father with a bookshop in disrepair, then I'll look into the matter. But if I find that you've lied to me, then I'll have them escort you right back here to the palace dungeons, where you can await trial for your actions."

Dakaran's face blanched.

So did mine.

But I had a feeling if it wasn't for Dakaran, I'd already be in the dungeon awaiting some form of execution, if for nothing more than all the lancers I had injured. I had broken into the palace, made it all the way to the king's personal chambers, got within weapon's reach of not only the king but the queen as well, and attempted to make off with the royal seal. If the king had been anything like the other nobles I'd run into, my head would be on the chopping block before mealtime.

I nodded. "I understand, Your Majesty." I bowed as low as my injured side would allow. "I will endeavor to earn back your trust."

The king turned and looked at Undercaptain Tolin. "How many men did you say were down?"

The undercaptain's jaw tightened. "Thirteen, Your Majesty. And four members of the High Guard."

"Seventeen." The king glanced back over his shoulder at me, then walked out the door.

The guards remained.

"As soon as you are capable of leaving, we should go," Undercaptain Tolin said sharply.

"Leaving? Already?" Dakaran looked put out. "He can't leave yet. Look at him. He's covered with wounds."

"Far less than what my men received," the undercaptain countered. I was suddenly hoping that Dakaran was coming as well, just to make sure the undercaptain didn't stick a knife in me and drop my body in some dark alley along the way.

"The undercaptain is correct," I said to Dakaran, grabbing my shirt from the far side of the bed. “The sooner I go, the better.” I held out my hands to Undercaptain Tolin, and he cut the bands so I could get my shirt back on.

Dakaran crossed his arms and glared at the two of us. “I demand you order him to stay. At least for the night.”

“I’m sorry, Your Highness, but your father’s orders were clear.”

I pulled on my runner’s boots and started for the door. I figured it would be best to make a clean break before Dakaran came up with a reason to keep me there. I needed to get back to the Temple, and we still had to stop by Master Fentin’s shop on the way to prove to the king that my lies weren’t lies. “It was nice meeting you, Your . . . What should I call you?”

“Dakaran,” the prince said, walking over and thrusting out his hand.

I took it. “Dakaran it is. I’ll never look at an armoire the same way again.”

Dakaran chuckled.

I released his hand and bowed, then followed the undercaptain and his guards out the door. There were at least a dozen armed men escorting me down the hall. People were quick to move aside when they saw us coming.

Undercaptain Tolin took me back to the storeroom, where I collected my belongings from Elfia, not taking the time to change out of the outfit I was wearing. I don’t think they wanted it back anyway, what with the rips, tears, and blood. They even let me keep the boots, which I was grateful for. They were good boots, after all. Good for anything but climbing.

We left the palace the same way I’d come in, except this time instead of hiding in the crowd, I was being given a full parade across the courtyard. Even the mounted lancers moved aside for us to pass. Once through the gate and across the bridge, the undercaptain had me move near the front so I could give him direction to Master Fentin's shop.

The march from the palace to Meadow Way was a pleasant one; at least, it would have been if I hadn't been sweating through my shirt about whether or not Master Fentin and Mistress Orilla would back up my story, and if my arm and side hadn't been hurting from the wounds I'd received.

We arrived just before the sun had fully set. The shop door was open, or as open as it could be, as it hung off the hinges to one side. Mistress Orilla had already lit the lanterns for the evening.

"This is it," I said, pointing at the broken front door. "You see? I told you I wasn't lying." I started for the shop, hoping to warn Master Fentin, but the undercaptain grabbed my arm. I didn't let that stop me. "Father!" I shouted. "There's some men here to see you."

Master Fentin peeked out from the front window. One look at the lancers and I thought he was going to bolt. "Father! It's all right. They just want to ask you about the shop."

"Quiet, boy," Undercaptain Tolin said, squeezing my arm even harder. "I can speak for myself." He passed me off to the next soldier in line. "Watch him."

"Am I not coming?" I asked.

The undercaptain didn't respond as he left the rest of us standing in the street while he went inside.

I don't know how long the undercaptain was in there—it felt like hours—but by the time he reappeared, my hands were clammy, and the back of my shirt was soaked. He waved me forward. "Bring him."

I followed three lancers across into the shop. It looked as though Master Fentin and Mistress Orilla had already started trying to clean up the mess but had only made it as far as the first aisle. I jerked away from the guard holding my arm and ran over to Master Fentin and gave him a big, loving hug. "Father, I'm sorry I didn't get the ring before they caught me," I said as fast as I could. "I hope Lord Gerrick doesn't try arresting you—"

The undercaptain grabbed my arm and yanked me back. "Hold your tongue!" He stared at me and shook his head, then looked at Master Fentin and Mistress Orilla. "He's quite the handful. How do you ever manage him?"

Mistress Orilla chuckled. "It's not easy, Undercaptain, I assure you. But all in all, he's a good boy."

Undercaptain Tolin looked at me like he didn't believe it.

Either way, I released a small sigh of relief. Apparently, whatever they had discussed while I was outside had convinced him of my adoption.

Undercaptain Tolin looked around the shop. "It seems, at least on this front, you were telling the truth."

"I told you I was. It was that street tribe that did it. They forced Lord Gerrick's hand."

"He speaks honestly, sir," Master Fentin said. "We don't feel safe around here anymore. Been here nigh on thirty years. Never had this happen. The city just isn't what it used to be; that's for sure."

The undercaptain looked at the three of us, then finally nodded. "I apologize for your inconvenience. I'll be sure the king hears about it." He turned me around and looked me in the eyes. "And if I ever see you in the palace again, so help me, not even the king will be able to save you."

I nodded, not knowing what else to do. The undercaptain had been humiliated in front of the king, and I had no doubt that if he ever did catch me again, I would rue the day.

With that, the lancers left, marching in file up the street with Undercaptain Tolin at the head. I was more than happy to watch them disappear.

"What in the name of Aldor have you gotten yourself into this time?" Master Fentin said as he plopped down on the stool beside the front desk and wiped his forehead with his handkerchief.

I looked at the two of them and sighed. "You wouldn't believe me if I told you."

Chapter 40

"IT'S THE PROTECTOR!" Toots shouted from atop the wall. "Hurry! Open the gate!"

The sun was just beginning to rise out of the east, but not enough for them to have doused the torches lining each of the makeshift turrets along the Temple wall. I waited patiently as those inside worked to get the bracer raised. My walk across town had given me time to think about what I was going to say to the others, but no matter how hard I tried, I couldn't come up with anything that would offer any amount of encouragement. The simple truth was I'd failed.

"You're back!" Mouse was the first to squeeze through the gate. He rushed ahead of the pack and latched on to my waist with a big hug. "I told them you'd make it back. They didn't believe me. But

I told them. No one can stop the Protector."

Petal and Squeaks were next in line. They released me just in time to miss being nabbed by the huge pair of arms that lifted me off the ground. "Tubby likes to eat."

Tubby squeezed me so hard, I nearly blacked out. "Put . . . me . . . down," I said, each word wheezing from my chest.

Tubby set me back on the brick pavers, and I took a moment to catch my breath, wondering what me being back had to do with him liking to eat.

"Boy, am I glad to see you." Bull pushed his way through the crowd and slapped me on the back.

I groaned inwardly as the impact sent lances of pain shooting through my arm and side.

"You really had us worried when you didn't show up yesterday." He tossed a quick glance over his shoulder at Sapphire and Reevie, who were just shoving their way to the front. "And I ain't afraid to admit it, but I thought you were a goner for sure. Figured you were on a boat heading for the salt mines." He smiled and slapped me once more. "Never so glad to be wrong."

The members of Hurricane poured out of the gate and surrounded me. Even Jayden and the other former Rockslide members gathered off to the side to hear what I had to say.

"Where were you?" Sapphire asked, concern on her face, if not in her voice.

"I spent the night with Master Fentin and Mistress Orilla. Didn't want to walk back so late."

Reevie looked me in the eyes. "Something's wrong."

I hated how much Reevie knew me.

"You didn't get it. Did you?"

Anxious chatter flittered through the group.

I stared at the sea of surrounding faces. Faces that just moments ago had been so filled with excitement, joy, and laughter, were now slowly transitioning to something else. The longer I waited to answer, the deeper that fear grew.

With a grief-stricken exhale, I shook my head. "No."

"No?" Mouse took a step back, almost as if he didn't recognize me. "You didn't get the seal? That's . . . that's not possible." He turned and started to chuckle nervously as he addressed the crowd, "The Protector is joking. Of course he got it. He's the Protector." The little picker laughed once more and turned around, waiting on me to reaffirm his declaration, because in his mind and the minds of most everyone there, I didn't fail. I couldn't. I was something akin to the faerie goddess Egla herself, or maybe even the Creator.

The look of despair in their eyes had my stomach turning. How could I let them down easy? How could I tell them that our life at the Temple was about to be over, the protection they'd been afforded gone? For many of them, this was life or death. I couldn't bring myself to do it.

I raised my arms and smiled. "You got me. Of course I got it." I laughed, full and loud and deep. "How could you have ever doubted?"

An uncomfortable moment of silence erupted into a chorus of cheers and applause. The only people not joining in were Reevie and Sapphire. Bull did clap, a little.

I waited for the ovation to die, then pointed back toward the Temple. "Why are you all standing around? Go get some breakfast!"

Shouts rang out as all the kids took off running for the gate, Tubby in the lead. I could actually feel the ground shake as the enormous kid tore through the barren gardens for the dining hall. I looked at my co-chieftains. "We need to talk."

Reevie was the last one to enter the study. Forehead closed the door behind him, remaining at his post in the hall. "Spill it," Reevie said. "What happened?"

"You didn't actually get the ring, did you?" Bull asked.

Sapphire passed him a frigid look as we all took our normal seats. Even Bull decided to sit down this time without complaint.

"Well, what are you waiting for?" Reevie asked.

I knew this was going to take a while, but I was anxious to tell it. So much had happened yesterday that I hardly knew where to start. I began with sneaking across the bridge and didn't stop until I told of my lancer escort back to Master Fentin's shop.

The others were so enraptured that they let me get through the entire unveiling without interruption. No one said a word for a long time, as if still waiting for a surprise ending where I tell them I had the ring all along.

"Let me get this right," Sapphire said, bewilderment on her

face. "Not only did you get caught trying to steal the king's ring, but you started a battle with the king's guards right in the middle of his own study . . . and you're still walking around with your head attached?"

Reevie slapped his forehead. "Only you would do something so stupid and somehow manage to walk out alive."

"Do you think the king will do what he said?" Sapphire asked.

"Which part?"

"Look into Rockslide and Lord Gerrick."

I shrugged. "I'd like to think he will. He seemed trustworthy." I reached into my pocket and pulled out the coins they'd given me. "He even let me keep the gold." Actually, in all the hubbub of what had taken place, he probably just forgot.

Reevie's eyes shone bright as he stared at the coins. "That's definitely something."

"So, did you pick anything else?" Bull asked.

Everyone turned.

"What?" He shrugged, looking all innocent. "The last time he invaded someone's home, he came back with a haul worth at least thirty gold."

"That was different," I said. "That was Gerrick."

"Yeah," Bull agreed. "And this was the king. He can certainly afford a lot more than a lord."

"The king hasn't done anything to me to warrant stealing from him . . ." I'd barely gotten the words out before realizing how stupid they sounded. "I mean, apart from the royal seal. But that's different. That was a life-or-death situation."

"It's going to be life or death for us if we can't provide enough to eat," Bull countered, making a lot more sense than I wanted to give him credit for.

"I was too busy fighting off an army of lancers to worry about picking trinkets. Besides, can you imagine what would have happened if I'd stuffed my pockets? They would have discovered my thieving while dressing my wounds, then I really would have been in trouble; probably would have executed me right then and there."

Bull scratched the back of his head, untangling some of the longer blond strands. "Yeah, that's probably true. Guess it was best you didn't pick anything."

"But what are we to do now?" Reevie asked. "We have Cutter's gold and daggers, Noph's hat, Red's usage of my skills"—his mouth twisted as he said it—"but no seal."

"I don't know."

"That seems to be an answer we hear far too often around here lately," Sapphire said, blowing out her lips in frustration.

"Maybe they'll be willing to give us some extra time," Bull said.

The others looked at him like he was crazy.

"Forget I asked."

"It wouldn't matter," I said. "It's not like I can sneak back into the palace and try again. That bridge has been burned."

"I can't believe I'm about to say this," Reevie said, "but maybe we should think about leaving."

"And go where?" Sapphire asked, shifting uncomfortably in her seat. "How do you plan on getting out of the city with an entire caravan of starving kids?"

"Who said anything about taking them with us?"

Sapphire tightened her grip on the arm of her chair. "I'm going to pretend I didn't hear that."

"Someone's got to say it. We need to be practical. Like you said, we can't just up and leave the city with a caravan of street kids. And if by some miracle we did manage to make it through the gates, then what? Where would we go?" He looked at each of us in turn. "It might be harsh, but we have to face the facts. When it comes to something like this, it's everyone for themselves. Some of them could at least go back to the orphan homes."

"They'd rather starve," Bull said with a sneer.

Reevie didn't say anything. Instead, he looked at me, as if expecting me to automatically side with him. The only problem was that both of them were right. Neither option was great, but only one of them left my stomach feeling queasy.

"We stick together," I said, "no matter what."

"Great." Sapphire drew her belt knife and began picking at her nails. "Now that we've determined we're going to stick together, how about filling us in on how we're going to make that happen? We need a plan."

"I agree," I said. "Let's look at what we know. The Guild meeting is set, there's nothing we can do to change it, and if we don't show up or we don't meet our price, then Hurricane loses its membership. But what does that really mean?"

"It means we can't pick," Reevie said.

"Which means we starve," Bull added.

"Is that all?" I asked.

They looked at me like I'd been into Reevie's mushroom stash.

"What do you mean, *is that all*?" Reevie asked. "I'd say that was pretty boil-popping bad."

"But what if we could survive without picking?"

Reevie shook his head. "What are you talking about?"

"I'm saying, what if there was a way we could fill our coffers without having to pick?"

"Like what?" Bull asked, as baffled as the others.

"Like I could take Senator Gerrick up on his offer."

"I think you scorched that bridge when you ratted on him to the king," Reevie said.

"Maybe. Maybe not. I get the feeling Gerrick is the kind of man who can see the value of my services whether he likes me or not."

"Are you crazy?!" Sapphire pointed at me with her knife. "He can't be trusted. Just as soon as he thinks you've outlived your usefulness, he'll have your throat slit and wouldn't think twice about it."

"Then I guess I'll have to show him the foolishness of such a decision. He knows I can get to him. At this point, we have nothing to lose and everything to gain."

"*Gain* and *Gerrick* are two words that don't belong in the same sentence," Sapphire grumbled.

"Do you have a better idea?"

Reevie cleared his throat. "I could try selling my services."

"Which would be a good thing but not enough to keep an entire tribe fed and clothed. Not without help."

"And you're forgetting the most important thing," Sapphire said as she ran her finger down the spine of her blade. "Losing

Hurricane's membership is more than just losing the ability to pick. We lose our territory, which means, no matter what we do, Cutter and Kore will be coming to lay claim to our home. The only thing stopping them so far has been our Guild membership. Take that away, and we're looking at a battle we can't possibly hope to win."

"They'd kill us all for sure," Bull said.

I sighed and leaned back in my seat. They were both right. We didn't have the resources to fight a battle with two tribes. Even if Red and Noph decided to get involved, which they wouldn't, it would be a war that none of us could afford. They knew a battle like that would not only bring the patrollers, it would bring the Lancers. And no one wanted that. Just another reason why the Guild was so important.

"What about the Granary?" Sapphire asked.

Both Reevie and I shook our heads.

"It's not big enough," Reevie said.

"Nor safe enough," I added. "As soon as they found out we were there, they'd push us right into the sea."

The room was quiet as we pondered our dilemma.

No matter how I looked at it, there was only one real solution. "As it stands, I think we can all agree that the most important thing for us is to keep our membership. Correct?"

The others nodded.

"Without it . . . I don't see how we survive."

"Then what do we do?" Bull asked.

I paused as a passing thought suddenly took root in the back of my mind. In truth, it was the only thing I could think of that could help us reach a solution. "The only thing we can do. We pay our entry fee."

Reevie rapped the arm of his chair with his knuckles. "And how are we supposed to do that? We don't have the king's ring."

"True. But no one else knows that."

"They flaming will when we don't show up with it," Reevie said.

Sapphire stopped fiddling with her knife and looked up. "You're talking about passing off a fake ring."

I nodded. "What does the royal seal look like? Describe it to me."

Everyone shrugged.

"Exactly. I'm the only person who's actually seen it."

Bull looked at the others, his mouth curling into a smile. "He's got a point. I wouldn't know the signet ring from a Delgan nose ring."

"Maybe not," Reevie said, "but I'm sure I could tell. It would have to look official or they'd see right through it."

Sapphire smiled. "And I know just the jeweler to pull it off. He deals in custom pieces, and he owes me a favor."

"What kind of favor?" Reevie asked, beating me to the question.

"The kind that should help us get what we want," she said curtly.

"Is his work any good?" I asked.

"I wouldn't have suggested him otherwise."

"Is he trustworthy?"

Sapphire snorted. "Of course not; that's why he's perfect for the job."

"What's the favor for?" Bull asked, not smart enough to realize he shouldn't.

She looked at the three of us and grinned. "Wouldn't you like to find out?"

We left it alone.

"How are we going to pay for it?" Reevie finally asked, breaking the awkward silence. "We used what was left of the gold we got from selling Gerrick's knickknacks to purchase those daggers for Cutter."

"We use the gold I got from the king," I said.

Reevie smiled. "Right. I'd almost forgotten about that."

I looked at Sapphire. "We've only got a couple of days till the meeting. Can your guy get us something by then?"

She laid down her knife. "He'll have to."

Chapter 41

WITH ALL OUR HOPES tied to this new ring, we started our long trek across town.

Sapphire's jeweler had done a remarkable job on the piece, especially in such a short amount of time. The crest looked almost believable. There was a crown. There was a sun. There were even decorative designs around the band. It wasn't what I would call a perfect replica, but it would do.

We were nearing the southern bridge leading onto the island when the hairs on the back of my neck pricked. I stopped and turned, which caused the others to stop as well. I scanned the street and sidewalk behind us. Something felt off, but other than the typical flow of citizens on either side of the cobbled lane, I didn't see anything out of place.

"What are you looking at?" Sapphire asked, her hand resting on the hilt of her blade as she tried to catch a glimpse of what I was looking at.

"I'm not sure. Just a feeling."

Reevie and Bull moved out of the road as a couple of carriages passed. "I don't see anything," Reevie said. "Then again, as short as I am, I wouldn't unless I was riding on Tubby's shoulders."

Tubby leaned down and grabbed Reevie's arms.

"No! Put me down," Reevie said, swiping at Tubby.

"But you said—"

"I was just making a point. I don't really want to ride on your shoulders." He shook his head and started forward once more, the rest of us following.

Bull quickly moved in front, while Tubby brought up the rear. The enormous boy kept the hood of his cloak up to hide his face, but one look at the lumbering giant and most moved out of the way regardless.

Before I knew it, we had already crossed over the island and were making our way east down one of the main avenues. We stopped just inside the shadows of the building across the street from where the Guild held its meetings, and I took a moment to look for any more of Rockslide's beaters. I wouldn't have put it past Kore to have set up another ambush just to keep us from reaching the meeting.

I barely even noticed the covered sky bridge above. I usually enjoyed staring up at the people, but today, entertaining myself with those passing by was a wasted effort. I did, however, give the bridge a momentary glance. This might be the last time I ever saw it. If we lost our status as an official tribe, we might have to leave the city.

I shifted the sword on my waist and turned to the others. "Are we ready?"

"Is that a trick question," Reevie asked, "or should I lie?"

Sapphire stepped out of the shadows and onto the busy street. "Let's get this over with."

"Guess that answers that," I said, and chased after her, the others right behind me.

We made it inside and started up the wide circular stairs, getting off at the same one we always did. I had to keep my arm around Reevie as we crossed the bridge, since he was determined to keep his eyes closed the entire way. By the time we reached the other side, his forehead was covered in sweat.

We took a moment to let him recover, which was fine with me, since I had no desire to get to the meeting any sooner than we had to.

Reevie finally nodded, and we started up another flight of steps, getting off when we saw the teal-and-gold runner. I tried to calm my nerves by slowing my breathing as we followed the long corridor back to the Guild Hall. We passed the second junction, and I felt that same prickling on the back of my neck. I turned, but the hall behind us was empty save for a couple of women we'd passed moments before. Both were too engaged in their quiet conversation off to the side to pay us any mind.

We rounded the final bend and I shivered. Red was there. I could feel Po's effects as my magic slipped from me. I shook it off.

The doors leading into the sitting area were open, but the ones leading from the sitting area to the meeting room were closed. I wondered if they'd started without us. We stepped inside the lobby to find it empty, save for the old scribe who was back in his seat, quill in hand, apparently waiting for our arrival.

He gave me a somewhat forlorn look as our group walked over to his desk. "Names, please," he said, dabbing the tip of his quill in a small jar on the right.

I gave him our names, even Bull's and Tubby's. The Guild allowed for two guards to accompany their chief, but with three of us holding that title, our party was larger than expected. Prior to today, I might have been worried about such a break in protocol, but right now, it was the last thing on my mind.

The old man finished scribbling our names in his ledger, then stood and walked over to the double doors. He gave us one more somber glance, then opened the doors. "Good luck to you."

I couldn't help but groan. Even he seemed to know what was about to happen. I straightened my sword once more, reassuring myself it was still there, then looked at the others to see if they were ready.

They nodded, and we walked inside.

Cutter's voice was the first to greet us as it rang out from the other side of the room. "Well, look who finally decided to show up." All the seats around the oversized circular table were filled. All but one. Cutter shifted the front of his brown wide-brim hat up higher on his forehead. "Hey, you're only allowed two guards! You can't bring them in here," he said, pointing at Bull and Tubby.

Tubby growled from behind his cowl, and Cutter quickly lowered his hand.

"There are only two guards with us," I said, trying not to show my irritation.

"Then why are there five of you and not three?"

"Because Hurricane has three chiefs," I said, fists clenched. "But you already know that."

"Whether Hurricane has *any* chiefs is yet to be determined," Cutter shot back with a nasty grin, not taking his eyes off Tubby.

Kore, who was sitting to Cutter's right, shifted in his seat, his muscular arms folded in front of his deep-green vest. He, too, held a disturbing sort of grin, as if the outcome of these proceedings had already been determined.

I couldn't wait to see their faces when we handed them their payment in full. I turned to Bull. "Grab two more chairs."

Bull nodded, and he and Tubby grabbed a couple from the sitting area by the right wall. The others at the table fidgeted nervously as Tubby lowered his chair, then took his place alongside Bull.

Before I could take a seat, both Sapphire and Reevie had plopped into theirs, leaving me the centermost spot.

"We were starting to worry something had happened," Red said with a nod in our direction. Her red shirt was a sharp contrast to the black-vested guards behind her. Po stood to the left of her chair, Toothless on the right; his smile hadn't improved.

"I assured them you'd be here, one way or the other," Noph

said, scooting forward in his seat. He tipped his purple hat in greeting. Unlike Cutter and Kore, his smile appeared genuine.

"Your hands look oddly empty," Cutter said gleefully. "Can we take that to assume you've failed to meet our requirements?" He looked at Kore and winked.

I smiled as well, as big and broad and carefree as I could muster, then nodded to Reevie.

Reevie opened his satchel. The others watched in silence as he removed a purple hat and placed it on the table.

Cutter grumbled something under his breath, his smile shrinking slightly. Noph, on the other hand, leaned forward to inspect the new hat, thumbing his chin.

"A hat for Noph," I said with as much dramatic flair as I could manage under the circumstances. "And our payment to Sandstorm has been met."

After a quick examination of the headwear, Noph rapped his knuckles on the table. "I concur."

I looked at Kore and Cutter, weighing their expressions. They didn't disappoint. Even with a forced grin, their eyes had tightened enough to let me know there was at least a modicum of concern. Red smiled, but more for Cutter and Kore than for us. I motioned in her direction. "Medical services for the next several months have been agreed to, which fulfills our obligation to Wildfire."

She struck the top of the table with the edge of a knife she'd been holding. "Agreed."

I looked at Cutter, and he leaned forward in his seat. His fingers drummed eagerly on the table while his face held a somber, almost worried look. The anticipation was killing me. I nodded at Sapphire, and she pulled out the leather purse and flopped it on the table, making sure it landed hard enough for everyone to hear the clanging inside.

"That's not possible," Cutter said. "How did you . . ." His eye twitched when Sapphire then proceeded to remove the two daggers we'd purchased and placed them on the table as well. Cutter's eyes bulged, and he pointed at the pouch. "Show us the inside. For all we know, it's filled with wooden knots."

Sapphire leaned forward and loosened the drawstring. She reached into the pouch and pulled out a small handful of gold coins, which she let clang on the table beside the pouch.

Kore lowered his arms, his smile disappearing altogether. Beside him, Cutter's hands were shaking as he gripped the edge of the table. I couldn't tell if it was from rage or excitement. "How did you get your hands on fifteen pieces of gold?"

"That's our business," Sapphire said. "Fifteen pieces of gold and two daggers was your demand, and that is what we brought, which meets our agreement with Avalanche."

"I'd hardly call those daggers worthy of a Guild requirement," he said with a sneer. "They're as ugly as your boots."

Sapphire snarled. "You said two daggers. If they aren't to your liking, that's your fault for not being more specific."

Red laughed. "She's got you there."

Cutter crossed his arms, his face red.

"Well," Sapphire said, "are you going to say something? You asked for fifteen gold and two daggers. We've brought you fifteen gold and two daggers."

Cutter looked at the other chiefs but eventually nodded and leaned back in his seat.

Kore's wide chest pressed against the edge of the table as he leaned forward and rested his huge arms on top. "Anyone can produce a silly hat and a bag of gold. I could have those by this evening if I chose. I want to see the ring."

I took a deep breath, my hands already sweating, and reached into my inner pocket. This was it. All of Hurricane was counting on us to pull this off. "The last time we met, you questioned my Upakan heritage and whether I had the prowess to pull off the impossible." I pulled out our fake ring and held it up for all to see. "This is my answer."

The other chiefs looked aghast. Kore's mouth actually opened, but only for a second, then it quickly snapped shut. "That's not the ring. Give it to me."

"The Pits it isn't!" I shot back before tossing it to him. "Look at it. You can't deny the royal seal."

Kore looked it over, carefully scrutinizing the crest at the top.

"Well?" Noph asked. "Is it the ring?"

Kore shoved it at Noph. "You tell me. You're more familiar with the royal crest than I am."

I gulped. How familiar was Noph with the ring? Reevie and Sapphire both looked at me, but I made a point of not looking back. There was no way Noph could have ever seen the ring before. I didn't know that much about the Sandstorm chief, but I doubted he'd ever been in the palace.

We waited as Noph examined every aspect of the ring, turning it over several times, even looking on the inside. My heart was pounding. Was there some sort of inscription that was supposed to be inside the ring? I hadn't thought to look that close at the original when I was in the king's study.

Noph finally finished his inspection and looked up. I bit my lip when he turned and looked at the three of us. I couldn't read his face.

"Looks genuine to me," he said, offering a faint smile in our direction.

Something in that smile told me Noph knew we were lying.

"I don't believe you," Cutter said. "Let me see it."

Noph tossed the ring across the table, and Cutter tried to catch it but missed, and it landed in front of him. He swiped it up, inspecting the crest, his face growing angrier with each passing moment. Finally, he looked up at me. "And how did you manage to get this?"

"I'm Upakan, that's how."

Cutter glared at me for a moment but eventually tossed the ring back to Kore.

"The price for admission from Rockslide was the king's signet," I said. "And as you can see, we made good on that obligation. All that's left is to—"

"Wait," Kore said, staring at one side of the ring. His mouth curled upward and the hairs on my arms stood. "This isn't the royal seal."

"Of course it is; you've all seen it."

"Then explain to me how the royal seal of Aldor has a chip?"

He studied the ring even harder, then placed the lower band in his teeth and bit down. His face darkened. "It isn't even gold! It's been plated."

I looked at Sapphire, and she quickly shrugged. Reevie looked on the verge of making a break for the door. All this work to find out that our infamous jeweler had cheated us with a gold-plated ring.

No one said a word as they stared across the table in our direction, no doubt waiting for an explanation that I didn't have. There was no way of talking us out of this one. There was no lie that could be said that would justify a fake ring now. It was over. Hurricane was through. "Fine," I admitted. "We don't have it."

The smirks of victory on Kore's and Cutter's faces had my jaw tightening.

"Actually, he did get it," Sapphire said.

Everyone turned, including me. What was she doing?

"You got the royal seal?" Red asked.

"No, you didn't!" Kore spat, holding up the ring. "It's a fake."

Sapphire's grip tightened on her dagger. "He did get it, but after fighting off half the palace guard, they managed to get it back."

"Fight off half the palace guard? Hah!" Kore slammed his fist on the table. "Not only are you a pack of liars but incompetent ones at that! No ring. No admittance."

Cutter leaned back in his chair and laughed. "Hurricane has been a thorn in my side for years. Spats, as stupid as he was, at least knew his place." He looked to the other chiefs. "The Guild law is final. They didn't meet the requirements, which means their tribe should be struck from the Guild."

I looked at Noph. "Is there nothing we can do? This entire process has been a farce from the beginning. Did any of you have such ridiculous demands placed on your tribes?"

Noph looked conflicted. "No," he admitted. "But, then again, you did agree to them."

"I didn't agree to them," Sapphire said. "They're absurd! I wasn't even here to cast a vote."

"That's your fault," Cutter said.

"No, that's his fault," Sapphire fired back, pointing at Kore.

Kore pushed his seat back from the table.

"Fine!" Reevie said. "If that's the way you want it!" He snatched the hat, the gold, and even the two daggers off the table and stuffed them in his satchel. "If we aren't admitted, then this returns with us."

Cutter shot from his seat and reached for his sword. "The blazes it does! That gold is mine!"

Sapphire was on her feet, sword in hand, before I could say anything. "I'd like to see you try to take it."

Kore and Red came out of their seats as well, their guards drawing their weapons and rushing in to protect them.

I got halfway out of my seat when the front doors burst open, and armed men in white uniforms came pouring in.

"Lancers!" Kore shouted, knocking his chair completely backward as he drew his weapons.

"We've been sold out!" Red echoed, moving to the back to join the others. She shoved Po under the table and raised her daggers.

Bull hopped in front of Reevie, a short blade in one hand and a cudgel in the other. Tubby joined him, quickly strapping on his leather mask and pulling his enormous bedpost club out from under his cloak.

I drew my own sword and dagger and stood with the others, the impending fight between the tribes all but forgotten as we faced this new enemy.

Elondrian soldiers continued to fill the other side of the room.

"I'm going to kill that old scrivener," I heard Kore say off to my right. "No one sells us out and gets away with it."

Where was Po? I was going to need my magic, and there was only one way that was going to happen. I turned to find him when a voice from the other side of the room pulled me short.

"Hold your place, Captain. No one moves unless I tell you."

I turned. How did he . . .

The lancers parted, and Dakaran took a step forward, wearing a proud smile. This time, he looked like a prince, with a gold vest and royal-blue sash, and a fur-lined, crimson cape over his shoulders. He didn't wear a crown. Then again, I wasn't sure if princes wore crowns.

My mind was racing. If Dakaran was there, that meant he knew that what I'd told them wasn't exactly true.

"I bet you didn't expect to see me again so soon," Dakaran said.

"Who are you supposed to be?" Kore shot back before I had a chance to speak. "And what in the flaming pits are you—"

"Silence, peasant, before I have you flogged!"

"Peasant?" Kore raised his blade and took a step forward. As soon as he did, the entire front line of lancers stepped forward as well, drawing their swords in perfect unison. Even Kore had enough sense to recognize a losing battle and quickly retreated.

I sheathed my weapons and walked out in front of the others. "How did you find me?"

Dakaran smiled as if it was all some kind of a game. "You didn't think I'd let you go without keeping an eye on you? How was I to reach you if I didn't know where you lived?"

"Where I lived?"

"He's the one who sold us out," Cutter said behind me.

"No, I didn't."

"I had Pathfinder Asa follow you," Dakaran said. "He's one of the best trackers in the kingdom." Dakaran pointed to a shorter man near the end of the first row of lancers. The man leaned against the wall and stared me down. He wasn't dressed like the rest of the company, wearing plain leathers instead of a uniform. He had a barrel chest and a noticeable ducktail beard that came to a point at the end, making his cheeks look even thicker than they were. He must have been the reason I'd felt as though someone had been watching me. Whoever he was, he would have given an Upakan a run for their gold.

I bit down on my lip. If he'd had me followed, that meant Dakaran knew I didn't live at the bookshop, which also meant he knew about the Temple. Were they here to arrest me?

"Who is this, Ayrion?" Red asked, as confused as everyone else.

"You don't recognize the crown prince?" Noph said, his hat in hand. He stepped forward and bowed toward Dakaran. "Your Highness."

I glanced at Noph. "How do you recognize him? I spent a

morning with him in an armoire and had no idea who he was."

Noph choked. "You did what?"

Dakaran chuckled.

The other chiefs looked positively dumbfounded.

"I told you he had the ring," Sapphire finally said, vindication dripping from each word.

I turned to Dakaran. "Why are you here? Not that I'm not happy to see you," I added with a gulp as I stared at the half-filled room of lancers. "Am I being arrested?"

"Arrested? No, you forgot something when you left." He walked out to meet me, flanked by four lancers.

I joined him in the middle. No one behind me said a word.

"I believe you were looking for this."

Resting in his palm was a large oval-shaped ring.

"Is that the . . ."

"Yes. It's the royal seal," Dakaran pronounced loudly, making sure everyone behind me heard.

I spared a quick glance over my shoulder, not wanting to miss their reactions. Again, I wasn't disappointed. Even Kore's mouth hung at the hinges.

I leaned forward so the others wouldn't hear. "I don't understand. Why are you doing this? Obviously, you know I'm not the adopted son of a bookshop owner."

"No, you're not," he said with a stern look, letting me know he wasn't pleased by my deception, "but I also know what you did was in the pursuit of helping others." He held the ring out to me.

I took it. Something about it looked different. It had a few less rays around the crown, and the crown seemed to have acquired a few more spires. I looked up at Dakaran, and he winked.

"They won't know the difference," he whispered.

He was right. It wasn't like any of them had ever seen the real ring, and I doubted Dakaran would have forged a ring with lower quality, like we had. Besides, who was going to argue the point when the crown prince himself showed up to deliver it? I turned around and held up the second fake ring for all to see. "Our obligation to Rockslide has been met."

Kore looked at the others, but they were too awestruck at the fact that they were standing in front of the High Prince to notice. He finally looked at the prince and nodded.

"You didn't have to do this," I said to Dakaran, turning back around.

"Sure I did. After you came to my rescue, it was the least I could do."

"It wasn't like you were in danger."

"You didn't know that."

"Won't you get in trouble for this? Your father didn't seem all that happy with me when I left."

"Whose idea do you think this was?"

I suddenly felt lightheaded. "The king knows that I'm a . . ."

"A street rat?" Dakaran finished with a smile. "Of course."

"Then why is he helping me?"

"Because when Undercaptain Tolin reported his conversation with your bookshop owner, and the extensive damages he'd seen at the shop, it proved that at least part of your story was true. And whether you live there or not, my parents were impressed by how far you were willing to go to help them." Dakaran leaned in. "Although trying to steal his ring might not have been the smartest idea."

I winced.

"Besides, I think he likes you. When I asked him to help, this is what he suggested."

I wasn't sure what to say. "Be sure to thank him for me," I managed, scanning the line of lancers behind the prince. "Did Undercaptain Tolin not accompany you?" I was surprised not to see him standing there glaring at me.

Dakaran shook his head. "I don't think he likes you much."

I smiled. I guess I couldn't blame him.

Dakaran stared over my shoulder at the other chiefs for a brief moment before turning to his lancers. "Captain, you can escort me back now."

We all watched in silence as Dakaran melted back into the middle of the ranks. A few moments later, the lancers exited, and we were once again left to ourselves.

"He's smaller than I thought," Red said with a slight grin.

"I can't believe that just happened," Reevie said, staring at the empty doorway.

"Yes, that certainly got the old blood pumping," Noph said sarcastically, sliding the hidden sword back into his cane.

Kore and Cutter remained silent.

I walked over and laid the ring down on the table, and Reevie placed the bag of gold, the two daggers, and Noph's purple hat beside it.

"Our obligations have been met," I said, turning to our party.

"Let's go."

I didn't wait around to see what happened to the ring and the gold. I walked out with my head high and a spring in my step. The euphoria was so overwhelming that I never even noticed my magic returning. One thing was for sure: now that the crown knew about our meeting place, the Guild was going to have to find new accommodations.

"I can't believe we pulled that off," Sapphire said as we walked down the hall.

Reevie held out his hands with a gleeful sort of laugh. "I'm still shaking."

"I can't believe I just met one of the royal family," Bull added.

"Tubby's hungry," the giant boy proclaimed as he unstrapped his mask and pulled his hood back into place.

I was still in too much of a daze to do anything more than focus on keeping one foot in front of the other. I hadn't felt this good since . . . since I'd made it to the top of Howling Gorge and won the Tri'Nephrin. All the pressure that had been placed on us to win our seat at the table had finally been lifted. The fear of not knowing how we were going to feed our tribe was gone. More than that, I had a friend in the palace.

The walk back across town was certainly far more enjoyable than the one we'd made earlier that day.

Toots saw us coming before we'd made it halfway down the brick drive and sounded the alarm. We were met at the gate by an energetic group of kids, not to mention a very eager Master Fentin and Mistress Orilla.

"I gather by the smiles on your faces that things went well?" Master Fentin said, looking quite pleased himself.

"They did," I said, unable to hide my excitement even if I'd wanted to.

"You'll never believe what happened," Reevie exclaimed.

"No more than what happened to us, I reckon," Mistress Orilla countered.

Reevie's smile disappeared. "Nothing bad, I hope?"

"On the contrary, my boy," Master Fentin replied. "An armed convoy arrived at the shop this morning from Lord Gerrick's. They'd been instructed to pay for damages to the shop." He waved at Forehead, and the tall boy stepped forward and opened the lid to a small chest he'd been holding. It was filled to the brim with gold coins. "Can you believe it? There's enough here to rebuild twice over, or even reopen the shop in a more prestigious part of town." Master Fentin was positively giddy. He closed the lid and stared at us over his spectacles. "So, what happened at the meeting? Got a feeling you'll have a hard time topping this."

The rest of us looked at each other and started laughing.

The End of ROCKSLIDE

Dear Reader,

I HOPE YOU enjoyed this third book in the Street Rats of Aramoor series. If you found the story entertaining and would like to see more, then please consider helping me reach that goal by leaving a quick review on Amazon.

Reviews are very important. They help encourage other readers to try the book while at the same time showing Amazon that the book is worth promoting.

~ Thank you in advance!

Want to be notified when the next book comes out? If so, go to this address: *www.michaelwisehart.com/join-the-wielder-council*

<< Keep reading for a FREE offer >>

Author Note

LOVE FANTASY MUSIC? Stop by the shop, *Aramoor Market*, and take a listen. Over 30 minutes of original fantasy score, inspired by The Aldoran Chronicles. You can also grab the digital hi-resolution images for each of the maps, as well as the character art.

« *www.michaelwisehart.com/aramoormarket* »

For the Latest News

« *www.michaelwisehart.com* »

« *facebook.com/MichaelWisehart.author* »

<< Keep reading for a FREE offer >>

Free Offer

IF YOU WOULD LIKE to get a FREE copy of the prequel to the Aldoran Chronicles series, go to the address below. The prequel is vital to the ongoing story.

« *www.michaelwisehart.com/aramoormarket* »

Born in a world where magic is not only feared, but outlawed, Ferrin's choice to use his abilities brings the Black Watch to his doorstep. Caged alongside a helpless band of half-starved wielders, he formulates a strategy to escape. Armed with nothing more than his sarcastic wit and a determination to never give in, Ferrin attempts the impossible.

Acknowledgements

I THANK GOD for the doors and windows He's allowed to open in order for me to reach this point.

I want to thank my parents *Mickey and Julie Wisehart* for their unending loyalty, encouragement, and support over the years. None of this would be possible without you—love you both.

I want to thank my Author Team, whose endless talent, time, and dedication have made this project possible:

AUTHOR TEAM

I want to thank my cover illustrator and sister, who gave us the initial sketch design for the cover—*Janelle Wisehart*

I want to thank my cover artist, who took a basic sketch outline and turned it into reality—*Dongjun Lu "Russell"*

I want to thank my interior illustrator for her creativity in designing the front gates of the Rockslide compound—*Elwira Pawlikowska*

I want to thank my cartographer, who managed to take a maze of jumbled ideas and turn them into the capital city of Aramoor—*RenflowerGrapx*

I want to thank my content editor, who has spent countless hours advising me on the proper structure of my thoughts—*Nathan Hall*

I want to thank my line editor, who managed to take a floundering script and turn it into something readable—*Danae Smith*

I want to thank my copy editors, whose careful eyes have made my book shine—*Richard Shealy, Crystal Watanabe*

I want to thank my *Beta Team*, who took precious time out of their busy schedule to suffer through the first draft in order to leave such valuable feedback as to help me make this book worth reading.

About the Author

MICHAEL WISEHART graduated with a bachelor's degree in business before going back to school for film and starting his own production company. As much as he enjoyed film work, the call of writing a novel got the better of him, and on April 14, 2014, he started typing the first words of what would become two epic fantasy series: The Aldoran Chronicles and the Street Rats of Aramoor.

He currently lives and writes in North Georgia.

Glossary of Terms

Street Tribes of Aramoor

Avalanche [*a-vuh-lanch*] Tribe color is white. Chief is Cutter.

Hurricane [*her-ĭ-cane*] Tribe color is blue. Chief is Spats.

Rockslide [*rock*-slide] Tribe color is green. Chief is Kore.

Sandstorm [*sand-storm*] Tribe color is purple. Chief is Noph.

Wildfire [*wild-fire*] Tribe color is red. Chief is Red/Kira.

Months of the Year

Aèl [*ay*-el] First month of the year.

Sòl [*soul*] Second month of the year.

Nùwen [*noo-win*] Third month of the year.

Manù [*mah-noo*] Fourth month of the year.

Toff [*toff*] Fifth month of the year.

Kwàn [*quon*] Sixth month of the year.

Nor [*nor*] Seventh month of the year.

Èldwin [*el-dwin*] Eighth month of the year.

Kùma [*koo-muh*] Ninth month of the year.

Akòsi [*uh-kah-see*] Tenth month of the year.

Èshan [*ee-shon*] Eleventh month of the year.

Zùl [*zool*] Twelfth month of the year.

Character Glossary

Ayrion [*air-ee-un*] Thirteen-year-old Upakan street rat. Born with two magical gifts. Banished from his home for accidentally killing another Upakan.

Bull [*bull*] Former Avalanche beater who fought Ayrion during a tribal battle. Becomes one of Ayrion's bodyguards.

Bracken [*bră-ken*] An Elondrian senator who has dealings with Wildfire.

Cutter [*cut-er*] Chief of Avalanche. Vindictive and cruel.

De'Witt [*dee-wit*] Noblewoman who was robbed by street kids.

Dorin [*dor-in*] One of Ayrion's instructors, who favored his whip as a method of teaching.

Egan [*ee-gun*] Rockslide beater with torch who catches them sneaking into the compound.

Egla [*eg-la*] Faerie goddess of the Temple. Her worshippers turned on her. Her creatures ate her.

Elfia [*el-fee-uh*] Daughter to Master Tripkin. Works with her father in one of the palace's storerooms.

Endle [*en-dull*] Pastry chef, along with his wife Smyrna, who own a shop on South Avis.

Eva [*aye-vuh*] Little girl standing in line with her parents to see the king.

Fentin [*fen-tin*] Husband of Orilla. Elderly bookstore owner and friend of Hurricane.

Tubby (Flesh Eater) [*tub-ee*] The Pit champion. Enormous kid known for biting. He fights Ayrion in the Pit.

Flon [*flon*] Upakan boy Ayrion killed.

Forehead [*for-head*] One of the Hurricane Guard. Best known for his ferocious head-butting technique. Large growth on front of head because of head-butting.

Fosner [*foss-ner*] Father of Eva. Meets Ayrion while standing in line to meet the king.

Gerrick, Lord [*gare-ick*] Overweight Aramoor lord whose carriage almost ran Ayrion over.
Jayden [*jay-din*] Watcher for the Rockslide tribe who helped lead Ayrion/Mouse to their pickers.

Kipp [*kip*] Hurricane member who dies from injuries during the battle at the Pit.

Kira (Red) [*kee-ruh*] Chief of Wildfire. Took Ayrion's father's ring.

Koal [*co*le] Shorter guard in Rockslide prison watching the rejects. Reluctantly joins Ayrion's tribe.

Kore [*kor*] Chief of Rockslide. Physically imposing.

Luiza [*loo-ee-zuh*] Wife of Senator Gerrick.

Melvin [*mel-vin*] Taller guard in Rockslide prison watching the rejects. Reluctantly joins Ayrion's tribe.

Mouse [*mowss*] Small reject boy from Rockslide. Small enough to squeeze in and out of tiny places for burgling. Friends with Squeaks and Petal.

Muriel [*myur-ee-ol*] Hurricane girl who tended to the pigeons. Her clothes are always covered in bird poop.

Naddi [*nod-ee*] Name of Eva's doll.

Nia [*ny-uh*] Wildfire healer with very little basic knowledge of the healing arts.

Noph [*noff*] Chief of Sandstorm. Great tactician.

Orilla [*or-ill-uh*] Wife of Fentin. Makes a fantastic mystery-meat sandwich.

Petal [*peddle*] Small reject girl from Avalanche. Her hair is as golden as a flower petal. Friends with Mouse and Squeaks.

Po [*poe*] One of Kira's head bodyguards. Short and pudgy with black hair. Has the ability to negate others' magic.

Reevie [*ree-vee*] Street rat who saved Ayrion and took him in. Healer in training.

Sapphire [*saf-fire*] One of Spats's bodyguards who befriends Ayrion. Good with the sword.

Spats [*spats*] Chief of Hurricane.

Sil [*sil*] Rockslide beater with pouch who catches them sneaking into the compound.

Squeaks [*squeeks*] Small reject from Avalanche. Friends with Mouse and Petal.

Steffin [*steff-in*] Picker hiding behind the barrels to keep from getting captured by the Rockslide Tribe.

Storella [*stor-el-uh*] Wife of Master Endle, the baker.

Striffus [*stry-fuss*] An Elondrian senator, and personal rival of Senator Gerrick. His family colors are orange and gold. His guards' uniforms bear the same colors.

Tripkin [*trip/kin*] Keeper of one of the palace storerooms. Known to all as Master Trip. Has a daughter named Elfia.

Toff [*toff*] The made-up name Ayrion used while in the Rockslide compound.

Toothless [*tooth-less*] Head guard of Wildfire.

Toots [*toots*] Head watcher at the Temple.

Willis (String Bean) [*will-iss*] A Hurricane picker known for his lanky height.

Stop by and visit:

www.michaelwisehart.com